Life on the Porcelain Edge

C.E. Hilbert

Life on the Porcelain Edge

COPYRIGHT 2017 by C.E. Hilbert

Contact Information: titleadmin@pelicanbookgroup.com

All scripture quotations, unless otherwise indicated, are taken from the Holy Bible, New International Version(R), NIV(R), Copyright 1973, 1978, 1984, 2011 by Biblica, Inc.™ Used by permission of Zondervan. All rights reserved worldwide. www.zondervan.com

Cover Art by *Nicola Martinez*

White Rose Publishing, a division of Pelican Ventures, LLC
www.pelicanbookgroup.com PO Box 1738 *Aztec, NM * 87410

White Rose Publishing Circle and Rosebud logo is a trademark of Pelican Ventures, LLC

Publishing History
First White Rose Edition, 2017
Paperback Edition ISBN 978-1-61116-939-3
Electronic Edition ISBN 978-1-61116-937-9
Published in the United States of America

Dedication

To God, Who makes all things possible - even the
dreams of a pudgy little girl from Ohio.

To my early readers - Mom, Jen, Paige, Leslie, Navin,
Alabama Ashley, Utah Ashley, Taryn, Brenda, Zoe and
Elise - you are a true gift from heaven.

And to the wonderful men in my life - Daddy, the
Uncles, and my BFF - who honor my dream by reading
romance novels.

About the Author

C.E. Hilbert lives in a 110+ year-old fixer upper with her dog Daisy and she believes that life goes best with Jesus, a cute outfit and SportsCenter!

1

Tessa Tarrington's life was in the toilet.

Job? *Fired.*

Dad? *Heart attack.*

Current residence? *Childhood bedroom.*

Love life? *Non-existent.*

Her life was swirling in the bowl, just waiting for the ultimate flush.

Until a few months ago, everything was tripping along at a wonderful pace. Great job. Fantastic apartment. Friends. Not a toilet bowl in sight. After graduating from college nearly one thousand miles from her childhood home of Gibson's Run, Ohio, she'd landed a job as a writer with Evanston and Evanston, a specialty publisher located in New Orleans.

The small print house specialized in untold stories and memoirs. But they had a dirty little secret: none of their authors wrote a single word, except their names at book signings. E&E relied almost solely on ghost writers.

Four years into her career as a ghost writer, Tessa's assignments were far-reaching. She'd written about a politician's wife's story of cancer survival and a bestselling song artist's memoir about rising from poverty in Canada. She'd shared stories that needed to be told while remaining neatly tucked away in the shadows—the credit for her beautifully crafted words resting on the stars of the stories themselves. The number one goal of a ghost writer: remain a ghost. And she performed her duties flawlessly until...*the terrible, awful day.*

While away at her college homecoming, her apartment was robbed. Notes for two current pieces and four future contracts were stolen—sold to the highest tabloid bidder. Her anonymity went from walking down a street unhindered to hiding from paparazzi. No longer the writer of stories, she *was* the story. Clients dropped her like a hot branding iron, leaving her unemployed and a pariah in the world of publishing.

While her professional life was falling apart, she received the phone call she'd dreaded since her mother's funeral three years earlier. Her father was in the hospital with a suspected heart attack.

One flight to Columbus and seventy-two hours later, she'd accepted a long term substitute position at her alma mater. She returned to New Orleans long enough to pack up her coupe and head home to the town she'd left in the dust. Being near her father was necessary. The lone bonus for returning to her hometown of nearly three thousand residents was that the publicity about her came to a screeching halt.

And now, the one threshold she'd promised to never cross again was about to become her daily purgatory for the foreseeable future. She was back in high school. Her years of matriculation in the Gibson's Run Local Schools were a series of embarrassments, humiliations, and harassments. All beginning with her sixth birthday when Ryland Jessup gave her "Days of the Week" panties.

Holding the seven pairs of egg-rolled undies in their long rectangle box, with embarrassment she had piddled in her white overalls from *Suzi's On Main*. From her sixth birthday through the seventh grade, she'd been known as Pee-Pee Tee-Tee. Thankfully, the when she'd entered McKinley Jr. High, the taunt became too long for the cool kids, but the ever clever Ryland shortened the dreaded nickname to T.T.

Throughout her Ryland-tortured adolescence, she sought the simple comfort of blending into the halls, the back row of class, and the loser lunch table for one. She'd been an above average student who only received knocks for shyness, and lack of class participation.

The one bright spot was Joey Taylor, the starting centerfielder for the GRHS Grizzlies and the center of her tiny universe. He was the lone reason she shoved the comforter from her face every morning. Not that he knew she existed beyond the praise band at church, and when the Grizzlies won the state baseball championship Joey Taylor had swung completely out of her orbit along with the last good thing about Gibson's Run.

Despite vowing never to return, she had a reoccurring fantasy of coming back to town to be honored as a Hall of Fame alumna. And, maybe she'd imagined Joey Taylor giving her introduction speech. And maybe, just maybe, she'd envisioned Ryland Jessup fifty pounds overweight and balding, sitting in the audience while she gave her acceptance speech.

"Well, as I live in breathe. If it isn't T.T. Tarrington."

A shiver ran down her spine at the sound of the voice she would recognize fifty years from now. Swiveling, Tessa locked her gaze with steely gray eyes that seemed to twinkle with a bit of the devil.

"Ryland Jessup."

Full head of hair and the evidence of a flat belly beneath his GRHS polo shirt.

Swirl. Flush.

2

Tessa's lungs burned as she sucked in a breath to keep her scream in check. Ryland Jessup. Of course her first day back at GRHS had to mirror her last with his smarmy grin and busting biceps blocking the hall. She resisted the urge to look down to confirm zero puddles. Once a piddler always a piddler.

"What brings you back to high school, T.T.?" Looping one thick, muscled forearm over the other, he leaned against the row of freshly painted lockers. His gaze raked over her body from the nothing heels of her sensible black flats to her simple ponytail before settling his overly inquisitive gaze directly on her face.

With a swipe of her hand over her forehead, she locked a stock sorority smile across her lips and spoke through clenched teeth. "I'm filling in for Mrs. Monahan while she's on short term disability for her hip."

"Huh, that puts you here for the rest of the semester."

She nodded. "I need to get to class." Without a word of dismissal she pivoted, taking long strides toward her classroom.

"Hey, wait up." His sneakers squeaked as he jogged to catch her. His hand clamped on to her shoulder and he spun her to face him. "That was kind of rude, T.T. We're colleagues now. Don't be all standoffish like when we were kids."

Her mouth dropped open.

"Yeah, kind of like this..."

A dangerous combination of twenty years of teasing and weeks of paparazzi pursuit exploded. "Are you kidding me? Standoffish? Rude? You've called me T.T. since I was six years old. You remind me *every* time I see you of the most humiliating three minutes of my life. You're a rude, insensitive jock who, I imagine, returned to high school because this is the only place bullying is still tolerated in America."

He slid away from her. His face reflected shock and maybe a little awe.

She knew it was rude. She didn't care. She just needed to get away from him. Running the twenty feet to her class room, she slammed the door shut.

~*~

Ryland walked toward the athletic office located outside the boys' locker room. Flipping the light switch, he ignored the buzzing of the bulbs kicking to life. His chair groaned under the bulk of his six foot, six inch frame.

T.T. Tarrington was back in Gibson's Run. She had just gone down the hall before disappearing around the corner to the upperclassman wing. He'd seen her with his own eyes.

She was still as pretty as a fairytale princess. Corn silk hair brushed the top of her waistband and eyes the color of spring grass sparkled. But gone was the shy waif who barely peeped outside of the church praise band. Somewhere between graduation and this morning, T.T. discovered a voice. And that voice was a shrew.

Ryland couldn't recall the last time he'd been torn

down so viciously in public. Coaches kept their yelling to offices and sidelines. His father was always more of a "teach by example" parent and only yelled when he was trying to get all six of his kids to the dinner table at the same time. Most people in his circle treated Ryland with kindness or at least good natured joking—which was what his old nickname for Tessa was. Just some good natured teasing. But when women were in the mix, good-natured and kindness were often worlds apart.

His late wife had been the master at the private cut and the public coo. When she was alive, Macy Collins-Jessup had been all about keeping private business private. Back then she was an NFL wife. He was the starting middle linebacker on a top ten team. They had an image to preserve. Macy and Ryland Jessup were the poster couple for success in professional sports; a couple with on-paper Christian values who attended church regularly, sponsored two local charities, and had the sweetest baby girl God ever created. Or at least that's what every Macy-approved press release touted.

For too long, Ryland bought the lie. He had loved his former cheerleader wife. She was beautiful and outwardly sweet. He thought she was his ultimate supporter, encouraging him to go into the draft a year early after completing his undergraduate work in three years. His mother balked at her only son's decision to forgo his final year of Division I ball and the chance at a graduate degree, but Macy convinced Ryland waiting for his NFL break could include a break to his body and the end of his NFL dream. At the ripe-old age of twenty-one, Ryland Tucker Jessup became the fifteenth overall pick in the draft, a husband, and less than a year later the proud father of Emma Grace Jessup.

Today, five short years after he walked on the stage and donned the hat of his new team, he was a widower, a single dad to a rambunctious toddler, and the coach of his former high school football team—his NFL career a near distant memory.

As topsy-turvy as the last five years had been, he wouldn't change a moment of them. Except the death of his wife. They had been heading to divorce court, but Emma would need her mother one day. He hoped the Lord gave him the strength and the words to help his wonderful daughter grow into the delightful beauty he knew was lying dormant inside her four-year-old tomboy frame.

He glanced out his two-by-four window—the only source of natural light or fresh air in the sardine container the school district called the athletic department head office—and his mind dropped back to Tessa Tarrington. When he was six years old he declared to his mother he would love Tessa Tarrington until the day he died. His mind replayed the day like a home movie.

Tripping over his too large feet, he ran through the back door of the four bedroom house, home to the giant Jessup family. "Momma! Momma! I just gots t-ta t-tells you something." He yelled, stumbling over his "T's" with his front teeth lost to the Tooth Fairy.

"Ryland, it is 'have to tell' you something. No one 'gots' anything. It's not a word." His mother had her PhD and taught courses on the impact of ancient masterpieces on modern literature, the early writings of C.S. Lewis, and her personal favorite, the complete works of Jane Austen. She did not tolerate poor grammar—even in her beloved youngest son, just starting kindergarten.

"Yes, Momma. Well, I have to t-tell you. I met my wife today."

She chuckled. "Really, Ryland. What's her name?"

"T-Tessa. T-Tessa T-Tarrington." He gave her a broad, toothless grin.

"You're planning to marry Reverend Tarrington's little girl? Why?"

That's what he loved most about his momma. She didn't think he was crazy even when he told her something she clearly thought was not quite right. She talked to him as if he were a grown-up. She talked to him just as she talked to his oldest sister, Elizabeth, who was thirteen and real grown-up.

"Because she's the prettiest girl I ever sawed. She looks just like a princess in one of those fairy t-tale books the t-twins have."

"The prettiest girl you ever saw."

"Yes ma'am. Prettiest next to you."

She slid a cookie onto a plate in front of him and asked him the most serious question of his life. "Pretty isn't everything, Ryland. Why else do you want to marry her?"

"She's real smart. She knew Columbus was the capital of Ohio. Who knows stuff like that?" He snatched the cookie and clumsily chomped down using his molars.

"Who knows stuff like what?" His father asked as he entered the kitchen wiping at the sweat dripping down his face.

"Stuff like Columbus being the capital of Ohio." His mother offered. "Your son has fallen in love with a beautiful and smart girl it seems."

His father nodded and ruffled the top of Ryland's curly brown head. "Well, like father like son."

Ryland chuckled at the memory and all of the days that quickly followed in kindergarten. After school, his mother would ask him about his day and he would start with a story about Tessa. Occasionally he talked about his friends Joey and Marshall but mostly his talk focused on Tessa Tarrington and his eternal love for her. When he received the invitation to her birthday party, he asked all his friends and his sisters what he should get for her.

His sister, Harper, said he should get her a doll; that way when she went to sleep every night she would think of Ryland. The twins—Marianne and Elinor—thought he should get her a football so they could play together. But his best friend, Joey Taylor, landed on the perfect gift. "Days of the Week" underwear.

"Just think Rys...she'll think of you every day and just about my favorite things on the planet, other than my baseball glove, are my superhero underwears. When I wear them I'm never scared of the third graders stealing my lunch. You give her 'em underwears and she'll never be scared of nothin'."

And so he'd ridden his first two wheeler four blocks into town and spent all his baseball card money at *Suzi's on Main* on the pretty box of rolled up underwear. He was thrilled. He went straight home and wrapped the box all by himself. Everyone at the party was surprised by his present, but no one more than Tessa. She reacted just like his new puppy, Bennett, and peed all over the floor. He wanted to warn her and so he tried to whisper to her, "You pee-pee'd T-T..." but he was too late.

All the boys at the party heard his stuttered attempt to warn the love of his life of her embarrassing moment. The warning devolved into a taunt. Tessa ran to her parents' bedroom and Ryland was dragged by his mother's bear claw grip from the party—out of Tessa's life. The whispered warning twisted into a nickname and the love of his life became his mortal enemy.

"Hey Coach," the soft knock and strangled voice of fifteen-year old sophomore, Jackson Murray, halted his trip down memory lane.

"Murray," he glanced at the wall clock. The school was fifteen minutes deep into first period. "Shouldn't you be in English?"

The gangly, three-sport athlete shrugged causing his overly long hair to flop in his eyes. "We got a sub. No bigs." He plopped in the chair opposite Ryland's desk.

"Major bigs, Murray." Ryland slammed his chair back to the wall with a squeak and a muffled thud. "And by the sound of your grammar you need all the time in English class you can spare. Maybe I should discuss a special reading assignment with your new substitute for you. Improve your take on the beautiful language of kings and queens. What do you say?" Without waiting for a response, he roughly guided the six-foot-two starting first baseman down the hall.

Ryland was about to see Tessa Tarrington for a second time in one day. Her response to him for round two most likely would not be improved.

3

The shrill of the bell announced the end of the school day and Tessa's eighth period Modern American Literature class.

"OK ladies and gentlemen, we'll pick up tomorrow where you left off with Mrs. Monahan. We'll be reviewing the potential titles to use for your papers on dystopian literature in the modern era. Have a wonderful evening."

The mix of juniors and seniors trickled into the hallway. The din of their conversations followed in their wake.

Her eyes flittered shut, the blessing of silence encapsulating her. Every muscle in her body felt as if she had run back-to-back marathons. Even her fingernails hurt. *How does one actually have pain in the fingernail?* With a long sigh, she pushed from her chair to wipe the giant white board behind her.

"I kind of miss chalkboards."

As if she wasn't already in enough pain. She plastered a long-practiced sorority smile on her lips and turned to find Ryland Jessup holding up the door frame of her classroom. "Coach Jessup, what can I do for you?"

"Well, Miss T., it's not what you can do for me. It's what I can do for you."

She gritted her teeth, but her smile never wavered. She had perfected the smile after three years of Rush, encountering hundreds of girls, and several sisters, who were less than genuine. Delta Alpha Psi, her chosen sisterhood, was not one of the crazy, partying kind of sororities that ended up on the news with black slashes hiding the identity of underage girls. Her sisterhood was more subdued—filled with girls majoring in English, Elementary Education, or something with the arts. They had movie nights featuring the latest British film, and book clubs discussing the finer points of Austen's heroines. She'd found her people. Bookworms in pearls.

Not that she liked all of her sisters—life in families never worked that simply. Bobbi Ann Risdy and Joanie Lee Wilston didn't make her post-college Christmas card list. But, within the sanctity of her sorority, Tessa found her most cherished friends. For an only child, small town loner, Lily Mae Benton and Ella Donavon were the water Tessa's parched soul desperately needed. And for Lily and Ella, she'd learned to plaster a smile and give a *'God bless her soul'* to her less-than-beloved sisters.

Her sorority days taught her hundreds of lessons. Everything from what table service to use when hosting a seven course dinner, to dealing diplomatically with individuals whose presence was similar to the scraping of nails down a blackboard. She learned to be surface sweet even to the vilest of people. Ryland Jessup was nearly as low on her list as Bobbi Ann Risdy. But as with her sisterhood nemesis, her smile never wavered while Ryland swallowed up the doorway to her room.

Despite returning the errant Jackson Murray to class and forcing him to apologize in front of all of his peers, Ryland remained at the center of all of her childhood pain. Tessa wished she had some petroleum jelly handy for her teeth when her lips dried from faking the grin too long. "Coach Jessup I don't believe there's anything I need, but thank you for asking."

He shoved away from the doorframe. With two steps into her classroom, Tessa's breathing went shallow. The man's mere presence sucked all the oxygen from the room. He was well over a foot taller than she was, with shoulders every linebacker in America envied. His hair was military short, likely to avoid the curl he'd hated as a child. His gray eyes twinkled with a smile, but she knew the devil was ready to pounce through those full lips.

"Well, Miss T., I think there is."

"Please don't call me that."

"Miss T.?"

"Yes, I buried that nickname under the fifty yard line when I was seventeen years old."

"What nickname? I've heard students all day referring to the new substitute Miss T. I think one of my football players told me that's what the 'cool lady sub whose letting us read regular stuff' asked to be called."

"Oh…" Her cheeks warmed, probably straight to fire engine red. She *had* told the students they could call her Miss Tarrington or Miss T. "I guess I did, but that was for the students. Not for the teachers."

"Well, what are the teachers supposed to call you?"

"Tessa…"

"Naw….that's no fun. You need a nickname. Everyone likes a nickname."

She lifted her dilapidated cross-body saddlebag from the floor and shoved overflowing folders inside. "Not everyone likes nicknames. Trust me."

He thrust a beefy hand through his cropped hair. "I'm sorry Tessa. I was trying to be nice. I seemed to have messed up again."

"Again?" She hoisted the near bursting bag on her left shoulder.

He yanked her coat and hat from the hook behind her, brushing her shoulder with his arm. "Yep. I've hurt your feelings more often than a rookie quarterback gets sacked."

"That many, huh?" She couldn't help the tug at the corner of her mouth.

"Yes, ma'am. It all started with a little boy who was head over heels for the prettiest, smartest girl he'd ever seen but he couldn't seem to ever get things right. And instead of making that little girl love him, he hurt her so bad, now she hates him."

Her heart warmed with the tender gloss of his gaze. Not a little devil in sight. "She doesn't hate you."

"Aww, but I think she does. And I need to start making it up to her."

She tried to slip on her wool jacket, but struggled with the balance of the saddlebag shifting sides. With his forefinger he lifted the bag, and shrugged her into her woolen coat, hooking her bag efficiently over her shoulder. Gently, he tugged the soft toboggan over her ears, scrunching her ponytail to her head.

She swallowed against the rising thickness in her throat. "How're you gonna do that?"

"Maybe we could have a coffee or something. And it's 'going to'. Just because you are from Ohio doesn't mean you should end your sentences with a preposition."

BAAM! He did it again! Ryland Jessup made her feel like an idiot. *Prettiest, smartest girl he'd ever seen.*

Bah! She stepped back, sidling around him to the door. "Coach Jessup, I don't think there's anything we have to say to one another. Good-bye." She zoomed through the door and was halfway down the back hallway leading to the associate parking lot, when the weight of five meaty fingers clamp onto her shoulder.

"What's your problem, T.T.? I'm trying to be nice. I wanted to properly welcome you back to Gibson's Run."

Pivoting to face him, she laced her arms across her chest. "And does mauling a co-worker on her way to the parking lot fall into the category of 'nice' or 'welcoming'?"

"When did you become so touchy?"

"I don't know. Maybe it was being humiliated when I was six years old in front of my entire kindergarten class—who all graduated high school with me because this town is the size of a cereal puff. Or maybe it was the years between junior and senior high when Pee-Pee Tee-Tee was shortened just to T.T. but you and Marshall Smith felt the need to remind everyone of the origins of the nickname. Or maybe it was during the praise band concert when you started shouting 'go T.T. like it's your birthday' from the back pew of church. Or maybe it was one of the hundreds of other days in the miserable thirteen years I spent in this town. Take your pick. But I can't imagine what someone as cool and awesome as Ryland Jessup has to say to someone as "touchy" as little old T.T. Tarrington. Good evening, Coach."

She spun out of his grip like a wide receiver avoiding a tackle, and for the second time in one day, Tessa Tarrington ran like an old toilet—noisy and erratic.

4

"Daddy," Tessa hollered as she stumbled through the front door of her father's parsonage. "I'm home. What do you want for dinner?" She dropped her bag and coat near the front door coat rack. Kicking off her shoes, she padded sock-footed to the paneled library-study her father used as his home office.

Since his heart attack four weeks ago while giving the third Sunday in Advent sermon on the shepherds being called to literally 'go and tell it on the mountain,' Thomas Tarrington had retreated to his private sanctuary every morning.

When Tessa was a child, her father's office was a place of reverence and peace. If the door was shut, her mother would say, "Tessa you always need to knock before you barge. More than likely the good Lord is in for a sit-down with Daddy. You wouldn't want to disturb them, now, would you?"

Until Tessa was sixteen, she was afraid to walk in too soon after her father opened the door for fear she would come face to face with The Lord. Not that she didn't love and cherish Him—she did—she was just trying to avoid a repeat of her sixth birthday party. Once a piddler…

"Daddy…" The door was cracked and she could hear the woeful tunes of the new country band she recommended filling the tiny space.

"Come on in, sweetie." Her father's voice, though no longer quite the interesting mix of booming volume and subtle tones, was still the greatest sound of comfort in her life.

Pushing the door, the vision of her father's mad-scientist hair, well-worn cardigan and holey socks, made her wince. "Daddy, have you left the office today?"

"I was reading some Lewis and lost track of time." He slipped his reading glasses from the bridge of his nose. "You know how that can be." He lifted a bushy eyebrow.

She slid onto the overstuffed leather ottoman beside her father's propped feet. "All too well. A dorm fire nearly took me because I was rereading *Pride and Prejudice*. I was desperately trying to correlate Austen's work to a modern romance novel I'd been assigned. I was so engrossed in Elizabeth's first view of Pemberley it took a firefighter tapping me on my shoulder to put the novel down."

Her father rubbed his forehead. "Tessa, you've always been an over-sharer. That was not a story this old heart needed to hear." His words reprimanded but his voice held a smile. He patted her hand. "How was the first day back at your alma mater?"

"How about we discuss what you'd like to have for dinner? We can't have grilled cheese and tomato soup again." She also knew how to make mac & cheese and scrambled eggs, but she'd exhausted both in the first two weeks. She didn't think her father was up to the Cajun cooking she'd learned in New Orleans, regardless of how mild she tended to make her etouffee.

"Why don't we take a walk and get a sandwich at *Only the Basics*? Maggie added soups and sandwiches with the New Year. Being a Monday night she's likely pretty quiet."

Tessa had met Maggie McKitrick at the small café her second day back in town. Maggie was the holder of the coffee. The coffee was what kept Tessa standing, upright and audible. Maggie also appeared to be a favorite of her father's parishioners. Bonus.

"Are you sure you can make it that far?" The coffee shop was on Main Street about a half of a mile from the parsonage.

"The doctor said I needed to walk a little every day. It's particularly nice for January in Ohio. We can't be wasting one of God's precious gifts because my heart isn't as strong as it was three years ago."

Three years ago…Mother.

Her father's spirit never fully recovered from her mother's untimely death.

Julie Tarrington contracted a summer cold she thought she'd shake with a little over the counter medicine and rest. By the end of August the doctor told her she had a rare form of lung cancer and less than six months to live. She made it to the Apple Festival in October before her eyes closed in prayer for the last time.

Pastor Tom pulled the celebration of his wife's life together while he was crumbling on the inside. He never took a break—not one Sunday—after her death. He just kept pushing until his broken heart cracked four weeks ago and nearly left Tessa an orphan.

"You're right. The weather is almost balmy for January in Ohio. Let me get your boots and coat. We'll leave right now. We don't want to run the risk of Maggie closing early due to a slow Monday."

~*~

Tessa snagged the one empty table in the middle of the bustling café. After settling her dad, she went to the counter to place their orders. She tapped her foot to the rhythm of the Christian Rock mix humming through the sound system.

The little café—formerly called *Taylor's*—was the same spot where she'd folded herself into empty-tabled corners when her mother shooed her out of the house. She'd sipped on coffee, nibbled cookies, and escaped to worlds as diverse as a raft on the Mississippi and a cold train bound for certain death. But of all the storied worlds of escape, her favorites were always the love stories. Tragic to joyful, love stories held the mystery of the universe for Tessa. Within their crumpled, worn pages, she became the heroine. The lead in fiction even if she was an edited character in real life. She'd prayed some of her more desperate prayers while sitting at the two person window table. *Taylor's* was the nearest place to a sanctuary outside of her father's church, and Mrs. Lorraine Taylor had been her priest.

Mrs. Taylor seemed to know when to talk and when to listen. Tessa's mother had been the most wonderful person in her life, but Tessa never wanted to reveal the true extent of her miserable alone-ness to former homecoming queen Julie Tarrington. Mrs. Taylor was a neutral party with zero expectations. And she baked the best chocolate chip cookies on the planet. Tessa missed Mrs. Taylor nearly as much as her own mother. A little café and bakery in the shop was a nice tribute to the woman Tessa still dearly loved.

"May I help you?"

The question tugged Tessa back to the present. She

narrowed her attention on the petite shop owner, Maggie.

"Hi, Tessa, what brings you in tonight? How's your dad?"

Tessa pointed over her shoulder toward her father who was talking with another patron. "He wanted to go for a walk. Suggested we head over here. I think the walk was good for him, but he'll feel it tomorrow."

"I'm so sorry I didn't see you both come in." She said with a wave toward Tessa's father. "We've been slammed since we added some savory dishes to the menu a few weeks ago. It's a wonderful problem, but unfortunately the extra business makes me a less hospitable host." She took Tessa's order with a smile. "I promise I'll stop by your table as soon as this wave dies down."

Tessa stuffed her change back in her wallet. Turning toward the coffee carafes, she slammed into a wall of solid muscle. Drawing her gaze from the size fourteen shoes and past the broad chest, she braced for the steely gray eyes and a glance at the devil. "Excuse me." She mumbled. She tried to edge past Ryland, but her path to the coffee was blocked by four juniors from her third period composition class. She bit her lip and glanced at her father to see if he was a viable pathway to caffeine.

"Let me do it." Ryland snatched the cup from her hand and plowed through the gaggle of teens who giggled as he passed.

He filled her cup with steamy goodness and she struggled to match him with the rude bully she'd known nearly her whole life. A tug on her pant leg drew her attention, and she dropped her gaze to the curly-headed face staring up at her.

"Do y'know my daddy?"

Daddy? Was Ryland Jessup a father? Was he married? Had the married Ryland Jessup almost attempted to ask her out today? Of course he was married. *Scum.*

"Yes, I do know your father. I've known him since...how old are you?"

Her fingers fanned to reveal four chubby digits. "This manys."

"This many." Her father corrected.

"Well, I've known your father since I was only a little older. If you'll excuse me, I need to get back to my own father." She lifted the cup from Ryland's hand. "Thank you for my coffee." Leaning up on her tip-toes, she whispered, "I can't believe you were asking me out today when you're *married*. You're...*hmphf!*" She dropped to her heels and spun toward her dad.

Their sandwiches waited in little woven baskets on the table. Presumably delivered by Maggie, who sat in one of the three empty chairs chatting with Dad.

"It's so good to have you back in the café, Pastor Tom." Maggie said. "I've missed seeing you for Make-Up Mondays."

"What are Make-Up Mondays?" Tessa asked, sliding onto a chair opposite her father.

"Make-Up Mondays are the tradition I started with Emma." Ryland answered. "When I missed church due to a Sunday game. We invited Pastor Tom to join us when we noticed him by himself on Monday's a few months back."

A wave of embarrassment coupled with a fresh shower of disgust, and mixed with a touch of dread, washed over Tessa.

Emma climbed on the seat next to Dad. Stretching

her toddler arms around his neck, she squeezed as if she was hugging a favorite teddy bear. "I missed you Pastor Tom. Make-Up Mondays have been real borings without you."

"Emma, we should leave Pastor Tom and his daughter to their dinner." Ryland tried to extricate his four year-old from her life sized toy.

"No!" Emma twisted in Tessa's father's lap and crossed her arms.

"Young lady, I'll not tolerate an attitude."

"But I wanna have a *real* Make-Up Monday. If we don't have hot chocolate with Pastor Tom, it ain't no real Make-Up."

"Isn't—do not let your grandmother hear you ever say the word ain't, or I might get my first switch to my backside." He held out her coat. "Now let's go. You can pick the movie tonight."

Emma scooted down and dropped to the floor.

Tessa glanced at her father. Sadness shadowed his eyes as Ryland help Emma with her coat. Guilt needled her. The love between a four year-old, her father, and her arch-nemesis was tangible.

"Ryland?" she whispered, with a soft touch to his shoulder.

He whipped around as if he'd been shot. His gaze locked with hers.

A long, quiet butterfly fluttered its wings within Tessa's belly. "My dad and I'd really like it if you and Emma would join us."

His face softened for a brief second, but he shook his head. "No, we should get home. This is your dad's first adventure out of the house. He doesn't need a four year old and her non-stop questions tiring him."

"I insist." She squatted to eye level with Emma.

"Would you like to have a sandwich with Pastor Tom?"

Her round cheeks puffed with a grin that took the whole of width of her little face. "Yes, please." Emma dropped her jacket to the floor, scooted a chair to within inches of her friend and climbed up. "Did you hear, Pastor Tom? I gets to stay."

Ryland puffed a sigh. "You get to stay."

But Tessa noticed the soft lift of his lips as his daughter and her father cuddled.

Tessa's chest tightened. "Emma, do you like ham?"

She nodded. Her curls bounced.

"Then you eat the sandwich in this basket. Your dad and I'll pick something else, OK?" Before Tessa could finish, Emma began methodically picking the sandwich apart, placing the pieces into separate piles. Tessa leaned into Ryland. "What's she doing?"

"She doesn't like the food to touch when she eats it."

"But isn't that the point of a sandwich?"

"Yes, and Emma will throw a little fit if you don't present her with an actual sandwich for her to demolish."

"Interesting kid."

"She knows what she wants and isn't afraid to go for it." His gaze drifted from his daughter to Tessa. The warmth and welcome she found in his dark gray eyes sent shivers of anticipation up her spine.

"From whom did she inherit that lovely trait?" Tessa chuckled.

He lowered his head, his breath warm on her cheek. "From me. I always get what I want."

5

By Friday, Tessa felt as though she'd been in a panini press baking on high. She was crunchy on the outside, but warming to gooey on the inside. The week had been a series of revelations, all beginning with the impromptu Monday night dinner.

Revelation #1: Emma Jessup might be smarter than every adult in her sphere of influence.

After recovering from the shock her father was a regular meal-sharer with Ryland Jessup, Tessa found herself falling under the spell of the enchanting Emma. The four year old was kinetic. Both Ryland and Tessa's dad were wrapped neatly around her plump toddler fingers. And if Tessa was being brutally, in-the-mirror honest, she was well on her way to being a card carrying member of the Emma Jessup fan club.

Revelation #2: Ryland Jessup was not the actual devil—he just played one from time to time.

Tessa's heart instantly softened toward her arch-nemesis when he was with his daughter. He treated Emma as if she were a precious jewel, encouraging her to shine and sparkle. Within hours of knowing the 'new' Ryland, Tessa quickly understood that the unspoken topic of Emma's mother was not to be discussed. Her father told her Ryland's wife died in a car accident a little over a year ago, about the same time he retired from the NFL, but no details beyond those two facts were shared with her. She didn't pry. But even with her near life-long distaste of all things

Ryland Jessup, she couldn't stop her heart from breaking a little for him—losing nearly everything he loved in such a short amount of time.

Revelation #3: Tessa Tarrington didn't hate Ryland Jessup.

The knowledge that the one person she'd single-handedly held responsible for her miserable childhood and adolescence was not the awful human being she'd assumed him to be was disconcerting. After Make-Up Monday, she continued to 'bump' into Ryland around town and at school. She saw him three out of four mornings at the café when she picked up her triple shot cappuccino. She walked headlong into him in the hallway outside of her classroom as he waited to escort a few students to their athletic physicals. And, following a treacherous exercise session, she cut through the park and crossed the battle lines of an epic snowball fight between Emma and Ryland.

He was everywhere. And yet, the loathing of him she had nurtured since she was six years old was losing the internal battle with forgiveness. In spite of the old adage that past performance dictates future behavior, Ryland Jessup was rapidly ascending her dislike meter. He now sat on par with a ten-minute mechanical flight delay: annoying but quickly overcome once the plane reached its soaring altitude. He was inching towards the like half of the meter, and she was struggling with how to cope with the rapid transition.

That she had thoughts falling into anything other than revulsion made her feel like the time she ate four beignets in one sitting—kind of nauseous and uncomfortable. Closing the novel her AP English class would begin next week, she watched the final seconds of the school day tick by as her eleventh grade American Lit class hurriedly finished their surprise quiz on Ray Bradbury. The bell shrilled and twenty-two heads popped up in unison. Tessa barely suppressed her grin. "Didn't finish?"

"Aww, Miss T. This was impossible!" Jared Noland whined, and twenty-one fellow victims, *err* students, bobble-headed behind him.

"Well," she said, shifting to the front of her desk. "I guess no one will refer to this class as a...let me see what was so cleverly written?" She lifted her tablet from her desk and swiped to unlock the hidden social media page dedicated to Slacker Subs in Central Ohio school districts.

Two days earlier, an incessant beep notified Tessa she was on the list placed there after Grady Bell and Bode Michaelson posted comments about their first class with her. Their reviews were not flattering.

"Yes, here it is: 'Tessa Tarrington hit the halls of GRHS this morning. She stutters when she's nervous and we clearly make her a bundle of nerves. We's toats gonna Bueller out of her class. We got her snowed. And no sweater's gonna keep out our white stuff. She thinks we care about all that literature junk, but if we play it right we's be able to convince the Newb that Mrs. Slow-Mo's plan for the semester was to watch the movie adaptations of the dumb books we's supposed to read. Slam! Here come da 'A'. Can't spell easy without it. Welcome to GRHS Miss. T. The Junior class was never so thankful for a hip surgery.'" She glanced at the back row of boys including Jared, Grady and Bode.

All three faces were bright enough to keep the town's fountain spouting water for the next three years.

"Would you like me to go on, gentlemen?" The entire back row of the class slouched in their chairs. "I didn't think so. You're dismissed. Please lay your tests on my desk."

Only the muffled sound of shuffled papers hovered in the room as each of the twenty-two students filed past her. Jared, Grady and Bode tried to sneak out with the masses. "Guys, I think you owe Miss Tarrington an apology."

Her head snapped toward the doorway. The air sucked from the room forcing Tessa to drag in shallow breaths.

Ryland Jessup leaned against the frame with the appearance of a man who had all the time in the world.

"Sorry Miss T." The culprits mumbled in unison.

"You three meet me in the gym tomorrow morning at six sharp ready to work. And skip hanging out at PaPa Pete's tonight. No pizza until your grammar steps out of the gutter and resembles something in line with those glowing letters of reference I composed last fall."

Work? Their grammar was atrocious, but what could the boys possibly retain in a gym at six o'clock in the morning? She could barely retain the cup of coffee she greedily gulped down at six.

"But Coach," Jared's voice rang out—the octave of a thirteen year old girl denied the latest boy band concert with her friends. "Tomorrow's Saturday. It's a holiday weekend. MLK's Monday."

Ryland straightened and all three boys visibly swallowed against what looked like baseballs in their throats.

Grady dropped a hand on either of his buddies'

shoulders, guiding them toward the doorway to move past Ryland. "We'll be there Coach. Six. On the dot. Promise."

With a flip of his chin, Ryland allowed the students to slip out of the room. His narrowed focus followed them until they'd disappeared.

Her heart twisted as he swung his gaze to meet hers. How had she never noticed his eyes were the color of the sky during a summer storm or that he had a dimple in his right cheek which seemed to wink at her with his slow grin? She grabbed the stack of unfinished tests. "Umm, thanks, but I had it under control. I think the pop quiz got their collective attention. I don't believe I'll have similar problems in the future." She shuffled the papers, stuffing them in a folder with shaking fingers. "I'm not as much of a weakling as I used to be."

"Whoever said you were weak?" he asked.

With a snort, she turned to face him. "Well, I wasn't exactly the picture of strength when I was a teenager."

"I don't know." He propped his hip against a front row desk, his weight causing the leg to squeak against the freshly waxed floor. "You always seemed pretty strong to me. And a little scary."

"Scary?"

"Sure," he said with a shrug. "You're the pastor's kid. From the time you showed up in kindergarten you were a mystery. This girl who seemed to appear out of nowhere with long blonde hair, and knowing green eyes. Who seemed to anticipate every wrong move one us would make. Back then, I thought you had a secret phone line to God in your house so you could rat me out."

"Rat you out?"

"Yeah, Joey thought you knew *the* Big Guy personally because your dad was the preacher. You were so quiet and kept to yourself—we were convinced the only One you ever talked to was God. And with that kind of connection, you could've spilled all of our dirty secrets in one not so long phone call. Pretty intimidating." The pull of his grin was nearly impossible to resist.

God *had been* the only One with whom she ever talked. Mostly she sought His comfort because she'd been lonely. Had they really been intimidated by her? Ryland Jessup? Joey Taylor…a vision of slightly overgrown locks and eyes the color of rich espresso flashed through her mind.

Joey Taylor would likely always be the one who got away. Of course she would have had to have him for him to really have gotten away, but the sentiment was still true. In theory.

"*Hmpf*," she puffed, trying to hide her rising blush. "So making me the recipient of your teasing-genius was your strategy to keep on the good side of God?"

"Genius, huh?" He snatched her bag from the coat rack and slung it on his shoulder.

"Criminals can be geniuses." She tugged her multiple layers of winter wear from the rack. She'd only been in Louisiana fulltime for four years, but her blood was thinner than the elbows of her father's favorite work shirt.

Wrapping the six foot scarf around her neck she tried to shake the near palpable pull of Ryland as he stood behind her. She'd been trying to ignore him all week, but the task was nearly impossible. He was everywhere. What was she to do with a problem like

Ryland? And not for the first time since returning to the purgatory she called high school, her eyes drifted shut and she lifted a silent prayer to her BFF. *Please Lord, help me find a way.* She wasn't quite sure what direction she preferred but she knew at the moment she desperately wanted *the way* to be far from jock turned coach, Ryland Jessup. Being in his presence was messing with her only strong muscle—her mind.

His snort drew her spirit out of prayer. "How many layers do you have there? Its only thirty degrees. It's Ohio. That's practically a heat wave in January."

Wiggling her cable-knit-sweater-covered arms through the double feather-down sleeves of her new winter coat, she probably presented as pretty a picture as sausage finding its new casing.

"Thirty is cold. Water freezes at thirty-two. I should be asking you 'where are your layers?' Polo shirts in the winter aren't a very good example." She wrestled with the zipper and silently cursed her new affinity for Maggie McKitrick's salted caramel brownies.

Her reflection in the window looked as if she should be advertising for a tire company. Why couldn't she look cool one time? Just one time. Especially when she was in the irritating presence of Ryland Jessup. Since the moment she crossed the county line four weeks ago, her hanging-by-a-thread confidence seemed to have slipped into winter hibernation.

"Need help?"

She faced Ryland. With her best Delta Alpha Psi smile plastered across her lips, she answered him. "Thank you for the offer, Coach, but as you can see I'm quite capable of dressing myself." She tugged on her gloves as her knitted cap fell to the floor. How would she fold twenty plus inches of down circling her middle to retrieve her hat?

Ryland swiped the cap from the floor. He tugged the scratchy hat on her head, flattening her ponytail to her scalp and trailing a stream of sparks down her cheek from his light touch. Ryland Jessup shoving her hat on her head was becoming a habit she needed to break.

He rested his hands on her puffy shoulders. "Everyone needs help, Tessa. It's OK to ask." He lifted her bag from his shoulder and looped it across her down-encased body. "I'll always be here for you. All you have to do is ask."

6

Ryland blew his whistle. Seven boys pivoted, sprinting to the opposite end of the gym. The wooden planked floor squeaked under the pounding pressure of the teenagers—all of whom were avoiding suspension, detention, or expulsion by participating in Coach Jessup's Saturday Suicide Session. A tradition he started soon after becoming the full-time Athletic Director and Head Football coach.

Within days of taking over the job, he'd received a stack of complaints from teachers, administrators, and the band director, claiming athletes were not following the same rules as the rest of the matriculating student population. The standard punishment did little to deter an occasional roll of toilet paper thrown across the town square or the rite of passage of mooning the band after football practice.

Ryland offered to take on the challenge of disciplining all athletes—male or female—for the balance of the year, without influence or intrusion of the principal or the school board. Frustrated with the ineffectiveness of the students' responses to the punishments delivered to date, the school board agreed. Ryland dusted off his dad's old whistle and went to work establishing Saturday Sessions.

After three weeks, the football team dubbed the non-stop sprints as Jessup's Suicide Saturdays and the name stuck. Student-athletes caught breaking school rules, circumventing the honor code, or crossing the line between joke and jerk were sentenced to two hours of hard labor: line to line suicide sprints in the gym.

The irony that he—Ryland "Jester" Jessup the mastermind of some of the greatest pranks in Gibson's Run's one hundred and fifty year history—was now the one doling out discipline was not lost on him. Considering he had been chastised by the best—Coach Carl Jessup—logic would stand he learned a thing or two. Ryland was more than willing to pass his knowledge on to the younger generation.

Blowing his whistle, he motioned all seven boys to the bleachers for a water break.

Grady, Bode, and Jared, the culprits behind the social media comments, limped toward the water cooler. All three boys were starters on the football and baseball teams. They were from great families, attended his church nearly every Sunday, and were the first to volunteer for the student council blood drive over Christmas. Why would they have written on that awful website about Tessa?

Tessa Tarrington. His reaction to her return was unprecedented. Not since he was a kindergartener and declared his unending love for a green-eyed little girl had he been this consumed by a desire to be in someone's presence.

When he met Macy at a friend's bonfire, he would go weeks without calling her. Even after they were married, he often went days on the road without contact, nearly forgetting he had a wife.

But with Tessa, his need to see her—to be near her –was overwhelming him. Not that his attention made a difference.

Tessa treated him as if she expected Ryland to

have a shock-buzzer in his hand, diligently keeping him at a suspicion-filled distance. If he hadn't deliberately stopped for coffee after dropping Emma off each morning this week or conveniently remembered a few students were in need of physicals, he wouldn't have seen her after dinner on Monday.

He rubbed his neck and regarded the seven student-athletes oozing the toxic aroma of locker room stench from their pores. All seven—including Ball, Michaelson, and Noland—were excellent athletes, but they were bored. The long stretch of short days between the end of football season and baseball try-outs was primetime for a wide range of practical jokes and general mischievousness for non-basketball players or wrestlers. Sprinting lines in the gym on a holiday weekend wouldn't be sufficient to keep them from lighting bags of doggie remains on fire or worse: crossing a line they wouldn't be able to cross back over.

"OK guys. I don't want to see you here again. Ever. You get one Saturday Session. One." He narrowed his focus on the first two boys in the row. "Simpson and Messing—did you write a note of apology to Mr. Tyler?"

Both boys nodded.

His starting QB, Blaine Simpson, and his best shortstop, Riley Messing, had painted Tony Tyler's auto shop windows with a series of interesting, comic inspired cars. The words painted above the cars were nearly as colorful as the neon window paint they'd used.

"One more thing…why don't you use your obvious love for art in a more creative outlet? There's an exhibit of Van Gogh at the Columbus Museum of

Art. They're open for the holiday. Enjoy Monday. I expect a fifteen hundred word essay on my desk before first period on Tuesday. Agreed?"

Expressions shattered across the boys' faces, but neither argued before jogging to the locker rooms.

"Morgan and Ray."

Freshmen Trevor Morgan and Mason Ray were clearly trying to find their places in the hierarchy of high school by "borrowing" the neighboring school's bulldog mascot. The dog was stuffed, but regardless, "borrowing" without asking was stealing. Both boys slouched over their thighs trying to fill their shallow lungs.

Ryland feared he'd have to keep them late to clean their puke up off the gym floor. He really didn't want to deal with messes of any kind, particularly vomit. He wasn't sure he'd be strong enough to keep his power bar and coffee in his own temperamental stomach. "Will you borrow anything without asking, ever again?"

Trevor and Mason both shook their heads, clearly fearful of opening their mouths.

"If either of you have a whiff of poor behavior near your persons in the next three and a half years, gentlemen, I'll personally call Chief Taylor and allow him to determine your punishment."

Trevor's and Mason's collective pallor fell to the color of paste.

Ryland shook his head and directed them to leave. Ignoring the limping fourteen year olds, he zeroed in on his real prey.

The three remaining delinquents in his gym at eight o'clock on Saturday morning—and the facilitators of hurt on Tessa Tarrington.

He dragged a folding chair over and stopped directly in front of the boys. Straddling the chair, he leaned his forearms on the backrest. The chair threatened to crack under the pressure of his two hundred and forty pound frame.

The three juniors were in varying states of misery. Grady's floppy brown hair, typically perfectly coiffed, was drowned in sweat. His cheeks were rosy with heat. Of the three, Grady probably felt the most guilt over the comments on the message board. Jared Noland and Bode Michaelson were disturbed at being caught, and likely hated having their good guy images tarnished in the eyes of the school, town, or even the church, but Grady Bell was a boy whose heart tended to live firmly on his sleeve. Not that he didn't try and hide it under jackets of bad jokes and harassing cheerleaders, but he definitely experienced life more deeply than the average teenage boy.

Ryland could identify. "And then there were three." He tried to keep his voice steady and clear, but his anger was coming to a boil. The thought of anyone hurting Tessa made his belly twist with fury. No more fear of chain reaction puking in front of students. Rage was a great antacid. "Gentlemen, of everyone who was sent to Saturday Sessions today, I'm most disappointed in you. You're called to be leaders—not just in school, but in our church. The teacher you violated with your attacks isn't any teacher, she's your pastor's daughter." He watched how his words impacted each of the boys' fallen faces. Guilt—he'd learned from his mother and five sisters—was a powerful weapon when properly wielded.

"Miss Tarrington left her job and her entire life to come back to Gibson's Run to help her dad—our pastor—heal. She accepted the position at GRHS because Mrs. Monahan specifically requested her to take over her classes. Mrs. Mo asked for Miss Tarrington because she knew Miss Tarrington's knowledge of literature and composition was better than a typical substitute. If Mrs. Mo couldn't teach you, she wanted you to have the best. Miss Tarrington has published a half dozen books, is finishing her masters in composition, and holds a Bachelors in Comparative Literature. You morons are extraordinarily blessed to have her as your teacher—no matter how long or how short her tenure is with the school.

"Instead of trying to take advantage of a new teacher, why don't you three use the brains I know the good Lord gave you and take advantage of all Miss Tarrington wants to teach you? Learn something. Be something other than immature imbeciles. I know you have it in you."

"OK, Coach…" Jared mumbled.

The other boys nodded their heads in agreement.

"You know you aren't getting away with one session of lines, right?" Their collective groan rattled the beams in the gym, and he couldn't suppress his chuckle. "No more running—at least not from me until baseball starts. But what I want you to do is call Miss Tarrington and Pastor Tom. See what they need." Each boy lifted his gaze to meet Ryland's, and the surprise he saw in their depths was a reminder that service was not second nature for the generation nipping at his heels. "You can do their grocery shopping, or clean the snow from their sidewalks, or go with Pastor Tom to a doctor's appointment, or something entirely different. I don't care what you do. I care that the three of you rediscover the leaders lurking deep inside. I know you each have a servant's heart. I just wish the seventeen year-old idiot didn't take over so often." He dropped his I'm-your-football-coach-don't-question-me stare before waving them toward the exit.

Jared and Bode shuffled as fast as their likely spaghetti legs would allow them, but Grady hesitated.

"Coach?"

"Yes, Bell. Is there something on your mind?"

The rangy teen scooted to face Ryland. He lifted his gaze to his coach, and the thick lashed, blue depths were brimming with tears.

Ryland sat a little straighter in his chair and nodded to Grady.

"Coach, I'm super sorry about hurting Miss T's feelings. She's really great."

"If she's so great, then why did you write all of those negative comments about her?"

He shrugged, dropping his focus to the super-sealed wood floor.

"Not a good answer, Bell. You never have permission to blatantly hurt someone, but if you like the person the last thing you should do is proactively injure."

The first tear drop hit the wood floor with a splash. And then they gushed like a tapped fire hydrant.

Shifting out of his chair, Ryland slid onto the bleacher bench beside Grady and waited for the seventeen-year-old to exorcize his teen angst. The wave of emotion was not uncommon for Grady. Ryland had sat beside him many times when tears flowed because the words were too confusing to comprehend.

Grady's father was a victim of friendly-fire while

stationed in the Middle East making the then pre-teen the man of his family. Sergeant Bell's death seemed to have shattered much of his son's childhood. Grady often seemed too old for his years, and yet made foolish decisions when he was faced with peer pressure.

With snuffled breaths, Grady began to speak. "I knew it w-was a b-bad idea, but the g-guys kept teasing me about l-liking Miss T in you know…that way." He glanced up to Ryland and his heart seemed to rip through his eyes. "I just had to do something, Coach."

He patted Grady's back. He knew how the kid felt. "I understand you made a bad choice in the face of a difficult situation, but Grady, it's never an acceptable solution to push someone else down so you feel better—or feel safer."

Grady swiped his giant wide receiver hands against his eyes. "I know. I need to be a leader. That's what my dad said to me every time he'd go in-country." He lifted his gaze to Ryland. "Sometimes it's easier to just go along, y'a know?"

Ryland's heart squeezed for the dozen years when it was easier to call Tessa, T.T. "Son, I know better than you could ever imagine."

"How do I fix it, Coach? I really like Miss T. She wants us to read all of these great current books—some stuff I've already read because it's so awesome—I know she's going to be a cool teacher. But now she thinks I hate her."

"She doesn't think you hate her, Grady."

Both Ryland and Grady swiveled at the soft sound of Tessa's voice wafting through the cavernous gymnasium.

Ryland's heart twisted at the sight of her long blond hair loose and messy around her shoulders. She was cocooned in that awful down coat. It looked as if twenty families could fit inside. She closed the distance, her booted feet leaving puddles of footprints in her wake. Except for the first moment he'd seen his daughter in his arms, Ryland didn't think he had ever seen anyone more beautiful. He shook his head. *Get a grip, Jessup.*

"Grady," she started, tugging at her gloves. She sat on the bleacher bench beside the teen. "I know those comments weren't really you. Any of the three of you." Her voice was soft with a bit of an early morning lilt. "You, Jared, and Bode seem to be wonderful young men. I just wonder why you wanted to hurt or discredit me with your words."

"Miss T. I can't really give you a good answer, I'm just sorry." More tears gushed down his cheeks. "You're a great teacher. Only a week in and I know you're gonna teach us a ton of great stuff."

"Well, I appreciate your apology. Although your diction and word choice need some help. Words exist beyond great to identify superior work. And 'gonna' will never be a word."

"Yes ma'am."

"Please don't beat yourself up about this situation, Grady." She lifted her gaze from Grady's and stared into Ryland's eyes. "We all do dumb things when we're teenagers. It's kind of like a rite of passage toward adulthood."

"I'm real sorry, Miss T." He rubbed his nose against his sweat drenched shoulder. "What can I do to show you?"

"Continue to work hard in class."

Grady lifted his speculative gaze between Ryland and Tessa.

"Even though I made the pop quiz nearly impossible to finish, or pass without a Masters in comparative literature, you earned a B+. The only questions you missed were the ones you didn't answer."

"Really?"

"Really. And, although your composition style is deplorable, I imagine if you apply the same effort you clearly gave to this morning's activity, you'll be able to excel in your writing as well. You have true potential, Grady Bell. Please don't do anyone a disservice by wasting your gifts."

"Yes, ma'am." His face lit as bright as if his heart was the core of the East Coast electrical grid.

"Get out of here, Bell, before my whistle finds my lips again." Ryland joked. "And don't forget to call Pastor Tom."

"Got it, Coach." He stood. His frame seemed to grow five inches with the simple and honest feedback Tessa poured into Grady. "See you at church tomorrow." He hollered over his shoulder as he disappeared into the locker room.

The echo of showers and muffled voices filtered into the gym, punctuating the silence between Tessa and Ryland.

Why was she here?

He straightened, reaching for his folding chair.

"Thank you."

He glanced over his shoulder at the muted words.

Based on her posture, Tessa was thanking the gleaming wooden floor.

"Tessa, the floor didn't do anything but take a bit

of a beating this morning. But go ahead and thank everyone and everything except me. I'm used to it." The whine was a little beneath him, but he was tired of extending olive branches. At the rate he'd been giving them to her, he could have started his own olive oil business.

"Thank you, Ryland." She stood, looking directly into his eyes. Her gaze glistened in the harsh fluorescent light. "I know you stuck your neck out to defend me."

The feeling of warm honey seemed to slide through his entire being with the intensity of her scrutiny.

Clearing his throat, he nodded and returned to straightening the gym, trying to dismiss her presence. He closed the small distance to the cart of folding chairs. The seemingly easy task of replacing one chair was unfortunately daunting. He struggled to straighten the shambled mess of metal and hinges. With brute force, he shoved the row of thirty plus chairs to the right in an effort to slide his chair behind the row. Like most non-football related things in his life, the chairs did not submit to his will and dominoed to the floor in a cascade of clangs, bangs, and sliding metal.

"Seriously," he muttered.

The cackle of laughter behind him shot his focus from the chairs to Tessa. He tried to summon his I'm-the-football-coach look, but her expression of pure delight pulled a chuckle from deep within his belly.

She struggled out of her enormous coat, dropping it on the bench. Sauntering toward him in skinny jeans and another two sizes too big sweater, he felt sucker punched. Only Tessa Tarrington could make no make-up and clothes that looked like they were selected in the dark gorgeous.

"So, was it your plan to get all the chairs on the floor?" she asked with a wink.

"I can't say that was my strategy." If he'd known he would receive help from her, he may have deliberately made himself look like an idiot. "Do you have any thoughts?"

She pushed her too long sleeves to her elbows. "Well, I think the best approach is to start at the very beginning." Her lips lifted to a sly grin. "Sometimes starting over is the only way to make things better."

7

Why was she at the school on a Saturday…at eight in the morning? Even when she was a student she'd barely made it to school on time. She truly believed only her dad's insistent prayers were behind her on time—barely—arrival each day her first week of subbing. Ghost writing was a perfect profession for her. She found many celebrities enjoyed sleeping late, so most of her in-person meetings were in the afternoon. And when she was actively writing, she could easily start at noon and wrap up around midnight. So, why was she giving up her only morning of zero alarms?

When Ryland dropped the six-in-the-morning gauntlet on her students yesterday, she was stunned. She thought she'd handled the whole new-teacher harassment effectively with the pop quiz. The quiz proved her secret-teacher-superpower: knowing all things at all times.

Of course the only reason she knew about the awful comments was because of the internet alerts she set up on herself after all of her clients' personal information curiously walked out her front door without protest. Regardless, to the students her superpower appeared to be firmly intact.

Yet, the always in charge Coach Ryland felt the need to add his own layer of punishment to hers. With his unwarranted intervention he undoubtedly proved to all of her students—particularly the athletes who held the most influence—she was incapable of delivering her own swift and just punishment. The more she contemplated his interference, the angrier she became until she found herself in the high school parking lot with a mass of messy bed-head hair and her morning coffee clamped to her hand.

From the other side of the gym doors, Ryland's no-nonsense voice firmly placed the fear of God into two freshmen, before turning his painful disappointment on her three troublemakers. Although his soliloquy on why her students should be grateful for her teaching wouldn't win any essay contests, without blinking an eye, he'd zoomed right past beignets with steamy hot chicory coffee on her like meter.

Now, twenty minutes later, she was cheerfully stacking folding chairs in a boy-sweat filled gymnasium on her one free morning. Being back in Gibson's Run had certainly off-kiltered her life more than she'd anticipated.

With one final clank of metal against metal, all of the chairs stood like neat soldiers ready for a battle—or the high school pep band's performance later that evening.

Ryland wiped his hands down the front of his wind pants. "Thanks for helping. You really didn't need to assist, but I appreciate it."

"How could I not after that speech?"

"You heard me?"

Was Ryland Jessup blushing? Not possible…or was it? Yep, definitely the fine hue of Gala apple pink flushing his perfect cheekbones.

She nodded and followed him back toward her coat. "You were very kind and generous with your words. Your tone could put the fear of God in the worst of sinners. Maybe you should've taken up preaching rather than coaching?"

"I like to think of coaching as teaching—not unlike what your dad does. We just have different pulpits." His dimple popped at the corner of his lifted lips. "Of course, I get the privilege of yelling a little more than he does."

"I don't know...you weren't his daughter." She cringed as the joke slipped through her lips. Settling on the bench she faced him. "That's not exactly true."

"Your dad never yelled at you? You were that perfect?" He raised an eyebrow.

"I'm far from perfect, but my parents—mostly my mother—resorted to nagging rather than yelling. I think my mother would've been on cloud nine if I'd been caught doing anything rambunctious or outside the lines when I was a teenager. I preferred sitting in my room and reading books. I think my dad only yelled at me once in my entire life."

Ryland chuckled. "Really?"

She nodded.

"I think my dad yelled at me once a day before noon until I left for college. And, then he would call to check-in and even his words of comfort were kind of yelling. But then again my dad was a football coach. Yelling was kind of his thing."

"I was sorry to hear about your dad's death. He was always nice to me. He never once made me run in gym, because he knew I didn't want to shower in the locker room." Carl Jessup, Ryland's dad, was a semi-legend in Gibson's Run. After captaining a Rose Bowl winning football team, he returned to his hometown with his fancy PhD candidate wife and led the GRHS

Grizzlies to their first playoff victory in nearly a decade. He remained the Head Football Coach and Athletic Director until his untimely death. His heart attack during her sophomore year at LSU—right in the middle of football season—created a nearly unfillable hole in his family and the entire town.

But it was Ryland's position as a starting linebacker for his father's alma mater that created the national story. A news segment, near Christmas of that year, reported about Ryland's tough transition back to football without his dad. Father and son had a relationship that was often heard as well as seen, but the love and respect between the two was undeniable.

"Thanks. Some days I forget he's gone and I pick up the phone to ask him advice about a play or how to deal with a student. I miss him every day. I just wish he'd met Emma. He would have loved being a Papa."

She squeezed his hand in comfort. The simple touch shot a sizzling current through her entire body. Snapping her hand from his, she rubbed her palm against her jean clad thigh. Curious to see his response to her touch, she peeked out of the corner of her eye but found his face draped in the pain of loss. "I'm sure he'd have been the best grandpa to Emma." Her lips tilted. "I know he's proud of you. He always was, Ryland."

He swiped a hand across his moist eyes, nodding his head in her direction. "Sorry. It's still pretty fresh even though it's been almost six years." He reached for her hand. "But I guess you understand that as well as I do."

Her chest tightened and twisted at his touch and the reference to their odd bond.

Losing a parent was expected, but not until one

was well into middle age. Parents were supposed to die when they were in a nursing home and called you Puddin' Tame because they couldn't quite place where they knew you. They were not supposed to die before you graduated college.

"Thanks." Her whisper was barely audible.

Ryland responded with a gentle squeeze of his hand. "I'm here for you, Tessa."

With the subtle link of their hands tethering them, she lifted her gaze to his and her heart flipped in its cage.

He slid along the bench until her leg was nearly touching his.

Her breaths quickened to shallow bursts. Flames burned her cheeks. Shoving her mass of not-brushed hair over her shoulder, he gently caressed her cheek with his long forefinger. Despite being overwarm in her sweater, shivers raced through her body and tingled like sparklers in her fingers. His eyes bowed, and dropped their focus to her lips. Her breaths escalated to a rapid staccato rhythm. With a quick turn of her head, she popped up from the bench and used every bit of her five foot four inch frame to establish a healthy distance between her and Ryland Jessup. She paced circles around the growling grizzly face painted at half court.

"Tessa…"

Throwing her arm in a Heisman pose, she kept her distance. "I can't think. Please stay where you are. My brain is mushy."

"Mushy brains? Sounds like something from a great horror flick we saw for my thirteenth birthday."

Tessa and Ryland pivoted toward the gym entrance.

Bathed in the soft haze of Saturday morning sun filtering through the skylight, with a grin worthy of a cereal box, stood Joey Taylor. He lifted a basketball from near the entrance and dribbled to center court.

Tessa blinked. Repeatedly. She pinched her thigh so hard she would likely have a bruise, but Joey "call me Joe now" Taylor did not evaporate into the ether. Nope, he stood two feet in front of her getting ready to shoot hoops. And not two minutes earlier, Ryland Jessup nearly kissed her. When had her life jumped from the toilet to an episode of *"As Gibson's Run Turns"*?

~*~

What just happened? Had he almost kissed Tessa? Ryland shook his head at the surrealism of the moment.

JT, his childhood best friend, professional baseball player, and eternal flirt, was bouncing a basketball as he stared intently into Tessa's upturned face.

After twenty years of waiting, Ryland Jessup was on the brink of kissing Tessa Tarrington and Joey Taylor zoomed in for the proverbial block. He flicked the back of Joe's head.

His friend whipped around and offered a grin of genuine warmth and friendship. "What was that for, Jess?"

"I don't care how fancy a ballplayer you are now, you still need permission to pick up GRHS property. We can't have just anyone playing basketball, can we?" Ryland swatted the ball into his hands mid-dribble.

Joe chuckled, casually draping an arm over Tessa's shoulders. "Well isn't he a big shot?" He guided her toward the bleachers leaving Ryland to follow in their intimate wake.

Tessa giggled. *Really, giggling?*

Releasing her from his casual embrace, Joe swiveled, plopping onto the bench. With the air of ownership with which he and all his buddies used to rule the high school, Joe leaned against the second row, stretching his long arms wide. "So, Jessup, now that I'm no longer breaking school rules, you wanna get in some trouble?"

"Want to..." Both Ryland and Tessa simultaneously corrected.

"Whoa, nerd alert."

Tucking the basketball between his hip and his extended arm, Ryland leveled his Don't-Mess-With-The-Linebacker-Pretty-Boy stare on his friend.

Joey responded with a lifted eyebrow and a single question. "Aren't you going to introduce me to your friend?"

"JT, don't be a dweeb. You remember Tessa Tarrington. You were in praise band with her for like five years."

Joe straightened and slowly drew his gaze from Tessa's booted feet up to her messy blonde hair. "T.T. Tarrington? Time has been very good to you."

Tessa's cheeks flushed petal pink in the breath of his words.

Without a thought Ryland reenacted seventh grade dodge ball when he socked Joe square in the jaw with the ball.

"Oww. Man, careful. I make a living with that shoulder."

Ryland missed Joe's jaw by nearly six inches. Although not as gratifying as messing up Joe's pretty face, he'd take a shoulder. "Well, then, don't be a pig.

Her name is Tessa not T.T."

"It's all right." Tessa actually twirled her hair around her forefinger. Seriously? When she'd imagined he'd called her T.T. she nearly decapitated him. But Joe got a hair twirl?

Joe lifted his lanky frame to standing, reaching for Tessa's hand in one smooth motion. Raising her fingers to his lips he stage-whispered his apology. "Please forgive me, Tessa. I'd never want to anger you."

If it was humanly possible, Tessa's blush deepened past sweet pea petals to hot pants pink.

Something angry and alien green rose in Ryland, on the edge of bursting forth. "What do you want, JT? I've been here since five-thirty this morning, and I'm not my usual sweet self."

"I stopped by your house. Mabel said you were here and that Emma was spending the holiday weekend with Macy's parents in Clintonville." Joe's million dollar arm once again found itself carelessly draped over Tessa's shoulders.

"So…" Man, he wished he had another ball.

"So…as I eluded, I wanted to get into some trouble. And since you're munchkin free I thought you might want to join."

"I don't do trouble anymore. I have plans." Ryland planned to watch tape of the middle school's last three games to see if any potential starters emerged. He'd actually contemplated walking to Pastor Tom's for a visit. Of course, he was only concerned about his friend. Seeing the pastor's daughter was just an unavoidable side benefit.

"Break them. I'm only home for a few more weeks before I report to Ft. Myers. And, Sean's coming. How much trouble could we really get into with law enforcement in tow?" He shifted, focusing his plea to Tessa. "We thought we'd head to Columbus. Maybe grab dinner in the Short North, and then to Grandview for open mic night at a new coffee shop."

"Sounds like a nice evening." Lifting her gaze to Ryland she gave him a soft smile. "You should go with your friends."

"Well, that includes you. Doesn't it, darlin'?" Joe tugged Tessa tighter to his side.

"I don't know." She said with a shake of her head. "I'm sure my dad will need something."

"He'd want you to be out and about. Catching up with your old friends. We can make it into a class reunion. Get a bunch of the old gang together." Joe twisted, squatting until he was eye level with Tessa. "Wouldn't you want to see everyone?"

Based on the reception she'd given him, Ryland guessed the only thing Tessa would want to do more than hang out with her high school classmates was to pluck every hair from her head while she watched hours of static on television.

"Joe, leave Tessa alone. She already has plans."

"I do?"

Both Joe and Tessa shot Ryland matching confused expressions.

"You do."

Tessa stepped away from Joe, lacing her arms over her middle. "And what, pray tell, might these grand plans be, Coach Jessup?"

Man, she was adorable when she was fired up. No more goofy grins up at Taylor now. "You are spending the evening with me."

Closing the small space between them, she forced her chin straight north, locking her gaze with Ryland's.

"I am, am I?"

He matched her arm crossed stance. "Yes."

"Who said?"

"I said."

"Well, I can't....I already have plans. And you're spending the night reminiscing along memory lane with your school chums."

"School chums?"

"You know what I mean." She said with a smack to his forearm. Swiveling away, she continued. "Thank you for the invitation, Joey, but I think it'd be best if you just enjoyed a boys' night." She glanced over her shoulder but didn't meet Ryland's eye. Apparently she'd used up all of her gumption for the day. "I really need to get back to my dad. Thank you again. I appreciate your support with my students."

"As they say, 'it takes a village'."

She nodded and turned to face Joe. "It was wonderful seeing you again, Joey. Maybe I'll see you at church. Dad's feeling strong enough to attend for the first time tomorrow. Your brother and Maggie have been wonderfully kind stopping by and encouraging him to take his time to get better."

"Well, if you'll be in church, how could I miss?"

"Well good...um, well, I guess I'll see you both tomorrow." She gave a little wave.

Ryland was pretty sure she bobbed a curtsy before she snagged her coat and skipped through the doorway. Shaking his head, he lowered his body with a thud to the bleacher bench. What just happened? Had Tessa Tarrington just rejected him? Again?

"Crash and burn." Joe slid onto the bench beside him.

8

Tessa let the front door slam as she kicked off her snow boots and wriggled out of her coat. "Daddy?"

"In the kitchen."

She padded the narrow, dark wood floored hallway to the bright and airy kitchen. The wide space was decorated exactly as it was in her first memory of sitting at the chipped yellow Formica table eating a peanut butter and applesauce sandwich. As an adult, she could admit the combination was weird, but the memory of her mother combining her two favorite ingredients to soothe the ouchy of a scraped knee was a classic.

Her dad and a young woman were sharing coffee at her childhood memory table.

"Dad?"

Both heads swiveled at the same moment and joy burst from the center of Tessa's heart. "Lily Mae!"

The barely five foot, dark haired beauty bounced to her feet, launching herself into Tessa's arms.

"What are you doing here?" Tessa asked.

Stepping back, she nearly blinded Tessa with her toothy grin and deep set of perfect baby-doll dimples. "*Cher*, you sounded just miserable on the phone this week. So, I looked up at Beau and said, 'Darlin' I just have to go and rescue my little sister from the dangers of those mean old Yankees.' And being the gracious Southern gentleman he is, he sent me up on his daddy's jet. And here I am. Ready to rescue you." Her high pitched voice was tinged with a mix of her mama's creole and her father's Northern Louisiana roots. The combination was heavenly music to Tessa's ears.

"Oh, Lil." Tessa chuckled. "Only you would commandeer a jet to come brave the cold and the Yankees to ensure your friend was OK. What would I do without you?"

"Turn into a little old lady with twenty-two cats and sixteen copies of each Jane Austen novel stashed around your one bedroom apartment." With a hand to her hip, she challenged Tessa to disagree. "You know I'm right, *cher*."

"Probably." Tessa scrunched her nose and leaned her forehead to her friends. "Sisters forever?"

"Delta Alpha Psi until we die."

They each lifted three fingers and tapped their hearts.

"Ahem," Tessa's father cleared his throat. "I see you girls have much to catch up on. I'll be in my study. The guest room is all ready for you, Lily Mae. Stay as long as you like."

"Thanks Reverend Tarrington, but Mama needs me home for wedding jazz by Tuesday morning. And I imagine Beau's daddy would like his plane away from all this nasty cold sooner rather than later. But I'll be sure to come back right quick."

"Well, dear, you're always welcome here."

"Thank you, sir." The sorority sisters and best friends linked arms as they watched Pastor Tom disappear around the corner and into his study.

Lily whipped around with a narrowed focus, dragging Tessa by the elbow up the stairs to her childhood bedroom. She nearly tossed Tessa on the bed before securing the old oak door in its frame. For a ninety pound, former cheerleader, Lily Mae Benton had the deceptive strength of a mid-afternoon storm in the bayou when a cloudless sky turned to a torrential downpour in seconds. "Spill it, T²? Why did you sound like your daddy took your favorite hound dog to the pound when I talked to you yesterday? Ella said you wouldn't give her a straight answer about that awful Ryland Jessup, and if he's back to torturing you again. Is he? I mean, the scary irony that you both are back at your alma mater as teachers now? Do teachers get in trouble for bullying other teachers? Or is it like the military—don't ask don't tell? Survive or die?" Lily Mae's chatter and active imagination made her an excellent writer of young adult fiction, but her bent toward the dramatic often left her two best friends—Tessa and Ella Donovan—speechless. Lily plunked onto Tessa's ancient double bed into a perfect cross-legged sit. Her over-sized blue eyes narrowed their focus on Tessa. "Well?"

She let out a sigh. "It's complicated."

"Uncomplicate it."

"That isn't even a word, Lil."

"In the world of YA, I get to create all sorts of new words and languages—that's why it's a perfect genre for me. And correcting my speech didn't work when you were trying to distract me from discovering that Bobbi Ann and Joanie were trying to stuff the ballot box in Joanie's favor to be the homecoming nominee over me. And it didn't work when you were trying to keep your shopping excursions with Beau for an engagement ring secret. And it won't work today—no matter how cold this place is. How does a brain function with this much frigid surrounding it?"

"I wear layers of down. And it's not that cold. It's been in the thirties all week. It's barely breaking fifty in Louisiana."

"Fair enough." Lily reclined against the center twist of the wrought iron footboard.

Tessa scooted off the bed and yanked her sweater over her head, suddenly overheated. Still clad in her LSU Tigers football t-shirt, her secret obsession, she folded the sweater and laid it on a small stack in her closet. She started fluffing her pillows and straightened the top coverlet. When she squared her stack of books on the nightstand, Lily whistled. Tessa flipped her hair over her shoulder. "What?"

"I flew one thousand miles—borrowed my almost father-in-law's plane to do it—and you don't have one word of explanation?"

Tessa shrugged, joining Lily on the bed. She tugged her childhood teddy bear to her chest. "My dad's been sick. I'm just worried."

"Wrong." Lily lifted a perfectly arched dark brow. "I spent the last hour chatting with your dad about everything from the weather to the potential of the Buckeyes basketball team making the Elite Eight— puke! And he told me his doctor thought with the right medication, increased exercise, and a slightly modified diet he'd be just fine. So, new answer, Tessa. That one's all played out."

A wet tear trickled down Tessa's cheek, landing on her hand with a splash.

The bed creaked with a little wave as Lily moved to place an arm over Tessa's shoulders.

With the touch of her best friend, water began pouring from her eyes like the flooding Mississippi cresting the river's edge.

Lily heaved Tessa and her bear to her tiny chest, stroking her back with the comfort of eight years of devoted sisterhood.

Tessa's whole body shook with pent up tears. She cried for her lost career. For her daddy's heart attack. For her mom. She cried because she'd left Louisiana. For almost kissing Ryland Jessup. For her flare up of crush with Joey Taylor. And for her best friend who flew one thousand miles to check on her because she knew something was wrong—even if Tessa wouldn't admit it. When the stream began to slow, she swiped at her eyes, and slipped out of Lily's arm. "Sorry." She sniffled.

"Best friendship means never having to say you're sorry, *cher*."

"I don't know what's wrong with me. I mean everything's wrong, but I can usually handle 'wrong'. But I just can't seem to control anything lately."

"Maybe it's because you've been trying to control everyone and everything for so long that one wrong move caused your entire world to crumble?"

"What do you mean?"

"When we met eight years ago, I knew I'd found a kindred spirit. I mean, you were quiet and kept to yourself and I'm neither quiet nor do I keep to myself. But you felt life as deeply as I did and I knew at eighteen that was rare. But the biggest difference between you and me is even though you feel life like I do you—you're afraid to live it."

"That's not true."

"Of course it is." She stretched her slim fingers and counted against them. "When you can't control a situation and everyone in it, you run and hide from life until the hard stuff passes. Life was difficult in high school for you, so you hid in this room, at the coffee shop, and backstage. You ran away to Louisiana because you couldn't control the world around you in Gibson's Run. You only rushed your momma's sorority, because you knew they had to take you. You chose a career where you write about other people's lives—not your own. Anytime you come close to feeling something bigger or deeper than what you're prepared to face, you run away." She dropped her hands to the bed. "Why do you think you are back in Ohio?"

"My dad's sick."

"That's an excuse and you know it. So what, you were fired? You should've stood up to both Evanstons. You can't help that someone targeted your apartment—but you could try and figure out who did it. And why. You could—for the first time in your sweet, uncomplicated life—fight back. Tessa, you need to come home. Find out who stole your files. Don't you want your life back?"

"I'd like to stop swimming in the toilet."

"That's the spirit." Lily rested her head against Tessa's.

9

Huddled in a darkened corner, Ryland gingerly sipped his decaf. The coffee neared a bearable temperature. The same couldn't be said for the musical entertainment.

When Joe suggested dinner in the Short North at one of his favorite college haunts, Ryland's spirit lifted a twinge at the thought of the macaroni made with five different kinds of cheese. But when they arrived, his beloved hangout had been replaced by a fusion restaurant. With utter disappointment filling his belly, they settled for high-end steaks out of everyone but Joe's price range.

Ryland made a decent salary and had a healthy savings from his short stint in the NFL, but he tried to be frugal by shoving every extra dollar he earned into a college fund for Emma. His one luxury was a fulltime housekeeper-nanny. Mabel had been with them since Emma was a baby. He would be lost without her.

After the mess up over dinner, he tried to bail and head back to Gibson's Run, hoping to catch a few hours of tape when the DVD player was his alone, but Joe was adamant about everyone hearing his soon to be sister-in-law sing.

The whole town witnessed the bickering turned to love story between Joe's brother Sean and Maggie McKitrick. And the residents were universally shocked by the horrors Maggie had endured, including a showdown with the man who had tracked her all over country last fall.

Correction. Everyone was shocked except Sissy Jenkins, Gibson's Run's answer to the gossip columns, who suspected everyone of everything. He glanced over at Sean and Maggie, who were casually leaning into each other as they listened to the karaoke. They oozed love, happiness and contentment.

"Are you having fun?" Joe asked as he straddled the seat beside Ryland.

"A blast. Did you get her number?" He lifted his shoulder to the blonde in line for a refill.

Joe winked. "Does Joe Taylor ever fail?"

Twack! "Don't be an idiot, Sprout." The woman's voice was friendly-scornful.

"Hey," Joe yelped, but his mouth spread to a wide grin. "What are you guys doing here?"

Ryland followed Joe's gaze and a soft grin touched his lips. He stood and reached to give his old babysitter, Jane Grey—now Jane Barrett, a hug. Her husband, Lindy, and her best friend Millie—the *thwacker*—were busy hugging Sean and Maggie.

Ryland stepped back with his hands still around Jane's waist. "I didn't know you were coming."

"Hands off, Weakside. That's my wife."

"Hey, Ice Monkey, I was always a Middle—never fast enough to be a Wilt." He stretched his arm to shake the hand of Lindy Barrett, former NHL legend, and Jane's husband.

"Ice Monkey?" Jane asked sliding into her husband's side.

Ryland shrugged. "My comebacks are a little rusty."

"They were never that crisp." Millie said, rubbing

her slightly rounded stomach. "You weren't just slow on the field, Jessup."

"Lovely to see pregnancy isn't softening any of your edges, Millie."

"Glad the presence of Sprout could bring you out of hiding." She said pointing Joe. "Maybe we can find a clever retort stuck inside that behemoth of a body, yet."

"Considering his greatest competition is a precocious four year-old, we should give him a pass," Maggie offered as she slid in the circular booth the expanding party was occupying.

"How's Emma doing?" Jane asked.

"Well. She turns five soon, and I'm a little shocked she'll be starting kindergarten this fall, but she's quite well." He waited for the obligatory questions about Macy, and how they were coping as a family. He hated the routine questions. The sorrow-filled looks and shade of misery blotted out the delight of any situation.

He was trying to move on from his failed marriage and his wife's death, but every time he was reunited with well-meaning friends and family the questions fell into a pattern. First asking about Emma. "How's she doing?" Followed quickly by, "How are you? Really?" He knew his friends' hearts were pure, but he wanted one night free of the guilt of not loving his wife.

He missed her and wished she'd survived the accident for Emma, but he'd never really loved Macy. She'd been a good mother—and a perfect PR wife, but the year before she'd died, when he'd proposed retiring from the NFL and returning to Gibson's Run to coach, she'd gone ballistic.

The next day she served him with divorce papers.

If he wanted to be married, to have Emma in his life, he would not bring retirement up again. She was an NFL wife—not some high school football widow. She didn't want him. Probably never did. She wanted the influence of those three letters: N.F.L. And she used his daughter as a pawn to keep what she wanted.

Since Macy's death, he'd been trying to forgive her—and himself—but he'd struggled to let go of the anger her felt toward the mother of his child. She'd been reckless the night of her accident—getting behind the wheel intoxicated after a night out with girlfriends. The only blessing was Macy's only victim was Macy.

"Earth to Jessup." Joe clamped his hand onto Ryland's shoulder. "Everything OK? You seemed to go on a little trip there and rudely didn't invite a single one of us."

"I'm sorry. What did I miss?"

"Nothing yet, but my musically genius soon-to-be-sister-in-law and yours truly are about to take this coffee house down with some wicked tunes."

"Brag much, Taylor?"

"Joe was born with confidence."

"Smack your own head, Sprout." Millie hollered from the booth. "You know it's ridiculous to speak about yourself in the third person."

"Millie, you are such a hypocrite." Jane chuckled. "You talk about yourself in third person all of the time."

"Yes, but that's me."

Ryland rubbed the bridge of his nose and suppressed a yawn. He sipped his coffee, and the now lukewarm liquid filled his belly, but the lack of caffeine did little to perk up his spirit. "I'm going to pick up an espresso. Would anyone like something?" He pushed away from the table.

"I'll take an espresso." Joe responded.

"No, you will not." Sean intervened. "You're so hyper tonight, you seem like you've had twenty cups of coffee. You don't need any help."

"Whatever." A frown creased Joe's brow as he slumped in his chair.

Ryland was annoyed by his friend's upbeat attitude because he couldn't seem to get his own feet firmly under him. Since Joe had returned home, Ryland had noticed a slight change in his friend, but he didn't want to imagine the root cause of that change. For the night, he'd rather wallow in ignorance where JT's life was concerned. Ryland placed his order, including a water for Joe, when the aroma of crisp linen and lilacs wafted through him. *Tessa.* He swiveled and caught sight of a mass of silky blonde hair. She was sitting with a woman Ryland didn't recognize. Lifting the diminutive cup to his lips, he tossed the contents to the back of his mouth as though he were taking medicine. The espresso burned a path down his throat and landed in his belly, firing every sense he had into overdrive. He flipped the bottle of water to Joe and nodded in Tessa's direction.

His best friend quickly picked up on the signal. Joe unfolded his six foot three inch frame to standing. In two strides, he was squatting beside Tessa and giving her friend a grin that sparkled with the brightness of every lake in the early morning sun.

Ryland pulled up the rear.

Joe slid onto a seat beside Tessa, but Ryland already lost the race. She was laughing at one of JT's dumb jokes, and the sound both warmed his heart and twisted like a knife to his gut.

"Hi, Tessa."

She raised her gaze to his, laughter spreading a genuine smile softly across her lips. "Hi, Ryland. Joey said you're going to sing tonight?"

"Umm…uhhh…" Heat scorched Ryland's neck. *Sing?* The last time he sang outside of church was during his freshman year in college when the upper classmen forced the rookies into a sing-off performing the fight song. After the first round, he was disqualified for being tone deaf.

"If you could see your face." Joe laughed. "Priceless. Trust me. No one on the planet wants you to sing. I'm trying to convince the lovely and talented Tessa to join Maggie and me up on stage."

Tessa shook her head. "No. I don't sing anymore. Besides, that wouldn't be fair to Lily Mae." She said, referencing the petite brunette sitting opposite her.

Ryland extended his hand. "I'm sorry to be rude. You must be a friend of Tessa's. We teach together. My name is Ryland Jessup."

"I know who you are." Lily Mae said, leaving his extended hand hanging above the table as she stuffed her arms like a pretzel across her chest.

Sliding his hand in his pocket, Ryland nodded. "Tessa, I hope you change your mind and sing. I was always blessed when you shared your gift. Nice to meet you, Lily Mae. Tessa." He padded back to his table.

Tessa's head bent forward and her shoulders started shaking. Joe had made her laugh—not holler, or overreact. Laughter was good. Everyone needed laughter—especially the all too serious Tessa Tarrington.

With a sigh, his eyelids fluttered shut and he

sagged into the chair feeling the weight of the last week in his very tendons. He rubbed circles over his eyes with the palms of his hands, simultaneously pressing out the last trickle of energy boost he'd received from the espresso. Coming tonight—being around Joe and his childhood friends—was a mistake. He should have stayed home, studied the tape, maybe visited with Pastor Tom. He should not be at some random coffee shop in Grandview vibrating from the last of his caffeine jolt and longing for the girl he'd been in full-on love with since he was six years old. Opening his eyes, he yanked his coat from the back of his chair and moved to stand.

"I wouldn't."

He stared at his surrogate big brother, Sean Taylor. "I need to get home. Macy's parents are bringing Emma to church and they'll take the opportunity to inspect the house. I need to be prepared."

"Mabel has that house so clean you could eat pudding off the floor. You're running away."

"I don't know what you mean. It's been a long week and I'm tired."

Sean slid onto the seat Joe had vacated. "I've known you since...well, since I can't remember when. And there are four things that are as true today about you as they were when you were a dopey fifteen-year-old excited about setting off a bottle rocket in Sissy Jenkins's backyard."

"Really?" Ryland asked, lifting a single eyebrow.

"Really." Sean stretched his hand and counted against his fingers. "First, you're a wicked competitor always willing to go the extra to win. Second, you're a family first guy—and that's holding true with how your love for your daughter infiltrates every aspect of your life. Third, you're a man of God. And fourth, you've been in love with Tessa Tarrington since you could first ride a two wheeler."

The heat chasing up Ryland's neck nearly burned his eyes with embarrassment. Was he that obvious?

"And with the exception of number two—which, by the way, I think you're using to hide behind— you're failing at living up to your truths. You need to fight for what you want. You get one life, Ryland. You need to try and live it with as few regrets as possible."

"I don't know what you are talking about, Sean. When did you go all touchy-feely-T.V.-doctor? 'Living up to your truths'. Seriously?"

"Jess, don't try and play me. You are more than my little brother's best friend. You're like a brother to me, and I'm being blunt for your own good." He stretched his long-limbed body and crossed his ankles. "And besides, I am a trained investigator. I read people for a living. You aren't the toughest nut to crack."

"Well, you must be going soft, Chief, because you're way off base. I need to get home *because* of my desire to win at all costs. I have game tape to watch. I'm scouting for next fall's team. Besides, we have early church tomorrow morning. Putting God first and all." Shrugging on his coat Ryland stood.

Sean's fiancé Maggie, Joe and Tessa were talking with the sound technician.

"Tell Maggie I'm sorry I couldn't stay to hear her sing. I'll see you in the morning."

"You're making a mistake."

"Well, then it's my mistake to make."

10

Tessa's heart beat with the steady weight of a bass drum. Sweat streamed down her back. Coughing against her narrowing throat, she settled onto the high stool beside Joe. What was she doing? One little wink from Joey Taylor and she was putty ready to be molded.

A sound tech raised the third microphone to the level of her mouth and Maggie adjusted her mic to a similar height as Joe tuned his guitar.

Lily settled into the wide booth beside Jane and Millie. Lily's mouth was clearly not slowed by the introduction to strangers as her hands took on the dramatic gesturing of one who made friends easily.

And Ryland shuffled toward the front door.

Hopping off the stool, Tessa scooted through the crowded tables and caught him as he opened the door, allowing a gust of chilled January into the cozy warmth of the coffee shop. "Ugh! Why is it so cold?"

Ryland pivoted and smacked Tessa with his elbow.

"Umm, ouch?" She rubbed her forehead.

"I'm so sorry. Are you OK?" Half squatting to her eye level, he grabbed her shoulders in his hands, nearly engulfing her upper back with their size.

"I'm fine." She dropped her hands, ignoring the gentle heat emanating from his touch. *Those eyes.* They seemed to shift color every time she looked into their depths. Tonight they were the color of the Smokey Mountains as evening sets.

"Are you sure? I hit you pretty hard. I'm really sorry."

A mysterious butterfly that seemed to only react to Ryland's voice, fluttered wings against Tessa's heart. Shaking her head, she forced her nearly smiling lips to a tight line. "I'm fine, but where are you going?"

"It's getting late. I need to go home." He dropped his hands, stuffing them in the pockets of his barn jacket.

"Don't you want to hear Joey and Maggie sing?"

"Maggie's pretty amazing, but I hear her nearly every Sunday in church, and JT likes to break out in song on a fairly regular basis."

"Oh, I just thought…" Why did she care if Ryland Jessup—her mortal enemy—stayed to hear his friends? She slid a step back towards the main room.

"Hey, Tessa, we need you." Joey hollered without the aid of a microphone.

"You thought, what?" Ryland asked, reclaiming the space she vacated.

"Nothing." She stretched her Delta Alpha Psi smile across her lips. "Have a good evening. Be careful driving home." She skipped back to the stage, shoving her disconcerting disappointment over Ryland's early exit to the back of her mind. "Sorry," she said to Maggie and Joey as she returned to her stool.

Joey counted down and strummed the opening chords to the well-known rock ballad.

The music began at her toes and travelled through her legs until it settled in her belly and began to grow. Maggie's rich tone wafted through Tessa's spirit, taking the melody. When her lips opened to join Joey on the chorus she countered with the harmony. The blend of their three voices propelled round after round of shivering needles over her body. The purr of the trio was glorious, and as the final strands of the song waned, Tessa's eyes slid open and she caught sight of the collective expression of awe in the audience a moment before they burst into riotous applause. Floating on nothing but raw emotion, her gaze shot over the jubilant crowd and caught the front door settling to close. The aura of the artistic beauty dissipated and she was once again falling into the pit of sadness she'd been residing in for months.

Joey tugged her off her stool, smacking a rough kiss on the top of her head. "We were awesome, T.T.! You're awesome." He released her along with a strangled battle cry.

She stumbled off the stage.

Maggie tugged Joey behind her.

Tessa wiped her forehead and locked gazes with Lily, then glanced toward the door.

"*Cho! Co!*" Lily exclaimed. "Well, wasn't that better than sweet tea on an August afternoon? Y'all sound like you've been plucked from the angels to sing together."

"Joe Taylor always knew he was meant to make beautiful music with angels." Joey dragged an empty chair to the table.

"Sprout, do you even know how to spell humble?" Sean said as he enveloped his fianceé in a body length hug.

Tessa narrowed her gaze to Lily, who nodded.

Lily offered an exaggerated yawn complete with a wide stretch of her short arms. "*Mais*, I'm spent like last month's allowance. I think I need to take a lie down. Tessa, I hate to rain on the party like midnight on Mardi Gras, but this little *boo* needs eyes shut for eight straight if I want to make it through anyone's sermon tomorrow."

Glancing at the dropped mouths and furrowed brows of the group, Tessa stifled her giggle as Lily pushed to scoot from the booth.

The Creole-Cajun Princess Lily Mae often shocked poor, unsuspecting Yankees into stunned silence. The CCP had aided the sisters in the escape of more than one uncomfortable situation. And like a comfy sweatshirt, CCP Lily Mae once again wrapped herself around the suddenly frigid Tessa. "It's just been a ball meeting every last one of you." Lily offered as she shoved her arms in her sleek leather jacket. "Miss Millie, biggest of congrats on the *bebe*. What a blessing. Hope if y'all ever make it to God's country you'll swing by for a little *fais do do.*"

Winding her scarf around her neck, Tessa was startled when Joey lifted her coat to her.

"You don't have to go, Tessa. I can give you a ride home, if you want to stay," he offered.

Her heart twisted against her inner sixteen-year-old who screamed, "YES!" But she suppressed the teenage yearnings and gave a soft shake of her head. "Thank you, but I drove Lily Mae. She wouldn't know the way home."

"OK." He held open her coat and she allowed him to drape the puffy bear around her shoulders. "How long is Lily in town?"

"She leaves Monday." Tessa's inner sixteen-year-old drooped her shoulders. He wanted to spend time with Lily. Of course, he did. She was beautiful, charming, and a former cheerleader. She was the picture of every girl Joe Taylor had dated throughout high school and beyond.

"So you'll be free Tuesday for dinner?" he whispered in her ear.

Her cheeks warmed. She nodded.

"You're staying with your dad, right?"

Another nod.

"I'll pick you up at six-thirty. Wear something a little dressy, OK?"

"OK," she croaked.

Zipping her coat closed, he tugged her scarf tighter around her neck and kissed her forehead. "You're quite the pleasant surprise, T.T. Tarrington. See you Tuesday."

11

"Do you mind explaining to me why we just left that fine young man, and all of the adulation that was about to be heaped on you like sugar on my little brother's cereal?" Lily asked as she fiddled with the radio in Tessa's ten-year-old coupe. "And how old is this car, *cher*? Do you need a hanger to get reception between the Columbus and the Gibson's Run?"

"Half the antenna broke off in the car wash two weeks ago."

Lily twisted in the passenger seat. "The elephant is still riding shotgun in this car and crushing me with his weight. Why did we skedaddle like your shoes were catching fire when that boy was clearly all about the Tessa."

"Could you please stop with the excessive use of articles?"

"I'll stop the overuse of 'the' if you quit evading the question."

"I just didn't want to be at the coffee shop any more. My dad finally feels up to going to church for the first time in weeks. I don't want to be the one who causes us to be late."

"Nine-thirty, Tarrington. It is nine…three…zero. Not buying that story. Not even picking it up for free off the wire."

"What do you want me to say, Lil?"

"I want to understand how the weeper I held this

afternoon is the same person who bolted at the chance to have a big, strong man wipe away her tears. You're hiding. Did I waste my thousand mile pep talk on you?"

"No. I just…" Why couldn't she say she was overwhelmed? That she couldn't put words to everything she'd experienced tonight. In less than one hour—sixty minutes—nearly every high school fantasy she had was realized.

Joey Taylor asked her on a date. She sang in front of a crowd that wasn't a congregation. Ryland Jessup apologized, and was nearly a human being. She belonged. At twenty-six she finally felt like she belonged. In high school. Of course, the fact all of her high school dreams could fit in a sixty minute segment should give her pause concerning her creativity. Transition from ghost-written memoirs to fiction was likely not an option.

"Yes? You just…what?"

"I don't know. Tonight was wonderful. And it was confusing. And I'm not sure what to make of it."

"OK. That's a start. Let's just waddle our way backwards and see what we trip over."

Tessa's stomach burned with the thought of a Lily Mae psychoanalysis of the evening's activities. She suspected Lil would be dissecting the minutia of the night long after Tessa needed her mind shut down for sleep.

"What did Joey say to you when he pretended to help you with your jacket?"

"He didn't pretend and he asked me to dinner on Tuesday."

"Joey Taylor—the man version of your teen crush, asked you on a real, honest-to-goodness sit down date?"

"Why can't you ever just say a simple sentence? Why must you use seven words when one will do?"

"How's that a good use of my birth family and fabulous education?"

"How can I argue with that logic?"

"Back to my question. Date? Man crush? Short enough?"

"Yes. And I don't think it's a big deal. Just dinner. We did graduate high school together."

"Are you sure he knew that before today?"

Tessa flipped her head, and stuck out her tongue.

"OK, so that would be yes. I'll need a full report postdate on Tuesday evening. Maybe we can conference call and yank in Ella. I'm sure she could add some adorable tidbits of advice."

"She starts a new ghost writing assignment Monday. She's been armpits deep in research for the last two weeks. I highly doubt she'll be up for air for some time." A wave of sadness washed over Tessa at the thought of all the new projects she would never start. Tessa was happy for her friend's increasing career, but she couldn't stop the envy creeping through her at the loss of her own writing.

She loved ghost writing; telling the stories that needed to be told. Loved sharing the intimacy of a person's life experiences. Translating them to words on a page and books on a shelf. She appreciated the sensitivity each project needed and quickly built trust with her clients. Trust was paramount to telling a well-crafted story. After the exposure *the terrible, awful day* caused, she couldn't risk trying to ask for trust to be given freely again. The burglar stole more than her files and her laptop; he robbed her of her spirit and drive.

"Well, you'll call me and we'll dissect your little sit down."

The idea of a real date with Joey Taylor—not one of the dozens she'd created in her imagination during the lonely hours of her teen years—banished the sorrow over her lost career and filled her with anticipation. Her teenage heart hoped for so much more than her woman brain expected.

Regardless of Lily's overactive romantic sensibility, Tessa anticipated decent conversation followed by a 'see-you-next-time-I'm-in-town' hug good bye. The date was a relatively known property.

Her evolving response to Ryland Jessup was not. Tessa couldn't quite understand the effect Ryland was having on her. She prayed Lily hadn't seen the curious exchange between her and Ryland. She wasn't ready to dissect her feelings for him now that her feelings did not revolve around disgust, distrust, or detesting. She needed time to process.

Beginning with her strange urge to confront him at the gym, and their near kiss, to the gentle concern she felt from him tonight before he left. She'd nearly told him she wanted him to stay and hear her sing. Hadn't he encouraged her? Why had he suddenly left without hearing Maggie or Joe? Why did she care? And why was she allowing herself to be consumed by what Ryland Jessup did?

Lily was right. Her father was recovering exceptionally well. Mrs. Monahan would be ready to return to her class soon. Her time in Gibson's Run was coming to an end. What was next?

Since she'd been in Ohio not one person—including her agent—had solicited her for a pitch.

One month.

One month without even the slightest hint of regaining her former career. Conversely, she thankfully hadn't seen any additional tabloid coverage using information from her files. Maybe the thief hadn't been able to crack all of the protection on her laptop. Maybe she'd be able to walk back to the life she'd once loved. Tessa needed to discover if she could resuscitate her writing career or if that, too, had been flushed with her breach of security and tabloid cover-girl status.

Rolling her car to a stop at the traffic light beside the "Welcome to Gibson's Run" sign, she rested her forehead against the steering wheel.

"Everything OK over there, *cher*?" The long, quiet Lily asked.

"Just wallowing…" And listening to the swirl of her life.

12

As the bell tolled its final *bong,* Ryland slid into the last pew of the church he'd attended nearly every Sunday—with the exception of his years in college and the NFL—since his baptism. The historic building held a kaleidoscope of memories. Each time he walked in for worship or Bible study or a turkey supper a new splash of colors would paint his heart.

He usually chose a seat near the front, but his in-laws consistently misjudged the driving time from Clintonville. They'd likely slide in near the pre-prayer music with some mild mannered complaint about how far he lived from them.

When Ryland had dropped Emma at their house Friday evening, his father-in-law, Gus, mentioned that one of the Division III colleges ten minutes outside of Columbus was looking for a head football coach. Friends with the chairman of the search committee, Gus offered to throw Ryland's name in the pool. Ryland quickly closed down the idea. He loved his in-laws, but the natural forty-five minute drive seemed a healthy distance—at least for his sanity.

The opening music started, a hum rolling through the sanctuary with the new music director motioning for the congregation to stand together to sing. Although he loved to sing, his was a voice only God could truly love, so he kept his lips sealed and allowed his heart to ride the melody. He lumbered to stand and allowed the worship to pour over him, but the usual peace he found was lost this morning. Instead of zeroing in on his Heavenly Father, his mind tortured him with a highlight reel of the previous evening.

Leaving the restaurant was a coward's path, but he couldn't watch his best friend ooze his baseball player charm over Tessa. He'd felt like a twelve year-old when she'd stopped him at the exit. For a brief moment he thought she would ask him to stay. And he'd clung to a thread of hope; but it slipped through his fingers when JT called to her. He'd stayed, just inside the café and listened to the sweet harmonies the trio made. The music wasn't perfect, but Ryland didn't know when he'd heard any band, group, or solo act quite as beautiful. As the applause erupted, he'd slipped through the door and sucked back the tears cresting in his eyes.

On the long drive back to Gibson's Run he listened to a book on tape his mother recommended and tried to lose himself in the story. But he could see only Tessa with her eyes shut, her face washed in the glow of pure delight, and his heart had ached with the loss of one who was never his to hold. Dropping his head forward, he gripped the pew to in front of him and sought comfort from the Great Comforter. *Father, please help me.*

A solid hand gripped his shoulder, and Ryland opened his eyes to find his mentor and friend, Pastor Tom, lending unspoken support as he sang with a voice that echoed his daughter's rich tones. The comforting, fatherly touch strengthened Ryland, settling a sense of peace around the ache. He straightened to his full height as Tom's hand slipped from his shoulder and he lost himself to the worship, blissfully unconcerned only his pastor separated him from the source of his longing.

The worship guide instructed the congregation to sit, and a collective moan seemed to release from the unseen mouths of the forty pews with the added weight. The substitute pastor began reading through the prayer concerns and Ryland felt a tiny tug at his hand.

Emma's cherub-cheeked face rested against his knee and her grin turned her wide eyes to tiny slits.

He lifted her to his lap and her fierce embrace around his neck filled him with all the goodness in the world. No matter what happened in his life, he loved his daughter and his daughter loved him. "How's F-train this morning?" he whispered.

She grabbed his face between her chubby four-year old fingers and landed a sloppy kiss on his lips. "I missed you, Daddy."

"I missed you, too." He kissed her forehead and held her tight against his chest. He twisted his head to the right and nodded to Macy's parents, who were discreetly pulling off their coats in the pew across the aisle.

"Please join me in prayer," the interim pastor offered.

Emma twisted in Ryland's lap to face the front of the sanctuary. Clasping her hands together she scrunched her eyelids tight and furrowed her brow. He couldn't suppress the chuckle deep in his belly. "Shush, Daddy!" Emma corrected. "We gots to pray to Jesus. G-ma will be reals mad if we aren't serious."

"I guess you've been told." Tom chuckled as he lowered his head to pray.

Ryland smiled at his friend and his breath caught

in his chest.

Tessa's eyes twinkled with mirth as she winked at him before bowing her head.

~*~

As the final strands of the closing hymn lifted, Emma sang with the full strength of her tiny lungs. In addition to her love of the pigskin she had inherited her father's singing ability. She stood on the pew with her hand gripping Ryland's forefinger, all while suctioning herself to Pastor Tom's side. Like her father, Emma Jessup was sweet on a Tarrington.

Tom's pulpit filler, retired Pastor Conrad, stood to give the benediction, and nodded toward the back row. "Many of you've already spotted our special congregant this morning, but in case you're unaware, our own Pastor Tom Tarrington has been worshipping with us this morning."

Sudden applause erupted, spreading a hint of pink to Tom's pale cheeks and delighting Emma, who seemed to think the clapping aligned with a football game as she jumped up and down on the pew, cheering with all of her four years of exuberance.

Tom nodded and raised his hand signaling for Conrad to continue. He leaned to his left and whispered in Tessa's ear before turning to Ryland. "I imagine it'll be a little long winded. Would you mind driving Tessa and Lily Mae back to my house?"

"Not at all." A thrill of anticipation bubbled in his chest. "I'll tell Macy's parents to meet me at my house."

"Thanks," Tom said with breathless relief as he moved to greet the hundreds of parishioners closing in on their pew.

"Come on, E-train." Ryland lowered her from the pew to the refinished wood floor. "Let's go find Grammy and Poppy. They can take you back to our house while I take Miss Tessa and Miss Lily Mae home."

"But I just gots you back and I haven'ts seen G-ma yet. She'll be awful heart-broken if I don't give her a smooshy kiss." Before he could answer, Emma scooted through the throng of adults and jumped headlong into his mother's surprised embrace.

An unseen drum began to play a deep bass rhythm against his skull and he rubbed the corner of his temple.

"She's quite something," Tessa said.

He glanced down at both women.

Lily didn't seem quite as aggressive after an hour of holy worship.

"I'm convinced my dad added something extra spicy in her mix before God sent her down from heaven. She is the most exaggerated version of me and all five of my sisters mixed into one tiny, combustible package."

"You love her very much." Tessa offered.

"Yes, I do." He caught sight of his in-laws walking toward his mother. He tilted his head toward Tessa. "Let me make certain Gus and Jackie can watch Emma for a few minutes while I run you home."

"We can walk." She glanced over her shoulder. "Or we could wait on Dad. He shouldn't be too long."

"Uh, *cher*, I don't know what rodeo you're watching, but Papa T will be stuck here until the next carry-in dinner. The least we can do is get on home and pull together a little lunch. He's gonna be as tired as an old coon hound after a two day hunt when he finally finishes all of this well-wishing."

"Maybe we shouldn't leave him. He's not as strong as he thinks."

"You need to let your father be Pastor Tom for a little while." Ryland locked his gaze with hers, brushing her hair off her shoulder. "Lily Mae's right. He'll be exhausted, but it'll be the good kind—like after a five mile run."

"What's good about running for five miles?" Tessa questioned with an air of disbelief, but she raised a quick hand. "But I get your meaning."

"I'll be right back."

He weaved through the milling crowd and found his daughter rapidly recounting her twenty-four hours away from Gibson's Run. "And then Grammy's new 'keet Skeeters squawked at me and I jumped'd seven feet off the ground."

"She means parakeet." Macy's mother corrected.

Without a single reference to Emma's horrific grammar, his mother kissed her only granddaughter's forehead. She glanced up at Ryland. "Emma, your father seems quite breathless. Do you know the cause?"

"Wells, G-ma," Emma offered with a tilt of her head. Her pigtail brushed her shoulder as she scrunched her forehead. "I'm guessing its cause he was jogging. But it coulds be he was looking at Miss Tessa agains. She seems to make him not so smarts."

Ryland drove his hand through his hair. "Emma Grace Jessup, gossip is a horrible habit to acquire from your grandmother. I'd hope she would use this quality time to give you boundaries around your abysmal grammar."

"Grandmothers are supposed to spoil and indulge, Ryland. Parents are intended to correct." His mother stood, setting Emma on her feet. "And apparently, your grammar lessons are not translating to your daughter."

"I'm glad to see you still feel free to correct your child." He kissed her cheek.

"Yes, well, your sisters are meeting us at McGregor's for lunch. I invited Gus and Jackie to join us, but they need to head back to Clintonville for a party." His mother's face reflected the genteel sweetness of years of practiced hospitality, but he knew she was relieved to have Macy's parents zipping back north of the county border.

"Are you sure you can't join us?" he asked, and saw the quick flicker of revulsion in his mother's eyes before Jackie shook her head.

"Thank you, Ryland. We've enjoyed having our little princess with us this weekend." She stepped forward and tugged him to her eyelevel for a hug. "Please think about the coaching position. You'd be so close. Emma could start kindergarten at CSG next fall, just like Macy. We'd love to be able to see her more often. And you, of course."

"Thank you, but I'm happy here."

"Please, just think about it." Her tears brimmed and he couldn't deny her the small request.

"Of course."

"Oh, thank you." With the quick wrap of her arms around his chest, she knocked the wind from his lungs."Well, Gus, we need to get back." She bent and wrapped Emma in a tight hug. "I love you to the moon and back, princess."

"I love you too, Grammy." Emma smacked a kiss

on her grandmother's lips and twisted to repeat the hug and kiss with her grandfather.

"We'll see you in a few weeks for your birthday, Em. You be a good girl for your daddy." He ruffled her hair. Nodding to Ryland, he slipped his fingers through his wife's and led her to the side door.

Ryland's stomach twisted with the ache he could feel trailing behind them. Macy was their only child. Their last link to her was Emma. If he was a more giving person he'd move to Columbus so they could see her anytime they wanted. His mother had five grandsons and all but one daughter in Gibson's Run. Maybe he should seriously consider the coaching job.

A tug on his belt loop pulled his attention to Emma's giant smile.

"So can they go?"

He squatted to her eye level. "Honey, Grammy and Poppy needed to go home. You'll see them soon."

"No, not Grammy and Poppy," she said, rolling her eyes and giving him a glimpse of his future teenage daughter. "Miss Tessa and her friend."

"I need to take them home then I'll meet you at lunch with G-ma. If that's OK?" He lifted his gaze to his mother.

"I believe your daughter is asking if your friends can join us for lunch."

He looked back to Emma, who nodded vigorously—her pigtails dancing around her ears.

"I'll ask, but I don't think they will."

"Jus ask, Daddy, OKs?"

13

Opening the door to McGregor's, the rush of conversations, clank of dishes and booming sound system slammed Tessa like a three hundred pound offensive lineman. The gregarious eatery was renovated a few years after she left for Louisiana and was a favorite spot of locals.

Emma tugged on her hand, dragging her through the entryway, past the paintings of 1950's pin-up girls and black-and-white photos of local sports teams nearly as old as her father. With each step the noise filled the remaining empty spaces of peace.

Her head was starting to thump with the underlying rhythm, and the anxiety that began rising the moment she slid into the front seat of Ryland Jessup's SUV overflowed.

Emma stopped just outside a glass door and yanked on Tessa's arm as though she were a door bell pull. Tessa bent down. The child cupped her hands around Tessa's ear. "You gots to open the door. It's to heaby fors me to get."

"No problem." She smiled, and shot a wink to Lily, who was scanning the rambunctious dining room as if she expected a comic book villain to pop up with a machine gun. Wrenching the cool stainless handle, she swung the glass door wide and exposed a haven of quiet tucked in the back corner of the restaurant's main dining room.

Four round tables stood in a square. Each was partially filled with a mix of a people from newborn to senior citizen. Emma raced across the cozy room and jumped into the waiting lap of Ryland's oldest sister, Elizabeth.

"Well, at least I don't feel like my head will implode from the noise," Lily said.

"Seriously?" Tessa asked with a lifted eyebrow. "This from the woman who singlehandedly caused us to have three noise violations and two visits from the local police during our senior year."

Lily waved her hand. "Pish. I was sowing my oats. I'm a soon-to-be-married lady of refinement. My gentle ears can only handle so much excitement. I'm parched." She sidled to the sidebar stuffed with carafes of water and tea. Nowhere was Lily a stranger.

"Hello, Tessa."

Tessa's smile stretched. "Mrs. Jessup." She stepped into the open arms of Ryland's mother.

"Oh, I think you're old enough to call me Nancy." Nancy Jessup stood eye level to Tessa's five foot four frame. Her coiffed bob was a silvery shade of blonde and her eyes were the same changing gray as her son's.

"Well," Tessa stepped out of her embrace. "Politeness was drilled into my soul by my mother—that included calling every adult by Mr. or Mrs. I'm not certain I'll ever be able to break the habit, but I'll do my best."

"I'd appreciate it."

The door swung open and the raucous sounds of the dining room rushed in with Ryland. Tearing off his scarf and jacket, he tossed them to an open chair just as Emma launched herself into his arms.

She really loves her daddy.

"Yes, she does." Nancy replied.

Tessa whipped her head to the right. She had spoken one of her wayward thoughts of Ryland out loud. Now she was losing control of her thoughts? Stupid toilet life.

"Don't worry dear. I won't say a word to Ryland. My son isn't perfect, but he's a spectacular father. Watching him and Emma together is a thing of poetry." She linked her arm through Tessa's and guided her to an empty table. "I'd love to hear what you've been up to over the last few years. Tom tells me so little. Men don't share as well as women."

"I should really help my friend, Lily Mae."

Nancy glanced over her shoulder at Lily and Ryland's sister, Harper, who appeared to have fallen into a deep conversation—evidenced by the lack of Lily's hand movements. "She seems to be OK for now."

"Lily doesn't really understand the formality of introductions. She tends to go straight from stranger to sister in one beat of the heart."

"You love her."

"She's the best friend anyone could have."

"I heard she flew up for the weekend to check on you."

Tessa instantly prayed a sinkhole would magically open and swallow her. Similar to the times she'd prayed the same prayer in adolescence—she was left with burning cheeks and a pit in her stomach—not a single hole in the space-time continuum in sight. "Yes ma'am."

"I also heard you ran into a little trouble with your writing." Nancy lifted a glass to her lips and sipped.

Why did people have to wonder about one's life? She glanced to her feet, but no movement. Hole? Come on…not even a little crack in the earth? Ohio has had earthquakes. Is it too much to ask for one at this particular moment?

"I don't know all of the details," Nancy interrupted Tessa's destructive thoughts. "But your father shared that you'd run into some difficulties. And I'm ashamed to say, Sissy Jenkins filled in some of the blanks."

At the mention of Sissy Jenkins, Tessa's heart sank. If Sissy knew what happened in Louisiana—the burglary, her firing, paparazzi following her every move, her clients' secrets sold to the highest bidder— every one of the two-thousand-nine-hundred and ninety-four souls in Gibson's Run knew. No wonder Mrs. Monahan asked her to substitute. She was officially more pitiable than when she was six years old and piddled in her pants. Tessa dropped her head to her folded arms.

"Now, dear," Nancy said with a pat to her shoulder. "You've nothing of which to be ashamed."

"Really? I failed at the most important part of being a ghost writer: being a ghost. Somehow, someone in New Orleans found out what I do and who my clients are. Besides an obligatory thank you in the acknowledgements, my name never should be associated with a client's. Now I'm a term searched on the Internet. I failed."

"Tessa, you didn't fail. You were violated." Her face twisted in concern. "I'm sorry for what you're enduring. I know this isn't the best place to talk, but I'd love to help any way I can—even if it's just using my excellent listening skills."

Tessa couldn't suppress matching Mrs. Jessup's grin. "Thank you."

Nancy patted Tessa's hand and stood. "Well, I need to see where our servers are. My grandsons will not be calm much longer if we don't stuff them with a few dozen chicken fingers and French fries."

Tessa leaned back and closed her eyes. She had designed her life to be simple and calm, but on *the terrible, awful day*, she'd stood in the middle of what seemed to be a Category 5 hurricane. Her reprieve to Gibson's Run was merely a hiding place until she returned to truly assess the rubble of what was once her thriving career. The floor shifted and her eyes shot open at the distant hope her prayer for the earth to swallow her whole was finally being answered.

Ryland sat in the chair beside her.

Her stomach dropped. "Can I help you?"

"I was hoping I could help you, but my mother skittered off before I could be your rescuer." The corner of his mouth lifted. "I'm sorry if she asked you too many personal questions. With six children, she seems to think she can mother everyone on the planet. Her mothering tends to include some serious doses of meddling."

"She didn't meddle. Not really. She just informed me of how my career humiliation reached the brain trust of Sissy Jenkins. So, pretty much everyone in the tri-county area likely knows details about my life I'm not even fully aware exist."

"I'm sure it's not as bad as you think."

"Sissy Jenkins, Ryland. Sissy. Jenkins."

He rubbed his chin and relaxed into his chair. "Well, when you put it that way, you might want to hide in your closet until the next millennium."

"Thanks," Tessa giggled.

"Why do you care what people say about you?"

"PK." She pointed to her father as he walked through the door. "When you're a pastor's kid, you have to be concerned with what people are saying about you. One poor choice has a tendency to bathe everyone in the family in your gunk. I hate my bad press is affecting my dad."

"Tessa," Ryland cupped her hand in his. "You didn't cause your dad's heart attack. The drama with your work is someone's sick attempt to find a new way to exploit overly exposed people. Your dad's heart attack was because he wasn't taking care of himself. Neither situation is your fault."

Her throat felt thick and tight. A single tear tore a cold streak down her cheek. Until this moment she hadn't begun to accept the unwarranted blame she'd been piling on since she'd received the call about her dad.

With a feather light touch, Ryland brushed the tear from her face. His fingers lingered on her cheek an extra beat. Her gaze locked with his. The comfort welling in the gray depths of his eyes fueled the flittering of the butterfly's wings in her stomach. She nodded, afraid a bullfrog's croak would escape rather than words.

"From where I sit, you've tried to make your life mistake-proof." His voice was a deep whisper. "Mistakes are a part of life. How we respond to the mistakes determines how well we live our lives. You've an extraordinary opportunity to respond with all of the grace and beauty God poured into your spirit. You just have to choose."

When had Ryland Jessup become wise? Shifting

her hand under his to connect palm with palm, she squeezed his fingers. Subtle heat emanated from the touch. She opened her mouth as the table rocked with the force of a fly ball to left center. She yanking her hand away.

Joey plopped onto the chair beside her—draping his arm over the back of her chair. "What I miss? You already order?" he asked.

Ryland stiffened beside her, before he shoved against the table, and stood. "I should find Emma and a server. I'll leave you two."

She reached out to stop him, but her fingers only grasped air. Her mind was fuzzy in regards to Ryland. The painting of him she was creating in her mind could hang in a cubist museum and easily be confused for one of the Masters. She couldn't match her childhood tormentor with the kindness he continued to shower upon her. And yet, every time she felt they were on the edge of a moment of clarity, he stomped off in the opposite direction.

Joey tweaked her shoulder. Pure joy was on his face with a delicious twinkle in his deep chocolate brown eyes.

She tilted her head to rest on her upturned hand, her sagging spirits lifting.

"So, T.T. what do you want for lunch?"

Teenage Tessa Fantasy #22: After-church lunch with Joey Taylor.

Ryland Jessup, who?

14

Ryland placed an order for a kid's chicken strip basket with applesauce, and a medium rare cheeseburger with carrot sticks, before sliding onto an empty chair beside his sister Elizabeth, who was chatting with Tessa's obnoxious friend Lily. How a sweet, timid woman like Tessa found herself attached to an outspoken, rude woman like Lily Mae was beyond his comprehension. He had a wide range of friends from college, most were other athletes, but they shared many similar qualities to him. He couldn't think of one friend in his life of a similar opposite nature to the friendship between Lily and Tessa.

From the corner of his eye, he followed the path of the server as she leaned down to take Tessa's and Joe's orders. Tessa closed her menu and shifted her gaze to the table, brushing a stray lock behind her ear. Joe's broad grin gritted against Ryland's spine—but the waitress visibly giggled, squeezing his upper arm. The man could flirt with a wooden pole.

Since they were kids digging pits around his backyard tree fort, Joe had a knack for turning females into molding clay. His superpower over women would be a horrible temptation for evil in the hands of most men, but Joe was barely aware of his hero worthy skills. He assumed all women were placed on the earth to charm and be charmed. The women in his life changed as often as Joe changed email accounts, but he always treated his woman of the moment as if she was a damsel and he was the rescuer.

Tessa Tarrington was the heroine of his current story, ripping a hole in the center of Ryland's own lifelong fairytale. Joe tucked another wayward strand from Tessa's ponytail.

Shaking his head, Ryland shifted his gaze across the table and locked eyes with his middle sisters—the twins, Elinor and Marian. Both sisters had mirrored expressions—squinted eyes and pursed lips—their heads tilted to the left. "What?"

"Isn't that Tessa Tarrington?" Elinor asked, jutting her chin toward Tessa and Joe.

"Of course that's her," Marian said. "Her father's talking to Momma."

"Why aren't you sitting with her?" Elinor stumbled over Marian's last words—the zigzagging conversation a standard with the two sisters.

"Yeah, why, Ry?"

"Didn't you have a crush on her when you were a kid?"

"I remember...you bought her some weird present?"

"What was that, Mar?"

"Underpants, El."

Marian's mouth dropped open. "You gave her underpants? How old were you?"

"He was like five or something."

"He was six." His sister Elizabeth jumped into the conversation. *Oh, joy! More sisters.*

"Six?" Marian questioned, her head falling opposite to Elinor's open-mouth chin tilt. "How did you talk Mom into buying underpants for a girl when you were six? I'm not sure you could get her to buy underpants as a gift from you today."

"Eeww, that's gross." His second to the oldest sister, Harper, offered as she sat next to him.

"Can we please stop this conversation?" Ryland pleaded.

"T's never gotten over the humiliation of those days-of-the-week panties." Lily Mae scolded him, her lips drawn into a thin, surly line.

"They were days-of-the-week underpants? Oh, Rys. How could you?" Scout—the sister one year his senior—offered in disgust.

"I...was...six." He rubbed his temples, his eyelids shuttering against the gaggle of women correcting his romantic misstep twenty years earlier.

An arm slid around his shoulder, as the debate about his ignorance grew in volume. "Your heart was in the right place, Rys." Harper's voice was low and laced with humor. "But if you don't want your kindergarten misstep to splat on the floor in front of the now very grown up Pee-Pee Tee-Tee, you should extract yourself from this...situation."

Tilting his face toward his second oldest sister, he squinted. "Her name's Tessa."

She cupped her hand around his cheek. "And don't ever forget that vital piece of information, little brother." Planting a sloppy kiss on his lips, she patted him on the shoulder. "Now go. I'll take care of this hen party. You distract that sweet girl from the charming sneak you call a best friend."

He shoved away from the table just as the waitress arrived with his and Emma's meals. Lifting both baskets with one hand, he hip checked his chair and sauntered toward the near empty table where Tessa and Joe appeared to be nestled in a private cocoon—

sequestered from the chaos of a Jessup Sunday lunch.

"Hey, giant, where do you think you're going?" Lily hollered, skittering to a stop a few steps behind him.

His shoulders dropped at the sound of her southern twang. Why couldn't Tessa have a normal friend? Why did she choose Miss Nosey Pants?

"What?" He swiveled, nearly knocking her head with his elbow.

"Watch it, bubba. You should understand your size and off putting proportions."

Cranking his chin, his neck popped. "I need to feed my daughter. Can you yell at me later for whatever imagined sin you think I've committed?"

"Listen, bub," her voice dropped to a near inaudible volume. Her finger emphasis in his chest was an adequate reminder she despised every bit of his person. "T's had her heart set on Joey Taylor since she chewed rainbow-striped gum and permed her hair. You let them be."

"Do you always speak in cryptic references to childhood?"

"I'm just saying Tessa seems like she has a real shot with Joey. I want her to have the room to pursue her dream. Don't mess it up or mess with her head."

"I want my daughter to eat some lunch. She needs her nap in about an hour." He glanced at the bottle cap clock on the wall. "I promise to stuff food in her face as quickly as possible and drag her away from her aunts, cousins, and grandmother so your friend can awkwardly flirt with one of the premier athletes in major league sports. OK?"

"*Hmpf.*" Pivoting, she stomped back to the table overflowing with sisters.

Not since he lived solo in his ten by eleven bedroom, had Ryland been so grateful to be male. Most days he loved his life—the copious females who seemed to ooze out of every crevice—but today they were too much. Too loud. Too pushy. Too southern. When his morning alarm demanded a stretch from his warm bed, he should have ignored its plea, played hooky from church, lunch, and life in general.

"Daddy? Is those my fingers?" Emma tugged him back to reality.

"Yep." He was too exhausted from the last few minutes to correct her four year old grammar. "Where do you want to sit and eat?"

Her hands shot to her mouth as if she was trying to keep the secret of Santa Claus from every child on the planet. "I knows."

Emma galloped toward Joe's chair and launched herself on his back.

"Great." Lunch with gooey JT and gushing Tessa. The cheeseburger would likely fight against the rising bile in his throat. But, he'd walk over hot coals or fight a Russian dictator for his baby girl. Gagging down a meal while he watched his life-long love lavish her affection on his best friend was only one of the many sacrifices he was willing to make for Emma.

Dropping the basket of chicken fingers on the table, Ryland snatched a napkin from the holder and lifted Emma with one arm from Joe's lap, setting her on an empty chair to his left.

"Aww, I guess I don't get to eat lunch with my best gal." Joe said with a tweak of Emma's nose.

"Buts I'm right here Uncle Joey. I didn't goes nowhere." She snagged a chicken finger and chomped the end with her molars.

"Emma..." Ryland said sliding onto the seat beside her.

"Oh, sorry, Daddy." She dropped her chicken on the table and clasped her hands together. Her face scrunched tight. "God, please bless this food. Bless our talkings. Bless my daddy. Bless my Uncle Joey. Bless G-ma, Grammy and Poppy. And bless Miss Tessa, cause she seems real nice. And PS, could you tell momma I miss her wider than the sky and deeper than the ocean? Amen." Swiping her loose bangs from her forehead, she reached for her chicken and resumed her gator chomp.

"That was a lovely prayer, Miss Emma." Tessa's voice held the tinge of a tear.

"Thanks. Sometimes, I forgets to pray. But Daddy says it's super importants to remember to thanks God for all our stuff. Helps us to remembers how much He does for us."

The burger in Ryland's hands melted. Pickles slopped into the basket, ketchup and mustard dripped down his fingers. He resisted the tug of Tessa's watchful eyes. He was so unabashedly proud of the tender steps of faith his daughter was taking, but he didn't want others—particularly Tessa—to think Emma was performing, or merely a parrot spouting out the words her father taught her.

"My daddy taught me the same thing, but I must admit I'm a bit derelict in that particular discipline." Tessa smiled.

After dunking a chicken tender in honey sauce, Emma chomped half the length in a single bite. "What's dare-licked mean?" She mumbled, sauce oozing down her chin.

"Smaller bites." Ryland said, dropping his burger

in the basket. Tearing open the foil packet of a moist towelette, the aroma of ammonia burned his nostrils countering the feel of the cool, damp cloth in his fingers. He tugged Emma's chin to him and swiped at the sticky honey residue. With a lowered voice, he locked his eyes with hers. "We don't talk with full mouths."

"Buts I just wants to know what the word means. You said know-wedge is super importants." She matched his whispered tone, her eyes stretched wide with emphasis.

"Yes, I did." He kissed her forehead. "Derelict means neglected or to ignore something to the point of forgetting."

"So are you dare-licked about having a wife?"

The power of Joe's snort shot Ryland's gaze to the table anticipating a soda stream from his friend's nose. Lifting a single eyebrow, he shifted his focus to Joe, and tried to ignore the sudden rise of heat blanketing his cheeks.

"Dude, your kid's got you pegged." Joe rocked in his chair, balancing on the back legs.

"I don't think that's fair." Tessa's brows pulled to a V over her forehead—her eyes filled with tender compassion, mixed with pity.

Locking his arms over his chest, he narrowed his focus and jutted his chin toward the door. "I do just fine. My life's not perfect—but it's a good life. You don't know squat about me, baseball hero. You're so consumed with your little life, you don't care about anyone else." He rested his forearms on the table, leaning towards JT. "You appear to be an expert on my pitiful existence, but you haven't been forthcoming with your own. You want to share what's going on with you and that shoulder? You seem to be doing much better. Taking any short cuts? Talked to Scott lately?" His stomach churned with the offensive attack on Joe. He didn't want to start with the questions that had been burning the edges of every conversation they'd had since Joe came home for Christmas.

JT was naturally hyper, but in the past month he seemed to be "on" all the time. His friend was nursing a nagging injury that never fully healed after a spring training incident when he collided head first with a catcher at home plate. The past season's numbers were well under his career average and his dipping stats had impacted his carefree, the-world-loves-everything-about-me, golden boy attitude.

The few times Ryland had taken advantage of his summer off and caught games, JT rarely wanted to linger over a postgame meal. Their conversations since Macy's death had transitioned from best friend to barely superficial.

Joe was in a deep valley, and as his friend, Ryland wanted to help him climb back to the light, but at the moment he was struggling for his own ego's survival and selfishness was rapidly winning. "No response? You're reporting in what, six weeks? Will you be starting in the Show or will you be back home licking your wounds and bouncing around the minors?"

Joe wiped his mouth with his napkin, swiveled to Tessa—shining his cereal box smile. "T.T. it's been wonderful seeing you again, but I nearly forgot I need to help my brother with a project this afternoon. If you'll excuse me." The table rattled as he stood. Kissing Emma's forehead, he whispered, "I'll see you this week, slugger, OK?"

"Do you hafta go, Uncle Joey?" Her head fell back

to make eye contact.

"I'm afraid so. Wouldn't want to disappoint my brother." Lifting his gaze from Emma to Ryland, twenty plus years of friendship transcended the need for words. His message was clear—*Back off.*

Joe bent to eye level with Tessa. "I look forward to a longer reunion on Tuesday." Tucking a stray strand behind her ear, he kissed her cheek with a subtle smack. Standing to his full six foot three, he nodded to Ryland. "Later."

Ryland scrubbed his face with his palm releasing a soft sigh. He'd crossed the unspoken line. The next few days would be a series of make-up hoop sessions and video game brawls. And he wouldn't be any closer to discovering the truth behind the change in JT.

"How could you?" Tessa hissed. "Every time I begin to think you're a better version of yourself you end up being Ryland Jessup all over again."

"He gots to be. Ryland Jessup is Daddy's name," Emma said, as she shoved a spoonful of applesauce in her mouth.

Tessa whipped her head to Emma—a look of shocked awareness splashed across her face. "I guess you're right, Emma." She lifted her gaze to Ryland. "I was just hoping your daddy was someone different."

"Then who'd he be?"

"My friend."

15

"Daddy, do you want to take a nap while Lily and I run to the market for dinner supplies?" Tessa asked as they walked through the front door of the parsonage.

"T, we just ate lunch. How could you possibly be thinking of food? Do you have a tape worm?" Lily unraveled the scarf swathed around her neck and face.

Really? Tessa said with her eyes.

"On second thought," Lily nodded. "We should get a head start if we're making Mama's mashed sweet potatoes, and chicken pot pies. How about a nice chocolate pie for dessert?"

"I don't think that's on my diet, Lily." Dad offered as he lowered onto the nearest overstuffed chair.

"Oh, Rev. T., you just leave it to me. Beau's daddy has a touch of the diabetes and we are constantly looking for ways to make good food healthy." She patted him on the shoulder.

Tessa crouched beside her father's chair. "Will that be all right, Daddy? A little nap and a nice home-cooked meal—not by me."

"That'll be fine, Tessa." Despite overgrown hands, his touch was as light as an angel's wing. His eyes shut before she stood.

A twist in her heart squeezed guilt through her whole being. Today had been too much for her father. She should have insisted on going home and waiting for him there so he could rest. But no, her recently awakened teenage hormones were in near constant control. If she had her grown up brain driving, she wouldn't be on the emotional roller coaster of allowing childhood crushes and unruly anger consume her. Her focus needed to be solidly on her father and his recovery; that was why she was in Gibson's Run. Starting now, she wouldn't be swayed by messy-haired baseball players, or enraged by ex-jock coaches. Her sole focus would be on helping her dad. She kissed his forehead and nodded to Lily. *Let's go.*

~*~

The steering wheel rattled as Lily slammed the passenger door on Tessa's ancient coupe.

"Careful."

"Darlin', not even Beau's best duct tape job could fix this horrible excuse for a car. I'm shocked the *po po* haven't yanked you right off the road for driver endangerment." Lily flipped the visor. Swiping lip gloss over her bottom lip, she gave a little shrug. "You know I'm right, *cher*."

"And just how am I supposed to buy a new car? My current employment consists of eighty-five dollars a day substituting for my high school English teacher. And that's pre-tax."

"That's highway robbery." Raising the visor, Lily swiveled in her seat. "But don't you even try to play me. You and I both know that rainy-day-I'm-going-to-Europe fund is burning a hole in your overstuffed bank account. You're forgetting I know how well your ghost writer self did before *the terrible, awful day*."

"I can't dip into that money. It's for Europe—or a

rainy day which seems to be much more likely than a whirlwind trip to the South of France or the hills of Tuscany. Either way the money stays far away from my car. Wilma's been just fine. We drove all the way from NOLA here didn't we?"

"I tried to forget you named this decrepit piece. At least you gave her a fitting name."

Tessa turned onto the open interstate connecting Gibson's Run with the outside world. They could have picked up everything on their limited shopping list at the local specialty market around the corner from her dad's house, but Tessa needed some time to think and some breathing room. Invariably, as soon as she picked up a basket at Dooley's Fine Meats & Cheeses she would run into at least four of her father's parishioners—and likely a Jessup or two. Ryland's sisters and their offspring seemed to have multiplied exponentially since the last time she'd visited her father. Heading forty minutes out of town to the closest chain grocery seemed like the simplest and safest route.

"You want to brood like a teen heartthrob or do you want to explain the urgent need to pick up dinner before lunch has fully settled in our bellies?"

"Again. Two words—'what's wrong?'—all you need, Lil."

"OK, boring much. What's wrong?" Lily offered her best imitation of Tessa's Midwestern accent.

"Everything was fine at lunch—nice even. I probably flirted a little more than I should have with Joey."

"Long overdue if you ask me."

"And Ryland seemed to be the man I've glimpsed for the past week. Adult. Kind. Generous."

"*Hmpf.* I don't know about all that, *cher*. He was pretty forceful when I threatened him."

Tessa swung her face to Lily. "You what?"

"Threaten is too strong a word. I suggested—with great emphasis—he shouldn't mess with you and Joey."

"Why would he mess with Joey and me? Ryland barely tolerates me."

"Umm...I think that's a negative, Will Robinson."

"Could you join us in the English language, Lil?"

"Mr. Jessup apparently had quite the crush on one Tessa Tarrington when she was six years old. It seems panty-gate was not ill intended. Rather, a diminutive Ryland Jessup was trying to impress you with his gift."

Slamming on her brakes, both women flung forward against their seatbelts whipping their hair about their shoulders.

"Glory be, T. You trying to get that trip to the good and plenty sooner than our young years deserve?"

"What did you say?"

"Are you trying to kill us? I want to be a young bride—not make Beau a widower. You might want to put the jalopy back in drive before this nearly deserted highway fulfills its destiny and cars actually start progressing on the pavement."

"Ryland was trying to impress me?" Pressing the accelerator, her heart thumped against her chest in a matching pace.

Patting her hair in place, Lily shrugged her shoulders. "That's what the gaggle of Jessup sisters shared. It seems nearly every day when Ryland was not much older than his daughter, he waxed poetically about one Tessa—the fairy princess—Tarrington."

"That doesn't make any sense. Ryland teased me

nearly every day of elementary and junior high school. The only thing that made his sing-song, tone-deaf shouting of 'here comes Pee-Pee Tee-Tee' worse was the consistency of the taunt. Every day, Lil."

Lily pulled a single leg to her chest. "Didn't you ever hear that when little boys tease you that's their way of declaring their undying love? Not that adult men are much more evolved—but seriously, your momma never shared that tidbit?"

"Well, sure, but she was more concerned with me not making a fuss with one of the most important families in the congregation. We moved here when I started kindergarten. For the first few years, momma felt we needed to always reflect the perfect, non-conflict family. So after a while, I stopped crying about the teasing to her. She was too busy to help." Tessa swiped at the soft dew of perspiration sprinkling along her brow. "Besides, that was when he was like six. It's not as if his crush survived elementary school. Right?"

"Umm. Sure. That's why he ran those boys breathless yesterday, left abruptly last night, and tried to make Joey look like an idiot over lunch. Sure—not a crush in sight."

The oxygen in the car seemed to evaporate. Breaths—shallow and soft—fought to grab air. Sweat poured down her spine. Ryland Jessup did not have feelings for her. What a ridiculous thought. She was his human teasing bag. Her rational, organized mine tore apart the story to diagram the plot—just as she had for dozens of projects—and Ryland Jessup as the villain didn't add up. Regardless of how the better part of thirteen years were clouded by his near incessant torture, she couldn't deny the kindness and generosity she'd witnessed and received of late. But kindness didn't translate to romantic interest.

Her breath steadied. Kindness was the gateway to friendship. Was she friends with Ryland? No. She was quite horrible to him, but he was consistently generous with her. Extending kindness that was beyond casual. And she rebuffed his outstretched hand at every turn. Tightening her grip over the steering wheel, her heart tripped. She needed to become Ryland Jessup's friend. She might as well. She was living out all her teenage fantasies. She might as well face all her nightmares.

16

"That was amazing, Lily. I can't believe the whole meal was low fat." Tessa's father reclined in his chair and rubbed his belly through his worn burgundy sweater.

"The secret's in the spices, Rev T. Beau's daddy's all about the spicier the better. I toned the chicken pot pie heat to a Yankee tolerated mild, but I believe the kick rounds out the flavor so you don't even realize your using skim milk or low fat cheese."

Gulping down her fourth glass of water, Tessa's eyes burned from the toned down spice mixture. Eight years in Louisiana—four in New Orleans—she could eat Cajun with the truest of natives. Lily's idea of mild was anything but.

"You OK over there, cher?" Lily reached for her hand.

All Tessa could offer was a quick nod and a point to the kitchen for more water. She flipped on the faucet and resisted the urge to dunk her head under the spray. She drank and filled her glass two more times before the heat subsided. Closing her eyes she rested her hip against the sink rim, the surface cool against her over-spiced body.

Lily was a creative culinary God-send—allowing her father to escape a swirling pool of macaroni & cheese and tomato soup—but she was hopeful there were no leftovers to extend past Lil's visit. With one additional glass of water, sipped rather than gulped, she filled her glass to the brim.

"Hey, *cher*," Lily shouted from the dining room. "You wanna cut the pie while you're in there lollygagging?"

"Sure." Tessa's voice held greater strength. Lifting the glass dome off of the cake plate, she sucked in the sweet, rich aroma of Lily Mae's Grandma Delta's Chocolate Meringue Pie. With quick efficient strokes perfected through decades of carry-in dinners, Tessa sliced the pie in eight equal pieces. An eighth seemed like a sensible portion.

Lily's baking magic created the pie and there was nothing low fat attached to the dessert.

She loaded up her mother's tea service tray with the pie, dessert plates, server, and her much needed water. If Daddy wanted coffee, she'd drop a pod in the one cup wonder, but she definitely didn't need any additional stimulation for the evening.

With measured steps, eyes focused on the delicate pie and its ride alongs, she tried to avoid the Thanksgiving debacle of age seven. She gently slid the tray onto the glossy surface of Grandma Jacobson's mahogany dining room table. Greedily grabbing her glass, she downed the water to drown the rising flame in her throat. The cool glass against her lips was a delicious relief. She quickly gave in to the temptation to wipe the clinging condensation from the glass, relieving the heat continuing to build up her neck.

"Ahem." Daddy cleared his throat. "Tessa, we have company."

Tessa lazily opened her eyes and the glass slipped through her fingers, shattering at her bare feet. *Ryland Jessup is everywhere.*

"Swizzle sticks," she mumbled as she dropped to snag the big pieces.

"I'll grab a dustpan." Lily scurried on tiptoes past the shattered mess.

"Let me help." Ryland was snatching chunks of glass before she could respond.

"Hey, Miss Emma," Pastor Tom said, "why don't we take our pie in the living room? I think I have a new DVD you haven't seen." Chairs scooted and little feet shuffled.

"You don't have to help." Tessa offered, but spoke to the floor, yearning for the scarred wood surface to open. "You should go watch the DVD with Daddy and Emma. Eat pie. Anything but put your hands and fingers in jeopardy of a bloody mess from my eternal clumsiness."

"These hands made it through three years in the Big Ten and four in the NFL. I think they can survive one drinking glass—but I appreciate the forewarning."

Holding the largest pieces, she rested back on her heels and lifted an eyebrow. "Forewarned is forearmed."

"True." A smile lit his face.

Her heart twisted with the warmth and welcome reflected in the now charcoal depths of his eyes.

"Found it!" Lily tip-toed back into the dining room holding the broom and dust pan as if one were a snake and the other was a dead rat.

Swallowing against the growing lump in her throat, Tessa reached for the cleaning supplies.

Ryland swiped them from her grasp.

"Hey…"

"You are not cleaning up glass barefooted." His voice dropped to coach-in-charge tone.

She glanced to her feet, surrounded by sparkling shards. "And just how do you think I will extricate myself from the sea of glass without a broom and dustpan? Fly?"

"Sure." He wrapped one arm around her waist and tugged her to his side, lifting her feet a good six inches above the floor.

Against his solid length, she felt small and delicate. His touch was light, and yet she never feared he would drop her. Needle pricks rose and fell in waves where their bodies touched. Her cheeks warmed—but she would be kidding herself if she thought she was suffering the lingering effects of Lily Mae's dinner.

Balancing her to his side, he toddled to the edge of the steps leading upstairs. With the grace of a dancer, he tenderly lowered her until her toes touched the bottom step. His fingers lingered against her side for a moment, his palm on her waist emanating heat.

Twisting to face him, her hands dropped to his shoulders. She drew her gaze up his broad shoulder to his sinewy, muscled neck. Licking her lips, she lifted her gaze to his. Standing just under eye level on the step, their mouths were less than a breath apart. "Thanks," she whispered.

"No problem. Glass. Feet. Bad."

"Daddy," Emma called from the living room.

Pushing a long sigh through his lips, he released her waist and slid a step from her.

"Comes watch the new princes DBD Pastor Tom's gots. She has hairs just like mines."

"Honey. I'm helping Miss Tessa." A smile tugged at his full lips. "I keep trying with her grammar. My mom drilled it into all six of us, but sometimes when she messes words up—like 'D B D' or adds an extra 's'— my heart twists. I try and lock the memories deep because I know she'll be proper in the flash of an eye, and I'll long for her horrible grammar and wonder at the world."

Tessa nodded. Unable to speak, her heart was doing some twisting of its own.

~*~

Pie with the pastor and his biggest fan—Emma Jessup—was turning into the most delightful evening.

Ryland had doubted the wisdom of accepting Pastor Tom's invitation for dessert, but when Emma overheard, he had zero viable excuses for vacating the generous offer. After losing her mother, his daughter struggled with any changes in her routine. And Pastor Tom's sudden heart attack in front of the congregation shot fear into his tiny daughter's soul. No number of Daddy'll-make-it-better kisses eased her panic. Each time Emma was able to physically touch Pastor Tom, she was reassured he wasn't going to fly away to heaven like her momma.

Ryland swiped the floor with a wet paper towel to ensure the final glass shards were in the trash bin. His mind flashed to the vision of Tessa wiping her neck with the glass, and his mouth went dry. The feel of her against his side lingered and filled him with a rising smoke of passion. He shuttered his eyes, resting his forehead against his fist. *Lord, help me. I can't do this alone.*

"The floor's not going to mop itself, Yankee." Lily's southern demand rolled over his spine.

His fingers clenched against the rag. Lifting his

gaze to her, he forced a broad grin. "Almost finished. Just saying a quick prayer."

"In the middle of the floor?" Her hand rested against her hip jutting her elbow out like a sail. Maybe she'd fly away sooner than expected. One could dream.

"Never a bad time to pray, is there?"

"Hmmm. Well, make sure you wipe up one more time. Glass can be a slippery little sucker. You never know when a shard'll sneak out, poke through, and make a big old mess." With a flip of her hair, Lily stepped over him and snagged a piece of pie on her way to the living room.

A final shove of the rag convinced him the floor hadn't been this clean since the day Mrs. Tarrington passed away. Pushing to stand he was reminded of why he opted to retire from the NFL. He wanted to be able to run with his grandchildren one day, but his knees and hips had other plans. He creaked like an old rocker against a cedar porch. "Ouch."

Tessa descended into the room. "Was that your knee?" She'd slipped her bare feet into cozy sheepskin boots and twisted her long hair into a lopsided bun.

He nodded. "What the NFL doesn't tell you is you enter with the body of a twenty-one year old and leave with the body of a fifty year old."

"Do you miss it?" She slid a piece of chocolate pie on a plate and offered it to him in exchange for the rag.

Accepting the pie, he sat on an empty chair, thankfully avoiding the princess DVD of the evening. A single twenty-six-year-old man could only handle so many hours of singing cartoons before losing street cred.

Wiping her hands against her jeans, she slid onto a

chair beside him. "So, do you miss it? I've had several former athletes as clients and walking away—retiring—is universally the hardest thing most of them do." She reached for her own piece of pie.

The room echoed with the distant high pitched twang of a cartoon sing along.

He shoved a large bite into his mouth, giving his mind the opportunity to process her question. For some reason, he didn't want to give her his standard reporter worthy answer: *I gave the NFL everything I had, and the NFL reciprocated. My time was done. I made the best choice for my family.*

The answer was solid and beautifully scripted to make a Sports Center clip, but the answer wasn't the truth. In reality, his body played a full season, maybe a season and a half, longer than its expiration date. He'd been shot up with every known substance to help him quickly heal. Pain killers were as common with his breakfast as coffee and vitamins. In the whirl of his career, his baby daughter saw him at photo shoots, or during an occasional off weekend. His marriage was an empty shell of what he'd thought it had been. The only glue holding it together was his professional athlete status. That was his truth. But was he ready to share his truth with Tessa? Was he ready to be weak and show her more flaws—real flaws? His fork tinkled as he tapped to the rhythm of the distant princess melody. Tessa's gaze tugged at him.

"If it's too hard to talk about you don't have to." Picking at the end of her pie, she lifted a shoulder. "I used to get paid to discover the heart of my clients' stories. I can be a bit nosy."

Dropping his fork, he massaged his temple. His eyes drifted shut as the last year washed over him like a stinging summer rain. "I just don't talk about it much." He opened his eyes and looked at her. "Macy's death is so tightly woven into the fabric and timing of me retiring from football. It's hard to separate the two."

"You don't have to tell me anything you aren't ready to share."

He scooped a heaping bite into his mouth and allowed the creamy richness of the chocolate to slide across his tongue as he wrestled with unlocking the secrets he held so close to his chest. Would Tessa think less of him?

Macy had said that giving up football made him less of a man. "A warrior fights, Ry. You're just a quitter. I can't be married to a quitter. Your choice. The NFL and me. Or retirement and nothing."

Her threat drove him to play—relying on chemical support to sprint towards three hundred pound O-Linemen designed to crush him. But nothing could save his marriage. Could he trust Tessa with all of his failure? Could he trust her with the wounds of his heart? Could he leap and land safely? With half shuttered eyes, he lifted his gaze to her clean green scrutiny; it offered no judgment, only comfort.

"When I graduated early, the move was fairly strategic. My body was beginning to show signs of wear. I was concerned I wouldn't make it through another brutal Big Ten beating without a career-limiting injury. My mom wanted me to quit. Get my Masters. Teach. Coach. Move home. She kept telling me it was just a game. The Lord had a bigger plan for me. But I convinced myself the Lord needed me to have the big stage of professional sports to tell His story. Can you imagine the arrogance?" He chuckled.

"God needing me to tell His story."

"God can use all situations and callings to His glory. I'm certain you've heard that from Pastor Tom a time or two," she said with a wink.

"True, but my heart was deceiving my mind. And my heart was being twisted by Macy. Don't get me wrong; she didn't have to bend far for me to be convinced her path was the right one. More money meant more mission work. More fame meant more glory for God. Bigger stage, bigger voice. When you want to believe a lie, there doesn't need to be a whole lot of convincing.

"I was beyond blessed to be taken so early in the draft—guaranteeing a signing bonus and a substantial rookie contract. Macy was right about the timing. The following year, ten potential top round linebackers entered the draft as juniors and three fell to the fifth round, one to the sixth and the others went undrafted." He pushed at his pie as the images of those years came flickering back.

"God definitely blessed my first year in the NFL. We had Emma and the veteran middle linebacker I was two deep behind was a man after God's own heart. Rick had a scripture for every experience, emotion or episode. He claimed God's power and mercy in a near miraculous way. I would rush home after practice bursting to share something I'd learned from Rick— either on the field about the game or off the field about the Lord—but Macy was too consumed with the charitable organizations of the other wives and girlfriends. She was busier than I was, and she asked if we could hire a nanny a few days a week to help her with Emma. Pretty soon two days turned into every day and every day became full time. My daughter knew two people extremely well: Mabel, and the driver who took them places. I was traveling, and Macy was..." Shaking his head he wanted to spit out the bitterness filling his mouth. He didn't want to hold anger towards his wife. He was afraid one day his mistrust and dislike of her would bleed into his conversations with his daughter—tainting the fading image she held of her mother.

He trailed a finger around the edge of his plate. Silence shrouded the dining room. The high pitched chirping of the sing-a-long video punctured the space like pinpricks, painfully reminding him of the commitment he'd made to The Lord, and to Macy, not to disclose. The weight of her secrets tethered him to her. Would he ever be free if he held tight to the life Macy fabricated?

"Macy was?" Tessa's voice, barely above a whisper, was a rope down the pit where he'd tumbled. Reaching for the lifeline, he hauled himself upward toward the light and glanced at her. The compassion, mixed with curiosity gave him pause. The question that kept him silence for nearly a year lingered. Could he trust anyone? Could he trust her? His throat constricted with growing thickness. A small trickle of cool perspiration raced down his back. He dropped his focus to the smooth glossy finish of the table.

"Ryland, you don't have to tell me, but you need to tell someone. Pain only has power when we hold onto it. But when we give a wound air, let it receive the treatment it needs, the pain lessens and that's where God does His finest healing. Even the best doctor can't cure a pain if we don't tell him where it hurts. He needs you to share with Him where you hurt. Let Him heal you."

A wave of calm knowing washed over his spirit. Pastor Tom had been gently nudging him to share since his return to Gibson's Run, but every time he was on the edge of exposing his failure in marriage and fatherhood, the weight of shame shut his mouth. What would his family say? His friends? Macy's friends? How could he face his daughter? The eddy of doubt nearly drowned him.

"That's a pretty hefty speech." His lips curled, the pressure in his chest growing and burning to be released.

"You learn a thing or two growing up a PK." She winked. "I may have stolen the sentiment—packaged it in my own dialogue."

"Good writing." His voice trailed on the breath of exhaustion. He was tired. Tired of hiding. Tired of protecting a life that was nothing more than carnival glass—warped and distorted images of reality.

"Macy was in love with the life of professional sports. She didn't care the price. Addicted to the rarified air breathed by the circle of premier athletes and celebrities. The more she consumed, the more she needed. But I loved her. Worked hard to give her the dream. She seemed happy and that made me happy. Playing was OK—different than high school or college. I love football for the game, but more for what the game represents. Eleven guys on the field all working together for the same goal. Layers of support from the bench all cheering in the same voice. Hearts beating together.

"The pros are different. Some guys love the sport. But it's like any other job. Many people are just in it for the money. Makes mission and purpose a far cry from everyday. After my second year, the team doctor gave me a clear warning. I should think long and hard about playing. The next hit would likely be last. My mom was right. Football wasn't worth my life. Before the door closed to his office, I called my agent and asked him to draw up my intent to retire.

"My determination was short lived. When I told Macy I wanted to stop playing and start coaching, teaching—get back to what I loved about the sport my father gifted to me—she didn't respond exactly as I planned. She gave me an ultimatum: football and her, or retiring and divorce."

"Oh, Ryland..."

"Divorce doesn't happen in the Jessup family. God first. We take commitment very seriously. So I did what I had to do. I went to the 'unapproved' doctor and started getting extra help. It started small. A shot in my knee by the team doc, and then a visit to Dr. Dex for some extra push through the pain pills. By the end of season three I was in a haze most of the time. Angry for no reason. Crying in rage. Going days without sleeping. Then crashing for twenty hours straight." His thick fingers zoomed against the smooth wood with enough force he was surprised a divot didn't follow in their wake. Bravery eluded him. He refused to lift his gaze to the anticipated judgment blended with pity in Tessa's eyes.

"I failed a random drug test at the end of the season, but because most of what was in my system was a mix of prescribed meds, the team and the league offered me private counseling and a one game suspension—listing me on the IR. I remember sitting in front of my locker. Packing my bag and knowing I shouldn't ever return. I called Rick and sought his counsel. He boxed my ears through the phone, but confirmed what I knew: I needed to stop before I couldn't.

"Macy's ultimatum was still in place, but she added to her threat. She said she would file for sole custody, claiming I was an unfit parent and a drug addict. Keep Emma from me, my mom, and my sisters. I couldn't let that happen, not if it was within my control. I went back to Dr. Dex but refused any oral pain medication. Just wanted shots. I could push through the pain if my swiftly aging body could stay in one piece. But I also had my agent working on a counter plan. I wouldn't be handcuffed without a way to have my child in my life.

"To the outside world, we appeared to be the perfect couple, cutting ribbons at Children's Hospital and eating pie at the State Fair; but behind closed doors the Cold War was friendlier. We stopped speaking during mini-camp. When training camp started, I thankfully lived onsite and was never so grateful for the guise of hotel room living than when the season started. On our first bi-week, Macy flew to the Bahamas with some friends and my mom came for a visit with Emma. She knew something was wrong, and in her infinite meddling wisdom she told me to fix it or let go. 'The shadow lands of doubt are no place to live, little boy.' And the message was cool relief in my barren soul.

"I went to our team chaplain and asked him for guidance. He gave me Luke 6:37 as a touchstone. '*Do not judge and you will not be judged. Do not condemn and you will not be condemned. Forgive and you will be forgiven.*' I knew I need to forgive myself and forgive Macy for the decisions that led us to where we were. From that moment I kept missing her. I'd pick up Em for dinner and Macy would be at a fundraiser. I left tickets for a game and found one of my sisters or Macy's parents in the stands instead of her. Two weeks before the end of the season, I decided to just drop by. I knew Mabel would have Emma at a play class downtown and the house would be empty. I needed to pray in the place where our marriage broke and hope the Lord could intervene. What I found…what I found…" The final notes of his tragic love story waned and his stomach curdled at the thought of rejection and disgust he would see reflected in the eyes he had loved his whole life.

How could he tell Tessa his wife, the woman who'd promised God she would love Ryland above all others had chosen someone else? That he wasn't man enough to keep Macy's love safe and protected. He sucked in a deep breath—filling his lungs to the point of burning. His fingers pressed against the table, the pressure flipping the tips to white.

Splat.

A tear dropped beside his hand. He swiped at the escaping emotion. How had he succumbed to the wickedness of his past yet again? Crying in front of Tessa. He plummeted. Head first into the pit.

"She was wrong." Tessa slid her hand across the table and squeezed his fingers sending soft billows of heat mixed with comfort through his spirit.

Lifting his gaze—cloudy with unshed tears—he looked at her. Deep green depths filled with sorrow and compassion. But no pity. Sadness wrapped him like a worn blanket, but his spirit felt free for the first time in over a year. The burden of Macy's betrayal no longer weighed. He glanced to the floor to make certain his feet were still firmly planted.

Healing wasn't instant. He knew years from now the prick of pain would likely revive the infidelity and the fear wrapped in its clutches, but he could see light and hope in front of him. He felt peace. All because he'd lifted his burdens out of the darkness of secrecy and allowed the healing touch of Jesus to sooth his pain. The healing touch of Jesus through one lovely blonde.

The gentle pressure of her squeezing fingers, shifted from compassionate comfort flowing through his spirit to waking desire swimming through his system like jelly fish sparking and stinging with passion. Shifting, palm touched palm. Tracing the edge of her hand with his thumb, electricity zipped through him pounding his heart in an erratic rhythm, instantly drying the tears in his eyes. "Tessa," he said, his voice crumbled through his lips. He laced his fingers through hers and felt content. At home. "Thank you for asking."

"Of course." Her words sounded brittle, on the wisp of a broken melody. She dropped her focus to their linked hands. Encouragement bubbled. She didn't pull away. Her hand remained firmly connected to his. No longer was she merely giving comfort. She had to be feeling the twist of burgeoning emotion too. Didn't she?

"Daddy. Daddy!" Emma screeched as she slid into the dining room.

Tessa snatched her hand out of his grasp, pivoting to stand, nearly toppling the chair beneath her. She scooted from his reaching grasp with a mumble of cleaning dishes.

Like a rock shot from a sling, his world zipped by him and he landed with a thud in front of his little girl.

Emma hopped onto his lap. She grabbed his jaw between her dainty hands, forcing his focus to her. "We's gots to get that new DBD of Pastor Tom's. It's the bestests video eber."

"Emma Grace," he sighed back to reality. "Bestests is not even in the realm of a word. We can discuss the video at home—after we read a book with all of the correct words." A full four year-old lip thrust in front of him and guilt gripped his heart. "Maybe you can ask for your birthday." Short arms squeezed his neck where once O-linemen tried to strangle. His heart settled and filled. Shifting his gaze over Emma's shoulder, he eyed the empty doorway connecting to the kitchen.

The rush of water and clink of plates echoed.

Standing with Emma in his arms, he held her tight to his chest. The unconditional love of his daughter was incomprehensible. Was it too much to hope he could also be blessed with the inconceivable love of Tessa Tarrington?

17

Tuesday morning, Tessa flipped her defrost heater to high trying to clear a visible line of sight in her ice-covered windshield. She glanced out the window—her car sputtered, battling against the frigid temperatures.

Snow blanketed the sidewalks, giving Elm Street an angelic quiet. The little girl inside her, frightened and hiding in the corners, missed snowy mornings. When she was small and the county gave her the rare gift of a snow day, she would race to the basement steps where her snow gear hung waiting. She would drop in the front yard and make angel after angel, closing her eyes and imagining the glowing white, delicately feathered creatures that she portrayed nearly every Christmas. The eerie stillness of a new snow fall allowed her the perfect canvas to create a world separate from the teasing and misfit casting of her own.

A few stray flakes scattered on the lawn and a slip of an idea trailed through her mind. *Snow angels...children's guardian angels come to life? Children's books?*

She grabbed her current journal from her bag and scribbled a few notes on the first blank page. The illustrations of a little girl in a puffy red coat with white fur trim formed in her mind. Her heart sped. She sketched the little girl and swirled notes about angel kisses and the uniqueness of snowflakes. The pen went dry against the parchment colored page. Tessa dropped her pen and journal. Shuttering her eyelids against the scene in front of her, she slowly drew in a lung-filling breath. The robbery had stolen more than her research and client files.

Her innate writer instinct had seemingly walked out the door on the thieves' backs. The drought of inspiration she'd trudged through in the last few months since *the terrible, awful day* compounded her out-of-control existence. Moments of inspiration had been so long in coming she'd feared they'd never bubble in her soul again. And yet, here on a snow-covered morning an idea for a children's book was plastered across her mind.

She couldn't remember the last time she'd even wandered through the children's section of her local bookstore, but she was grateful for any inspiration. One of her friends in New Orleans was an illustrator. She could pass her wisp of inspiration on to John. Maybe the idea was a non-starter, but at least she had an idea.

With the release of her long held breath, her eyes flickered open and she stared straight through the dripping circle on her windshield. The ice peeled back, cracking and sliding down the window, releasing her car from the cocoon. The day was beckoning her. Her classes of not so eager students—disappointed by the lack of a county-wide snow day—awaited her.

And Ryland Jessup.

Despite two texts asking to talk, a voicemail invitation to Monday Make-Up dinner from Emma, and the near constant inquisition from Lily Mae until the airplane door sealed for her flight, Tessa had managed to avoid confronting the churn of feelings that Ryland stirred in her. His transparency about his loss and the struggles he'd faced tugged at her heart. The fixer in her wanted to jump in with both feet, break-out the bandages and ointment, treat every ouchy he had. And yet, the memory of adolescence stood tall and cast a wide shadow over her life.

She was leery to trust him. She needed to resolve her conflicting emotions regarding Ryland. But for now, she had to face the snow covered streets of Gibson's Run, class after class brimming with irritated teenagers, and then dinner with Joe Taylor. She shifted her car into drive. Ryland Jessup would just have to wait his turn.

~*~

"Students..." Principal Jamison's voice crackled through the ancient intercom system.

Buzz. Buzz. Buzz. Dozens of phones vibrated against jean pockets, purses and backpacks. The students in Tessa's sixth period ignored the principal's announcement and sought their appendages.

"Yes!" Connor Avery pumped his arm. "Early dismissal." His announcement was followed by a series of whoops.

"Students," the principal's voice was barely a torn whisper above the din of excitement pulsing through her class. "Your parents are currently being notified. School is being released early today due to the inclement weather. All after school activities are cancelled this evening. Please leave your classes in an orderly fashion..." The balance of his instructions were lost behind the shuffle of desks and squeaks of rubber soles against the tiled floor.

"Don't forget to write five hundred words on the essence of being a teenager. Your assignment is still due on Friday." Tessa hollered as students scurried out of her class. She slumped against the edge of her desk with a sigh. "Good bye..." Scrubbing her face, tension melted from her body and she allowed the pull of inspiration that had been tugging all day to overwhelm her.

Snagging her journal, she snatched a pen from the cup holder and dropped into a front row desk—plowing into her snow angel story. Images of winged creatures filling the outlines of the snow covered grounds of a Midwest town flowed through her fingers onto the page. Her main character became three dimensional—a four-year-old, motherless girl with a broken heart. The story, simple and true, began to take root, no longer a wisp, but a twisted thread creating a beautiful tapestry. She sketched and wove. Her heart pounded as the story branched and twirled with adventure. Her outline intermingled with prose and swift drawings of the main characters. Sweat beaded against her forehead. Flashes of scenes trailed through her mind, quickening her pulse and breath. Flipping the page of her journal, she pressed her pen against the page and scribbled another scene. A jolt of pain shot through her hand, contorting her fingers. The pen slipped, landing against the floor with a clink. She massaged the cramp even as the pen rolled across the floor and under the bookshelf against the far wall.

"Ugh." Maneuvering the desks, she knelt, her pencil skirt constricting her movements. With her cheek pressed to the gritty floor, she pushed down the bubbling bile threatening to race up her throat as the toxic mix of melting-salt, floor cleaner, and teenager burned her nostrils.

Swatting through the cobwebs and dirt lining the hidden recesses of the underbelly of the bookshelf she reached for the lost pen. The vision of dozens of unknown species of insects racing up the hollow of her sleeve flickered. "Mind over matter, Tarrington." She whispered. With a puffed breath she snatched the pen and swiftly wiggled away from the horrors of the hidden filth of a public high school mid-semester.

"Well, this is an interesting view." Ryland's voice cut through the lingering silence of an empty classroom.

She spun on her hip, cracking her temple against the cinderblock wall. "Oww." The sparkle of white pins sprinkled in her sight. Her hand shot to her head expecting to find the trickle of blood.

"Hey," Ryland knelt in front of her. His hand gently lifted her chin. "You OK, bruiser? I'm not sure, but you may have gotten the better of the wall. He's definitely not fighting back."

"Funny." She shoved his hands from her face. "I'm fine." Pressing against the floor, she moved to stand, but found his hands clamped on her shoulders.

"Listen, you hit your head pretty hard. Let me take a look at your eyes."

"For what? I hit my head, Ryland, not my eyeballs." A wave of nausea crashed in her stomach, triggering another one the size of a tidal wave to grow. *Please Lord, I don't want to vomit on Ryland.* The opposite of many a teenage prayer.

"I want to look at your 'eyeballs' to see if you overachieved and gave yourself a concussion."

His long fingers were feather-light against her chin. Tingles raced against her jaw and down her spine, chased by a line of heat warming her cheeks. "I'm fine, Jessup." She swatted his hands from her face and moved to stand. Wobbling, she fell against Ryland's broad chest.

He wrapped his arms around her, guiding her to a chair.

Her head swam. The burn in her belly warned that the contents threatened to exit. Lifting her palm to Ryland, she drew slow breaths. Her eyes shut against the florescent, suddenly brighter and pulsing light of the room. One breath. Two breaths. In. Out. Slow. In. Out. With a deep inhale, her eyelids flickered open and she pushed the lungful of air through her lips, a slow whistle accompanying the release. The nausea continued to threaten, but she was in control. A few more minutes and she would be fine. At least her head and stomach would be fine.

She still had to look Ryland in the eye. Maybe he wouldn't want to talk about Sunday? Maybe he was ready to give up the charade of being friends and they could return to being frenemies. Revert to high school and the perverted stability she knew. Forget about the ascribed Ryland's-been-in-love-with-you-his-whole-life theory of Lily Mae, and go back to the status quo: Ryland the Bully. Tessa the Victim. She almost longed for him to call her Pee-Pee Tee-Tee.

Almost.

She glanced his way and looked into his eyes, her hand slowly falling to her lap.

He squatted beside her chair, his face openly reflecting concern. Not a bully tease in sight.

"Tessa," he rested a hand on her knee, sending a surge of tingles through her leg, awakening the butterfly in her chest. "Let me look at your eyes. I just need to see if they're dilated. You whacked yourself pretty good."

Swallowing against the thickness in her throat, she turned in her seat. Her knees brushed his.

His gray eyes reflected a mix of concern and sad longing that she'd never before seen.

Her breaths became shallow as she fought the rising current of the butterfly wings in her chest. His palms cupped her cheeks, burned against the pulsing heat of her blush.

"What's your full name?" his voice was low and tender.

"Tessa Natalie Tarrington."

"What day is it?" His face inched slowly closer to hers.

"January twenty-first." She licked her lips, her breaths quickening.

"Where are you?" Ryland's lips were an angel's breath from hers.

A fog clouded her mind that had little to do with the bump on her head. "Gibson's Run High." Her voice rasped, nearly foreign to her ears.

"Why do you hate me?"

"I don't hate you." She looked down.

His thumb stroked her cheek—slowly—forcing her attention back to him. His steely gaze drew her, beckoning and weary.

"I don't hate you, Ryland." She whispered. Her hand covered his.

"Then why are you avoiding me?"

She tried to break from his tender hold. A tear streaked down her cheek. Her eyes shuttered against the intensity of his gaze. She couldn't think, couldn't breathe. Every cell in her body vibrated with his closeness. What was she doing? A spark shot through her lips as his soft mouth pressed against hers. The touch, as light as a sigh, rippled through, stirring something she couldn't grasp. Her lips parted, and she leaned toward him.

"Ryland?" Her skin quivered and her eyes flittered open.

He stood and strode toward the wide expanse of windows. "I'm sorry. I shouldn't have…" He drove a hand through cropped hair, turning away from her.

Shivers raced through her body as she moved to stand by him. Drawing in a lung-filling breath, she inhaled his scent—a mix of the crisp wind of winter and the tawny rich aroma of leather. Her butterfly found friends and they swarmed from her throat to her belly.

Standing rigid—both disciplined with their focuses toward the high brick wall surrounding the football field five hundred yards in the distance—neither she nor Ryland moved.

The wall clock ticked. Each second echoed off the sterile walls of the empty classroom.

Her shoulder was near level to his—thanks to four-inch, stacked heeled boots. The temptation to lean against him overwhelmed and confused her. Comfort from Ryland Jessup?

When she'd escaped the intimacy of the dining room on Sunday night, her feelings had been like an assorted bag of jelly beans—some tasting sweet, some bitter. In the wake of his transparency, she wasn't certain if what she felt was compassion or something more. Something deeper and potentially dangerous. In cowardice, she'd stayed in the kitchen, avoiding good-byes and probable pitfalls as she scrubbed already-clean dishes and pans.

Before her head had hit the pillow, Ryland's "good-night" and "sorry" texts had scrolled across her phone, both embracing and embarrassing her. How could he be so open about the most tragic moments of his life? Tessa's clients shared stories ranging from drunken nights hanging from balcony ledges to hidden pregnancies, and drug-induced binging. She'd always been able to remain compassionate yet professional, the wall between her clients' stories and her personal boring, beige life firmly intact.

But hearing Ryland's story,—*feeling* Ryland's story—transformed her from a good, kindhearted listener to a warrior wanting to protect Ryland and Emma from all the pain the world wanted to impress upon them; and Tessa was not prepared to care about Ryland Jessup. She wasn't sure she was *able* to care for him. But at the moment, standing in the aura of his intoxicating mix of brute strength and gentle warmth, she wanted nothing more than to step into his embrace and seek his comfort. "Ryland..." Her knuckles brushed against his, shooting sparks through her. She turned to face him. She knew what she wanted.

"Knock, knock." Tessa jumped from Ryland and swiveled to the doorway.

Joe Taylor leaned against the frame.

"Joey." she plastered on a smile. "What are you doing here?" She glanced over her shoulder to the snow covered window, not allowing her gaze to linger on Ryland, who continued to stare toward the vacant football field.

"I called your house to make plans for tonight. Your dad said you were still at school." He shoved away from the door, ambled into the room and rested his hip against a student desk. "Tried calling your cell, but no answer. I was a little concerned, and didn't want to worry your dad. I had my brother drop me here to check in on you."

The blush she'd been fighting flamed her cheeks. "Phone's off." She reached for her shoulder bag to retrieve her phone. "I don't keep it on during school. I try to be a good example for the students." She swiped the screen and saw the flash of two voicemails. "There you are." She pointed the phone toward him.

"There I am." His answering grin was wide, but she could see the question in his eyes. "Why are you two still here? This place is like a ghost town. I don't even think Jamison is still in the building."

"Ryland came in to check on me. We were just leaving." She reached for her coat and saw Ryland link his arms tight across his chest, widening his stance but never pulling his stare from the field in the distance.

"They announced a Level two snow emergency over an hour ago. The roads are a mess. I'm planning on hoofing it back, but if you want, I can drive you home." Joe picked up her journal from the front desk. "What's this?" He flipped through the pages.

"Nothing. Just some notes." She reached to snatch it from his grasp but his touted wingspan that made snagging fly balls from the mouth of a homerun lifted her treasured thoughts out of her grasp.

"I think I should get a peek at what you're working on if the mystery is what kept you from me."

"It didn't keep me from you."

"Really?" He lifted an eyebrow and glanced toward Ryland. "If it wasn't your musings, then what kept a substitute teacher at school long after the final bell rang?"

Ryland's back muscles rippled in response to Joe's question.

The head-bump nausea rolled through her. Was he sorry he kissed her? Of course he was—he said as much. Blinking back tears, she stretched her grin wider and closed the distance to Joe. "I'll admit I was inspired this morning, and when class was dismissed early, I thought I could get a few extra notes down in the quiet." She slipped on her coat and slid the journal in her bag.

He nodded. Dropping his arm over her shoulders, he tucked her to his side. "What's your story, Jessup? Seems like you'd want to get out of here as quick as possible. I'd think Emma would want to go sledding or snowman building or whatever. Don't you need to be a dad or something?"

Steam from Ryland's breath fogged the window before he pivoted to face them. His arms remained locked across his chest. "You're right. I was just stopping to see if Tessa needed a ride home, but you can clearly take care of her." His gaze landed on her. "Watch your head."

Her hand instinctively shot to her temple and the firm bump beginning to form. "Thanks. Have fun making snow angels with Emma."

He turned back to her. "Why do you think we would make snow angels?"

"I don't know." She shrugged. "Just something my daddy and I used to do when it snowed."

His lips drew to a tight line. "They're her favorite thing. Good night." His sneakers squeaked against the tiled floor, echoing as he walked down the hall.

"Night." Joey hollered. "What's wrong with your head?"

18

"Here you go." Tessa handed a cup of steaming hot chocolate to Joe.

She curled her legs underneath her as she settled on the opposite end of the overstuffed couch in the sun porch and then propped her own cup of chocolate on her knees.

"Ouch. Hot."

"It's called hot chocolate." She giggled, taking a tentative sip.

Joe licked the whipped cream off the top of his cup.

When she'd briefly explained the bump on her head, he insisted on driving her home. The roads were barely touched and the snow was falling nearly an inch an hour. She was surprised when they made it to her house without having to abandon her car.

With the crazy weather, she'd assumed Joe would cancel dinner, but instead they ate a frozen pizza with her dad. Her father retired to his study before the paper plates where in the trash can. Daddy was sweetly trying to give her and Joe space, but he left his door cracked just enough to hear them in the house.

"I had a good time tonight, Joey."

"Me, too." He swiped a finger through her whipped cream and patted her lips with the sticky sweetness.

"Hey," she licked her lips, the cream sugary to the

taste. "Keep your fingers on your own cup Mr. Baseball Player."

With a chuckle, he shifted on the couch, draping a long arm along the back, and nearly touched her shoulder. "So Miss T.T. why don't you tell me what you've been up to the last eight years—give or take the last few weeks."

"Not much. Went to college in Louisiana and stayed. I'm a ghost writer." *Or I was until* the terrible, awful day *my life went down the toilet with a break-in and a flush.*

"You write ghost stories?" His brow pinched together. "You don't seem like someone who would be into all of the creepy creature of the night stuff."

"I don't write ghost stories. I'm a ghost writer."

"What's the difference?"

"I write other people's stories—generally biographies, too many parties, bad celebrity choices, and the like. No one but my publisher and the client know I banged the words together." Eyeing him over her mug, she waited for his reaction. Most people thought her career choice was interesting, but for a celebrity it could be perceived as one step up from gossip journalist.

"Huh…" He drew his arm back off the couch and clutched both sides of his mug, staring at the contents.

Tessa bit her bottom lip. For someone like Joe, who endured the plastering of poorly shot photos of him in compromising positions throughout his career, she imagined he was quietly condemning her. Her clients often felt a similar repulsion when they first met her. How could she make a living capitalizing on sharing the darkest parts of their stories? But quickly, all her clients learned she was trustworthy—a human vault who released only the stories her clients wanted to share. At least she'd been trustworthy until her refuge—her loft in the warehouse district of New Orleans—was breached. Tears burned the edges of her eyes, threatening to spill. "Joey, I don't tell stories without permission. I'm not that kind of writer. I help people with a story to tell, tell their story. And until recently, I was very good at my job."

His shoulders relaxed and he lifted his gaze to hers. "How do they find you—the people with a story?"

"My publisher specializes in celebrity tell-all's. They give various clients the opportunity to share their sides of their stories. Too often, someone in the press is giving a pretty one sided view of a tragedy or event. E&E allows celebrities of all kinds to share their stories in their own words. I'm just there to help put the words together in a way that allows for a readable book."

He nodded, setting his mug on the coffee table. "I should probably get going. It's been real nice catching up with you, Tessa."

Her heart pinched at the use of her name. She reached, clasping her slim fingers around his formidable man-hand. Suddenly she was filled with an urgent need for him to stay. To understand her. "Please Joey, let me explain. I love writing people's stories. But I also understand the weight of responsibility attached to knowing the deepest, darkest secrets of someone's life. I only write what I'm given permission by my client to reveal. I don't sell secrets. I don't share. I listen. I record. I write. I don't pass judgment or give an opinion on life choices. I truly try to be their pens. Nothing more. And hopefully, through me, each of my clients ends up with a book on which they are proud to have their name."

"I get it." With his free hand, he twisted the small space connecting his neck and his shoulders, where his unruly hair hit.

Squeezing his fingers, she drew his gaze back to her. "Joey, I want you to understand. I don't sell secrets. I don't tell stories unless someone wants me to share." She stroked the back of his hand with her thumb. "You can trust me." She needed him to understand. She didn't know why, but she was desperate for Joey Taylor to know he could trust her.

With a slow, smooth move, Joe wove his fingers through hers and matched the gentle stroke of her thumb, sending soft feathers of heat floating up her hand and arm. "Tessa Tarrington, I want to trust you. But I've had a couple bad trust situations in the past few years. You seem kind and earnest. I'd really like to get to know you better." He tugged her to his side of the couch and wrapped his free arm around her shoulders. His dark chocolate stare melted through her. "Do you mind if we start now?"

Nodding, her breath quickened.

A soft smile tilted the corner of his full mouth. He drew a single finger over her cheek, lifting her chin, his focus dropping to her lips. His mouth brushed hers with the barest of pressure.

A sweet pool of light flowed through her at his touch. Warm and gentle. No fireworks, only tender comfort. Kissing Joey Taylor was not the dream of her teenage years, but it was deeper, richer, than any fantasy she could have concocted on her loneliest day.

"Well, that was a nice hello."

"Joey…" She wasn't sure what she wanted to say.

Did she tell him just this afternoon his best friend kissed her with sweet tenderness contrary to their troubled past? Wait…had she really kissed two men in the same day? She couldn't remember a time when she'd kissed two men in the same year, let alone the same day. How could she kiss someone—two someones—she barely knew and with her father just a cracked door away? Sucking in her bottom lip she twisted away from Joe—pulling her legs to her chest.

"Hey, Tessa, look at me." The low timbre of Joe's voice tugged her focus. "Are you OK?"

She nodded. She was OK. Well, at least as OK as a PK feeling the burn of a Scarlet Letter splashing around in her toilet bowl life could be.

"Listen," he shifted to face her. "I'm guessing you don't typically kiss on a first date."

She shook her head, resting her cheek on her knees and lifting her gaze to his. "Not that I've been on many first dates."

"I find that hard to believe." He brushed a stray blonde lock off of her forehead.

"Being known as Pee-Pee Tee-Tee until I was thirteen didn't lay the groundwork for a healthy teenage dating frenzy."

"But what about college? After college? I can't believe someone as beautiful and smart as you hasn't been the target of every male in New Orleans."

"I don't know," she said with a shrug. "High school taught me to keep to myself and I wasn't very adventurous in college. I joined book clubs and hung out with my sorority sisters. I had dates to formals— the standard events—but those were mostly friends from class or the brothers of friends. I wanted to excel in school since it was costing every penny I had saved since childhood, and a fair number of my parents' pennies. It just seemed safer to study."

"Doesn't seem like much fun."

"I imagine your college experience was different."

"I definitely didn't focus on book studying. Studying my swing, yes. Studying for exams, nope. I didn't graduate. I jumped straight from the college World Series in Omaha to the Double A system for Minnesota. I played one season of Triple A ball. When I was called up that September, I never looked back."

"But I bet that didn't stop you from dating."

"Dating is a loose term." He winked. "I definitely traded phone numbers with a fair number of women. But none are quite like you, Tessa Tarrington."

"No man I've ever met has quite lived up to you, Joey Taylor."

"Really?"

"Really. I had a pretty big crush on you when we were in the praise band." She buried her face in her knees.

He brushed his hand tenderly over her hair, his warm breath caressing her cheek. "I had a pretty big crush on you, too." He whispered in her ear.

Her heart sped. She tilted her head to face him. "What?"

A soft grin deepened his ever present dimples. "I spent most of high school trying to figure out how to ask you on a date."

"Get out!" She punched him in the shoulder.

"Oww!" He rubbed the point of contact. "Bad shoulder, remember?"

Her hand shot to her mouth. "I'm sorry."

"It's OK."

"I don't believe you really wanted to ask me out.

You dated Mary Lou Bennett most of high school." Her mind flashed to the yearbook photo of Prom King Joe and Prom Queen Mary Lou.

"Doesn't mean I didn't want to date you. Why do you think I joined the praise band?"

"Your mom made you."

"She thought she made me. I refused until she told me there would be other kids my age in the band. You, Emory Grey, and Jessup were the only other kids my age in church. We all know Jess sings about as well as a tone deaf hoot owl, and Emory wouldn't be bothered with something as trivial as a church obligation." He winked, stretching the smile that made him the cover of every major league baseball promo.

"OK, let's say I believe you—which is a pretty wild 'let's'. Why didn't you ever say a word to me other than, 'hey T. T., is that my stool.'?"

"You made me nervous."

"BAH!"

"Seriously. You were the pastor's kid. You were one of the best students in school. You never talked, so *no one* knew what you liked and didn't like. Getting intel was nearly impossible. I bet if you ask, nearly every male in our graduating class had a crush on you at one point."

"And yet I sat at home alone on prom night."

"Not saying the male of the species is quick or brave. You were one tough nut to crack, T.T."

"Hey, enough of the nickname."

His head tilted to the side—an expression of complete confusion marring his brow. "What's wrong with T.T. I think it's cute."

"How would you like being reminded of the most humiliating moment of your life nearly every day for over thirteen years?"

"Why didn't you say something?"

"To whom? You? Marshall Smith? Ryland?" Heat chased up her neck at the mention of Ryland. She had told him that the nickname hurt her feelings. Actually she'd yelled at him. And then she let him kiss her. *No.* Shaking her head, she focused on Joey. She would deal with Ryland another day.

"Why not? You know we teased you because we all wanted to ask you out. Of course, none of us had it quite as bad as Ry." He chuckled. "I can still remember how many people he asked to find just the right present for you when we were six."

"And yet, he bought me 'Days of the Week' underpants."

"Hey, that was my idea."

"What?"

"Sure. I thought it was pretty genius. Of course, I was six years old so in retrospect the idea of giving a little girl underwear for her birthday doesn't seem as awesome as it did when I was six and my favorite thing in the world next to my baseball mitt was my superhero underwear."

The heat that had raced up her neck flared against her cheeks. "Twenty years later, and I'm still embarrassed." She tried to hide her face from him, but he seized her jaw in his wide grip.

"I like you embarrassed. You are an excellent blusher."

"Really? Blusher?"

"Yeah." He leaned forward and brushed his lips against hers.

Warm pools of light washed through her, heating her from belly to fingers. With a hand on either side of her face, he deepened the kiss rolling waves of shivers through her body. She slid closer to him, tentatively draping her arms across his shoulders. He heaved her to his chest, tightening his grasp as he lifted his lips from her mouth, peppering her cheek with feather-light kisses.

Her breath quickened, short staccato rhythms rushing through her mind and filling her ears.

"Ahem."

She jumped out of Joey's arms at the sound of her father's cough. His entrance drowned her in humiliation. Staring at the worn rug beneath her feet, her breath burned her lungs with compromised mortification.

"Snow's let up some. You might want to get on your way, son." Her father offered from the doorway.

"Yes, sir. Pastor Tom, sir." Joey coughed, folding himself into the far corner of the couch.

"I think you've both said enough good nights for the evening. No need to dawdle."

"OK, Daddy." Tessa said to the floor. "Do you mind checking to see if the walk was cleared by Bode and Jared?"

From the corner of her eye, she could only see her father's form, not his face, but she recognized the tentative hesitation before he turned toward the front of the house, leaving Joey and Tessa alone.

"Man," Joey shoved his fingers through his unruly hair and kneaded the small space between his neck and shoulder. "I haven't felt that put in my place since...well...I don't think I've ever been shamed over kissing in my life."

"Your face is ghost white. 'Yes, sir. Pastor Tom, sir.'" She mimicked his voice.

"Hey," he tossed a throw pillow at her. "I was just reprimanded without a word, and I feel like I'm sixteen years old. It's tough for the ego."

"You're the one who said he wanted to know what it was like to date me in high school."

"Yeah, I just didn't know we would be recreating an intimidating-dad scene a decade later."

"Was it worth the wait?"

He engulfed her hand in his, stroking her palm with his thumb. "Every humiliating second. I can't wait for date number two."

19

Buzz. Buzz. Buzz.

Tessa's phone vibrated across her nightstand, falling into her trashcan with a clank. Stretching a hand from under the mound of comforters and blankets, she yanked the phone up by its charger cord and swiped the screen open.

School cancelled for Gibson's Run Local. Teachers and students do not report. Emergency personnel only. Level 2 snow emergency remains. Please watch news for additional updates.

Rolling over, she pushed at the covers and struggled to sit. When she was a teen, she would have languished in the extra hours of sleep and delinquency. But at twenty-six as soon as her eyes opened, her mind raced in rewind over the past few days.

Last night, after watching a little T.V. with her father, she'd dragged herself up the steps to her bed. Rest eluded her. Her treacherous mind compared and contrasted her evening with Joey to Ryland's Sunday confession and Tuesday afternoon kindness.

Being with Joey was more than her limited teenage mind ever conjured. He was funny, caring, and flirtatious. She wanted to know him more. Teenage Tessa deserved the opportunity to explore and challenge her infatuation.

But then there was Ryland.

She'd definitely misjudged him as an adult,

unfairly cloaking him in the sins she'd thought he'd committed in his adolescence. Caution needed to be her path with him. The pain and betrayal he'd endured at the hands of his wife pricked her heart and triggered a desire to comfort. His love for his daughter lit his entire world, shoving his sorrow-laden past into the corners. Drawn to the openness of his emotions, she feared she would lose her control.

The balance between being his friend and allowing those feelings to cloud how she reacted to him would be a careful tightrope. Joey was the second person to tell her Ryland had feelings for her extending well beyond teasing and adult friendship. His casual reference to Ryland, gripped her tighter than Lily Mae's near constant nagging.

Could Ryland really be in love with her? Had he truly been infatuated with her since they were six years old? The thought overwhelmed and flittered awake her butterfly that only seemed to respond to Ryland. The tickle of wings sent shivers through her entire being. The concept of that kind of devotion sped her heart to a rabbit racing beat. Could she be falling for Ryland Jessup?

"Knock, knock."

Her door creaked open.

Her father held a mug in his right hand. For the first time in weeks he looked more like Pastor Tom, his hair neatly combed and a sweater vest already in place.

"Daddy, what are you doing up so early?"

"I saw school was cancelled and wanted to make sure you knew before you rushed around in a panic getting ready."

"Text." She lifted her phone.

"Oh. I guess things have changed since you were

in school."

"Modern technology."

"Well, I'll leave you to get some sleep."

She patted the side of her bed, inviting him to sit.

He sat on the edge, his back to her.

"Daddy, how long have you been up this morning?"

"I was restless. I thought I'd get up and pray."

"It's six o'clock in the morning, Dad. You're showered, dressed with at least your second cup of coffee in your hand. How long?"

"I guess about three hours."

"You've been up since three? Why? You know the doctors said you needed rest."

He shifted to face her. "Tessa, I've been home and out of the hospital for nearly five weeks. I'm about rested out. I've decided I'm going back to work next week."

"I don't think that's a good idea."

"I'm feeling stronger every day, and there's only so much strength I can regain here in this house. I need to pastor. My work is more than a job to me. I need to lean into my calling to get back to me." Longing coated his words.

"Daddy," She reached for his hand. "I don't think you're ready. You need more time."

"Rest can be good. But too much rest can be the enemy. Too much time away from a calling can lead to complacency."

"Daddy. You could never be complacent in your walk or your work."

"I wasn't talking about me." He squeezed her fingers.

"What are you saying?"

"Tessa, why are you still in Gibson's Run?"

"I'm here to take care of you."

"Honey, I love having you here, but you know you could've gone home a few weeks ago. I've been strong enough to take care of myself for a while. Let's not hide behind that excuse."

"It's not an excuse. It's a reason. A very good 'I'm the only child' reason."

"Fair enough..." He shifted to stand, but Tessa knew the challenge would be revisited. He only ever pushed as far as a wall, and then he searched to find a doorway to walk through. "What do you plan to do with your free day?"

"I would sleep, but I'm no longer a teenager who can drift for hours." She shrugged. "Maybe I'll take a walk. Make some cookies. Order Lily Mae's wedding present. Free days have limitless possibilities."

"What about writing?" He'd found a door.

"I don't have anything to write."

"Tessa, you always have something to write. You're a writer."

"Not anymore."

"Sweetie, one setback doesn't change the course of an entire life's work."

"Dad, I'm twenty-six. I hope my writing career isn't the full compass of my life."

"Your calling to write is no different than mine to pastor. You're only partially alive if you aren't walking on the journey you were called to walk. Just because you've had a bump in the road doesn't mean you cannot turn right. Roads are not straight. Your journey has been violated. You need to reclaim what you are called to do."

With a sigh, she rolled off the opposite side of her

bed to stand. Padding to her closet she lifted a sweatshirt from college, barely held together by the faded image of a snarling tiger. "It's not that easy. I lost all of my credibility with one act. An act I didn't have any control over." Dragging the sweatshirt over her head, she returned to the bed. "Dad, you have to understand. Dozens of people trusted me with their deepest darkest secrets. Most I'd never agree to write. They shared because they knew their secrets were safe with me. I didn't judge them or correct them. I only wrote what they wanted to share. Without that level of trust, I can't do my job. Without my job, I can't write."

"That's ridiculous. Writing has nothing to do with whether you have your job or not."

"Yes, it does. It has everything to do with whether or not I can be employed. I need to make a salary. I have student loans calling. Rent. Food. I have savings, but not enough to sustain me very long. I need a job. And if I can't write, I don't know what kind of job I'm qualified to do." Tears began to pool. She hadn't truly faced the void of nothingness *the terrible, awful day* had created in her life. Her father's heart attack had followed so closely, another link in her chain of unfortunate events. Her career was lost and she didn't know what she would do next.

"Just because that company doesn't want you on their staff anymore, it doesn't mean you can't write. Write something different. Write the same thing. Just write. The faster and further you run from what God created you to do, the more miserable and hopeless you'll be."

"Daddy, I wouldn't even know where to start."

He reached under his vest and pulled out her journal, tossing the three by five notebook in her lap.

"There's a story in there, Tessa."

"You shouldn't have looked in my journal." She pressed it to her chest.

"You're right. You're an adult and your privacy is very important. But you're also my little girl, and you're suffering. I thought I might be able to find something in those pages that could help me ease some of your pain. Give you some direction. Sweetheart, that story of the snow angels is brilliant."

Tears trickled over her cheeks. "I can't, Daddy," she whispered.

"Yes, you can. And from what I read and saw in those pages, if you don't allow yourself to share your gift you're sinning."

Swiping at her tears, she released a shaky sigh. "Not writing is not a sin. I might not be as up on my church as you are, but I don't think not writing is one of the seven deadly sins."

"Not using the gifts God has given you is disobedience. Would you categorize disobeying God as a sin, Tessa?"

His question was like icy water in her face. His words of conviction stirred her soul. But despite the stinging message, her dad's tone was full of compassion.

"Being complacent can lead to ambivalence. Jesus reprimanded the Church of Laodicea for being neither hot nor cold. Lukewarm is the worst temperature to be. If you aren't walking in your calling, then you're wasting your gift."

"But Dad, Paul said to be content in all things."

"That's true, but spiritual contentment simply means you are so rooted in Christ that your spirit is not troubled by troubles. To be content no matter the situation and to be complacent are not the same. And, I know you know, Tessa, because you're my daughter, that the greatest contentment—both spiritual and physical—is achieved by being settled in your calling, still on fire for what The Lord is doing. That level of contentment requires sacrifice. Complacency allows the outside world to determine what steps you will take. You've been complacent, Tessa. Even before the robbery, you were complacent in your calling. Leaning on a career path you fell into—not taking the harder road. You always wanted to write fiction. To tell stories that entertained, and yet glorified God. What happened to that young lady? Huh? She would have taken this challenge and run. You turned and hid."

She sucked in a deep breath. Her chest felt as if it was caving. But she had no argument. Everything her father said was true. She'd accepted the job with E&E because of safety and security. She knew she would do well. And she'd never be challenged. By telling the stories of others, she didn't have to worry about the ridicule that would come with being transparent with her own words. Crafting someone else's story seemed less threatening. Safer.

She'd chosen a path that kept her as a backdrop. Since she was six years old, her desire to blend into the background had driven nearly every decision she'd ever made, culminating with her choice of career. She wrote other people's stories. Their memories. Nothing of her own.

"Stop hiding." With his pocket handkerchief, he dabbed her cheeks. "Be brave."

"Daddy, I don't know how."

"Just start. You just have to start." He handed her a pen. "I'll be praying for you." The click of his shoes as he left echoed in his wake.

Rolling the pen between her fingers, she stared at her journal. Could she do it? Could she write something of her own? Splaying the journal wide, she flipped the pages of notes from yesterday morning. The images and words she'd sketched were disjointed and unrealistic. The scenes unimaginative and stilted.

With a snap of her wrist she ripped the story pages from her notebook, slamming it against the door of her closet. The sheets crumpled into a tight ball under the pressure of her pounding hands. A sigh rolled through her body. The paper ball fell limp. Drawing her knees to her chest, every muscle in her back stiffened and relaxed.

She couldn't do it. She wasn't creative enough to write an original story. Her dad was wrong. She only had talent. No gift. "Lord, help me. I don't know what to do. If I can't write—what will I do?" Her prayer broke through her tears, falling into puddles, dripping down her knees and legs.

Sucking in breaths between sobs, she folded herself under her comforter and squeezed her pillow to her chest. She cried without purpose or reason, the tears soaking her sheets, blankets and pillow. A dam released a flood of worry, self-doubt, and recrimination held at bay for months.

What would she do?

Her dad was right. Her life was in New Orleans— but did she really have a life left in the Crescent City? Her career was gone. No number of idea wisps, sketches, or momentary lapses into inspiration would bring back her purpose. What was she now? A substitute English teacher who barely had the respect of her students? A misty image of her teenage self who was finally getting to live out dream date scenarios? A scared daughter who worried her father would abandon her like her mother? Who was she now? "Who am I, Lord? Who should I be?"

Buzz. Buzz. Buzz.

Rubbing her eyes, she glanced at her phone.

One new text. From Ryland.

Without moving from under the covers, she snagged the phone and swiped the screen.

Em and I are making snow angels today. She wanted you to come and play. Interested?

Snow Angels. "Huh."

20

"Watch out! Here I come!" Emma raced as fast as legs would take her.

A giggle bubbled up through Tessa, who squatted behind a tree beside Ryland.

He tapped a finger to his lips. "We're supposed to be hiding."

Emma wobbled through the snow—nearly as deep as her waist—with all of the delight and joy Tessa remembered from her own wobbling days. The distraction of playing in the snow for hours with a four year-old and her father was the perfect tonic to oppressive self-doubt. Between the fresh air, wet mittens, and loss of feeling in her toes, she felt free. For the first time in months.

Her tilt-a-whirl life was still swirling, but at the moment she was playing hide and go seek with a four year old who had snatched a giant piece of her heart—along with the hearts of most of the residents of Gibson's Run.

Ryland crawled around the tree and snagged Emma by the waist. "I got you."

Her squeal warmed Tessa better than the hot chocolate she'd been promised with this adventure.

Emma wrapped her arms around Ryland's neck as he swung her in swooping circles.

"I thought we were making some snow angels." Tessa stood with her hands on her hips.

Swaying to a stop, Ryland rested Emma against his hip. "Well, nugget, are you ready to show Miss Tessa why you are the best snow angel maker in all of Ohio?"

"All of Ohio, huh?"

"Yep," Emma wiggled to the ground. "No one's better than me. I knows how to make the bestest snow angels cause I'm littles."

"Oh, I didn't know being little was a prerequisite for making snow angels." Tessa fell to the ground and began sweeping her arms and legs against the fluffy snow.

"What's pre-reckisits mean?" Emma dropped to her left, mimicking Tessa's motions.

They brushed against the snow in smooth rhythm. The swishing of their nylon encased bodies echoed in the silence of the early evening stillness.

Tessa's eyes flittered shut as snow wafted from the sky, pricking her cheeks with pops of chilling wet.

"Prerequisite means something you need to have before you can accomplish a task." Ryland offered.

"What's 'complish mean?"

Tessa sat cross-legged in the center of her angel. "To accomplish means to make something happen."

Emma matched her sitting style. "So we 'complished snow angels?"

"Something like that. Do you want to make a few more? We could make a whole host of angels on your front yard."

"Can we's, Daddy?" Emma's face contorted in earnest hope.

"May we, Daddy?" Ryland corrected. "And yes, you may."

"Yes!" Emma pumped her fist and tumbled to an

unblemished patch of snow. "Over here, Miss Tessa. We's can make loads of snow angels here."

"Yes, ma'am." Tessa stood and clapped her gloved hands together to dust off the crystalizing snow.

"Do you mind if I run inside for a second, Tessa?"

She faced Ryland. "I think I can handle a few snow angels. Besides it'll give Emma and me time for girl talk without some smelly boy around."

"Hey. I'm not just some boy, I'm 'Daddy'." His mock offense triggered a chuckle in Tessa.

"All boys are smelly. Even Daddy-boys." She lifted a packed ball of snow and hurled it toward him, missing by a foot.

"Watch it, Tarrington. Don't pick a fight with a professional athlete." He looked over his shoulder where the snowball sank. "Also, please don't teach my daughter to throw. That's just pitiful." He turned toward the house, and Tessa squatted, packing a softball size mound of snow in her hands, torqueing her arm to a throwing motion.

Ryland peeked over his shoulder. "You miss me, you hit my house. Either is a declaration of snow war. And I don't play fair."

Her breath caught in her chest at the sparkle of his smile. The snowball limply fell from her hand.

"Come over here, Miss Tessa," Emma shouted.

"Looks like you are being summoned." Ryland slipped through the door and into the house.

Tessa was unable to stifle the flutters rippling through her middle.

"Miss Tessa...you comin'?"

"Wild horses couldn't stop me."

Emma was lying near a wide, near-barren oak tree that likely gave shade for days in the summer. Her short legs chopped the thick snow leaving divots rather than sweeping snow angel skirts.

"How's he looks?" Emma huffed as her arms and legs struggled against the white weight.

"How do you think he looks, Emma?"

"I can't tells. I'm in the middle."

"Well, stand up and take a look." She reached out her gloved hand to the sopping wet, mitten covered fingers.

Emma stood and tilted her head to the side as she surveyed her creation. "I think he's a war-e-or snow angel."

Tessa scanned the frosty outline. "Why do you think he's a warrior?"

"Look," Emma said pointing to a long ridge near the waist of her angel. "He has a sword and his pants are made of armors. He's wearin' a helmet and I think he has a shield behind his back."

"A shield?" Tessa asked as she squatted to Emma's eye level. "Why do you think you made a warrior angel instead of a regular snow angel?"

"Miss Tessa, there ain't no regular snow angels."

"Well, what about the ones your daddy and I made over there? They look pretty standard to me."

"Nope. Ebry snow angel's special. Just like peoples." With a sodden mitten pressed to Tessa's cheek, Emma forced her focus to the myriad snow angels made only moments earlier. "That's a daddy snow angel 'cause he's so bigs and can protect little snow angels from bad stuff. And the angel you made, she's a momma angel 'cause she's soft and smooths and pretty. The angels I made are all different, too. One's a baby angel. Another's a big sister angel. And the last one's super impordant."

Tessa narrowed her focus to the angel that was widest across the middle. Emma's tiny hand prints circled the angel in an overlapping pattern, but to her clearly stunted imagination, she couldn't comprehend why Emma thought this angel was the most important.

"Why is she so important?"

"She's my Guard-Ann angel. See her hands comes out all over so she can protect me from hurting myself or she can give a hug when I'm reals sad and missing my momma. Guard-Ann angels are the mostest impordant 'cause they help little kids feels better."

Warm tears cut straight paths over Tessa's cheeks. "I think you're right. Guardian angels are very important for big kids, too." Tessa pulled Emma into a soft embrace and kissed her forehead. "What else does your angel do for you?"

"Well," Emma said, biting her bottom lip and rubbing her chin, reflecting a mirror image of her father's deep thought. "Sometimes when I gets real scared that Daddy's not comin' home like Momma, my Guard-Ann angel whispers in my heart that he's OK and will be home reals soon, and then like magic he walks through the door."

"Is she only a snow angel?"

"No, we just gets to see what the angels look like in the snow—like pit-chers. But we can't sees them for too long—that's why their pit-chers are out of snow. They goes away real quick. But you still have the memory of what the angels look like."

"Emma, how would you like to help me write a book?"

"But I can't read too much yet. How's can I writes a book?"

"You help me with the story, and I'll write the

words. Maybe I can come over after work some evenings. How does that sound?"

Emma launched herself at Tessa and they both tumbled into the snow mound piled near the partially cleared sidewalk.

"I'll take that as a yes."

"YES!"

"Well, we need to ask your Daddy, before its official."

"Let's go. Let's go. Let's go."

~*~

Ryland leaned against the frame of the large window, watching Emma and Tessa squatted in deep discussion. His daughter's quick affection for Tessa was a welcome sight. Prior to Macy's death, Emma loved swiftly and often. The strangers his daughter encountered became family within moments and even at her precious age, she had a wisdom that seemed to sense the words of kindness and care others needed. The sudden loss of her mother had shaken her to the core.

The outgoing toddler who climbed onto the laps of three-hundred-pound linemen with the same ease as she'd embraced her slip of a grandmother descended into a sullen and shy little girl who spent hours watching videos, or playing alone in her room, not wanting to talk to anyone aside from Mabel or him.

The introduction of Pastor Tom into their weekly routine was a welcome healing salve for Emma's broken, skittish spirit. Within weeks of sharing Monday dinners, the sparkle began to resurface in her. Watching her with Tessa, warmed Ryland's own dusty spirit.

"They make an adorable picture. Don't they?"

Glancing over his shoulder, he caught the broad grin of his part-time nanny and full-time housekeeper. Mabel held two steaming cups of coffee in her hands and extended one to him.

"Thanks," he said with a tentative sip.

"Emma has really taken to her."

He nodded, focusing his attention back to the living picture. "Tessa came with street cred. She happens to be the daughter of Emma's favorite person on the planet."

"Well, I don't think Pastor Tom outranks her daddy."

"I wouldn't be so sure. She told me a month ago she was going to marry Pastor Tom. I haven't broken it to my future son-in-law yet."

Through the thick pane of glass, he watched Emma tackle Tessa. "Well, something's pretty exciting."

"I should go put some hot chocolate together for those two. They'll surly be ice pops by the time they trample through my kitchen." Mabel nodded toward Tessa wrapped in Emma's embrace. "It's a good thing she has so many people who love her and make her a priority," she said over her shoulder as she shuffled back to the kitchen.

Alone again, his coffee fueled breath fogged the window.

Emma tugged Tessa across the front lawn toward the side porch and the kitchen door.

Muffled voices wafted into the living room from the kitchen.

A grin tugged at the corner of his mouth. Setting

his coffee cup on the end table, he reached for a skinny log to add to the fire. Sparks scattered with the added wood. He stoked the flame shoving the partially burned logs beneath the fresher ones.

The floor beneath him shook with the power of a child's size six feet.

"Daddy. Daddy. Daddy." Emma's voice was breathless with delight.

Kneeling, he turned to face her as she skidded to a stop in front of him. "That's my name. What can I do for you, slugger?"

"Daddy." She cuddled to his side, placing small chilled hands on either side of his face, drawing his gaze to hers. "Miss Tessa asked me to writes a book with her. Can I? Can I?"

"Well, I think your grammar might need a gargantuan leap from four-year-old to write a book with someone like Miss Tessa." He glanced over Emma's shoulder as Tessa settled on the edge of an overstuffed chair. "She is a phenomenal writer."

"What's fee-nom-nal mean?"

"It mean's extraordinary or amazing. But your father overstates my writing. I'm OK at best, but I'm not as creative as you." Tessa offered.

"See Daddy, Miss Tessa needs me."

"So what kind of story are you writing?" Ryland relaxed onto the floor, settling Emma on his lap.

"Wells, Miss Tessa thinks we should write about my Guard-Ann angel and all the other angels."

"I had this idea yesterday"—Tessa slid from the chair to the floor, matching Ryland's position—"about a little girl who sees snow angels come to life. But it was barely an idea until Emma told me about the different kinds of angels."

"I didn't know there were different kinds of angels."

Emma sighed. "Of course you do. I tolds you all 'bout them when it snowed a'for."

Last winter.

Last winter, weeks after Macy's accident, he'd taken Emma to the park near their home in Pittsburgh to play in the snow. He'd desperately wanted to distract his tiny, little girl from the pain of losing her mother. She'd been nearly silent since Macy's death a month earlier. He'd tried sweets, movies, and books but nothing was reaching her. She was adrift in her solitary pain. Watching her suffer only amplified his own grief and anger.

His mother had suggested a walk in the snow—something simple.

He grasped the idea like a drowning man. They'd built a snowman Emma's size, and then swished snow angels until they nearly filled the abandoned baseball field. When the snow from the dozen angels seeped into their clothes, he'd wrapped Emma in his arms and she'd told him the names and occupations of each of the angels. Her biographies were elaborate and bubbled out of her like a hot spring.

He was so thrilled to see a glimpse of his once vibrant daughter that he barely registered her words. But he was no longer peeking through the shadows of grief to find his child. She was now almost wholly healed, and the memory of the joy she'd shared through the telling of the angels' stories flashed through him.

"I remember. Sometimes daddies forget. Not because it wasn't important, but they have so much shoved in their brains, they have to be helped to remember. You do a great job helping me remember."

"See," she smiled at Tessa. "I tolds you he would 'members."

"I never doubted you."

Delight shined in Tessa's eyes, stirring his heart. Not out of an old seeded crush on an unattainable girl, but for the love he saw a woman was openly showering on his daughter. "*Ahem*," he cleared his throat, tearing his gaze from Tessa's. "So you two want to write a book. How're you planning on accomplishing such a lofty endeavor?"

"Daddy, that's too many words for me to ask."

"Sorry E-train. How will you write the book together?"

"Well, I thought I might come over a couple days a week after school." Tessa interjected. "I promise not to be here more than an hour a day."

"Are you sure it wouldn't put you out too much?" he asked.

"Are you kidding? Emma is helping me. I'm not too proud to say I've been struggling with writing since the unfortunate incidents in New Orleans. This is the first time in months I've been inspired to write anything beyond a lesson plan or a grocery list. But I want to make sure you're OK with her helping me."

He hugged Emma. "Em, why don't you run into the kitchen and see if Mabel has the hot chocolate ready."

She slowly stood, dragging her sock covered feet to the doorway. "Miss Tessa?" She swiveled, draping her upper body across the back of the chair. "Please don't lets Daddy talk you outs of the book?" Her tiny brow twisted in worry. "He can be 'suasive when he wants."

"I'll be tough. Don't worry."

Emma raced into the kitchen hollering, "Mrs. Mabel, me and Miss Tessa gonna writes a book togethers!"

"She's amazing." Tessa chuckled, stretching her legs near the fire.

"I am blessed every day God chose me to be her father." Massaging his temples, he shifted his focus to the fire. "I am scared to death of her teenage years."

"Are you kidding? She worships you. She'll be an angel."

"I hope you're right. When Macy died I just tried to push through every day. Take a shower. Feed Emma breakfast. Drive her to preschool. One step in front of the next. But now that the immediacy of grief has passed, I wake in the throes of panic over her first date, where she'll go to college, teenage girl drama...all of it. I'm a dude. We just punch stuff out. I'm not sure I'll be enough to help her through."

"Emma will have the benefit of all of your sisters, your mom, and this whole town to help keep her on the straight and narrow. Her dad is just the icing on the cake."

He lifted an eyebrow. "Are you sure you want to try your hand at fiction? Your storytelling could use some work."

"I'm much better at sharing true life stories, and yours is one that'll have a happy ending. You're a wonderful father, Ryland. Emma is very special."

"Yeah, she is."

"How is she? With your wife's death, I mean."

"Why do you ask?"

She shifted, pulling her knees to her chest. "Emma mentioned she gets scared that you won't come home."

"What?"

"We were talking about the different kinds of angels and she told me guardian angels are the most important angels because they help alleviate the fears of little girls."

"My four year-old daughter told you her guardian angel alleviated her fears?"

Shoving her hand through her hair, she shook her head. "No, not exactly, but she said her 'Guard-Ann' angel helped ease her worry when she started fearing you wouldn't come home like her Momma."

A burn like sulfur flamed in the pit of his stomach. "Really?" His sweet little girl was worried he would die too? How did he not know?

"I think it's probably normal. I remember when my dad went on a mission trip when I wasn't much older than Emma. I woke up every night convinced he was never coming home. When you are small your world is only as big as what you can see in front of you, or inside your mind. Your little girl has an unbelievable imagination helping to bridge the gap between her fears and reality. She's coping, but I wanted you to know what she was going through. Losing my mom was by far the hardest thing I've ever endured, but I was a young adult. I had somewhat mature emotions to deal with her loss. But at four years old, I don't know how your brain and heart can reconcile your mother never coming home again."

Her friendly touch of his hand slipped through his defenses and soothed the blistering heat in his belly. "I thought she was doing better." He shifted his body, angling toward her. "She doesn't wake with nightmares anymore. She rarely asks to sleep in my bed. She smiles most days and is back to talking to every stranger she meets as if they're long lost soul mates."

"She's coping. It's pretty miraculous if you think about it."

"How so?"

"She's four years old and she created an entire world of angels to bring her comfort and explain all of the things too big for her mind to comprehend."

"Just another of God's answered prayers."

With a soft smile, she slid her hand from his and wrapped her arms around her drawn legs.

They settled into the silence peppered by the crackle of the fire. The blanketed warmth of the room made his desire to sidle up to Tessa nearly overwhelming. From the corner of his eye he glimpsed her tousled hair and cheeks flared pink by the contrasting heat of the fire against the cold she carried from the snow. If he shifted a couple inches to his right, his shoulder would be pressed against hers. One little scoot, and he could touch her. He would know if she was still cold from the frigid January storm. Inhale her sweet fragrance. Lace his fingers through hers. Draw her to his side and…

With the power of years of training he shot to standing, yanking the fire poker from its holder with a clatter. He stoked the fire—shooting sparks across the tiled hearth.

"Watch it, Daddy. That's how Sparky the Fire Dog says fires start," Emma chastised. On tip-toes, she slowly made her way into the living room balancing a wide rimmed mug of steaming hot chocolate brimming with mini-marshmallows.

"Can you handle that chocolate, E?"

"Daddy, I'm super bigs now. I can handle a cup of

hot chocolate." The mug rattled against the coffee table, sloshing drips of its contents on to the glossy wood surface.

"I guess you are."

The doorbell sang as Mabel sat the tray with three additional mugs and toppings on the table. "I'll get the door."

Emma plopped onto the floor, stretching her legs under the table. Swiping a spoon across the bowl of whipped cream, she dolloped a heaping mound on her hot chocolate.

"Whoa, slugger, that's more sugar than even Joe can handle."

All the females' faces lit up at the sight of Joe Taylor's lanky form and crooked grin. Even Mabel wasn't immune to his charm.

"Uncle Joe!" Emma shot up and shuffled around the couch, enfolding her arms around his legs.

He lifted her with one arm and settled her on his hip. "You're awfully cold, E. Were you making snow angels without me?"

She nodded vigorously, the ends of her static-filled, lopsided pony tail sticking to her cheek and Joe's. "Miss Tessa and me mades lots of angels and we's gonna write a book."

Joe's gaze went to Tessa and the gentle heat exchanged in the glance pricked a pin in the burgeoning hope building in Ryland.

"That's awesome, Em's." Joe carried Emma back to the couch. "Why don't you tell me about your book while I steal your Daddy's hot chocolate."

As Emma chattered through the story, Ryland slipped from the room. He couldn't endure watching his daughter completing the perfect couple of Tessa and Joe.

Grabbing the pot Mabel used to make her magical hot chocolate, he poured the remnants in a mug and tossed the pot into the wide country sink. He scrapped and scrubbed the goop from the base, slopping soap and scalding water onto the floor.

"Watch it." Mabel scolded. "It might be your house, but this is my kitchen. Don't be messing up a perfectly mopped floor and a decades-old pot, just because your little, ole heart got a little mushed."

"I don't know what you're talking about, Mae."

She linked her arm around his waist, flipping the water faucet off. "Darlin', I've known you for almost five years now. Your heart lives all over your face. I knew the day Macy broke it into a dozen little pieces. I knew the moment you decided to move back here and quit a job you loved. I knew when you felt as if you were failing Emma after Macy died. I knew all of that without you ever saying a word. Now don't you try and tell me I don't know your heart is firmly in the hands of that sweet young lady in the living room. Even if she is curled up beside your best friend."

He released the pan from his grasp and turned away from the sink. "Mae, I've known both of them my whole life. JT's the best friend I've ever had."

"But..."

"...but, nothing." With a shove against the sink, he pulled a tall kitchen stool from under the island and lowered his body with a sigh. "Tessa barely tolerates me, but JT seems to make her happy."

"Barely tolerates you?" Mabel dragged a stool to face him. "If what I saw outside this house and in front of the fire constitutes 'barely tolerating' someone then I need to find someone to barely tolerate me."

"Mae, be serious."

"How can I be when you're being ridiculous? You are currently displaying the emotional maturity of a thirteen year old girl who just found out her favorite boy band broke up."

"Harsh."

"You know me. I only speak truth." She slid the untouched mug of hot chocolate to him. "Now tell me why you're in here whining to me when a beautiful, intelligent, generous young woman is enjoying the warmth of your fire, the comfort of your couch, and the overt intentions of one fine specimen of athletic manhood."

Ryland rolled his eyes and took a deep drink of the lukewarm chocolate. "It's stupid."

"Honey, nothing's stupid if it impacts your heart."

"Tessa's the one…" He paused, unsure of how to share the feelings he'd been nurturing and sheltering for twenty years.

"The one?"

"It's complicated."

"Either you have a thing for someone or you don't. The heart is a pretty simple organ. It's the brain that complicates matters."

"We've known each other since we were not much older than Emma."

"History is a good thing. Helps to build a solid foundation."

"Not our history."

"What did you do to that poor girl?"

"What makes you think I did something to her?"

She lifted a single eyebrow.

"I may have accidentally given her an unfortunate nickname in elementary school that followed her through graduation."

"Oh, boy. What was the nickname?"

He dropped his focus to the thick grains of marble swirled on the surface of island. "Pee-Pee Tee-Tee," he whispered.

"Oh. you didn't?"

"It was an innocent mistake, but some things just stick." He told her the story of Tessa's birthday, the years of trying to get her to notice him that backfired, and his most recent attempts to find a tentative friendship.

"You've had a crush on this girl since you were six years old—finally kissed her yesterday—and you still are allowing some dude to usurp your home turf?"

"Usurp, Mabel?"

"Hon, fancy word or no, you need to get your cute butt back in that living room and lay claim to what's yours. That's if you even want to be with her. Do you care?"

"Of course I care, but I'm not fighting JT for her. If she wants to be with him, then I'll have to be grateful for her friendship. Besides, she's leaving as soon as her substituting job is finished. It's not wise for Emma or me to get too attached."

"Yeah," Mabel went to the kitchen sink, yanking the spray nozzle from its holster. "I guess that book won't attach Emma to her. And her being in the house nearly every day won't affect you at all. Good plan."

21

"Thank you, Mabel." Tessa blew a cooling breath across the top of her cup. "I think I've gained five pounds in the last three weeks. Your hot chocolate is the best I've ever tasted."

"You could stand a few pounds."

"I'll be lucky to fit into my bridesmaid dress for Lily's wedding on Saturday."

"You'll fill that fluffy monstrosity just fine."

"Thanks again for doing the alterations for me. I never thought I'd be in Ohio this long." She set her mug on the kitchen island and drew her laptop closer, typing updates to her story outline from the ideas she and Emma worked through over the last hour.

"My pleasure. When do you leave for New Orleans?"

"Tomorrow night. I have so much to do." She closed her computer and swiveled to face Mabel. "Can you keep a secret?"

Mabel threw her towel over her shoulder and laced her thick arms over her rounded belly. "My late husband Cal used to call me Fort Knox. Still makes my sisters crazy."

Tessa glanced over her shoulder toward the stairwell Emma had raced up minutes ago to retrieve more coloring paper and crayons. "I have an appointment with a children's literary agent on Friday before the rehearsal dinner."

"Really?"

Tessa nodded. "I'm going to pitch him Emma's story idea. I have most of the framework built and I've been pulling together rough sketches every night. I have a mock-up just about finished. I think this idea could be more than one book—maybe even a series of books based on the angels Emma described—all centered on the main characters Guard-Ann, the guardian angel and Shelby, her charge."

"Oh Tessa, that's wonderful. But why do you want to keep it a secret?"

"I don't want Emma to get her hopes to high. Publishing is a tough industry. You have to have more than just a well written, creative story. You need a marketing plan. Publishing goals. Target markets…"

"Here I thought the hard part was writing a book."

Tessa chuckled. "As hard as it is, writing the book is the easiest part of the entire process."

"I gots it!" Emma's voice bellowed into the kitchen—seemingly unattached to the little girl. Her tiny feet and legs slid to a stop at the top of the steps. With halted movements, she stuttered down the stairs with intent focus.

Anticipating the clean sheets, Tessa placed her laptop, notebook, and sketches in her shoulder bag on the floor. The last three weeks of collaboration with a near five-year-old were the most creatively invigorating of her life. Emma's tireless energy zapped Tessa's hibernating writing muse back to life. Beyond the snow angel stories, she had written book proposals for a political thriller set in New Orleans, and a biography on Elton Gibson, Gibson's Run's founding father. Although she trusted Mabel, she didn't share her biggest secret—she had a meeting with her former publishers when she arrived in New Orleans. She feared their rejection, but the hope she clung to flowed on the inspiration she'd been riding.

Between fruitful writing sessions—alone, and with sweet Emma—living out her teenage fantasy of being courted by Joey Taylor, and her father's daily improvements, her once swirling life seemed to be on an upswing. She'd been so consumed with her work and social life she hadn't had a single free minute to think about the teeter-totter her heart was on weighing the affections of Joey with her unexplainable attraction to Ryland.

Since the afternoon of snow angels and hot chocolate, she'd seen him in passing at school, and for doorway waves as she rushed out of his house in the evenings. If she didn't know better she'd guess he was avoiding her, but that would be silly. Why would he avoid her?

"Are you ready to draws Guard-Ann, Miss Tessa?" Emma asked, yanking Tessa from her thoughts.

"Yes, ma'am." She lifted the wide sheets of translucent drawing paper, spreading them on the marble counter. "Now we said that Guard-Ann had long hair—but no halo, right?" Tessa swept her pencil from top to bottom with wide curves in the middle of the sheet.

"Yep. She's gots long, blonde hair that gots big curls and is kind of..." She propped her chin on her upturned palm, twisting her lips in deep concentration.

"Kind of wild and crazy, like someone I know?" Ryland's voice was deep and flowed through Tessa like warm tea on a cold night. He scooped Emma into his arms and shuffled her hair with his wide palm.

"Daddy, angels ain't wild and crazy." She shook her head with authority.

"I don't know. The one angel I know is pretty wild and crazy."

"You knows an angel?"

"I'm looking right at her." His grin was wide, oozing love and pride for his daughter—tipping the teeter-totter in Tessa's heart.

"Daddy, don't be sillys. I'm not no angel. I live heres. God's gots all the angels living in heaven with Him. They just gets to come here when someone needs their help."

"Well...did you ever think that God sent you to me so that makes you my angel?"

A soft grin tilted the corners of her mouth. "That's real nice, Daddy." She wrapped her arms around his neck and squeezed.

Tessa was convinced she'd cut off Ryland's airway passage, but she leaned back and gave hima kiss.

Setting her back on the stool, Ryland smacked a kiss on her cheek. "I'll leave you to your work." He turned without acknowledging Tessa, and whispered to Mabel. He tossed his wet shoes into the mud box by the door and padded down the hall, likely disappearing into his study or workout room.

In the time Tessa had been collaborating with Emma, he hadn't said more than two words to her: "hello" and "good-bye". Maybe she'd misread Ryland's feelings for her. Misinterpreted his kiss nearly a month ago. Surely, if he was interested in her—beyond a glorified babysitter for his daughter—he would engage her in conversation. Had she angered him? Was he mad about the time she was spending with Emma?

"Miss Tessa, we gots to draw. Mrs. Mabel's making biggie stew and I won't be con-trating after I eats it. It's my favorite and my brains gets all mushy after I eat it. I can'ts think of nothing."

"Well, we can't work with a mushy brain. Let's get to drawing."

~*~

Music pounded through Ryland's headphones blocking the cheerful giggles and chatter from the kitchen.

Three weeks. Three weeks he'd endured Tessa invading his home and every waking conversation he had with his daughter.

Miss Tessa likes chocolate cookies like you, Daddy.
Miss Tessa thinks angels are reals too.
Do you think I'll be pretty like Miss Tessa?
When Miss Tessa laughs she kinda snorts.
Miss Tessa. Miss Tessa. Miss Tessa.

His daughter's fixation with his own personal obsession was not helping him be the bigger man when it came to Joe's pursuit of Tessa. Each day he walked through the back door and spied Tessa's blonde locks intermingled with Emma's curls, and his heart twisted with longing for weeks upon years of walking into similar scenes. Tessa helping Emma with her homework or reciting lines for the school play, or sharing secrets—preferably not about some future boyfriend. Her fixture in his house, with his daughter, was allowing his unimaginative mind to create a tidal wave of images that would likely crash and leave the pool dry.

He tugged his sweat-soaked T-shirt over his head

and tossed it in the corner of his workout room. When he'd purchased the house, the room was outfitted with a treadmill, elliptical and stationary bicycle. He'd added his extensive free weight system, heavy weight bag, and benches. The room had been his refuge since the Tessa Take-Over started—allowing his bent toward grueling exercise to free his mind and untangle the longing in his heart.

He wrapped his phone in a case around his bicep, strapped on sparing gloves, and then rhythmically punched the center of the bag. With each whack he vented his romantic frustrations. Distancing himself from Tessa was the best form of self-preservation. In a fair fight, he would never be able to beat JT for Tessa's affections. And Tessa was good for Joe. She'd had him in church every Sunday since the two went on their first date and his friend was starting to show glimpses of his old self.

Although JT remained tightlipped about the source of anxiety nipping at his heels, after two decades of friendship Ryland knew JT's happy-go-lucky demeanor was actually shadowing secrets. His game was not up to his stellar rookie year performance.

The baseball commentators—who had celebrated Joe's early success and thirty home run first year in the majors—lambasted his .285 batting average last season as he vacillated between the injured reserve and the starting line-up. The knocks on his professionalism and athletic ability weighed heavy, showing in his performance on the field.

But Joe's time with Tessa seemed to give him a renewed sense of self.

Despite his feelings, Ryland wouldn't do anything

to destroy his friend's fragile recovery. Instead he would work himself into the best shape of his post professional athlete life. A tap on his shoulder caused him to swing with instinct—barely missing Tessa's jaw. "I'm sorry. Are you OK? Did I hit you?" Ripping his earbuds from his ears, he stripped off his gloves and tossed them near his T-shirt. He rested his hands on her shoulders, guiding her to sit on the bench.

"Ryland, I'm fine." She chuckled. "You totally whiffed."

"Are you sure?" He squatted in front of her, examining her face for the chance of defect.

"I'm sure, but if I knew nearly getting cold-cocked was the way to get you to say more than two words to me, I'd have startled you three weeks ago." Her smile twinkled through her eyes, causing a sudden awareness that his palms were still pressed against the thin fabric of her sheer blouse. A steady simmer of heat flowed from her through him.

He tore his hands from her shoulders, quickly stood. "I'm sorry. Did I mess up your top thingy?" Grabbing a clean towel from a stack beside the weight rack, he tossed it to her—afraid if he stayed too near his self-control would race out the back door.

"It's just a shirt. Regardless of what Lily Mae says, I have plenty. A toss in the wash and it'll be good as new." Standing, she closed the gap between them and handed him the towel. "But I do need to talk with you."

Ryland swallowed against the growing thickness in his throat, he nodded.

"OK…" She turned, slowly pacing the room—dragging her hand across the weights. She stopped at the elliptical and leaned awkwardly against the machine. "So, you know I'm going to Lily's wedding this weekend."

He nodded.

"Well, I'm going down tomorrow. I was able to get an appointment with a children's literary agent." Her eyebrows lifted, waiting for a response.

But being close to her for the first time in weeks—after trying to squash his desire—caused a flood of yearning to flow through him and a sudden case of mute.

"Nothing? How about, 'That's great Tessa' or 'What does this mean for Emma?'"

He nodded.

"Well, I'm so glad you asked, Ryland. I wanted you to know about the meeting, because Emma has a stake in any contract I sign. As her legal guardian you'll need to review the book deal—if we get one—and decide how you want to account for her royalties and payments."

The talk of money for his daughter released his tongue. "Why would Emma receive royalties? It's your book, Tessa. I mean I'm happy for you, but she didn't write anything. You did."

"That's not true." Pushing off the elliptical, she crossed the space in two long strides. "I wouldn't be anywhere in this project without Emma. She's the one who developed the character sketches for the angels and their vocations. She's the one who sees the images of the angels in her mind and transcribes them to me. She's the one who thought of the first adventure for little Shelby—Guard-Ann's charge."

"She did?"

"Didn't she tell you what we've been working on for the past three weeks?"

She had, but one too many mentions of Tessa forced Ryland to flip on his parent nodding reflex as a defense. He knew his daughter was talking, but nothing she said registered. "I guess I didn't realize."

"She's very talented, Ryland. Her creativity is amazing." Her cheeks flushed full bloom pink as she recapped the writing sessions. The pure delight Tessa exuded, and Emma's input into the story puffed his prideful heart. His daughter was a writer. Who knew?

"When my friend set up the meeting with Terrell I knew I had to jump on it."

"Wait." He shook his head. "Who's Terrell?"

"Haven't you been listening? Terrell Bergstrom— the agent. He's the one I'm meeting with on Friday to discuss Emma's book."

"Right. Contracts. Royalties. Etcetera."

"It's kind of a big deal. The timing is beyond quick, but I think the proposal is in decent shape." Wringing the towel in her hands she began to pace the small room. "I've not pitched a children's book before, but I'm hoping the process is similar to other projects. It can't be that different, can it?" Her pace quickened and her words sped, but held little coherence.

The subtly confident, and strong woman disintegrated before his eyes. With each step her mind seemed to unravel through her lips, and the vulnerable little girl he'd known since he was six years old took control.

He caught her as she passed and wrapped his arms around her. "Shhh…" With long, smooth strokes of his hand, he trailed a path from her shoulders to her back, intending to soothe and calm. She sighed into his chest, and relaxed in his embrace. He swallowed, desperately trying to ignore the intensity of emotion trilling through every cell of his body. Her fragrance flowed with his senses. He deeply inhaled. She smelled soft and delicate. Not sweet like most women.

She was calm now; her breath slowed against his chest. He should step away. But the feel of her, her gentle weight, wrapped protectively in his arms, was nearly his undoing. He wanted this. Tessa in his arms. Protecting her. Comforting her. Loving her.

"Hey, did I miss something?"

Tessa jumped as if she'd stepped on a firecracker at the sound of Joe's aw-shucks chuckle. She went over and casually wrapped her arms around his waist. "Just a typical freak out moment. Ryland calmed me down."

Joe tucked her in the crook of his arm. "Must have been some freak out."

"Epic." A smile didn't quite reach her eyes.

"Yep," Ryland echoed. "Epic."

"You always comfort topless, Jessup?"

Pivoting, Ryland yanked a hoodie from the weight bench. "I was working out when she interrupted. How was I supposed to know I needed to put on my Psych 101 hat?"

Joe chuckled. "I'd have liked that kind of class in school. I'd have had an 'A' for sure."

With a quick smack to the gut, Tessa stepped out of Joe's arms and stalked to the door. "Excuse me. I'll go say goodnight to Emma. I believe she may hold the majority of the maturity in this house at the moment—Mabel the obvious exception." She disappeared into the hallway.

"Whew," Joe shook his head. "Who knew T.T. Tarrington was such a spitfire?"

The rip of Velcro answered him. Ryland wrapped his weight-lifting gloves together and tossed them on the small corner counter, ignoring Joe's one-sided conversation as he extoled the wonders of dating Tessa. Similar to Emma, the only conversations he'd had with his best friend in the last three weeks were Tessa-centered. For someone who was desperately trying to avoid her, he was surrounded by all things Tessa.

Lifting the disinfectant spray bottle and soft towel, Ryland methodically began to clean all the equipment as Joe continued to prattle on about the double date he had planned with Tessa, and Sean and Maggie that evening. Somewhere between wiping down the bench and the mats, Joe switched discussion topics to the status of the failing Ohio State Buckeyes basketball team. Without missing a beat in his one-sided conversation, Joe stepped onto the elliptical and absently swished the footholds back and forward.

"Dude," Ryland dropped to the bench, the spray bottle dangling between his fingers. "What's your problem?"

Joe swished to a stop. "What do you mean?"

"Why are you still here?"

"I thought I'd visit with you."

"I'm cleaning my workout room, JT. Don't you think that's weird since I have a full time cleaning lady?"

"Maybe you're a little more OCD than in high school. To each his own."

Ryland rubbed his forehead.

"I'm sorry I bugged you. I'll catch you later," Joe said.

"Wait. We need to talk."

22

New Orleans fed Tessa's soul.

The city's sorrowful melody trailed every street; her spicy aroma lingering. Despite the three weeks of anticipation still separating the city from her annual "carnival", NOLA was alive with preparatory Mardi Gras celebrations floating between cafés, clubs, and corner street bands. The revelry was a mere shadow of Lily Mae's elaborate wedding event strategically scheduled to overshadow New Orleans' most famous of parties.

Waiting in the famous French Quarter café for the bride-to-be Thursday morning, she sipped her chicory coffee, well diluted with fresh cream, and contemplated soothing her wounded pride with the warm sugary goodness wrapped in a traditional beignet. Her breakfast meeting with the co-founders of Evanston and Evanston, Jim and Cheryl, yielded disappointing results.

They would be delighted to have her return, provided she could bring one or two "juicy" clients with her. Somehow her gossip-fed former leaders discovered she went to high school with Joe and Ryland. The prospect of signing either a current baseball player with a well-documented party-at-all-costs-lifestyle, or a retired NFL linebacker whose wife's death was less than straightforward made the two salivate.

When Tessa refused to offer any details around either man, Jim and Cheryl cut the breakfast short. The offer was clear—sign a book deal with either athlete or don't return to E&E.

She hoped her meeting the next day with John's friend reaped better results.

Gingerly sipping her coffee, the tension of the last forty-eight hours began to settle. Was it just two days ago she'd asked Joey to attend Lily's wedding as her guest? Just hours after being plastered against Ryland's very naked and sweaty chest. What was she doing inviting Joey to the wedding? They'd only been dating for a few weeks. One didn't invite a newbie to a wedding. Too much pressure. Too many expectations. Too many slow dances. Too many bridal bouquets and garters. She knew why she'd invited him.

Ryland.

If Ryland hadn't stirred up every female hormone in her body with one shirtless embrace. Or if he hadn't acted as if she was a pariah for the last three weeks. Or if he hadn't smelled like fresh wood and clean air every time she'd passed him in the hallway at school. Or if her heart hadn't cracked a little each time Emma excitedly shared her daddy's near super powers, ranging from killing a spider to reading the same book five times before locking said book with its strange googly eyes in a drawer for the night. If he wasn't so...the opposite of everything she thought was Ryland Jessup, she would never have invited Joey to a wedding—let alone a wedding one thousand miles from home where he would be a virtual stranger to everyone in attendance. She lowered her forehead to her arms crossed on the rough-hewn table. She was an idiot.

"Well this is a picture. You'll never make it through to Sunday brunch if you're pooped Thursday morning, *cher*." Lily Mae chuckled.

Tessa rested her chin on her crossed arms. Her heart warmed at the sight of her two best friends—Lily and Ella, her sisters from other misters.

Lily's face was obscured by oversized sunglasses. Her dark locks were blown out and as big as her southern roots would allow. Draped in a rich green sweater dress, she was accessorized with layers of thin gold chains in varying lengths.

In stark contrast, Ella's short brown curls cuddled her pink, rounded make-up free cheeks. During her time in New Orleans, the former ballet dancer discovered that the heady freedom of not being restricted in her diet coupled nicely with the delicacies of New Orleans' cuisine. The combination had transformed her petite, five foot one, size zero frame to the comfortably soft, oversized-sweater-wearing writer she'd become during four years of college. Today, Ella remained curvaceous.

Tessa often feared her friend hid behind her frame rather than embracing her plump body or committing to changing it. Either way, Ella's perfectly porcelain skin, chocolate brown hair and nearly clear blue eyes were striking—but Ella's features were nine hundredth on the list of what made her a wonderfully dedicated friend.

Ella sat on the seat nearest Tessa and cupped one tiny hand over hers. "Why are you so forlorn?"

A smile tugged at the corner of Tessa's heart. Only Ella would rely on a phrase better suited for an Austen character than a strong, modern woman. "Well, do you want the short version or the essay?"

"Short." Lily interrupted sliding a coffee in front of Ella and plopping her half-dozen shopping bags on the empty chair. "I love you, T, but your dramas already consumed the better part of a holiday weekend this calendar year. I can only give you an hour per day of this wedding to sulk, wallow, or whine about your life. We can focus on you again after I return from Belize and before carnival."

"Your compassion overwhelms, Lil." Ella rolled her eyes at the bride-to-be.

"I'm just saying. This one weekend is supposed to be all about me." Lily slouched against her chair.

"And Beau," Ella said.

"And Beau, of course. All about me and Beau." She mumbled.

"I don't want to make anything about me. Let's just go do all of the bridal duties that need doing."

"You said duty." Both Lily and Ella said it simultaneously. "Jinx."

Tessa's heart floated with the fullness of a helium balloon. "Short version. My life's back in the toilet."

"What's the long version?" Ella asked.

"Well, it all started with snow angels." Tessa shared the ups and downs of the previous weeks from her inspiration to write a children's book with Emma, to her essential rejection by E&E, culminating with her curious feelings for Ryland. How he had all but ignored her during every writing session—making her see-saw emotions all the more inexplicable.

She recounted her building romance with Joe. Her heart softened as she told the story of him sweetly walking her back to her father's house Tuesday night. He'd insisted he wanted to spend the evening alone, suddenly cancelling their plans with his brother and Maggie, opting for a chilly moonlight picnic in the backyard. Something weighed on him after his conversation with Ryland, but he said it was nothing for her to worry over. She'd tried to believe him, but his smile never reached his eyes as he entertained her with clubhouse stories and childhood anecdotes. When she'd probed, he'd claimed he was tired, but something was troubling him. She hoped when he arrived on Saturday for the wedding, she would uncover his worry.

"Let me get this straight. Hottie football coach was half-naked and you didn't dissolve into a pile of ash from the heat of your blush?" Lily challenged.

"I tell you I've been denied my livelihood. That I'm writing a book with a four year old. That one of my childhood friends—"

"Soon to be official suitor." Ella interrupted.

Tessa sighed. "I don't know about that, but he's definitely in trouble. That I can't define the feelings I have for either Ryland or Joe and all you focus on is I saw Ryland without his shirt?"

"I love my fiancé, but I'd like to see that one without his shirt."

"Lily!"

"Well, *cher*, he's one mighty fine specimen—even if he is a Yankee. And rude."

"Regardless," Tessa said. "None of it really matters. My career is essentially over. I'm probably over fixating on Joe's potential problems so I don't have to deal with my own."

"Darlin', if the gossip rags haven't wrangled the story, I don't believe we'll discover the issues of the seriously dreamy Joe Taylor."

"Agreed." Tessa tossed the last of her coffee in her mouth, dropping her cup with a clank against the saucer. "Let's get this southern belle married!"

~*~

Four hours later, her hands wrapped in tinfoil and her face caked with a green concoction that smelled faintly of menthol, Tessa wished she'd stayed in Ohio until two hours before the wedding. Her face itched. Her back itched. Sitting still this long made her brain itch.

In the whirlwind of the last four weeks, she'd been able to shove her thoughts about Joe and Ryland into tightly locked compartments in her mind. The distractions of school, the book, the potential revival of her career occupied her. But now, sitting for hours being poked and yanked in the name of pampering, her mind let loose, and the compare and contrast skills she'd acquired in Modern English Lit systematically evaluated each man.

Joe was sweet. He was everything she dreamed when she was sixteen and longed for him to notice her. Their dates were filled with laughter and stories, but something was missing. His stories seemed to graze the surface—never going deeper than his bio on the team's media page. His eyes held a sadness that rarely evaporated. One of the qualities she'd always admired in him was his light-hearted approach to life.

Over the last few weeks, he'd appeared more strained than easy going. He was working hard to ensure no one noticed, but Joey Taylor was one of her favorite subjects in high school. Back then she noticed when his overlong hair was slightly out of place.

Today, she'd definitely noticed his lack of joy. From her side of the glass, his life appeared to be one splashy scene after another. The press dubbed him the Shindig Slugger for the countless parties, premieres, and playmates connected to him. But that wasn't the Joey Taylor she knew.

Over the last few weeks, she'd glimpsed the old Joey; the sweet boy who helped her learn new music in the praise band and always said 'hi' to her in high school. Her Joey—the real Joey—was sweet, a little flirty, and desperately broken hearted.

And Ryland noticed, too.

During the few times she'd seen the two in the same room, she'd recognized the shadow of concern eclipsing his tightlipped glances. Joe and Ryland's bromance was larger-than-life. They'd been friends since the two could walk and hold baseballs in leather mitts. If anyone—including Joey's two overly protective older brothers—was going to know what was driving him to depression it would be Ryland.

His obvious concern for his best friend softened Tessa's heart in places she was unaware existed.

She was diligently trying to remain single-hearted—focused solely on her budding romance with Joe—but with each passing day she couldn't deny the ebbing attraction to Mr. Baseball while her fascination with a certain enigmatic football coach continued to grow. If she was honest, her worry for Joe's mysterious behavior spawned not from a deep abiding love, but from a place of concern for an old friend. She wanted to help him. She wanted to see the twinkle spark in his eyes once again.

Dear Lord, I don't know how to help Joey. He's hurting but he doesn't want to share his burden with anyone. He's a lost soul in desperate need of Your tender healing. Help me to know how I can help him. Is there a clue to what is causing his pain?

Moments clicked by. The faint mutterings of other spa clients humming above the synthetic nature melodies piped into the room. Tessa breathed in the sounds and expelled a slow and steady...peace. Her eyes flittered open. Peace.

Joey needed peace. He didn't need more dates or surface conversations. He needed to rip off the bandage and allow his wound to heal. "With healing, peace always follows," her father had said.

Through peace Joey would rediscover his joy.

How could she convince him to willingly reveal the pain he was concealing? She wanted so much for Joey—just not her. "Huh," a soft smile cracked her green caked skin, echoing the scales slipping from her heart. She didn't want to be with Joe. Her sixteen year-old-self had motivated the dating whirlwind of the last month. She'd enjoyed nearly every minute, and in line with most teenage relationships—the expiration date was under thirty days. Knowing she didn't want to pursue a relationship with Joey gave her new direction. She wouldn't need to worry about any romance with Joe ever again.

She only had one snag: in less than twenty-four hours she would be attending her best friend's over-the-top, romantic wedding with him.

Her first order of business when he arrived Saturday morning would be to establish the new boundaries of their relationship. She didn't want to elongate the confusion—and the fixer in her itched to help him solve whatever was drawing lines at the corners of his beautiful brown eyes.

23

Calling Literary Agent Terrell Bergstrom's building a place of business was a stretch. The garbage-strewn entryway greeted visitors leading them directly past cardboard patched windows. The once black and white tiled lobby was hidden beneath several years of dirt and mildew. The turn of the Twentieth Century charm existed. It was just on a very long coffee break. The elevator leading to his fourth floor agency, likely original to the building, was as out of order as the lobby.

With no other option, Ryland jogged the stairs in twos.

On the fourth floor, he was greeted by a buzzing security light illuminating the landing in a halted staccato, the eerie aura of a horror film. Twisting the handle to open, the door barely shifted. Using the force of his entire six foot six frame, he slammed against the door. The frame splintered with a crack, showering his head and shoulders with strips and bits of paint layers.

"Seriously?" He mumbled, brushing his light gray sweater.

"Ryland?"

Every short hair on the back of his neck stood at the sound of his name slipping through Tessa's lips.

"What are you doing here?" She stood, absently brushing paint chips from his sweater.

"You said it'd be a good idea for me to know the

details of the book deal—for Emma's sake."

"Ryland, we don't have a deal, yet. This is just the first meeting. The first agent." Her soft smile signaled his ignorance.

"Oh…" Words were lost in the light touch of her hands against his shoulders. A slow burn spread from her fingers up his neck and down his chest warming his heart and mudding his mind.

Yanking away her hands, she shuffled back to her seat.

Ryland glanced at the curved back wooden chair beside her and lifted a silent prayer of safety before lowering to sit.

The hum from the security light offered the harmony to the subtle tick of the wall clock offset by the rhythm of Tessa's heel tapping. Her hands smoothed the flat surface of the wide leather case resting on her lap.

"Like you said. This is the first meeting." He squeezed her fingers.

"But what if it's awful. What if he hates the story? What do I do then? This is my last shot. I don't have any other options beyond returning to Gibson's Run and waiting for Mrs. Monahan to retire so I can take over for her for the next thirty years until I die because I've choked on my oatmeal and no one finds me until the smell fills the halls of my decrepit apartment building five days later."

"Whoa. How long did it take you to come up with that story?"

"The last seven minutes waiting for Terrell's door to open."

"Then clearly this isn't your last chance. You obviously have plenty of fiction writing ahead of you."

The corner of her mouth lifted, pouring calm relief through him. Cupping her fingers in his large grip, he continued, "If this Terrell guy doesn't see how great this story is, then he's an idiot and we'll find someone else who knows how special it is."

"We will?"

The crash of dozens of books and glass against a tile floor snapped their attention to the opening office door.

Tessa ripped her hands from Ryland's grasp as she shot up. Wiping undetectable lint from her skirt, she stretched herself to a willowy height he didn't know she possessed.

Ryland stood behind her, resting a light hand to her shoulder.

A man—presumably Terrell Bergstrom—emerged from the closeted space in a cloud of dust and mutterings. He barely reached Tessa's shoulder and his girth made passing through the narrow doorway a challenge. His tightly curled salt-and-pepper hair spoke of an age his cherubic cheeks did not register.

"Mr. Bergstrom?" Tessa asked.

Lifting a forefinger to his ear, he jiggled it as if to clear unseen debris. "Miss Tarrington, I presume. John Samson speaks highly of your work." He shuffled back through the door. "Come. Come. Let me see this story."

Snagging the portfolio, she followed in Terrell's wake.

Ryland trailed them, rubbing the back of his neck.

Twenty minutes later, after enduring Tessa's attempt to share Emma's vision as well as her own with the apathetic agent, Ryland shifted in his seat and rested an elbow on the edge of Bergstrom's paper strewn desk. "So do you like the story or not?" he asked.

Tessa's eyes shut. Tension stretch across her shoulders.

"It's got some promise."

"But do you want to represent Tessa and Emma?"

"Ryland," Tessa whispered through a clenched jaw.

"No, no, Miss Tarrington. I like a man who doesn't tiptoe around a question. Just jumps in with both feet. No life preserver." Clasping his hands over the middle of his body, Bergstrom gently rocked his chair, a high pitched rhythm filling the small space.

"Forget this." Ryland stood and yanked Tessa to stand. "Let's go."

"What are you doing?" She tugged against his grip.

"I'm removing you…us, from a situation where we are clearly not wanted."

"Now, now, son, no one said y'all weren't wanted."

"You clearly don't have the same passion for this book Tessa or my four year old has, which makes you the wrong person to represent them. Have a good day." He pivoted but Tessa wouldn't budge.

"I'm so sorry Mr. Bergstrom. I don't know what's gotten into him."

"No worries, *cher*. Clearly, he's passionate about his daughter and you. Leave your proposal and any bits you want me to take a closer look at. I'll get back with you in a few weeks or so to let you know. OK?"

With her free hand, Tessa handed him the packet, including Emma's sketches. "Thank you. I'm so sorry for all of this."

Terrell stretched a wide smile. "Darlin', I love to see people as passionate about children's literature as I am. I'll look over the proposal and let you know if it's something I can pitch."

She nodded, turning to Ryland. "Let go of my arm."

He dropped his hold and followed her.

Silence hung heavy over their descent. Throwing open the door to exit, the damp air clung to Ryland's skin. The sun barely burning through the early fog.

"I can't believe you." Tessa whirled and punched him in the shoulder.

"Hey. Violence isn't necessary."

"Really? Terrell Bergstrom's one of the leading Children's Lit agents in the country. The country, Ryland. Do you know how blessed we were to even be in his office today?"

"Tess, if that's the office of a leading agent, Children's literary agents need to find new jobs."

"Ugh." She stalked across the cobblestone street.

Ryland jogged after her opting for silence. They zigzagged through alleys and off street sidewalks for nearly fifteen minutes before stopping at a misplaced door along a city block-long wall of brick.

"Hold this, please." Tessa shoved her portfolio into his hands. She rummaged in her shoulder bag and lifted out keys unlocking the mystery door to reveal a narrow stairwell.

"Are you coming?" She jogged up the stairs not waiting for his answer.

Following her up four flights, and two landings, they stopped before a wide metal sliding door. She fitted another key into a hidden slot in the frame and shoved the door to the right. Her heels clicked against the cement floor of the open space. Dropping her handbag on the wide bar connected to the small galley kitchen, she kicked her heels under a chair and disappeared behind another sliding wall. "You can put the portfolio on the table by the door."

Ryland laid the folder on the table. "What's this place?"

"My apartment. Have a seat. I'll just be a minute."

The room was an expansive stretch of floor to ceiling windows, an L-shaped couch and a corner desk nestled between two file cabinets. The apartment wasn't big, but the understatement was one he'd seen in the luxurious downtown lofts of his single teammates. Simplicity was expensive.

Resting his shoulder against the windows, his gaze landed on the winding Mississippi River. Tessa Tarrington's life wasn't one he recognized. As much as he was fighting it, Tessa was bigger than Gibson's Run. She needed to be with someone like Joey. Someone whose life was still on the rise, not someone whose life peaked at twenty-one. She deserved more than a small town football coach.

"Would you like something to drink?" She'd swapped her professional garb for torn sweats and an oversized sweatshirt. Her hair was tied in a lopsided ponytail, and yet, she was as pretty as the day his heart first opened his eyes to her.

Sucking in a steady breath he shook his head and shifted to the door. "I should get back to my hotel. I'm sure you have wedding stuff before Joe gets here. I'm sorry about today."

"Hey," she said, stopping him with a light touch to his shoulder. "I thought we were going to fight this thing out. Now you're running away like a girl? Pretty poor conflict management for a coach, don't you think?"

Heat flamed up his neck to his cheeks. "What's there to argue about? I messed up. You lost your contract. It's all my fault."

"Ryland, please. Today is no one's fault. I put too much on one little pitch. Please, come sit. Let me make you some lunch and we can plan our next pitch."

"Our?"

"Sure. You're the best proxy partner I could ask for. No one will protect Emma's—and apparently, my—interests as well as you. Terrell wasn't taking us seriously today. And I'm not sure I want someone representing the book who can't see the potential for what Guard-Ann and Shelby can be. Your daughter created amazing characters for a series of stories, not just one little children's book. Please stay."

"OK."

She smiled and dropped her hand from his shoulder. "Have a seat on the couch and I'll get some lunch pulled together. I dropped by the farmer's market and picked up some veggies and stuff. How's a little jambalaya and rice sound? I made it ahead for Joe's visit. There's plenty."

The clang of pans and clink of dishes drowned his answer as Tessa began cooking. She prattled about Lily Mae's wedding, her meeting with her old publishers, and her idea for a second book based on Guard-Ann's adventures with Shelby.

Ryland barely registered a word. His mind swirled. Why was Tessa so relaxed? The vulnerability she'd showed him this morning seemed counter to the carefree attitude of the moment. She rarely showed him a side of her that wasn't controlled or ordered. But then again, over the last few weeks Tessa Tarrington was consistently inconsistent.

Since the first moment he'd seen her at the high school, he was struck by the contrast of confidence she'd displayed compared to the timid mouse he'd known through adolescence. The compassion that oozed from her when he'd shared about Macy or when he'd watched her with Emma, her seemingly unending patience, were all various sides to a multifaceted woman. And now the comfortable ease she wore in her own world was intoxicating.

Swaying between the stove and a cutting board, she continued her conversation.

He straddled a barstool, and watched her work. Worn sweats and lopsided hair were no match to seeing Tessa completely comfortable in her own skin. He'd never seen her sparkle quite as blindingly as she was chopping green onions and stirring soup. She belonged here in this urban, slightly exotic setting, not bound to six hundred teenagers and dozens of ungraded midterms.

"What do you think?" she asked.

"I'm sorry. Think about what?"

"Haven't you been listening?"

He shrugged. "My brain's kind of swirling."

She lifted a single eyebrow. "Do you want to talk about it?"

Hmmm. I've been in love with you since I was six years old and I'm just now realizing I can never be with you because our lives are too different... Not exactly a lighthearted lunch conversation. "Nope. I'm good."

"OK. But there's something I wanted to discuss with you." She said, ladling the thick stew over brown rice. She handed a bowl to him and gestured to the wide sectional. Carrying her own bowl, she balanced a carafe of water and glasses in a single hand, with a long loaf of crusty French bread cuddled in the crook of her arm. Setting the water on the oversized ottoman, she folded her legs under her facing him on the couch.

Tearing his gaze from her graceful movements, he scooped a mounded spoonful of jambalaya into his mouth. The heated spice filled every sense, warming a line of perspiration on his brow.

"Water?" She offered him a tall glass.

He swallowed nearly half of the contents to simmer the heat in his mouth.

"A little too hot for you." She chuckled as she dug into her bowl. "Make sure to get some of the rice in each bite. It takes a little of the edge off the heat. And the bread is a good counter. I usually can't take much spice, but jambalaya is a classic."

He ripped the end off of the bread and chomped the chewy center. "The dish is really good. I'm just a little tentative around spicy food."

"Well, you might want to take smaller bites."

Tearing another chunk of bread, he lifted his gaze to the top of her head. "Can I ask you a question?"

"Sure," she said, lifting her hand to cover her mouth as she continued to chew.

"What happened with your publishers?"

She stirred her spoon through the thick soup, ladled a bite to her mouth, and slowly chewed.

"You know what, forget I asked." He dug his spoon in his bowl, chomping another bite. Sweat pooled at the base of his neck.

"It's all so weird…" She started slowly sharing the story of the break-in. Her notes stolen. The invasion of privacy. The fear of returning home.

"Someone went through all of my drawers. My closets. Read every email—all of my notes. He not only invaded my privacy but the three clients I was in contract with and every other client I had partnered with in the past. Everything was taken."

"Do you have any suspects?"

"I asked the building management for the videos during the weekend of the break-in, but there was a power outage and the memories were all erased."

"This happened over a weekend? Were you out of town?"

She nodded. "It was homecoming and a bunch of us go back to school. Visit the sorority house. Pretend we're still young."

"Tessa, we are still young."

"Not if you go on a college campus, we're not. We're ancient—barely days away from Medicare, Social Security, and sitting on the front porch of the nursing home gumming our food."

"Beautiful picture."

"Writer."

He smiled. Tried to temper the expansion of his heart. "How long were you gone?"

"Just two nights. I left Friday afternoon. Stayed for evening worship at The Chapel and then headed home. I guess I returned around 9:30."

"And was the place ransacked?"

"No. Just a little mussed, but I can be kind of a freak about leaving for a trip. I have this morbid fear someone will have to come in and clean out my apartment."

"What?"

"If I die or something tragic happens. I wouldn't want to have dirty dishes in the sink or dirty clothes in the hamper. How embarrassing."

"Tessa, I don't think anyone who loved you would care."

She shook her head. "You'd like to think so, but I remember when my Momma's great Uncle Leopold passed away—God rest his soul. The old *church* ladies who cleaned up his place were vicious. Talking about his stacks of car magazines and old oil cans. You'd think he was a horrific hoarder the way they carried on. But it changed the way I leave my house every day. I don't ever want to look down from heaven and hear a bunch of old birds chirping on about how I had dirty T-shirts in my hamper and unfiled papers on my desk."

"I don't think you'll care when you're in heaven."

"But do you know that for sure?"

"Revelations 21:4, 'He will wipe every tear from their eyes. There will be no more death or mourning or crying or pain, for the old order of things has passed away.'"

"What does John's vision have to do with my dirty dishes?"

"I think Jesus's promise of no more tears, includes your dirty dishes. You won't care, because it won't matter."

She narrowed her bright green gaze and laced her arms tight across her chest. "Well, let's just agree to disagree."

"Fair enough. So you got home and noticed things out of place. Did you call the police?"

"I called Lily Mae first and she told me to call the police. She actually told me to call the 'po po' but that translates. They poked around for a couple hours, but the only thing of value missing was my notes. And since the door wasn't jimmied they assume it was someone with a key. Which makes zero sense—the only people with keys to my apartment are Lily, Ella, and the manager of the building. Why would he want jumbled notes only another writer could understand?"

"Yep, does seem like a mystery."

She shrugged. "When Jim and Cheryl first found out they were super supportive. 'No worries.' 'We've got your back.' And all of that nonsense, but as soon as one story leaked directly tied to the notes, they yanked my contract and that was it. I had about a week or so to wallow before my dad's heart attack. And...well you know the rest of the story since then."

"Did the police ever do anything?"

"Not really. None of the prints that came back were out of the norm."

"I'm so sorry, Tess."

"Thanks, but as a ghost writer all you have is your integrity. Your ability to keep a secret. When *the terrible, awful day* happened, I lost my credibility. I lost my power to be an effective writer of others' stories. I kept fooling myself, believing that if enough time passed, Jim and Cheryl would think I was too good of a writer to lose, but after meeting with them yesterday I realized talent has little to do with what they want in a writer."

"What did they ask?" He scooped another spoonful of jambalaya in his mouth—balancing the spicy stew with the cooling rice.

"They wanted me to bring them a juicy gossip filled story. They don't care if they have the consent of the subject. They just want a tell-all they can turn into a blockbuster."

"That's horrible."

"I guess that's the business I associated myself with for the last four years. I thought I was doing something good. Being the fingers that typed someone's story. I think I did that part of the job with honor. But what Jim and Cheryl want to turn E&E into isn't a business I want to be associated with, regardless of the payday." She tore a chunk of bread, tugging the soft inside into a ball.

"You can't think of anyone whom you've made an enemy out of? An old client who didn't like the finished product? A rival writer? What about your publishers? Maybe they thought you were holding back on the 'gossip gold'?"

She shook her head. "I guess the thief—whoever he or she is—did me a favor. I wouldn't have left this job and may've been forced to compromise my beliefs. I hate to think what I would've done if I had to choose between being a ghost writer and a gossip writer."

They fell into companionable silence as they ate.

He drank two more glasses of water, forcing Tessa to refill the carafe with a chuckle.

"Hey, before we sat down you said you wanted to discuss something with me?" He scraped his bowl for the last of the rice and stew.

"Yep." She set her half eaten bowl on the ottoman and pulled her knees to her chest. "I'm not really sure how to start."

"The beginning always seems best."

"It's about Joey."

His heart slammed against his ribcage. Ryland didn't want to talk about Joey. The idea of her with anyone else—including his best friend—scraped at his soul. "What about Joey?"

"Have you noticed anything odd about his

behavior?"

Odd? Ryland thought about the confrontation in his gym a few days earlier. In those moments Joe confirmed Ryland's greatest fears for his friend, but he wasn't certain how to answer Tessa's question without betraying long held confidences. "What do you mean odd?"

"I don't know. He seems cagey about how his career is going. He just doesn't seem his old self. He doesn't sparkle."

"Well, speaking as a man, I'm sure Joe is glad he doesn't sparkle. Sparkle isn't exactly the description most men are striving toward."

Throwing a pillow at his head she grunted.

"Tessa Tarrington. Who knew you were so violent?"

"I'm being serious and you're joking. Maybe I shouldn't talk to you about Joey. I just thought since you've been best friends since the beginning of well, the beginning, you would want to help him with whatever he's going through…but I guess compassion wasn't something they handed out in the coaching line, was it?" She burst to her feet.

With a flick of his wrist, he tugged her back to the couch, tucked neatly to his side. "Enough. You really need to learn how to take a little good natured teasing, Tarrington."

Her sigh melted into his body. He tried to remember they were better apart, but her fragrance filled his lungs and wrapped around his heart jumbling his mind. He could be content to sit on this couch with Tessa stretched against his side for the rest of his life. A flash of Emma's broad smile shot across his mind and gave him the strength to make space. He couldn't burden Tessa with his readymade family. After seeing her today, he wouldn't be the barrier to her flourishing.

She scooted to face him with her legs laced under her. "I'm sorry I overreact. Years of response. I guess I'm as guilty as any of Pavlov's dogs. Forgive me?"

"Forgiven. And the same to you. I over-tease. Will you forgive me?"

The corner of her mouth lifted in a devilish grin. "Forgiven."

"Now...how do we solve a problem like Joey?"

24

The waning sun blanketed her loft as she and Ryland continued to chat. Hours had passed and she felt she was closer to understanding the source of Joey's pain, but she was still unsure of how to best help him move forward. Ryland was guarded about what he shared, but reading through the lines was her specialty. Joey was dealing with lingering injuries and instead of owning them he was relying on medication—only he didn't have prescriptions.

"Would you like a little more coffee?" She lifted the tray holding their empty dessert plates and coffee mugs.

"Naw, I'm good." He glanced at his watch and straightened to stand. "I should really get out of your hair. You probably need to get ready for a rehearsal dinner."

"What time is it?" She loaded the dishwasher.

"Nearly 4:00 PM."

A wave of dread flowed through Tessa. She needed to be at the church by 5:30 to be told how to walk—something she'd thought she'd mastered at two years old—and she would have to see Bobbi Ann Risdy-Jones for the first time since she'd lost her writing career.

She could almost feel the superior sneer from her sorority sister. Why had Lily insisted on having Bobbi Ann in the wedding? Just because her father had rented all of Bobbi Ann's sorority sisters high end loft apartments for next to nothing after graduation, shouldn't make every sister indebted to her for the rest of their young adult years.

"You OK?" Ryland asked, leaning a shoulder against the fifteen foot pillar flanking her kitchen.

"Sure. But I'm out of time."

"Well, I'll get out of your hair." He turned to leave.

She watched the muscles of his broad back ripple as he reached for the sliding door, and Spontaneous Tessa spurted again. "What are you doing tonight?"

~*~

The din of the small army of guests and attendants grew as Tessa led Ryland to the backroom. The private event facility would be transformed into a fairy tale reception in less than twenty-fours. A server greeted them with champagne, but both declined.

"I just really need a giant glass of ice water," Ryland answered.

"Mouth still have a little lingering heat?"

"Funny. Would you like anything to drink?" He nodded at her order and wove his way to the bar that dominated the back of the room.

Tessa watched him retreat.

Turning from him she walked to the windows set deep into the high brick walls. The rehearsal was smoother than she'd anticipated.

Lily Mae placed Bobbi Ann at the front of the processional, keeping two cousins and one sorority sister between her and Tessa. Now if she was strategic about her seat at the long family style table, she could reduce her potential interaction with her nemesis to mere minutes waiting for the pre-wedding photos and the church vestibule line-up tomorrow. Her eyes shut in a silent prayer of thanks.

"Well, as I live and breathe."

Ice poured through Tessa's veins.

"If it isn't little T-squared Tarrington. It's just been months and weeks since I've seen you last."

Puffing a sigh through her smile stretched lips, Tessa turned. "Well, hey, Bobbi Ann. Long time." She stepped into Bobbi Ann's outstretched arms.

At barely five feet tall, Bobbi Ann never tipped the triple digits on her scale unless her hairspray was slightly more generous or her sequins were double-rowed over her entire dress. Balancing on four-inch heels, the top of her hair nearly scraped Tessa's cheek.

"Where've you been? I mean after the *scandal* it must have been just awful to show your face around town, but surely you know your friends wanted to support you." Bobbi Ann stepped out of the air hug.

"My father had a heart attack. I went home to Ohio to help him. I'm planning on returning as soon as he's better."

"Oh, joyful day!" She sipped her cocktail through a teeny red straw. Oversized, violet hued eyes dominated her face. "Then the rumors I heard about you and E&E splitting aren't true. Wonderful to hear. You know I just deplore gossip. I couldn't bear to ask Cheryl whether you were still on staff."

Quick beads of perspiration bubbled along Tessa's forehead. Heat flashed up her neck. Using her clutch as a fan she scanned the room for an escape and saw Ryland break through the crowd balancing two tall glasses filled to their brims. "Oh, here's Ryland." She stepped forward and laced her arm through the crook of his elbow. "Bobbi Ann, this is my *friend*, Ryland Jessup." Her heart slowed to a steady pace.

"The football player?" Bobbi Ann asked.

"Retired." He handed Tessa her glass and clasped Bobbi Ann's outstretched hand.

"Didn't you play with Everett Tanner, the quarterback?"

Tessa felt Ryland stiffen. "When did you become such a football aficionado?" she asked Bobbi Ann.

"Oh, I'm not. Not really. I'm acquaintances with Everett Tanner's wife. I mean we know each other from this board and that...nothing more." She waved her hands dismissing the thought. "I just find it so intriguing. Little T-squared snagged herself a bona fide stud-muffin." Bobbi Ann said as she dragged a hand down Ryland's chest.

"Umm, excuse me?" He turned to Tessa.

"Bobbi Ann I'd appreciate it if you'd keep your hands to yourself." Tessa lifted Bobbi Ann's rhinestone encrusted fingers from his chest. "Where's Billy?"

Lifting her cocktail, she slurped her drink for several seconds. "Billy? Oh, he's around somewhere. You know how he loves a good party. Don't you?"

"Bobbi Ann," Tessa started. Her voice dropped a few octaves. "You know Billy and I've only ever been friends. He pinned you sophomore year. He's been head over for you since the first moment he saw you."

"*Pfft.*" She pivoted, leaving Tessa and Ryland alone.

Tessa unlinked her arm from Ryland's and repositioned against the window. She shut her eyes against the tears threatening to spill. Why tonight?

"Do I even want to know what that was?" Ryland

leaned against the brick wall.

"It's not exciting. Bobbi Ann and I are sorority sisters. Same pledge class. She's hated me since sophomore year when I tutored her boyfriend—now husband—in an Old English lit class. Billy made some comment about me to Bobbi Ann and no matter how much I protested, she was convinced I was in love with Billy."

"Were you?" There was a slight crack in Ryland's deep resonate tone.

"No. Billy's a wonderful person. A good friend. But I've never thought of him as anything other than Bobbi Ann's. Period."

"That's sad."

"I know." Tessa sipped her water. After a few seconds she tilted her head to Ryland. "Wait. What's sad?"

"It's sad she's not confident in the love she shares with her husband. That's a horrible way to live." A shadow settled over his gray eyes shifting them to the color of a summer storm.

"But she's holding some unnecessary grudge against me. I'm lucky she didn't convince her dad to forfeit my deal on the apartment when we graduated."

"What deal?"

"Bobbi Ann's dad's a big time developer. He was trying to get a few new warehouses he converted to apartments and lofts rented out. They weren't moving as quickly as he liked, so he offered every one of Bobbi Ann's sorority sisters rent for a quarter of the price to help make the buildings seem attractive. Lily Mae lives in a building three blocks from mine, and Ella lives in the same building as Bobbi Ann off of Decatur Street, when she's not on assignment."

"I was thinking I made the wrong life choices when I saw that slick place today."

She chuckled. "Don't get me wrong. I do OK, but I couldn't afford my loft without the Delta Alpha Psi discount. And now, because of the unfortunate *scandal,* E&E doesn't want me back. My discount is good but not that good. I'll probably have to give up my place. At least Bobbi Ann will be happy. I'll leave New Orleans and she won't have me threatening her marriage or her career."

"What do you mean? Threatening her career."

"Bobbi Ann was trying to get on with E&E for the last four years, but every pitch she made was turned down. I heard she was picked up this past fall for a top secret project. My job at E&E was just another reason for her to hate me."

"Huh…"

"What?"

"It's just weird that…"

Clink. Clink. Clink.

"Toast time, people!" Lily Mae shouted from her perch atop a wooden bench. "As you all know this wonderful man beside me will be gaining an equally wonderful wife tomorrow at St. Louis—y'all are invited, of course—except maybe you Bubba Ray. That shirt has to go. Now, about my nuptials." Lily continued, her speech spiraling down a black hole.

"I need to rescue her from herself." Tessa whispered. "Her mouth tends to be bigger than Lake Pontchartrain when she's the center of attention." She glided toward the bench, nearly colliding with Ella.

"What shall we do?" Ella whispered.

Tessa gave her a wink. "I'll take care of it." She sucked in a deep breath and began to sing, "*Where stately oaks and broad magnolias shade...*" Before she made it through the first verse, nearly the entire room—including wait staff—began singing the LSU alma mater. Arms slung around strangers shoulders, a collective sway began.

As the song came to a close, Tessa hollered, "Let us raise our glasses to our two favorite Tigers, Lily Mae and Beau. Blessings for a beautiful wedding and an amazing marriage. *A votre sante!* Cheers, everybody." She downed her water, lifting her gaze to check Lily's wrath, but her friend was melting into a deep kiss with her soon to be husband.

Ella smiled. "Crisis averted."

"There's always tomorrow."

Several more toasts went around the room, including Beau's to his groomsmen and his parents, before the microphone was given back to Lily Mae.

"Oh, dear..." Ella muttered, her grip on Tessa's hand rivaling the best pliers on the planet.

"Thank y'all for sharing this special day with Beau and me. We were super blessed to meet the first week of freshman year, but I was equally blessed to meet two of my best girlfriends who became my sisters of the heart. Ella and Tessa." A soft applause rippled through the room. "I'd have been lost at school without all of my sorority sisters—Bobbi Ann and Talia included—but Ella and Tessa made my college years and every day since graduation an experience. Life isn't life when we don't have people to share it. Along with Beau, you two are my favorite sharers. To Ella and Tessa."

"Ella and Tessa."

Tessa swiped the warm wet streak on her cheek. Lifting her arm around Ella's shoulders, she hugged her quivering body to her side. "What are you going to be like tomorrow, Miss Romance?"

"A blubbering idiot," she said with a snort.

Tessa smacked a kiss to her forehead. "I should go find Ryland. I've left him to the wiles of the single ladies long enough."

"Tess, wait a sec."

She looked into the upturned angelic face of her friend. "Yes, ma'am."

"Don't waste it."

"Waste what?"

"It. I've watched you tonight. Something near magical exists between you and Ryland." She laid a petite hand to Tessa's cheek. "Don't waste the opportunity to have love because you are chasing a dream God placed in your past." Without another word, Ella left Tessa standing in the middle of a bustling dinner.

The thumping of her heart deafened her to the conversations and laughter.

Ella was right.

This afternoon at her apartment, every tentative feeling she had for Ryland expanded to the size of a Thanksgiving Day balloon. Glancing around the room, she caught sight of him in the same spot where she'd left him, but now he was cornered by no less than three knock-out blondes—one of whom was Bobbi Ann Risdy-Jones.

Tessa stalked across the room. *Nope, not happening tonight.*

25

"Are you sure Lily Mae won't be mad we didn't stay for dinner?" Ryland asked.

"Lil's twenty-seven shades away from caring whether anyone but her is at the party about now." Tessa hailed a cab and gave the driver her address. "Do you mind riding back with me to the loft? I know you've an early flight, but I'd like to chat a little."

He shrugged, shifting his focus to the rolling changes of the Crescent City at night. He couldn't put a pulse to Tessa's tangent personalities. In one day she'd switched from yeller to hostess to soothsayer party saver to a friend. Ever since he'd busted through the door this morning and heard her soft voice, he'd been valiantly trying to suppress his feelings. Now she was asking him back to her apartment to talk? Nothing good could come from this conversation.

His buzzing phone interrupted spiraling thoughts. Glancing at the screen he was surprised to see JT's name scrawl across. He answered. "What's up?" He chose not to wade through pleasantries.

"Joe has a huge-o favor to ask." His words were slightly slurred. The sound panicked Ryland.

"JT, what's wrong."

"Awe man, nothin's wrong. Jus' need a favor."

"What do you need?"

"You still in N'leans?"

"Yes."

"Do ya think you can go to May Belle's wedding with T.T.?"

"Lily Mae's. Where will you be?"

"Ummm...I've to go to Ft. Myers earlier than I thought. Miscalculated the days. No big. Just wanted to give Tessa a stand-up stand-in. Ha. Get it. Stand-up. Stand-in."

Ryland didn't respond. He knew this JT. This was the ugliest version. He rarely came out, but when he did nothing but a blackout or a brick wall could stop him.

"Rys, you still there?"

"Yes."

"So will you? I mean I need an answer, man. I don't want to disappoint T.T."

"Sure."

"Aww, thanks, man. You're the best. I'll pay for any extra costs. Hotel, whatever."

"Not a problem. I need to call Emma. Tell her I'll be late getting home."

"Sure. Sure. Do you mind telling Tessa? I can text her but I'm getting ready to go into a team meeting. Not sure how late I'll be."

Ryland glanced at his watch. East Coast time was later than any team meeting.

"JT..."

"Yeah, Rys, what's up?"

"Be careful. Don't do anything stupid."

"What could happen in a team meeting?"

"Don't lie to me, Joe. You and I both know you aren't in Florida and you aren't going to a team meeting. You need help. Help I can't give you over the phone. Help I'm sure you won't find in the backroom of any club you're going to with one of your 'friends'."

"OK, Granny. Just tell Tessa I'll call her next week."

The phone went dead.

Anger poured through Ryland. With a single punch to the back of the empty passenger seat, the car rattled like a tin can.

"Hey, buddy. You break it. You buy it," The cabdriver said.

"Sorry."

Tessa slid her hand over his knee. "Ryland?"

He shoved his hand through his crop of hair. "Joe's not going to make the wedding tomorrow. Gave me some lame excuse about reporting to Spring Training early. He sounded as high as a kite."

"What?"

He shifted in his seat.

Terror blanketed her face.

He couldn't give a pat cover-my-best-friend's-six answer. Not to Tessa. "Can we talk about it at your loft?"

She nodded. Sliding her hand off his knee, she laced her arms tightly across her middle, caving her shoulders toward her knees.

"Everything will be OK. I promise." He hoped he wasn't lying.

~*~

After a brief conversation when they'd arrived, Tessa had slipped into her bedroom to change clothes, giving Ryland space to set the plays in motion addressing the immediate problems. Just like game day: read and react. Only one difference. He never thought he'd be riding point on his best friend's intervention.

Now, two hours later, he had arranged for his flight to be changed to Sunday, talked to Emma—who thought he was on a grand adventure with Miss Tessa—extended his stay at his hotel, requested an early morning appointment for a suit to be tailored, and talked to Joe's brothers. Not bad for one hundred and twenty minutes.

Finished with his conference call with Sean and Mac, Ryland rested his forehead on his folded arms. *Lord, please help my friend. He doesn't know what he's doing. He's running from the difficulties of life and only making them worse. Please Lord, keep him safe.*

"How're Sean and Mac?" Tessa set a cup of crisp mint tea on the ottoman in front of him.

The bright aroma seeped through his tired frame, soothing some of the bumps of the last few hours.

"Unfortunately, they aren't surprised. JT had a flirtation with drugs and excessive drinking during his brief stint in college, but all of us thought he'd kicked it. The injury last spring forced him to take pain killers and led him down a familiar path. I understand. As an athlete you'll do anything to get better. If someone tells you one shot will make your knees not hurt or suck the pain from your shoulder so you're able to throw a ball, you'll take it—no questions—but drugs for any other reason make zero sense. An athlete's body is his trade. How you get to play a game meant for kids every Sunday afternoon for money. We all know we're living on borrowed time fulfilling the fantasy of every ten-year-old. Why do anything to risk living the dream?"

"Are you sure of what you heard? He's seemed out of sorts the past few weeks—not his old self—but I can't imagine Joey taking drugs for recreation."

"I don't believe it's for fun. I think Joe's running away from more demons than you or I could ever imagine."

"But his life is so…perfect."

"No one's life is perfect. Not even Joe Taylor."

"Don't feel like you need to stay. If you want to go home please, don't worry about Lily's wedding. Taking care of Joey is more important than holding my handbag while I have pictures taken tomorrow."

With a slight stretch he clasped her hand. "I can't think of anyone's purse I'd rather stand around and hold. I'm just sorry that Joe won't be the one to be there for you."

"About that…" She pulled her hand from his and wrapped her arms around her drawn legs. "I was going to tell Joe in the morning I wanted us just to be friends. I've been chasing an unrequited teenage crush. Trying to fulfill a shy sixteen year-old's fantasy. And I'm not sixteen anymore."

Ryland's heart grew three sizes bigger and beat with the pace of a rabbit. Thoughts swirled through his mind, but he couldn't allow himself to get distracted by the potential of Tessa. She was leavimg Gibson's Run. Her life was in New Orleans. He was sitting in the ultra-cool evidence. Focusing on finding JT tomorrow would be paramount. His friend needed him. His rabbit heart would have to wait.

~*~

Tessa's heart thumped in her ears, snuffing out the music of the city wafting through her windows. Squeezing her legs tight to her chest, silence hung between them. Only the sound of Ryland's deep breaths filled the space.

Why wasn't he saying anything? Had Lily and his sisters been wrong about Ryland's feelings? Had the kiss they'd shared weeks ago faded from his memory as quickly as yesterday's headline? Was she now the holder of the unrequited love stick?

The flex in his jaw moved at a steady rhythm as he stared into the foggy night, his expression as revealing as the eerie sky.

The teensy brave part of her wanted to lean into his side and whisper the words she'd been trying to ignore for weeks. The ones that motivated their early exit from tonight's party. But brave Tessa Tarrington wasn't. She was a piddler. Playing it safe was how she stayed dry. Sharing her true feelings about Joey was as far as her shaking legs would take her. She needed Ryland to do the heavy work. If he was willing.

Ryland wiped his hands against his pant legs and slowly stood, the creaks from his football aged body bounced against the brick walls. Glancing down at her, his lips lifted and his dimple deepened. "It's been a long day. I'll leave you to those much needed hours of shut-eye." The heels of his shoes clicked against the concrete floor.

Tessa's heart screamed for her mouth to open and ask him to stay. To listen. To talk. But her mind overrode her heart. Asking Ryland to stay. To take a chance on whatever was growing between them was risky. She didn't do risk. Risk equaled hurt. She'd endured enough hurt at the hands of others to ever willingly leap off the edge. "Good night Ryland."

Stepping across the wide threshold, he glanced over his shoulder and nodded. With a flick of his wrist, the heavy steel door slid closed.

Falling back onto the couch, she snatched a throw pillow, pulled it to her face and screamed into its muffling down. "Stupid toilet bowl life…"

26

"A little to the left. You. Yellow hair. Tall girl. You move to the left." The photographer shouted.

Never in her life had Tessa been referred to as the tall girl, but she obediently scooted a half step closer to Lily Mae's cousin, Paley, another five foot brunette beauty. After hours of hair teasing, shellacking, and painting of faces, each of the six bridesmaids was wrapped in a blue silk confection masquerading as a dress. The February morning was unseasonably warm and the humidity synonymous with New Orleans wrapped the group three hours into photos—transforming Tessa into the cotton candy she resembled—fluffy and sticky.

"Smile. Smile. Smile." Her cheeks had been twisted and tugged so often she felt as if her face had run an ultra-marathon. If only smiling burned more calories.

"OK, lovely ladies. You're through. Now just the bride and her father. Go. Go. Go." He shooed them like pigeons out of his path.

The bridesmaids, two flower girls, various mothers, and a few bridal party dates scurried from Jackson Square and up the steps into the church to wait for Lily Mae.

"Oh, I am always overcome when I enter this sacred place." Ella fanned her face as she slowly spun on her ballet flats. The ornate sanctuary overwhelmed as it welcomed one into the presence of the One Who was the ultimate Comforter.

Ella was in awe, but Tessa was strangely at home.

The famous cathedral—a hallmark of her adopted hometown—was the unequivocal opposite of her father's minute clapboard church, but there was a familiarity in the space. The Holy Spirit dwelt here.

"Hey, sisters," Bobbi Ann's high pitch bounced off the walls and scratched the back of Tessa's spine.

Tessa greeted her with a wide compulsive hug.

Between her four inch heels and her piles of hair, Bobbi Ann nearly towered over Tessa in her Ella-matching flats.

"Can you all believe how many pictures Lily Mae demanded? I know she's particular but I only had a few dozen shots taken prior to my wedding." Barely flicking her wrist, she popped open her compact and patted imperceptible shine on her nose.

"I don't think it was too many." Ella offered. "Today's Lily Mae's special day. She'll only have one wedding. She wants it to be perfection—top to bottom. I can understand why she'd want to capture the moments."

"And I seem to remember your wedding starting forty-five minutes late due to some malfunction or other." Tessa cringed. Why did she allow this woman to yank her down to a level on par with snakes and lizards?

Snapping her compact closed, Bobbi Ann pivoted and scurried to a gaggle of unsuspecting cousins of Lily May.

"Why do you let her bother you so, Tessa?" Ella asked.

"I don't know. How could she pick on Lils when

she was generous enough to invite her to be in the wedding? I really don't know how Lily Mae puts up with her."

"Didn't she tell you?"

"Tell me what?"

"I really shouldn't say. Lily Mae pinky swore me to secrecy."

Ella admitting she'd been pinky-sworn to secrecy was tantamount to her spilling the story, chapter and verse.

Ella bit off the minimalist soft pink lipstick from her bottom lip. "Well...I imagine she'll tell you after the wedding. But you must act shocked, surprised, and utterly amazed when she does."

"OK..."

"Bobbi Ann threatened to have her father revoke all of our leases and raise the rent to market value if she wasn't a bridesmaid. Starting with yours. She insisted Billy was one of Beau's dearest friends—which we all know isn't near the truth—but she placed Lily in quite the quandary. Once she's married she doesn't need her apartment anymore, but both of us do. And with all of your difficulties, she knows it could be months before you're able to pay the steep rents Mr. Risdy could demand."

That woman! Fingers of flaming fury curled and stretched from the pit of Tessa's belly to flash hot white in her vision. "Of course she used the one bit of leverage she had to make Lily Mae's day about her. I wish Lil would've said something to me. I'd have told her to tell Bobbi Ann to stuff her leases. I could find another place to live. Lily only gets one wedding."

Ella's lips lifted to a soft grin shining through her eyes. "She knew what you would say. She also saw you only hours after *the terrible, awful day* and heard your panic when you called her from the road on your way to Ohio to take care of your Dad. She refused to pile on to your worries. Having Bobbi Ann in the mix for a few hours is worth a bit of suffering to know you could return to New Orleans when you're ready."

Tugging Ella into fierce hug, a quick tear slipped down Tessa's cheek. "I don't know what I'd do without you."

Like an angel appearing to give comfort, Lily stretched her diminutive arms around Tessa and Ella. "We feel the same." Her normal over the top southern was a choked murmur.

"Now I'm really soggy." Ella said, stepping out of the sister hug.

Swiping at her falling tears, Tessa smiled. "I love you both. You didn't need to make the sacrifice for me. I would've figured a way back to the city. Back to my life. I wouldn't have been stuck in Gibson's Run forever—no matter how hard Bobbi Ann Risdy-Jones tried."

"Ahem."

Tessa turned at the rich baritone and drank in Ryland's presence. "Hey, when did you get here?" She stepped forward to give him a hug, but he quickly folded his arms across his middle.

"A few minutes ago. Where should I go and wait?" He glanced over his shoulder.

"Ryland, are you OK? Did something happen with Joey?"

"Haven't heard anything. Is there some place special you want me to sit or am I supposed to stand in the corner until you need a glass of water or your purse held?"

"Umm, you can sit anywhere on this side." He nodded, walking in the direction she pointed, sitting in the third to last pew of the mammoth sanctuary.

"Everything OK between you two, *cher*?" Lily asked.

"I don't know." Tessa turned. "But that doesn't matter. We need to get you hidden before anymore guests arrive." Swatting the air near Lily's wide dress, she led the bride's party to her special room. She was not a multi-tasker. She could only deal with one drama at a time. Ryland's cool greeting would need to be put on hold until the wedding party was sauntering back up the aisle.

~*~

Rubbing the bridge of his nose, Ryland allowed the haunted melodies wafting above the din of the cocktail hour to flow through his spirit. He'd left the rambunctious post-ceremony photo shoot as the Delta Alpha Psis and Chi Delta Taus waded knee deep into the fountain at Jackson Square. The joyous splashing sliced his worn patience.

Beginning with the taxi ride to his hotel, the arguments for why he shouldn't capitalize on Tessa's decision to break-up with Joe ran a loop in his mind. They began and ended with her life in New Orleans. Around two in the morning, the thousand mile commute lost its heavyweight battle against twenty years of unrequited love and the cycle of "why-nots" transformed into "why-yes's".

By the time he walked into the ornate church, he'd practiced his "can I take you to dinner…for the rest of our lives speech" roughly fifty times. Four little words from Tessa's lips snuffed his hope: "Back to my life."

How could he have allowed his heart to be oblivious? He'd suffered from don't-ask-don't-tell syndrome for the nearly four years of marriage to Macy. Without even a blinking an eye, he'd been infected once again.

He'd ignored all the clear warning signs: Tessa's struggles with writing. How she'd talked about her friends as if they were family. Her freak-out with the potential rejection by Terrell. Even her decision to stop seeing JT pointed to her goal of returning to New Orleans. Ryland had mistakenly allowed his hope to be fueled by Tessa's relationship with Emma, her desire to care for Tom—even the connection he'd seen evolve with her students. If she stayed through the spring, maybe Gibson's Run would once again feel like home. Then he'd have the time he needed.

Time to woo her. Time to convince her that the life he offered was better than the life she once lived. But he was wrong. He never had a chance.

The squeal of the speakers drew the collective attention of party-goers. "Where y'at?" The DJ's nasal southern twang grated against Ryland's thoughts. "We'en fixin' t'ave a *fais-do-do* to wake d'em all! *Laissez les bon temps roulet!*"

Whoops and hollers rolled through the room at the brash announcement to let the good times roll. Raised hands popped skyward, waving white napkins and swaying to the rhythm of a trumpeter's warble who led a tiny parade—with the help of a half a dozen band members rounding out his sound—through the cramped cocktail party quarters. The French doors to his left flung open revealing the wedding party led by Lily Mae and her new husband, who danced the street band and the napkin-wavers through to the dance floor.

Ryland lingered in the anteroom while streams of guests bopped and twirled through to the main dining room. He caught a glimpse of Tessa pirouetting through the throngs of partyers, her head tilted back in delighted laughter. She was in her element—with her truest family. If he loved her how could he ever think about dragging her from where she was happiest?

Lifting his soda to his lips, he stepped out onto the balcony running the length of the building. The cool air hugged him in a damp embrace. Why was he sulking about Tessa? He should be focused on trying to track down Joe. His friend needed him.

Joe was dangerously hovering on the edge of a slimy pit and he required a hand to hold.

Ryland wanted to be the hand to help drag him to safety and point him toward salvation.

The muted sounds of the city twisted with the excitement seeping through the doorway leading to the party. He leaned against the wide concrete ledge and soaked in the mix of horse drawn carriages, taxis, and Saturday revelers swarming the city street. Shutting his eyes against the moving painting, he lifted his thoughts to heaven.

Dear Father, if You are in the midst of this, let Your will alone succeed. I've stepped off Your path too many times and pursued my own agenda. Lord, tonight I give myself to You. Let me see Your will as clearly as I see the street before me. In Your name. Amen.

Dampness chilled his cheeks against the cold night air. Scrubbing his face with his palm, he focused on the party in the street, trying to block the revelry behind him. How could so much excitement bubble around him while every dream he'd ever hidden was bursting?

"Penny for your thoughts?" Tessa's soft voice flowed through him, awakening his senses with a spark.

"Why aren't you inside? Seems like there's some pretty significant bridesmaid duties afoot." He shifted to face her.

"Funny thing. I was looking for my purse carrier and water fetcher, but he abandoned me in front of the church." She shrugged. "Seems to be a grand mystery as to where he ran. But now I'm responsible for my own purse and not a single glass of water to be found. The horror. Guess I'll have to steal your soda." She swiped his glass and downed the watery contents in a single swallow.

"What do you want, Tessa?"

Setting the glass on the wall, she straightened her shoulders. "I don't know what's up with you today, but I'd like to see the friend I thought I knew, not this surly version."

"I'm sorry I'm not exactly who you want me to be." He turned from her, focusing on the moon hiding behind a cotton-pulled cloud. "I shouldn't have come for the meeting yesterday. I certainly shouldn't have jumped through hoops to get a suit to stand in a corner and watch you from a distance at a wedding for someone who barely tolerates me."

"Lil likes you just fine." She softly punched his shoulder. "She even told me you looked mighty fine in your brand new suit. High praise indeed from her southern highness."

"Regardless, I knew what I was in for. I've been standing in a corner watching you for the better part of twenty years. Why should tonight be any different?"

"What's up? You've been moody since you got to the church today. I thought I'd give you some space, but that clearly hasn't worked."

"What's up?" He swallowed the space between them with one step. Annoyance twisted to something he couldn't identify. "What's up? How about the fact I'm a stand-in date for my best friend who's doing only-God-knows-what as we speak? Or that I left my daughter with my mother to come traipsing after you on the whim you might need my help. Or the fact I've been in stupid love with you since I was six years old only to hear today you'll do everything you can to get back home—to get to New Orleans—never giving Gibson's Run or anyone there, including me and Emma, a second thought. How's that for a start to what's up?"

"What?" she whispered. Her brows tightened to a V.

"Forget it." He stepped around her and stalked toward the door.

"Wait!" Her arms locked around his waist, plastering her body against his back. "Don't go. Please, Ryland." Her breath was warm through his suit jacket.

The sparks sizzled, flowing molten heat under his skin zipping from his core through to his fingers. With aching determination, he turned in her embrace, cupping her cheeks in his hands.

Tears streamed as her bright eyes glistened with untold stories. "Please don't go. I want you here with me. Stay. Stay with me."

"Why?"

"Because," her voice broke. Her eyes shuttered.

His heart plucked like a standing bass. With a slow breath, a tremor ran through her and flowed into him. Her fingers traced his jaw. She opened her eyes. "Because I'm in stupid love with you, too."

Her confession was a whisper, but the words sang through Ryland's veins. "You love me? That doesn't make any sense."

"Of course it doesn't make sense. But love never does. I started falling for you when you shared your story with me. You were so open and transparent. The naked honesty reached inside my heart and unlocked the gate. For the first time in my life I saw you. Not the you I created—my enemy. But the you I know in my heart that you are. And every day since...I don't know? As hard as I tried not to love you, I just couldn't stop. You're pretty hard not to love."

"What about JT?"

"Joey was the dream of a teenage girl no one noticed. He erased a childish dream. And he was a good decoy—even for me. The longer I allowed him to pursue me, the longer I could avoid the feelings ready to consume me."

"What about New Orleans? Your friends? Your career?"

"I don't know about any of it, Ryland. I don't know about where I'll live or what I'll do beyond teaching on Monday. What I know—what's irrefutable—is I'm in stupid love with you, too. And stupid love always wins. Ryland I didn't want to fall in love with you. But the heart wants what the heart wants."

"And what does your heart want, Tessa?"

Resting her palm against his cheek, she swallowed. "You...my heart wants you. My heart wants you so desperately."

With a yank, he lifted her to meet his eye level.

Consuming her in his embrace, he brushed his lips to hers as light as mist. He breathed her in, blending the years of longing to one single sweet memory.

The fear of waking to the misery of knowing he was only dreaming closed his arms around her, deepening the kiss. She shoved her hands through his short hair, driving desire through him. A low murmur hummed through her and he commanded his arms to loosen their hold. Breaking his lips from hers, he pressed his mouth to her forehead.

Sliding down to standing, she trailed her hand over his chest to rest against his heart. "Wow."

"I've been waiting twenty years to hear you say you love me. The declaration deserves an epic kiss."

"Maybe the next one will be even better?" She raised to tip-toe, grazing her lips across his. The tender touch rolled through him buckling his knees and tightening his embrace. With the kiss threatening to cross a line his discipline wouldn't be able to recover, he tore his mouth from hers. Tucking her under his chin, he held her tight. He rested his back against the balcony ledge, allowing the chaos of sound to create a precious cocoon. Only moments before, the music had salted his open wounds.

Tessa's hand traced the outline of his bicep. Her warm breath heated his chest and oozed into his heart. He knew he couldn't hold her much longer. He would honor God and Tessa. Even if stepping out of her arms would be near torture.

She lifted her chin to rest against his chest; a slow tug of her lips to a grin. "Hey…"

"Hey."

"What do you want to do now?" Her focus fell to his lips.

"I'm guessing there are a few people wondering where you are." He stood tall, gently pressing her away from him.

She nodded, sliding a step back. Wrapping her arms tight around her waist, her shoulders rolled forward. A shiver ran through her.

"Come here." He pulled off his jacket, dropping it on her shoulders. "Better?"

"Yep. I'm surprised I'm this cold. It's been so warm all day." Resting her elbows on the balustrade, she chewed on her bottom lip, staring into the murky night.

"Tessa, please look at me."

She twisted to face him.

"I had to slow down. I respect God and you too much to put either of us in a situation we aren't prepared to face."

A soft smile dawned in her eyes. "Oh. I thought I did something wrong. I haven't done this much." She circled her hands between them.

"You didn't do anything wrong. In fact, you were a little too right."

"Oh…"

"Oh, is right." He gave her a slight hip check.

Metal scraping against metal caused them both to turn. Ella toddled over the threshold, balancing two tall glasses of ice water. Her cheeks flashing a gentle flush. "I'm sorry. I hope I'm not interrupting. I finally found glasses that could hold more than four ounces."

"You're not interrupting. How's the reception going?" Tessa reached for the second glass.

"Beautiful. Nothing short of spectacular."

"Exactly how Lily demanded it to be."

"Rightly so." Ella downed half her water in one

swallow. "Whew. I believe it's warmer than Houston in July in the ballroom."

Ryland was captivated by the two as they fell into their own universe chattering about the various friends and frenemies in attendance, the lovely day and the extravagance. He was so intoxicated by the moment that he barely registered the vibration in his pocket.

Taking a few steps away from the sisters, he answered the phone with a swipe.

"Ryland, its Sean. Sprout needs your help."

In a breath, his world somersaulted.

27

Tessa glanced over Ella's shoulder.

Ryland had stepped away, seeking privacy for his call.

"Things seem to be going along with the two of you," Ella said.

Tessa bit the side of her cheek. "He told me he loved me."

Ella tugged her into a crushing hug. "Oh. my! Isn't that wonderful?"

"I like breathing, Elle."

"I am sorry." Her curls bopped around her head. "But isn't this exciting? What did you say to him?"

"I told him I am in stupid love with him, too."

Ella's hands shot to her mouth in a fruitless effort to stifle her romantic glee. "But how did this happen? When did you know you were in love? Did he kiss you? This all seems so sudden, don't you think? Wasn't he the bully who caused you difficulty through school?" Her stream of questions bubbled over and the truest Ella swam to the surface of her carefully reigned personality.

"Elle, the wedding will be over before I can answer all your questions. Let's just say, I'm as surprised and delighted as you by this turn of events."

"It's quite delicious, don't you think? Star-crossed lovers never quite fitting until one day..." Ella released a sigh. She linked her arm through Tessa's and they leaned against the railing, watching the mix of natives and tourists weave the crowded street below. "If I'm not too intrusive…what was the kiss like?"

Tessa chuckled and leaned against her friend. "Better than the best writing could ever describe."

"So I guess New Orleans is on hold?"

"I want to take time. Not rush anything." Tessa glanced back to where Ryland paced in deep conversation. "But if I let my mind wander, I could conceive of only being a tourist ever again."

"Ahh…I do love love."

Chuckling, Tessa turned at the soft click of Ryland's shoes on the concrete. With one shot of his drawn features, her smile faltered. Her heart sped. "Is Emma OK?"

He reached for her hand and squeezed. "Emma's fine. Sean called. Joe's been in an accident."

"Oh, no. Is he OK? What can we do?" She tried to ignore the slight trill of pleasure running through her at the mention of her and Ryland as "we".

"All I know is he's in the hospital. The hospital couldn't give Sean more information, because Joe's still being evaluated. Sean hasn't been able to get hold of Mac, and Sean can't get a flight until tomorrow, so he asked if I could go to the hospital and manage any decisions or possible press."

"How will you get to Joe faster than Sean on a plane tomorrow?"

"He's here, Tess. He's in New Orleans."

~*~

Orderlies and nurses zipped through the waiting room in Tulane Medical Center Emergency Room calling patient names.

Ryland was at the central nurses' station speaking to a doctor.

Tessa clutched his suit jacket tight against the chill racing through her system. She didn't care what Joey had done. She just wanted him to be OK. *Father, please be with him. Help him.*

A wide palm encompassed her praying hands. Without a glance, she released her grip laying her palm open.

Ryland laced his fingers through hers. "Holy Father," Ryland said, his voice low and intimate. "We lift up JT to Your loving, healing hands. We don't know the details of what brought him here tonight, Father, but we trust Your holy embrace can heal the brokenness in any life and we claim that tonight for him. We thank You for Your gift of grace and healing. In Your Son's holy name. Amen."

Ryland's prayer was a salve to her flayed spirit. She leaned against his shoulder, seeking the comfort she'd once coveted. "Thank you. What did the nurses say?"

"They haven't received a copy of the emergency medical power of attorney from Sean. They won't tell me anything other than he's in the hospital. He could be in surgery. ICU. CCU. Or just have a broken collar bone. I feel so helpless."

"I'm sorry." She squeezed his hand. "He couldn't be in better hands. This is one of the best hospitals in the city. I had my appendix removed a couple years ago and everything was wonderful."

"You don't have an appendix? I've waited all this time and you're a chopped up model? I guess no one's perfect."

"Hey?" She slugged him in the shoulder. The shadow of a grin tugged at his lips. "You're teasing me. Still a little touchy, I guess."

"I think you're perfect. Appendix or no appendix."

"Ugh, did you read that on the back of a greeting card?" She tugged her hand from his.

"No, you bring out the poet in me."

"Really?"

"Really. Listen. Roses are red. Violets are blue. To T.T. Tarrington, I will always be true."

She chuckled. "That's awful."

"I should probably leave the writing to you and Emma." He brushed his lips to her forehead.

"Sound plan."

"Excuse me, Mr. Jessup?" A doctor draped in scrubs loomed over them.

"David?" Tessa recognized the tall, lean, slightly tan doctor from church small group. "When did you start at Tulane?"

"Tessa?" She stood and he immediately enveloped her in a tight embrace. "When I finished my residency they recruited me to be the emergency attending. Where have you been? I was hoping to debate this month's book with you. "

"Taking care of my dad in Ohio." She stepped back from his hug, sliding to Ryland's side.

"You two know each other?" Ryland asked.

"Umm, yeah. We're in small group together. Ryland Jessup, this is David McCullen." Tessa said. "But we can catch up another time. You have news on Joe?"

"Yes. We received Mr. Taylor's medical power of attorney and his brother's consent to discuss his condition and course of treatment with you. Would you follow me?" He led Ryland and Tessa through the maze of gurneys and waiting patients to a small span of rooms with frosted glass doors.

Through the door sat two overstuffed chairs and a small love seat. David sat on the arm of one of the chairs but Ryland leaned against the open wall consuming the majority with his broad shoulders. Tessa hesitated entering the room, unsure of her place in this moment. She wasn't dating Joe anymore. She shouldn't be privy to his secrets.

"I'll wait outside."

Ryland shook his head. "JT and Sean will be fine with you knowing. Please sit." He guided her to the small love seat.

David leaned forward and shut the door with a slight push. "Mr. Taylor was admitted roughly two hours ago with multiple lacerations, a broken wrist, a torn ACL and some internal bleeding forcing emergency surgery. The team was able to successfully stop the bleeding; however with the mix of amphetamines and alcohol in his system, we'll need to monitor him for at least the next forty-eight hours."

"Do you know what happened, Dr. McCullen?" Ryland asked. "Was he driving?"

"No. He was the passenger. The driver had minor injuries and is set to be released in the next few hours. The driver was just under the legal limit. The police are choosing not to pursue action at this time as no one, aside from Mr. Taylor, was injured."

"Has anyone called asking about Joe?"

A fog floated over Tessa. Ryland's and David's conversation hummed in her ears. Her mind zoomed through questions she couldn't answer. *Amphetamines?* Why would Joe take a drug banned by major league baseball? *Drinking?* At least he wasn't driving, but was the driver intoxicated? This was not the Joey Taylor she'd known since kindergarten or the sweet man who'd courted her the past few weeks. What kind of pain was he enduring to be trying to escape it with extremes?

"Tessa?" David's voice broke through her haze. "Tess, are you all right?"

Both David and Ryland squatted before her.

Ryland brushed his fingers across her cheek.

The touch registered the dampness. How long had she been crying? "I'm OK." Her voice was a mix between a croaked frog and laryngitis.

"You're sheet white," Ryland said.

"I'm fine. Really." She pushed his hand aside and straightened to as tall as her body would allow. "When can we see Joey?"

"He's in recovery, but he won't be moved to a room for a few hours." David said with a pat to her shoulder. "Visiting hours will be done before you've an opportunity to see him. Why don't you go home? If there's an issue the hospital will contact you."

"David, please isn't there any way?"

He dropped his focus to the chart. "The nurses in recovery are friends of mine. I might be able to swing something for you, but I can't promise."

"Thank you." She squeezed his hand. The room tilted to the left. Stumbling forward, Ryland snatched her into the crook of his arm, tucking her to his side.

"Are you OK?" he whispered.

She nodded. "Just a little lightheaded."

David's face twisted to a frown. "When was the last time you ate? You know how you get when you don't eat."

Ryland's entire frame stiffened and his grip on her tightened.

"I know. As soon as we see Joey, I'll make Ryland take me to get some food. Deal?"

"Deal. Let's sneak you on up."

Ryland and Tessa followed David through the emergency room to a bank of elevators. The trio rode to the third floor—the ding of the floors punctuating the whine of elevator tunes. She sucked in shallow breaths. The buzz of her brain fought against the swell of nausea rolling in her stomach.

Ryland stood stiff beside her, his arm wrapped protectively around her shoulders, but his silence cascaded a waterfall of worry through her. What was he thinking? Feeling? Her old memories of jokester Jessup clashed with the clenched jawed man holding her. If his intensity matched his concern, what had she missed in her fogged state in the consultation room? She released a slow breath as the doors slid open.

David ushered them to a quiet corner to the left of the nurses' station. He chatted in low whispers to an attending nurse.

Ryland stared forward, his jaw pulsing.

"Are you OK?"

He nodded, shifting his focus to her, anxiety shadowing his steely gaze.

She lifted her hand to his chest—resting lightly above his heart. "He'll be OK. I know it. Things will get back to normal."

"What's normal, Tessa?"

She opened her mouth to respond, but David motioned them forward.

"He's sleeping in the third bay. Since he's the only patient in recovery, Jill's being gracious enough to let you visit him." David winked at the petite redhead hiding a smile while she shuffled papers behind the desk. "You'll only have five minutes. I want to warn you. He probably won't wake up. He looks worse than his condition. He has bruising from the accident, and he's pretty bandaged, but he's stable. We expect him to make a full recovery."

Beeping machines and the drip of medicine through Joe's IV broke through the silence.

"Oh, my." A soft gasp seeped through Tessa's lips.

The beautiful man, who, only days before walked her home and kissed her good night, was engulfed in layers of crisp white cloth. His head was wrapped with gauze and the bit of face she could see was swollen and scraped, beginning to show signs of transitioning from red to bruised purple. Tears sprang from her eyes, flooding her vision. Stepping out of Ryland's grip, she rested a hip on the side of Joe's bed and brushed his bangs from his forehead. "What did you do, Joey?" She whispered.

"I'll give you a few minutes." David's voice dropped low. "Be careful of the wires and his wrist." The subtle squeak of rubber against the floor signaled his retreat.

She swallowed against the surge of weeping wanting to bust from her body. Joe looked so weak lying in the sterile bed, his face devoid of the joy-filled spark.

Ryland hovered at the curtained entrance. With legs spread wide, his arms were laced across his middle and his narrowed gaze observed the full length of his best friend.

"He'll be OK." She said.

Ryland turned to her. His eyes crested with tears

unshed. "I should have stopped him. I knew. This is my fault."

Tessa stepped to him, forcing him to drop his focus to her. "Listen to me. This is no one's fault but Joey's and the driver's. Joey made his choice tonight. For reasons we may never understand. It was his choice. We can love him through to healing, but healing will be his choice too."

"Thank you." His hand brushed her hair over her shoulder, caressing the length of her neck with a slow, steady cadence waking her dormant butterflies and reviving her sagging spirit. With a quick peck to her forehead, he whispered. "Let's get you some food. I'll take care of everything else in the morning."

"We will, Coach. We will."

28

When Ryland had left Tessa's twenty-four hours earlier, he'd never believed he'd again cross the threshold. And yet, he sat legs outstretched on her L-shaped sofa staring into the distant chaos, a recap of the day's events playing on his mental highlights reel. Six months ago, if he'd been given coffee by his future-self, complete with the accounting of this day, he'd have snorted the scalding beverage through his nose and recommended a good psychologist. How was a person to balance the realization of a lifelong dream against the near destruction of his best friend?

"If I keep offering you pennies for your thoughts you'll have Emma's college paid before she enters elementary school." Tessa handed him a glass of water, setting her cup of tea on the ottoman. Scrubbed clean of the layers of caked make-up and dressed in threadbare sweats topped with a plain white tee, she embodied every simple, soft dream he had.

"You look amazing," he whispered.

"*Pfft.*" She shook her head. "I look ready to crawl under my covers and sleep for six years—but six hours will do. How are you? Did you talk to Sean?"

"His flight arrives at ten-thirty. He's heading straight to the hospital. I extended my hotel room until Friday. Hopefully, he and Mac will sort this situation long before then."

"Are you staying?"

"No. I need to get back to Emma and school. I just wanted to take something off of Sean's plate. He's always doing for everyone else—especially JT."

She stretched her arm across the sofa and squeezed his shoulder. "I don't know how I blinded myself to your generosity all these years."

"If I'd only known at six that being nice to JT's big brother would get you to smile at me, I would've totally skipped *Suzi's On Main* and written you a list of all the nice things I planned on doing in the future."

"Oh, those stupid underpants…"

With her chuckle, the breath he held released a flood of relief through his body.

"I may never fully forgive you for the thirteen years of torture. What a horrible nickname."

"One day, I'll explain how good intentions are similar to the best laid plans."

"They do often go awry." She lifted her mug to her lips, blowing soft to cool the steaming contents.

His phone chirped, drawing his attention. He swiped to answer a number he didn't recognize. "This is Ryland Jessup."

"Whew." The voice cracked. "I'm glad I finally connected with you, Ryland. This is Charlie Messing, JT's agent."

Ryland remembered meeting Charlie at a Spring Training game a few years earlier.

"What can I do for you, Charlie?"

"Sean said you're running point on the JT situation until he gets down to New Orleans. I'll be there on the red eye out of Las Vegas tonight. Any updates on his progress?"

"I'm sorry Charlie, but if you've talked to Sean, he would've told you how JT was doing. I'm not comfortable sharing my friend's medical status with someone I've met one time."

"Understood. Appreciate your discretion. Not everyone in your situation could be so trusted. Sorry to put you in a tough spot. Just worried. JT's my best client and I consider him a friend. You can imagine how the news shook me up."

"Well, if you want to do something for your friend and client, I suggest you ensure you are the last person to hear this news until JT decides what to do."

"Roger that. Night."

Ryland tossed his phone on the ottoman and walked to the broad expanse of windows.

"What did he say?" Tessa asked, her reflection just to the right of his in the window. Two silhouettes with nothing but time. How different reality was from an image. She slid her arm around his waist, resting her head against his bicep.

"Charlie's just worried. We all are. How could JT be so stupid? Riding with someone who'd been drinking? Not caring about anyone but himself. I knew JT was self-centered but I never thought he was selfish. His brothers have dealt with enough loss for a lifetime. They've cleaned up after JT for decades, and now almost ten years after their mom died, they're still mopping up his messes." He kicked the wall four times shaking loose mortar like snow on their heads.

"Hey. I have a security deposit I'd like to get back."

"I'm sorry..." Resting his forehead against the glass, the tears he'd checked since early this morning burst through to sobs. Body shaking, he slid to the floor. Shedding the coach's armor he diligently used to keep the world at bay, he wept.

Tessa cradled him to her chest. "It'll be OK." She said. Her arms tightened around his shoulders, her fingers not quite touching.

But in her half hug he felt more comfort than years of marriage or friendship. She gave and asked nothing in return.

Moments turned to minutes. Minutes turned to he-didn't-know-how-long, but finally his tears shifted to a trickle. His breaths came in a steady stream rather than gulps. He pushed himself to sit, resting his back against the rough brick wall. With little thought to propriety, he lifted Tessa in his lap and held her tight to his chest, unwilling to release his one source of comfort.

"Joey isn't Macy." Tessa broke through the silence with a bomb.

"I know." He felt his settled anger bubble to the surface. "I never said he was."

"Yes, you did."

He tried to shove her from his lap. He wouldn't let his anger out on a woman. He used punching bags. But she resisted his pressure, setting her hands on his shoulders and forcing him to look her in the eye.

"Listen." Her voice low, laced with strength. "I may be overstepping my bounds. I know what Joey did tonight was stupid and reckless, but he had the sense not to drive himself. He may not have been aware the driver was intoxicated. No matter what kind of spiral Joey is spinning he would never intentionally hurt anyone. But I think Macy would have."

With the strength of twenty years of football training, he shifted Tessa to sit on the floor. He brushed unseen wrinkles from his pants, reached for his jacket and phone. His hand was on the door handle, aching to slam the heavy metal sheeting open.

"Don't run away from this, Ryland," Tessa said.

He closed the five foot gap between them in two steps. "I don't run away. That's your MO, lady. I stick. I stick by my best friend regardless of his choices. I stick in a marriage that used up all its love to create the perfect little girl. I stick by my wife's memory of perfection so my daughter won't have to know who her mother really was. I stick, Tessa. You run." He backed her against the wall. "You ran away from high school. Hiding in libraries, backstage, and coffee shops. You ran so fast and far from Gibson's Run, you ended up below sea level. You ran away from a job you loved because you faced one obstacle. You are the runner. Not me."

"I know I am. So trust me when I say—one runner to another—you are running so fast you don't even feel your feet moving." Stroking his cheek with her soft palm, his pulse sizzled through his skin. "You need to address the pain of Macy before you see Joey tomorrow, or you may say something you can't take back. Anger has a way of feeding anger like oxygen to a fire. Let me help you let it all go." She linked her fingers through his and tugged him toward the couch.

Sitting knee to knee with Tessa he released her hand. He swirled his fingers through the plush gray fabric hoping she would start. Say something. Anything to clarify his emotions masquerading as a ping pong ball.

"Why did you say Joey was selfish?"

With a shrug he lifted his gaze. She was a beauty. But she had a strength hovering under the surface encouraging him to flay open the barely healed wounds from his last Macy laced conversation. "He should have been at the wedding. If he'd followed through with his responsibilities he wouldn't have been in the position to have to make a decision."

"Coulda, shoulda, woulda. Three great words of 'if only'. We can't play the what-if game, Ryland. We have to focus on what happened—facts will clarify your feelings. Why did you say Joey is selfish?"

"He…" Ryland closed his eyes and rested his head against the pillowed top roll of the sofa. "When everything isn't coming up Joe, he chooses avoidance over acceptance."

"And that's wrong. But most of us chose a similar path at some point in our lives."

"Not me. From the time I could walk, my father instilled the need to own my mistakes. Face my problems. Life becomes complicated when you lie to yourself."

"True. But most of us don't have the discipline of a Jessup. We need a little grace."

He stared at the vaulted ceiling. "I've given JT pass after pass. When he missed Emma's baptism to meet his girl of the moment. When he was a day late to my wedding. When he bagged college because he couldn't make it to class." Shifting his head to the right, he stared into Tessa's bright green eyes. "When he chased after the one girl he knew I've been in love with since I saw her on the playground." A flush of pink stained her cheeks and stirred a yearning deep in his spirit.

"OK. Let's say you've shown him ample opportunities to get his life right. Why are you angry with him?"

"As I said, he's selfish. He doesn't take ownership. Avoidance instead of acceptance."

"Why is that bad? Who else did the same thing?"

Thump. An unseen fist smacked his gut. He wasn't angry at Joe. "Macy." He shoved his hand through his hair. "Macy spent our whole life together avoiding reality. She wanted a bigger house. A bigger car. A bigger star. She wouldn't accept the life I offered her. She threw it away like day old bread and went in search of...I don't even know, but her selfishness left my daughter without a mother and future questions with no answers. And who can I tell, huh? My mom, who never wanted me to marry Macy? Or how about her parents, who've built a shrine in their living room to their only daughter? I can't tell anyone. My wife—the mother of my child—chose Everett Tanner, my teammate, over me."

"Everett Tanner the quarterback? That was who you found..."

"She spit in the face of God and our family to feed her ego. My wife hated me so much she drove her car into a ravine rather than stay married to me. How could she choose anyone or anything above Emma?" *Breathe. Breathing is good, Jessup.* Every limb felt like jelly. If he stood he would just collapse into a pile of limp on the floor.

The smooth length of Tessa's fingers wrapped around his clenched fist. His breath slowed to steady.

"I don't know the whys of Macy's choices," Tessa said. "but you'll never be free of the weight of them if you don't let go of the anger you're shoving into compartments in your mind. Every time someone disappoints, you'll be right back in this pit. You're stronger and braver than Macy's decisions."

"I thought I had let it go. I really did."

"Healing is a process. It requires discipline and

recognition. One day—hopefully before Emma does something really teenager-esque like miss curfew, go to a party, or take your car without permission—you'll have healed. And you'll be able to be plain old disappointed in Emma without bringing old hurts into it."

He nodded. Unclenching his fist, he laced his fingers with hers. "But to be clear, Emma will never do anything wrong. My daughter is perfect, and will not even think about disobeying me. Including not dating until she's thirty."

"Now that we've covered projection, would you like to discuss denial?"

With a chuckle he hauled her into his arms resting her back against his chest. Her head tucked neatly under his chin, he pressed a light kiss to her temple. "Thank you."

"Anytime." She snuggled into his embrace.

"How did you become so insightful?"

"Years of wading through other people's history has a tendency to create a need to recognize when the truth is being hidden behind a wall. The walls come in varying shades—grief, anger, regret, and so on—but rarely is the wall the destination. A good story is about digging beneath the layers."

"Thank you for not letting me brick in my wall."

"Anytime."

He closed his eyes and pulled in a deep breath.

"Ryland?" Tessa's voice barely a murmur above the street din.

"Mmhmm…"

"What will we do about Joey?"

29

The elevator doors swooshed open. Tessa stepped across the threshold and was hit with the pungent aroma of disinfectant mixed with body fluids. The sting in her nose drowned the subtle fragrance of the petite glass bowl filled with gardenias she carried. Glancing at the numbered signs for guidance, she walked down the narrow hall toward Joey's room. The click of her low heels against the tiled hall hardly registered against the clamor of a dozen new imagined scenarios regarding Joey.

She was happy she'd reduced the number from the hundreds of possible outcomes she weighed in the last five hours. On her three mile walk, she'd vetted options including Joey making a run for the border, charming his way out of the hospital and into another drunken car ride, or his elopement with the mysterious driver from last night's joyride. She assumed the driver was female. The only logical reason for Joey to ride in a car driven by an intoxicated driver was she was...well, a she.

After a long discussion, neither she nor Ryland were aligned on what would happen when Joey was confronted. They both agreed, regardless of the outcome, Joey needed all of the support the two of them could rally. Part of the support menu included her and Ryland arriving separately at the hospital. Even if Joey's feelings toward her were barely present, they didn't want to allow him the opportunity to deflect. Instead of meeting Ryland at his hotel, she followed her normal Sunday routine in New Orleans. Read. Walk. Coffee. Shower. Church.

The normalcy of the morning refreshed her worn spirit. Worshiping amidst the comfort of a familiar setting with friends who were her family in the city centered her heart on God. Discerning His will regarding Joey's situation would require all of her spiritual fortitude and a few of her PK tricks. Scanning the room numbers, she weaved between medical carts, gurneys and the pool of doctors on rounds. His room number beckoned twenty steps in the distance.

The hall seemed to narrow, tilting to the left.

Her legs locked. The burning simmer in her stomach rumbled, threatening volcanic eruption. Resting her back flush to the wall, she closed her eyes. *Holy God, how did we get here? Help Joey get the help he needs to be the wonderful man You created him to be. Please don't allow my selfishness to interfere with Your will. If this isn't Your will. If you desire some other path for Ryland and me...and Joey, I pray that Your will be done Father. Amen.* She opened her eyes.

The hall straightened. Nurses bustled. Sunlight softened the austere floor.

With a quick knock, she entered Joey's room on a muffled response. "Oh, Joey." Tears sprang to her eyes.

Stretched across the bed, one long lean leg was encased in a series of straps and metal from ankle to hip. His right arm rested cross body in a sling and the faint beginnings of a purple and gold smudge spread across his beautiful jaw.

"You should see the other guy." His voice was muffled through swollen lips adorned with a jagged split.

Setting the stout vase of gardenias, impulsively purchased in the gift shop, on the window ledge, she perched on the vinyl covered chair beside his bed. Avoiding the myriad of beeping boxes and dangling IV drips, she lightly cupped her hands around his unbound arm. "Why were you in New Orleans? I thought you were in Florida? Do you want to tell me what happened?" She kept her voice soft and low.

He tilted his bandaged head into the stack of pillows supporting his injured body. "I came in a day early. Take a break from my big brother's nagging. But didn't want to bother you. Thought you'd be busy doing wedding stuff. I'm sorry I missed the wedding. I bet that little firecracker was a gorgeous bride. But she probably couldn't hold a candle to my tantalizing Tessa."

"Lily Mae was lovely."

Shifting his gaze from the ceiling to connect with hers, he lifted the corner of his cracked lip. "Modest much?"

She remained silent.

The twinkle on the surface faded, revealing etched pain mirroring his injuries. "I'm sorry," he whispered.

"I forgive you." She squeezed his left hand. An unnoticed tear trickled from the corner of his eye.

The drape of hushed peace fell around them.

"Tessa, would you pray with me?"

She swallowed against the growing lump. "Of course. Always." Lacing her fingers through his, she sandwiched his hand. "Would you like to start?"

"Lord," Joey started. "In all of this mess, I know I'm wrong. Please forgive me. Please..."

She sensed his exhaustion was overwhelming his

will. With a squeeze of his hand, she interceded. "Father, we trust in Your will. I lift up Joey to You and Your care. I pray, Father, forgive him. And help him to forgive himself. We love You, Lord. Thank You for loving us more. In Your Son's Holy Name. Amen."

"Amen." The resonant voice seeped into her spirit. She twisted on the chair.

Ryland was leaning against the doorframe, barely inside the room, but his presence quivered and revived better than a steaming cup of chicory coffee. A smile stretched her lips. Every prickling sense urged her to jump into his arms in a single leap, but his gaze cautioned.

"Glad to see you've finally woken from your beauty sleep, JT." He closed the brief distance to Joey's bedside in a stride. "From the look of you, a few dozen more hours should get you back to pretty boy form."

"It's a burden only some of us can bear."

"Have you two had a chance to chat?" Ryland asked.

"A little, but more than enough," Tessa responded.

"JT, Sean's in the cafeteria. I think he finally was able to track down Mac. Do you want me to go and get him?"

Joey's shook his head. "I need to talk to you." Glancing to Tessa, his lips tightened to a straight line. "Both of you."

Ryland tugged a chair near the bed, the scrape of the legs echoing against the barren walls.

Joey glanced from Ryland back to Tessa, releasing a sigh. "I screwed up. I've been screwing up for months—maybe years. I know you know about the PED's and the uppers. I know you know about the car, and the drunk girl. You know all of my recent dirty laundry. But my biggest mess isn't what happened last night, or bailing on the wedding, or even trying to salvage my career in the stupidest better-living-through-chemistry way possible. The biggest mess I made was inserting myself between the two of you."

"Rys, I know you've been in love with T.T. since we were six. My ill-fated attempt at fashion gift-giving advice caused a rift back then. Six weeks ago, I jumped in when I should have been the best wingman on the planet. I'm sorry."

Ryland nodded, keeping his focus on Joey.

"My sweet Tessa," Joey said, reaching for her hand. "I've been trying to fulfill some whacked high school bucket list by dating you. From the time you were thirteen—man those long braids killed me—I wanted to find a way for you to notice me. Took thirteen years, but here we are."

She clasped her free hand around their linked fingers. Tenderness poured through her.

"But you weren't mine. Not then. Not now. God has been drawing you and this lug head together since the day He brought your dad to our church. Gibson's Run needed the Tarringtons. But I have a feeling, that the Tarringtons needed Gibson's Run too."

He rested her hand atop Ryland's wide thick fingers.

"You two belong with each other. I knew it the moment Rys left the coffee shop instead of listening to us sing. And I saw it in your eyes, Tessa, the instant you knew he was in the room today."

The burn of salty tears slipped down her cheeks and across her lips. She leaned forward and pressed the barest of kisses on an unbruised cheek. "How'd you get to be so observant?"

"Lots of time on the IR, watching the stands from the dugout. Darlin', everything you ever needed to know can be learned through baseball."

"Noted."

Ryland's face was blank, Coach Jessup firmly in place. "Don't use this noble gesture as an excuse, JT."

"What are you implying?" Joey sat as straight as his broken body would allow.

"I'm saying you're pulling a JT. You're being overly generous, kind, shifting the focus off yourself and on to someone else–or in our case someones. Magnanimous doesn't look good on you, Joe."

"Ryland!" Tessa hissed.

"No Tess, let him finish," Joey said. "He obviously has something to share."

Ryland shot up from the chair.

Tessa's hand fell from his.

"JT, this is a pattern. You mess up and turn contrite." Ryland began pacing the tiny width between the bed and the white wall. "You've been allowed to smooth over every mistake with charm. But not this time. Not this time, JT. Today you have to take ownership of your actions. You have to see what your choices cost you. You'll lose everything if you don't make a complete one eighty. Do you understand?"

Tessa swiveled her gaze between Ryland and Joey, but she didn't need to look Joey in the eye to know how Ryland's speech was impacting him. "Ryland, enough," Tessa whispered. "I think half the hospital heard you."

"But did he?"

"I heard you." Sean said from the open door. "And you're right." Sean turned his focus to Joey. "Sprout, you have to take responsibility for this situation. The whole situation. From last spring through last night."

Joey tensed.

Tears bubbled in Tessa's chest. An awkward joke rested on her tongue, aching to cut the heavy tension. But she remained silent. She only knew the Joey of her teenage crush and the man who wooed her these past few weeks. These men—one a brother of blood, the other a brother of choice—knew the demons Joey was fighting and what weapons they needed to destroy them.

Sean stepped to the end of the bed beside Ryland. Tall and lean, a shadow of Ryland's muscled football frame, but both equally oozed intimidation.

"I spoke with Mac. He has a facility his team uses to help rehab players."

"I don't need rehab for one stupid night." Joey huffed.

"It's primarily for physical rehab. Have you looked at your body?"

"Trust me, I feel it. But I don't need some fancy rehab facility. I'll just go to Florida and work with the team doctors and trainers."

"That's not an option. Charlie called me last night. He'll be here late this afternoon." Sean stepped forward and clutched his hands to the footboard. "The team is suspending you. They're listing you as IR. They don't want the spin during Spring Training. But based on your long track record of screw ups, they've invoked the morals clause in your contract."

"They can't do that." Joey argued.

"They have every right. According to Charlie, they warned you last summer after the lake party you had one strike left. Last night you struck out."

Joey tilted his gaze to the ceiling, kneading the small space between his neck and shoulders with his left hand.

"Sprout...Joe,"—Sean moved to the open side of the bed. His voice low—"this is bad. I'll not sugarcoat it, but you can crawl out of it."

"How?" Joey's voice was a whisper.

"One step at a time. The honest, generous, kind-hearted, caring brother I know and love is still in you. You just need to let him be in control—rather than the guy who's been pulling your strings the last few years."

Tessa chewed on her bottom lip, lifting up silent offerings to the only One able to transform Joey. *Please help him.*

"When do I go to Mac's place?" Joey asked.

"He's sending the corporate plane tomorrow. I'll fly with you to South Carolina. Help you get settled. There's one other thing. The facility offers a program we both think you need to pursue," Sean said, leaning back in his chair.

"I'm not a drug addict or an alcoholic, Sean."

"I didn't say you were, but I think, we think, you have some stuff to work through. Why you were so willing to take a shortcut to try and help your shoulder or why getting in a car with a complete stranger you knew was intoxicated was a good idea. You need to deal with the underlying reasons for why you're making these bad choices."

"Whatever. I don't want to sit around a circle and discuss my feelings. I'm a professional athlete, Sean. I need to do. Hit a ball. Run some miles. I don't need to feel."

"Maybe that's part of the problem." The words

tumbled from Tessa's mouth before she could seal her lips.

"You, too?" Joey asked. A deep crease dented his marred forehead.

She gently laid a hand over his. "Joey. You've so much joy hidden deep in you. Joy you let out for fits and spurts. But it mostly remains buried under mountains of pain you aren't willing to sort through. I understand, because I hate feeling the hard stuff, too." She sucked in a deep breath. "But lately, I've realized, avoiding the hard stuff only allows for more garbage and junk to build. The faster you run away from your feelings the more dangerous they become. The junk in our lives wants to be thrown away. That's why every time we try and ignore it, the junk rears its ugly face in weird and sometimes awful ways. You don't know why you keep messing up? You keep messing up because you aren't willing to clean out your junk drawer. Instead, you keep piling more junk in it until one day it'll explode. Then, we won't have the privilege of having this conversation."

Ryland's thick fingers squeezed her shoulder. When had he moved behind her?

Sean began describing the facility to Joey. The details buzzed around her head, but Joey appeared to be absorbing each one. Pleasantly in a fog, she leaned her head softly against Ryland's chest, his heat warming the places chilled with emotion.

"How long will I be locked away?" Joey asked.

"The doctors think it will take about ten to twelve weeks for your leg to recover. You may need additional surgery on your shoulder. Could set you back another half dozen weeks. Then the real physical therapy begins."

"I'm not staying in a hospital for six months, Sean."

"We'll figure something out. First things first. You need to get that leg on the mend. All that down time will be the perfect opportunity to work through... what'd you call it, Tessa, his junk drawer?"

She smiled. "He may have like a chest of drawers, but yeah, they all have some junk that needs cleaned out." The Lord was working a miracle right before her eyes. Joey would be OK. His recovery wouldn't be easy, but he would be OK.

As the two brothers began to negotiate through the details of Joey's next adventure, Ryland whispered in Tessa's ear. "We need to talk."

30

Nearly dragging Tessa through the hospital lobby, Ryland barely noticed the warm sun on his cheeks as they hustled outside. "Where'd you park?" Ryland asked.

"Umm…Gibson's Run?"

No car? Huh, hadn't really thought that through. Cab. He made a sharp pivot toward the cab stand. Stumbling forward, his arm yanked as he tried to pull an immovable Tessa with him. "Hey."

Tugging her fingers from his grip, she scowled. "Hey, yourself, Coach Jessup. What's your damage? Where's the fire?"

"Come on, Tessa," Ryland sighed. "We need a cab. We need to go."

"No. You said we needed to talk. So talk, bubba."

Scanning the sidewalk, he shoved his hand through his short hair. No cabs. Not a trolley or a bus insight. "I'd rather do this in private."

"Jessup, there's no one out here but you and me. Sunday. Remember? This is the South. We take it very seriously." Glancing at her watch, she shrugged. "It's one. People are either sitting down to Sunday supper or they're still catching the Holy Ghost. They won't be rounding out the day with visitations for another few hours." Shaking her head, she closed the few steps to a slightly rusted wrought iron bench and sat. With the demure grace that drove him crazy at sixteen, she crossed her ankles, tucking her skirt around her knees.

"Why don't you take a little sit down? Draw a breath. Or two. Maybe that talk you said we needed will rediscover its words." She patted the bench.

Sitting beside her, every lecture from his mother rushed through him. *Always keep room for the Holy Spirit, Ryland. God gave man woman to respect, love, and honor her. Not for any other reason. Remember she's a child of God. Like a sister.*

The electricity vibrating through him simply by sitting beside Tessa did not remind him of any moment he ever had with any of his five sisters. Not even close. Sucking in a deep breath, all he could see was her. All he could think was Tessa. Her delicate scent wafted through his senses clouding his foggy mind. The love bursting through him trounced every rational thought.

"Ryland?" Tessa's voice whispered—asking the unasked question.

Reaching for her hand, he laced his fingers through hers. "Tessa, what you did for JT...how did you take something we've been struggling with for years to show him and make it so simple? You were magic."

A soft curl of her lips tempted him to kill the talk.

"I didn't do anything. Definitely wasn't magic. At first...at first I was so angry with you and then Sean. I thought you were so unfair. He had one bad night. He was trying to mend fences with you. He seemed so unselfish. And you were so harsh."

"I know. But I've tried compassion before. Compassion fails with Joe. He's a charmer. Has been his whole life. But he's also an athlete. After I talked to him earlier this week, I knew he wouldn't be able to make the tough choices he needed to make without a little coach pressure."

"I just don't see the Joey you see."

"You see the man-child you had a crush on all through high school."

Thick lines marred her forehead. "I think that's what I saw a month ago, but over the last few weeks, I've seen a desperately sad child of God in need of help. I know what I see because at times I feel as if I'm looking at myself when I see the light fade from Joey's eyes.

"Ryland, I've been so lost for the past few months. Probably more like the last few years. *The terrible, awful day* when my whole career was stolen from my apartment was the flush, but my life was already swirling the toilet bowl. I just didn't know it. After Momma died, I felt this overwhelming need to control everything in my life. No mistakes. No judgment. I needed to be perfect.

"My job gave me the ability to control a story. But no one knew I was the writer. Never risk anyone but my editor and the seven people who knew I was ghost writing judging my work. But with *the terrible, awful day*, the gift of anonymity was stolen from me." Her lips twisted. A single tear raced down her cheek. "So, you see, I can empathize with Joey more than you know. What I said to him wasn't magic or some unique wisdom from years of writing others' stories. I was talking to myself."

His heart twisted. The robbery evoked fear and failure in her. Returning home was merely an escape from the life she deemed a catastrophe.

She shifted across the bench, her leg leaned into the length of his. Her cheek rested against his bicep. "In the past few weeks, I've discovered more junk in my drawer. It's at capacity. I desperately want to throw it all away. I'm just not certain where to toss it."

He wrapped an arm around her shoulders, drawing her to his side. "Someone recently told me recognizing the situation was the first step."

"Very wise advice." Lifting her chin to rest against his chest, she smiled. "Well, hello, Coach Jessup."

"Hello, Miss Tarrington." Brushing his lips tenderly across hers, a flash zoomed through his system, setting off his caution light. "You're amazing. You know?" He said, resting his chin atop her silky hair.

"I know, but why do you think I'm amazing?"

"Too many whys to count."

"Let's just try a few." He could feel her smile against his chest.

"Fishing for compliments?"

"Well, if they were freely given I'd have no need to go fishing."

He lowered his lips to the crown of her head. "You're wise. You shower a four year-old girl with affection. You care for your dad. You care for your clients. You love me."

Twisting, she rested her palms against his chest. "I'm awesome because I love you?"

"Didn't I mention how wise you are?"

"*Hmph.*"

The subtle sounds of Sunday afternoon at the visitor's entrance of the hospital enveloped them. Ryland trailed his hand down Tessa's spine, her silky hair gliding under his fingers. Drawing a deep breath, her scent flowed through him. Closing his eyes, he tightened his arm around her.

"What time is your flight home?" she asked.

"Same as yours."

"So, 9-ish?"

"Yep."

"We need to be at the airport in five hours."

"Yep."

"So...are we going to sit here for the next five hours while random folks pass by and stare at the odd Yankee couple cuddled on a bench outside the trauma wing? You know everyone probably thinks something tragic happened."

"Tragic?"

"Of course. They probably think I lost the love of my life to some horrible disease, or an awful accident, and you're his dear friend trying to console me before you move in on his territory." She shrugs. "Quite tragic."

"Indeed. And you're worried about writing fiction?"

"Just saying...two people...nearly conjoined outside a hospital. Either we're really weird twins no one would medically be able to explain or tragedy. Only two options."

"How about a young couple in love stealing a moment?" Ugh! He sounded like a greeting card wrapped in a two pound box of Valentine's candy.

"Seriously? When did you become the romantic?"

"Guess you bring it out in me. I'm so gallant and romantically spontaneous I stopped by your apartment this morning, hoping to take you to breakfast, but you were already at church."

She propped her chin on her folded hands resting on his chest. "How'd you know I went to church?"

"Sunday. Deductive reasoning. And Bobbi Ann was leaving your building just as I was crossing the street. She told me you were at church."

Her brow furrowed. "How'd Bobbi Ann know I was at church?"

"Don't you go every Sunday? Haven't you been attending the same church the entire time you've lived in New Orleans? She probably figured you would want to get back in a routine."

"Huh? Makes sense. It's just disturbing…"

"What's disturbing?"

"The thought of Bobbi Ann Risdy knowing anything about my life. One can't give ammunition to a woman like Bobbi Ann. And why was she in my building? She lives across town."

"Doesn't her dad own your apartment? Maybe she was running an errand for him."

"Yeah," she said, cuddling against his side, all thoughts of big-haired Bobbi Ann Risdy-Jones slipping from her mind.

31

Tessa's life tumbled into a new normal. By the following week, every moment of normalcy revolved around the universe of Ryland Jessup. She continued to stop at Maggie's shop for coffee, but each morning she discovered her beverage paid for and waiting her arrival. On Monday, she asked about her mystery donor, but Maggie simply winked, handed her the to-go cup and helped the mayor with his order.

Tessa found small notes in her desk drawer and scribbled in her journal. She and Ryland had lunch together every day. Sitting in a corner of the teacher's lounge, she discovered the subtle likes and quirks of Coach Jessup. Turkey, no bread for lunch. Liked grape juice. Hated apple juice. Bad sixth grade boys' camp-out experience. Twelve carrots he treated as dessert— Bizarre. But with each new revelation, she plunged deeper into a warm pool of love for the man. The misery clouding her childhood evaporated into a thin smoke.

Friday morning's note lay in a neat one-by-one square at the center of her desk. Unfolding the striped notebook paper, her heart trembled. Across the top was scrawled, "Will you go to dinner with me? Check your answer below." A quarter of the way down the page were three squares:

Yes, tonight.
Yes, tomorrow.

Yes, for the rest of our lives.

Clutching the note to her chest, she leaned back in her chair. Her eyes shut against the glare of the florescent light and her mind added thread to a story she'd been weaving since Saturday on the balcony. Long walks in the snow. Hands locked with Ryland as they trailed behind Emma. Quiet swings on the front porch. Laughs. Celebrations. Tears. Peace. And love. All linked solely to the addition of Ryland to her life. She swiveled in her chair, her feet trailing along the floor. A sigh slipping through her lips.

"Uh, Miss T?" Jackson Murray's croaked words sliced through her bubble.

Her eyes slammed open, tumbling back to the reality of first period.

Scanning the room, every eye was on her.

"You OK, Miss T?" Gabrielle Harrington, a withdrawn freshman who tested into advanced English but rarely offered insights aside from her exquisitely written papers, asked from the middle of the left row.

"She got another love letter from coach." Riley Messing, star athlete, guffawed. The room rumbled with laughter.

Heat scorched Tessa's neck, burning her cheeks and flickering at the edges of her eyes. Quickly folding the note back to a square, she slid the paper in her top drawer and stood. "Ladies and gentlemen, let's take this opportunity to share our essays on one of the five William Blake poems I assigned. Mr. Messing." Her gaze fell on the lanky six foot shortstop. "I believe you have *Love's Secret*. Would you be the first to share your wisdom on the lovely works of Mr. Blake?"

"Aww, man," he mumbled. Tugging a folded

piece of notebook paper from his binder, he swallowed. His Adam's apple bobbed like the fishing lures Tessa was forced to use on summer camp-outs.

Riley stood to the left of his chair and began to read his five hundred words on the poem.

Forty-five minutes later, the shrill of the class bell cut through the presentations. "OK students. For those of you who didn't read today, I've taken note, and you'll be up Monday. Remember half your grade for this assignment is reading the essay in front of the class." A groan floated through the students. "Please leave your essays on my desk for evaluation."

Papers slid across the corner of her desk. The din of student chatter filled the room as friends collapsed together for the ten minutes of freedom between periods.

Gabrielle, the last to lay her paper on the stack, hesitated. "Miss Tarrington?"

"Yes, Gabrielle. What can I do for you?"

"Do we really have to read the essay in front of the whole class?"

Reaching for the jumbled stack of papers, Tessa smiled. "Gabrielle, part of this class is presenting your composition."

"But can't I just write another essay. Would that make up for not reading in front of the class?"

Her mind flashed to a similar conversation she'd had with Mrs. Monahan ten years earlier. "I'm sorry, Gabrielle. Part of your grade is your ability to share your words. Speaking in front of people is a needed life skill. And at least in class, you're among the safety of your classmates." Tessa regretted the message before it slipped through her lips.

"But Miss Tarrington, reading in front of the class

will be the worst. The boys already tease me, and the girls act like I smell of rotten eggs doused with drugstore perfume. I don't have any friends in class. Even when I thought I might have a friend...well, I just don't think I can do it."

Tessa slid to the front of her desk, resting against the edge. "You can. Even if it's a horrible experience, reading in front of the class will make the next time you need to talk in front of a room of harsh critics much easier."

"But I'll never have to talk in front of a class again."

Tessa chuckled and squeezed Gabrielle's shoulders. "Trust me. Talking in front of people is kind of like algebra. It's something you never think you'll need, and then you find you use it every day of your life."

Tears threatened to spill down Gabrielle's cheeks.

"I hear what you are saying. And trust me...I understand wanting the anonymity of the back row more than most. Let me see what I can do. OK?"

Gabrielle's face lightened. A smile stretched to pop the tiniest dimples on either side of her chin. "Thank you, Miss T. Thank you so much." She spun on her heel and raced down the hall.

Tessa closed her eyes, thankful for the free second period. She prayed for guidance on how best to protect and promote Gabrielle.

"It's only second period," Ryland's voice wafted through her classroom. "Nothing can be so bad that you are already in prayer."

Her gaze grazed the length of his broad form. "Hello, Coach Jessup. Don't you have a baseball tournament to schedule?"

He shut the door to the hall, sauntered across the room and tugged her to him. "I realized I hadn't said hello to you yet this morning."

"Oh," she whispered. His lips lowered to hers and branded her with their heat. His mouth curled to a subtle grin. "Hello." His eyelids bowed over the smoky depths.

"Hi." Her mind slipped from foggy to fuzzy. His hand trailed her spine, melting the strength from her legs.

"Did you get my note?" he asked, distracting her with feather-light kisses along her exposed collarbone.

A knock on her classroom door shot ice through her veins. With a weak muscled shove to Ryland, she skidded behind her desk. "Come in." Her voice sounded low and husky to her ears.

The door cracked open and Principal Jamison banged through the threshold. Toddling into the room on ill-placed cowboy boots, he made an unforgettable cross-section of authority and cartoon. He stood nearly a foot shorter than Ryland. His partially bald head reflected the harsh lights of the room and his wide painted tie flopped to the side of his rounded belly "Hey Tessa." His full lipped smile was filled with warmth. Swiveling, he nodded to Ryland, lifting a single eyebrow. "Coach Jessup."

"Principal Jamison." Ryland shoved his hands in his pockets.

"Ahem. I was hoping to talk to Miss Tarrington for a few minutes." He turned to Tessa. "This is your free period, right?"

"Yes, sir. Coach Jessup was just down here... ummm..." She lifted her gaze to Ryland.

Pulling his hands from his pockets, Ryland

snatched a folder from the top of her teetering stack. "Miss Tarrington has been working with my daughter. I was stopping by to see if she was still available to help Emma tonight."

"Oh, well that's nice." Jamison said, resting a hip against the front corner desk. "I didn't know you had an interest in elementary education, too."

"Not specifically. Emma is a unique talent. She is helping me with a children's book idea."

"Splendid."

"Well, I'll leave you two alone. I need to be on my way," Ryland said.

"I'll see you tonight."

"Of course, Miss Tarrington. Counting down the minutes until we say hello again." The twinkle in his eye sent shivers racing under Tessa's skin. She struggled to shift her focus from his exiting form to Principal Jamison's knowing grin.

"I'm sorry, Mr. Jamison, what can I do for you?"

"Well, as you know we hired you as a long term sub for Mrs. Monahan based solely on her recommendation. I was leery, I admit. You have zero high school teaching experience."

"I was a TA for two years in one of the best English Lit programs in the country."

He waved a hand. "College and high school are like China and Australia. The main two things they have in common is they are both on the planet and have human inhabitants."

"OK…"

"Regardless, we trust Mrs. Monahan, and she was once again perfectly in tune with what her students needed. After a bumpy start, you've managed to gain the trust and near admiration from your students."

"Thank you?" Tessa glanced at the clock on the far end of the hall. Fifteen minutes before the next bell.

"Yes, well, you don't need to thank me. We keep track of the student-run message boards, and since the first incident, you've received nothing but praise. Match that with some of the assignments I've read from your students and you've made amazing strides."

"How did you read what my students wrote?"

"Skimmed through your files while you were out this past weekend for that wedding. Good stuff. Well written. Much improved from what I read before Mrs. Monahan went on leave."

"OK…" Tessa slid onto her chair, lacing her arms over her chest.

"Yeah, well, as I said, Mrs. Monahan was right in guiding us to hire you short term. Now, I'd like to make the offer more permanent."

Tessa sat straight. "What do you mean?"

"Mrs. Monahan has decided to retire. Her hip hasn't healed quite as well as the doctors would like. They're afraid she won't be able to handle the intensity of standing most of the day teaching. She has forty years in so she's well past the retirement qualifier. With her out, we have an opening in the English department. I'd like to offer you first crack at the job."

"But I'm not a certified teacher."

He waved his hands. "Yes, I know, but if you sign up for the accreditation courses beginning this summer, you should be able to complete your certification by the end of the next school year. You'd need to be probationary until then, but I've little doubt you'd be able to complete all of the work necessary for us to make the position official."

Tessa stared at Jamison. Teach fulltime? Move to

Gibson's Run permanently? Wasn't that what she was daydreaming? She, Ryland, and Emma—one happy family. Her stomach churned. Acid percolated. "Mr. Jamison, I'm flattered. But aren't there already qualified teachers who'd want this position?"

He shrugged. "Sure. But they don't have a rapport with the students. They don't have credibility. They also don't have a relationship with the coach of the football team."

"Principal Jamison!"

"Hey," he raised a hand to her. "I have two eyes and two ears. Nothing gets by me. You two have been in a gaga relationship for the last month. Hearts are flying overhead every time I see the two of you together. If I can secure you here, I've a better chance of locking Jessup into a multi-year contract. There are some schools up in Columbus sniffing around. Offering him the moon to come and coach their teams. But I can't have it. Nope, he took the Grizzlies to the state playoffs for the first time since he donned the uniform. There's a bunch of money in football in this state. I won't allow any of it to seep in to Columbus if I've a say about it."

"Mr. Jamison, this seems a little like blackmail."

"Naw, just a little friendly push in the right direction. I wouldn't offer you the job if you weren't an excellent fit for our students. You're a good teacher, Tessa." He tossed a stack of papers on her desk. "Read through the contract. It's all pretty straightforward. Let me know if you've any questions."

She reached for the papers, the weight of the moment beginning to seep through her spirit.

"But there's an expiration date on the offer. Monday morning. If you're not interested I need to begin a search for Mrs. Monahan's replacement."

"OK." She flipped through the pages—the black words blurring in her vision.

"Monday, Tarrington." Jamison said over his shoulder.

Monday. Forty-eight hours to decide if she wanted a life in Gibson's Run—forever closing the door on New Orleans. If she taught full time, what would happen to her writing career? Would she be happy teaching students the same poetry and classic literature year after year? What if Ryland didn't see a true future for the two of them? What if his feelings were like Joey's and he was only pursuing a high school crush? What if she wasn't really a good teacher?

The class bell rang over the loudspeaker launching the countdown for her decision.

Stay or go?

32

"I'm home." Hip-checking the front door closed, Ryland dropped his oversized nylon duffle to the floor and kicked off his shoes. Padding toward the kitchen, the spicy aroma of marinara wafted to him.

"Daddy, Daddy, Daddy!" Emma launched into his arms, her tiny weight thrusting the wind from his lungs.

"Hey, E-train. How was school today?" Cuddling her to his chest, he inhaled the subtle scent of girlhood—a mix of watermelon soap, peanut butter, and play-dough.

"School was greats." Emma leaned back in his arms, continuing to play with the tiny hairs on the back of his neck. One day too soon, he'd call up this memory because his grown daughter wouldn't want to be in the same room with him, let alone cuddle after school.

"We learnt all about some turtles and how they swims in the waters and walks on the ground. Theys called them rep-styles. I think I needs a turtle. Don't you think we needs a turtle?"

"Reptiles." He kissed her forehead. "Last week you wanted a dog because you read a book about puppies. Remember? From what I hear, you begged Miss Jane's niece to keep her puppy when you were at the Grey's farm with G-ma playing with their grandchildren on Saturday."

"Well," she paused, wiggling to be released. Climbing onto the barstool, she rested her chin in her upturned palms. "Gordie—the puppy—sure seemed to like me best of all the kids. Even better than Lizzie. I think he really wanted to come homes with us. And Miss Janie's niece is super busies with school. I just knows Gordie needs me. I could tells by all the kisses he gave me."

"Emma, just because someone or some dog likes you doesn't mean they want to come and live with you."

"So does that mean Miss Tessa doesn't want to come and live with us? She likes me real good."

Waves of uncertainty crashed into growing mountains of love with the thought of Tessa. He hoped the path they were walking led to permanency. He was walking that way, but was Tessa on the same path? "It smells like Mabel almost has dinner ready. You better go upstairs and wash your hands." He glanced at her white t-shirt with a giant pink sparkly bunny in the center. "Why don't you change your t-shirt, too?"

"But I loves my bunny shirt. I wants to wear it e'ry day till Easters."

"Well, if you don't want it splattered with red dots from the spaghetti and marinara Mabel is making, you should put it in the hamper and pull on one of your old play t-shirts."

Her eyes doubled in size. She slid off the chair and scrambled up the stairs, using her arms for leverage.

"How was your day?" Mabel asked as the echo of Emma's footsteps receded down the back hall.

"OK. I'm having trouble convincing some of the schools around Columbus to come to the baseball tournament in April. They seem to think the caliber of competition isn't as high as what they would find closer to home."

"That's silly. The boys around here are great ballplayers."

"I know. We'll get it worked out." Grabbing a water from the refrigerator, he leaned against the counter by the stove. "Are you certain you're fine with babysitting tonight?"

Mabel's lips curled at the corners. "Of course. I love the idea of helping your romance chug along. I must say, I've been pulling for you two since the first moment she came to the house. She's a special young woman." Patting his cheek, she continued. "You've had enough heartache. It does this old woman good to see the sparkle of little hearts swimming in your eyes."

"Ugh, Mabel. I'm still a man. Please don't reduce me to a greeting card image, or a made for TV movie." He shoved away from the counter and started down the back hallway towards his bedroom.

With a shrug, she turned back to her sauce and stirred. "You had a phone call today."

"Oh, yeah?"

"Someone from the *Dispatch* calling to confirm a story on *The Tattler Zone*."

"What did the reporter ask?"

"Confirmation on the details surrounding Macy's relationship with that quarterback, Everett Tanner."

~*~

Tessa swiped bronzer over her cheeks. The contract, dog-eared and highlighted, lay to the left of her make-up bag. She'd read every word after Jamison left. And again during the essay test she gave her seventh period class. And again when she arrived home and found Daddy locked in his study.

Dropping the brush with a clink on the glass surface, she reached for the contract. With a flip of the pages, her gaze landed on the signature line. By signing she would be sealing her fate—at least for the next few years. She would officially have to move.

Leave New Orleans. Leave her friends. Leave her career. Leave. Leave. Leave. That one word flashed like a neon sign. With a sigh, she closed her eyes. *Dear Lord, please let the answer be crystal clear. Help me to know Your will in the midst of my own confusion. Help me to not run away simply to find safety, but guide me toward the path of Your choosing even if the journey is filled with twists and turns of uncertainty. Amen.*

Calm washed over her. The decision of whether to stay and teach or keep her life in New Orleans didn't need to be determined tonight. She had forty more hours before Jamison required an answer. Tonight would be filled with learning more about Ryland and if his intentions matched his ardor.

Her eyes fluttered open; her gaze landed on the pink and white confection masquerading as a dress. She'd bought the tiny, tulle laden, little number on a shopping spree in Chicago two weeks after Lily Mae's engagement. At Lily Mae's insistence, she'd purchased three lovely dresses during the journey along Miracle Mile, and had worn exactly zero. Tonight was one of the few times she was ridiculously thankful she'd listened to her crazy friend.

With one quick zip, she turned to the mirror taking in her full length. Swirls of pink in varying shades twisted around her body flaring just above her knees. Thin strips of dark pink satin edged the top, middle and bottom of the dress. She slipped into three inch nude pumps and reached for a rich, platinum cropped cardigan layered in bugle beads. The cardigan transformed her outfit to subtle modesty with a hint of glamor. Her long blonde hair was lose around her shoulders—touched with slight waves.

A swipe of clear gloss on her lips and she was ready. Her first official date with the man she loved. Trembles rippled through her body. Part excitement. Part nerves. Tonight would be perfection.

~*~

Ryland hesitated.

The muted voices of the Friday evening news wafted through the Tarrington front door. He'd dreamed of standing in this spot most of his years, a fistful of wildflowers in his hand, sweat pouring down his neck. Deep breaths in and out before finally knocking on the marred oak door with a burnished cross blazoned in the center; a calling card of the household: "Beware: we love Jesus."

He'd imagined every moment from the first knock to the good-night kiss under the porch light. In a thousand daydreams his heart was never freshly bruised nor did his stomach burn with acidic anger from his former wife's indiscretions. But here he was. Standing at the doorway to his dream, a passageway quickly transforming to a gateway to his most dreaded nightmare.

The reporter digging into his and Macy's past riled every part of his protective instinct. Macy hadn't been the wife of his dreams, but her memory deserved to be left untarnished, if not for her, then for her parents and

Emma. He'd returned the phone call with the sole intent of simply saying, "No comment" but what he discovered was beyond his imagination.

The reporter divulged that a tell-all gossip novel about Macy's former boyfriend, quarterback Everett Tanner was in the works. Ryland had cut the call off in under two minutes, but it was enough time for the reporter to share some of the key points that would be published about Macy's carelessness. A book, the reporter shared, to be published by Evanston & Evanston, Tessa's former employers.

His blood boiled and his stomach burned with rage. How could anyone be so cruel? Macy's death was nearly two years ago and yet some sick need for gossip was going to drag his daughter's mother's name—and by proxy his daughter's—through the muck and grime of tabloid magazines and reprehensible talk shows.

He released a slow sigh, lifting his fist to knock. Before his knuckles wrapped against the wood, the door whipped open and the pain aching in his heart soothed with the glorious sight.

Draped in what appeared to him to be a giant tutu, Tessa shined. Her hair was loose and long against her shoulders. Standing nearly four inches taller thanks to teetering heels, her sparkling green eyes met his gaze— requiring the barest of head tilts. "Hi," she whispered.

With a thick swallow, he stepped through the doorway, closing the gap between them. "Hi."

"Hello, Ryland." Pastor Tom's deep voice splashed him and chilled better than a bucket of ice water.

Sliding back, he glanced over Tessa's head. "Good evening, Tom. How're you tonight?"

"Just fine, son. Where will you and Tessa be going

this evening?" The once formidable pastor, whose illness seemed to age him overnight, stood tall and strong behind his daughter. Gone was the wiry, misshapen hair and untucked wrinkled shirts of the past several months. Tonight he was once again the bigger-than-life preacher who'd caused a seven-year-old Ryland to tremble with the sound of his voice. Pastor Tom tugged his reading glasses from his the bridge of his nose and tucked them in the chest pocket of his roll-neck cardigan. "Not too far, I hope."

"Up to Columbus."

Tom nodded. "Do you have any students this Saturday?"

"No. Fortunately we're in the prime time of spring try-outs for baseball, track, and tennis. Miraculously, during try-outs, the students are often on their very best behavior."

"Who's watching my little Emma this evening?"

"Mabel. They're having spaghetti."

"Emma's favorite. I'm sure she's tickled."

"Why don't you join them?" Ryland suggested.

"Oh, I wouldn't want to be an imposition."

"It wouldn't be an imposition. Mabel always makes double what the three of us will eat—even with my appetite. She'll have plenty. I'm certain Em would love the surprise. If you haven't already guessed, you're her favorite person on the planet. Kind of hurts my ego to have another man trump me so early in her life, but if I had to be pushed over, I'm glad it is by you."

Tessa laced her arm through her father's. "Dad, why don't you go? You don't have any plans tonight expect practicing your sermon. And what I've heard so far needs no additional tweaks. Emma asks about you every day I'm at the house."

"Well...I do miss spending time with her. She's quite the rascal." The slight lift of the corner of his lips warmed Ryland's heart. "Do you really think Mabel will have enough?"

"I'm certain."

"Well, it sounds as if I have a date myself."

Tessa lifted her gaze to Ryland. The love reflected in her eyes tripped the beats of his heart. "Sounds as if you do."

33

The decadent aroma of chocolate crème brûlée billowed around Tessa and seeped into the deep dessert recesses of her brain, miraculously creating room after the three course dinner she and Ryland lingered over for as many hours. With a gentle tap of her spoon, the crystalized surface cracked revealing the dark creamy texture of the custard. She dug her spoon into the stiff pudding, scooped a heaping bite. Closing her mouth around the velvety indulgence was bliss. For a moment, she didn't see Ryland or have the nagging question of staying in Gibson's Run or returning to her career in New Orleans or wonder what was next—she simply melted into the dark lusciousness of silky chocolate goodness.

"Tasty?" Ryland asked.

Her eyes flittered open and she caught his subtle grin. "It's stupid good."

"Stupid good? When did you revert to a sixteen year old girl?"

"If you can't beat them. Join 'em." She scraped the surface of the crème brûlée and shoved another bite in her mouth.

"How can you possibly have room in that tiny body for more food?"

She shrugged. "I've been training since I moved to New Orleans. I rarely eat out, but when I do, I want to enjoy every taste and nibble on my plate—and occasionally on my friends' plates. In the Crescent City, food is nearly a religious experience. If God eats, I think His chef is from New Orleans."

Ryland chuckled. "Don't let your dad hear you reference God so casually. He might just ground you." He slipped the tip of his fork into the edge of the dish and tasted the dessert. "Aww, man, that is good."

"Told you."

"I should never question your judgment."

"Keep that in mind, would you?"

"Always. I'll always trust you. Promise." Lacing his fingers with her free hand, he lightly stroked his thumb against her palm. Warm liquid seemed to seep through her fingers, sliding down her arm and settling in a pool around her heart.

With an involuntary head tilt, her loose hair brushed the edge of the table. How had she spent so many years hating Ryland? Now all she could see were the years stretched out before her—each day including Ryland and Emma—hopefully with his hand linked with hers.

The discreet waiter slid their bill on the table and Ryland reached for it before she could balk.

"Thank you."

Lifting his gaze from the bill, he smiled. "I invited you to dinner. I've only been waiting twenty years for this night. Who knew praying for patience would develop into such a long term strategy." He refocused on the bill.

She scanned the half full dining room. Until this moment, she hadn't realized how busy the German Village establishment was. Couples and parties ranging from two to twelve were in various states of meal consumption. She glanced from the tables to the bar jammed with business men. A few were watching the basketball game on the TV's. Some were chatting with each other. But one, dressed in rumpled khakis and a polo, appeared to be directly staring at her. Fear sent cold footprints racing down her spine.

She shot a glance over her shoulder to see if polo-man was really looking at her. A few famous musicians and artists made their homes in Columbus for the blissful anonymity. Maybe he'd spotted one of the local rich and famous. But the only person behind her was a woman in her near eighties shuffling to the bathroom.

"Ryland…"

"Hmm…" He slid his credit card on the tray. His relaxed expression quickly transformed to concern. "What's wrong?"

"Do you know the man sitting at the bar? The one in the blue polo shirt."

Ryland glanced over his shoulder and his entire body tensed. With a quick shove against the table, Ryland shot to stand and his chair teetered, threatening to crash to the ground. He closed the distance between the bar and their table in three strides. A single hand clamped around the man's shoulder as Ryland encouraged polo-man to follow him outside.

Tessa snatched her handbag from the table and scurried after them, stopping briefly to tell the waiter they'd be back. She pushed open the 19th century door.

Ryland' voice was low but held a palpable threat in each word.

Polo-man was pinned to the brick wall—his feet barely touching the broken pavement.

"Ryland."

He didn't turn, but maintained his steely focus on his prey. "Tessa, go back in the restaurant. I'll be finished in a few minutes."

Sliding behind him, she rested her palm against his broad back—taut with the pressure of holding polo-man still. "Ryland, do you want to introduce us?"

"Tessa, go back inside."

"I'm not leaving you alone. Not until you tell me what's happening."

He shifted to face Tessa. Polo-man remained firmly attached to the restaurant's brick wall. "Tess, I don't want you in the middle of this."

"But she is," Polo-man choked through his lips.

"What?" Tessa and Ryland said in unison.

"I'll explain, but I'll need more than a sip of oxygen to talk."

Ryland released his hold and Polo-man slipped to the ground.

"Talk." One word. Arms folded tightly, shirt straining against bulging muscles, Coach Jessup wasn't going anywhere.

Rubbing his neck, the man reached in his pocket and pulled out a folded piece of newspaper. Handing the paper to Tessa, a sneer stretched his lips. "It's all there, beautiful."

The creases from the quarter folds made the paper delicate, masking the age of the paper dated three days earlier. The headline from that morning's issue read:

Troubled Taylor? Or Wicked Woman?

Under the headline was a picture of Tessa cuddled to Ryland's side outside the hospital in New Orleans. The brief article described Joey's accident, including details around his night at the casino with the unknown driver. The article from the *Times-Picayune* went on to hypothesize Joey's off the rails night was a result of his best friend stealing his girlfriend. The writer hinted at a torrid love triangle started in high school, but ultimately surmised Tessa was stringing both men along to gain access to their dirty secrets to sell to the highest bidder, supporting her career.

Waves of nausea billowed and crashed in her stomach as each word poured through her mind and broke her heart. Blinking back tears she tried to focus on the man. "Did you write this?" she whispered.

"Tessa, sweetheart," Ryland said as he touched a finger to her chin, "what does it say?"

The concern displayed in his gray eyes broke the dam holding her tears. Warm streaks mingled with the cold night air, instantly chilling her cheeks. Wrapping her arms around his waist, she rested against his solid chest. The warmth of his strong arms enveloped her, shielding her from the worries and fears that pounded her at the reading of five hundred words. Five hundred words that dragged her back to the swirl of the toilet.

"It says she's a black widow mercenary." Polo-man answered. "Willing to do anything for a buck and a story."

"What?" Ryland stepped back, staring at her.

She handed him the crumpled paper.

Shoulders straightened. Jaw pulsed. Fingers tightened. Controlled anger oozed. But he remained silent. No words of protest. No words of defense. Just silence.

Tessa sucked in a deep cleansing breath against the tears threatening to resume. She stepped to Polo-man. "Who are you? Why are you here?"

"Babe, it's all about the story. And you're it."

"How am I the story?" But with the question, the weeks of hiding in her apartment after *the terrible, awful day* crashed against her. The incessant photographers capturing her every move bombarded her memory. Flashes of running from paparazzi with her groceries scattering along the brick-lined street. Articles subtly claiming she crafted the break-in to cover her trail of deceit. *Not again. Please, dear God, not again.* Her breaths shortened. Lungs wouldn't fill. The throb of a migraine began at the base of her skull.

"You are the ultimate player. Pastor's kid who spent her life in the shadows. Piling up peoples' secrets. Waiting for the perfect moment to let them loose. You have that innocent girl look about you. Makes men fall for you. You draw them in close enough to stab them in the back."

Polo-man slithered, loomed over her, the breadth of him blanketing her from the street light. His sneer sent chills racing over her flushed skin.

With barely a breath, Ryland yanked the man from Tessa and tossed him to the street.

"Hey, that's assault!" He lifted his gaze to the valet watching the scene. "You saw him. Didn't you? I want to press charges."

"I didn't see anything but three people having a conversation." He nodded to Ryland. "Good to see you, sir."

Ryland tilted his chin to the young man with a smile of recognition. "Nice to see you, too, Gage."

"You'll be hearing from my attorney." Polo-man shouted as he scrambled to his feet and ran down the alley.

Tessa rested against the brick wall, afraid she was moments from collapse.

Ryland watched the alley as if he was waiting for an attack by reinforcements.

What must he think of her? He must know the article was all conjecture. None of it was true. Right? "Ryland?"

His shoulders rose and fell with a deep breath. "We should get going." He handed Gage his valet ticket.

"Ryland?"

"I need to settle the bill." He reached in his pocket and pulled out a five dollar bill. "Do you mind waiting for the car?"

Before she could respond he disappeared through the door. An invisible weight settled on her chest. What if Ryland didn't believe her? Was this the moment? Were they done before they ever really started?

34

The drive back to Gibson's Run was stiff with silence, punctuated with haunting melodies floating through the radio.

Tessa was tempted to talk through the altercation, but she didn't know where to start. Fear kept her lips vacuum-sealed—fear of what Ryland was thinking. Fear of what Ryland now believed of her. She'd come to rely on his consistent strength. His unwavering support. Even in the wake of her dreadful treatment of him, he was a good man. A man after God's own heart who professed to love her. And if she could really fathom it, he had loved her since he was barely older than Emma. But could his love be so tenuous that someone's lie built on a house of lies could cause his love to disintegrate in a moment?

The steering wheel was swallowed by Ryland's hands. He was hunched forward, and yet his head nearly brushed the top of the SUV. The pulse in his jaw kept time with the music. The *tick, tick, tick* of the turn signal sliced through the cabin, the sound heralding their arrival in Gibson's Run.

If she didn't talk to him about the reporter now, she wouldn't have a chance. They'd be swept into the whirlwind of her dad and Emma. Of keeping the conversation light and happy the way they were over dinner. Only an hour ago, when they were laughing about the size of Tessa's pork chops compared to the petite fillet set in front of Ryland.

"We need to talk about what happened."

Silence.

"I didn't tell any reporters anything. I haven't spoken to a reporter since I released a statement about the break-in last fall. And even then all I said was my apartment was burglarized and I lost all of my clients' notes. Nothing else. Nothing about who my clients were or their stories. Nothing. I'd never tell anyone anything I wasn't given permission to share."

Tick, tick, tick. The turn signal announcing the shift onto Main Street.

"I didn't tell anyone anything, Ryland. You have to believe me."

Ryland slammed the car into an open spot in front of the police station.

Her neck whipped her head to the left with a jolt. "Whoa!"

"Sorry." Ryland mumbled, his fingers flexing against the steering wheel.

"Why are you stopping in the middle of town?"

"You wanted to talk. So talk."

She unbuckled her seatbelt and shifted in her seat to face his profile.

He focused straight ahead—staring into the murky gray of small town evening.

"When *the terrible, awful day* happened, Evanston and Evanston released a statement that one of their writers had been violated allowing for several clients' secrets to be exposed. Within two, maybe three days, I had reporters camped out on my front step looking for a statement or some slip of gossip, but I never said anything. Nothing."

Scrubbing his face with his hand, he released a

sigh. "I was contacted today."

"By a reporter?"

He nodded.

"Is that why you grabbed Polo-man?"

"Polo-man?"

"He needed a name. Butt-face Miscreant seemed too long."

Her joke tugged a subtle tilt of his lips. "I thought he was following me. Not you."

"Why?"

"The call today was about Macy and her relationship with Everett Tanner."

Tessa's heart twisted. "How did a reporter find out about Macy?"

"Apparently there's a tell-all coming out about Tanner, his wife, and his women."

Stretching her hand across the console, she linked her fingers through his. "I'm so sorry, Ryland. I know you wanted to keep Macy's actions in the past."

"But what I don't understand is how anyone found out."

"You said the reporter said he was confirming a story from a book?"

"It appears they know everything. Including her state of mind the night she died." He met her gaze. "I've only told one person other than my mother about Macy. And that's you."

"Ryland, what are you implying?"

"I don't know, Tessa. What am I implying? You were the only one who knew about Macy's indiscretions and about Joey's accident. The article has a picture of the two of us in the paper. You're the common link."

Yanking her hand from his, she hugged her arms

around her middle. "How am I the common link?"

"You knew both stories in their entirety. And that book coming out about Tanner? Your publisher's printing it."

"Former publisher. Remember. They fired me. After my apartment was robbed. After my home was violated, they kicked me to the curb without another thought. Why would I give them any information? How could I ever trust them again? How could *you* not trust *me*?"

"What a perfect way to get back in the game? Sell them a big story. Create another one."

"Create one?"

"Ex-NFL linebacker jilted by his wife steals best friend's girlfriend—also a famous athlete—while he's recovering from a near death accident. Sounds like bestseller to me."

"Are you kidding me? Do you think I've been lying to you? Who do you think I am?"

"I think you're someone so desperate to get back into full time writing you've maneuvered yourself into my home by writing a children's story with my daughter. I saw you in Terrell's office. You were a crazed person with the thought you wouldn't get back to your precious career. I think you were scared enough—desperate enough—to do anything. And the bonus. You get to pay me back for all of the years of torment you blame me for."

"Watch it. You're starting to sound like middle school through high school Ryland."

He turned to her his face ravaged with grief and pain. "Isn't that how you see me? How you see all of us? Haven't you been judging me since we were six years old? All the while I've been trying to prove my heart to you? And now this…"

"Now this, what? I didn't do anything."

"Really? I want to believe you, but every single sign points to only one person. You."

Sucking in her cheeks, she bit down. The acidic taste of blood flowed into her mouth, her tears threatening to burst over the edges. But she wouldn't cry. She'd been a victim for too many years. She wouldn't be one now. With a thick swallow, she dropped her hand to the door handle. "Ryland, you have to make a choice. Right now." She kept her voice low, but clear. "Do you really believe I could do all of those things? Do you love me? Or do you love the idea of me?"

"I love you." His tone didn't match his words.

"If you love me. You have to trust me." She stretched her left hand to him—palm up. "All in or all out."

He dropped his focus to her hand.

Breathe in. Breathe out.

Slow steady.

He'll take your hand. He has to.

Love means trust.

Belief.

Hope.

Her right hand clutched the door handle.

35

Inhale. Exhale. Inhale. Exhale.

The crisp tang of bleach tickled her nose. Dragging her quilt under her chin, she drew another short breath and snuggled deeper into her pillows. Breathing was the height of accomplishment.

Her eyes flittered open. Sun peeked through her curtains slicing across pale yellow walls. Her childhood alarm clock flashed. She'd slept nearly ten hours, and yet her skin yawned with weariness. Had it been only twelve hours since the end of her future? When Ryland refused her hand, she'd opened the car door and walked. She hadn't run. She hadn't cried.

She'd buttoned her coat and walked the three blocks to her father's home. Three blocks and across the threshold to a life without the love she'd come to require like basic sustenance.

Rolling to her side she stared at the faded rosebuds floating over her pillow case. Momma had surprised her with the fancy sheets when they'd bought her bed for her thirteenth birthday. Momma said flowers were always a comfort. *"When you're happy they enhance your joy. When you're mad, sad, or a little blue, flowers lift your spirits. Breathe deep, baby girl, can't you smell their sweet aroma?"*

Momma's magical flowers were failing miserably.

A soft knock at her door was followed by the

squeak of the hinge in desperate need of some oil.

"Tessa?" Her dad's whisper glided over her. The soles of his shoes scuffed against her floor until she felt the weight of him on the edge her bed.

"Sweetie? Are you sick?"

The touch of her dad's wide palm to her shoulder triggered her first tear. With a swipe at her cheek, she pushed a slow breath through her lips. "I'm just tired."

"OK." The bed creaked as he stood. "I thought you might want to tell me why Ryland seemed as if he'd seen a ghost when he returned to his house last night. Or why I had a reporter greet me at the front step this morning with my *Dispatch* in hand?"

Thrusting the blankets from her face, she shoved herself to sitting. "What reporter? What did you say? What did he ask?"

"Well, that woke you up." He dragged her desk chair to sit next to the bed. "I think we should talk about what happened between you and Ryland last night."

"Nothing happened." And nothing ever will. "We realized we don't see life quite the same way. Tell me about the reporter."

"He said he was looking for a quote about how you destroyed Joey's life." He patted her hand. "We both know that isn't true. You couldn't hurt that boy if you tried. I don't know if anyone can hurt Joe as badly as Joe hurts himself."

Throwing back the covers, she jumped out of bed and scurried to her closet. Grabbing a pair of flip-flops and her favorite sweatshirt, she hustled to the door. "Dad, I have to go."

"Tessa Natalie Tarrington. Where do you think you are going in your pajamas?"

36

Tessa lifted her clutched fist but hesitated to knock on the worn door. She sat on the porch step, tightened her wool coat around her middle and laid her head against her long-legged lap, curling her bare toes against the brisk early spring morning. What was she thinking? Running around town in her pajamas and flip-flops? She hadn't thought. She went straight to fixing. Sprinting from her own misery and diving into another's pool of problems. Her go-to solution to dealing with her life: avoidance.

"Sleep walking, Tessa?" Sean's authoritative voice broke through the bubble of pity.

She looked up.

A sweat-drenched Sean sat down beside her.

"I wanted to help Joey."

"Don't you think you've 'helped' my brother enough?"

She stretched to meet his gaze, her spine taunt with frustrated anger. "Listen. I didn't do anything wrong. I didn't tell a soul what happened in New Orleans. Not even my father."

"How'd you explain you and Rys making goo-goo face the last week? Only two weeks ago you were making goo-goo face with my brother. Pretty quick recovery."

"My dad is aware of Joe asking Ryland to 'fill-in' for him at the wedding. And he's also aware I've been struggling with my feelings…wait I don't need to tell you anything." Scrubbing her cheeks in frustration, she leaned against the porch pillar. "Goo-goo face, Sean? Why am I telling you about my feelings?"

"I'm a cop. People tell me stuff." He shrugged, matching her position against the opposite column. "Now, you want to tell me how you think you can help Joey?" His tone softened a notch, shifting from cop to confidant.

"Sean, I'm so sorry about the photograph, but it was taken after we'd spent the morning with Joey in the hospital. After he'd given us his blessing. Ryland…I….we wanted to talk. In that moment I felt the freest I'd felt since I was a little girl on the Planter's Park swings. I could finally see the path God had been clearing for me my whole life. The reasons behind *the terrible, awful day*. The reason I had no choice but to return to Gibson's Run. At that moment I just wanted to revel in the newness. The perfection of the moment. I never thought we were in danger of causing a stir. We were alone."

"Obviously not.'

"Obviously…" Silence hung between them. How would she fix this? What could she do? Where could she go? Four months ago she'd run home to Gibson's Run. Now, she had nowhere left to run. Nowhere to find sanctuary.

"Tessa," Sean's deep timbre broke through her spiraling thoughts. "I know you didn't do anything."

Her head popped up. "What? But you just said…"

"I know what I said. It's what I thought when I saw the paper. But Maggie talked me off the ledge. She helped me think of options for what happened. She's good for me. Helps me to find clarity when things hit to close to the brotherly bond. I also know Sprout gave you his blessing. Regardless of how amazing you are, he would never be able to give you a fair shake with his heart. He needs to heal it first. Maybe he'll find his own Tessa Tarrington. Or Maggie McKitrick."

"Pretty deep for eight in the morning."

"Second run of the day. Helps with the focus. You should try it."

"Second? I can't remember the last time I ran a first."

"The first one landed me at Maggie's, and in the process she gave me some new things to consider. She gave me a little fuel to get back here and since I'm on the late shift today, I thought I'd mull over her considerations while in motion. I do my best thinking and praying while moving."

"I do my best thinking and wallowing elbow deep in a pint of rocky road ice cream."

"We all have our methods."

The first twinge of a smile pulled at her cheek. "Seriously, what can I do to help Joey? Do you want me to release a statement or write an article? Run away?" *I'm really good at the last one.*

"Don't worry. This'll blow over. Six months out of the year Joe's in the middle of one catastrophe or another. He'll survive. What about you?"

"What about me?"

"I passed Ryland on my first run this morning. Kind of early for the coach when I know for a fact he doesn't have anyone scheduled for his Saturday morning of suffering. Heard you two had a fancy date up in Columbus. I'm surprised he didn't want a little shut eye. I'm also a little shocked you're up and over here—straight out of bed—trying to fix a situation you didn't break."

Shrugging, she tucked a piece of her bed-worn hair behind her ear and stared at the well-manicured street, quiet on a Saturday. "I don't know why Ryland was up and going so early."

"Last night not go according to plan?"

She swallowed against the thickness growing in her throat, praying her tears would stay in retreat mode. "I don't know what the plan was, but I don't think the sleazy reporter who stalked us all through dinner anticipated being thrown into the street. And I didn't plan to watch my future swirl the toilet bowl after falling from such a wonderful height."

Sean kneaded the space connecting his neck and shoulders. "I think I understood four of the bevvy of words you just spewed. What reporter?"

"I think he's from the New Orleans paper. He showed us the article."

"How'd he track you here? How'd he even know who you are?"

"Well, about six months ago I had a...*the terrible, awful day*..." From the moment she stepped across her apartment threshold, to reaching for Ryland's hand in the car the previous evening, Tessa dumped all of her problems on the unsuspecting chief of police. To his credit, he barely flinched when she mentioned the links between her washed up writing career and the notoriety of Joey's current state. "And then when I realized I messed up Joey's recovery, I had to try and fix it. That's why I'm here."

Scrubbing his face with his palm, Sean released a soft sigh. "I'm really sorry you've had to endure all of these obstacles. I had no idea."

"I'm surprised Mrs. Jenkins didn't tell you all

about *the terrible, awful day*. The first time I saw her in Maggie's café she asked me how I was able to show my face after I let all of those secrets 'run out of my apartment'."

"Well, if I'm being honest, Sissy cornered me the day after the news hit that your apartment was burglarized."

"How could she have known?"

"She has a Google alert set up on everyone who has ever lived in Gibson's Run."

"Seriously?"

"We're talking about Sissy Jenkins. What do you think?"

"You're right." Rubbing the bridge of her nose, she shifted to face Sean. "But I really am sorry. I think I may have drawn the drama to Joey. Just like Ryland. It's all my fault."

"OK. You've lost me. What does all of this have to do with Ryland?"

"Another reporter called him for a quote yesterday about his wife, Macy."

"What about her?"

"I can't say. He told me in confidence, but I can't imagine a reporter would've found Ryland if he hadn't been in my swirling orbit."

"Tessa, you can't blame yourself for every bad thing that happens to your friends."

"Why not? I seem to be the only common denominator."

"That's a little self-centered don't you think?"

"Perhaps, but that's what I was told, anyway." And she had to admit: facts were facts. Ryland had lived in near anonymity since Macy's death and his retirement. Now Tessa was connected to him, he'd ended up a gossip headline in the sports section of the *Times-Picayune*. The secrets surrounding Macy's life had come quickly to the surface when Ryland claimed he'd told no one else. Tessa would love to believe all of the flushing around her was coincidence, but reality was reality. Hers just happened to live on the porcelain edge.

"Tessa, I don't know what made Ryland transform into an idiot last night. The guy has been in love with you since he stuttered. But you need to forgive him."

"Forgive him? I need him to forgive me."

"Maybe. That's the thing about relationships. One person is often in the process of forgiving the other. But this situation is pretty clear. Ryland jumped to some dangerous conclusions. Granted, the circumstantial evidence was pretty heavy against you. But the straight up facts are clear. Anyone who has known you longer than a minute knows you wouldn't intentionally hurt another person. Especially someone you care about."

"Maggie?"

"Like I said. She's good for me." Sean squeezed her hand. "Ryland is stubborn. He's kind and generous. And still really angry about Macy. I don't know what happened between them. It's not my business. But I've known him since he was like a week old, and something changed in him within months after he married Macy. His joy seemed to evaporate for anything other than his daughter. Then you came back into his life. And he seemed lighter. I thought my idiot brother messed it up, but when God is in something, nothing and no one will stop His will. Not even Sprout."

A warm tear raced down her cheek, splattering

against their linked hands. "I don't know. Yesterday. Before dinner. Before that reporter and the picture and the news...Before everything, I would've staked my life Ryland was my one. I could see him and Emma in every day of the rest of my life. But now...I just don't know."

"He's a thinker. He'll need to brood. Punch the weight bag. Make some poor sophomore run laps 'til he pukes. But he'll realize his mistake. Sooner, rather than later. The question is, when he discovers he was wrong about you, will you be ready to forgive him?"

37

Rolling her exercise mat in a tight cocoon, Tessa swiped at the beads of sweat racing across her forehead. The hour session at the community center was led by Eloise Mayweather, a lithe former ballet dancer who graduated with Tessa.

Tessa remembered Eloise as being kind to everyone in school, often writing notes of encouragement to other students and staff. She even baked sugar-free cookies for the janitor when she discovered he was insulin dependent. For all her grace and cavity inducing sweetness, Eloise was a terrifying taskmaster when she led class.

After her heart-to-heart with Sean, Tessa had opted for mind numbing pain rather than folding herself under her covers for endless cycles of what-if scenarios. With sweat chilling against her skin, and her mind settled for the first time since dinner the night before, she knew she'd made a wise decision.

Tugging her threadbare Tigers sweatshirt over her head, she nodded to Eloise, who closed the distance between them. Her head barely reached Tessa's shoulder, but every muscle was clearly defined. If she had fat, she kept it stored in a closet somewhere to be used only on special occasions.

"Great class. I don't think my instructor in New Orleans could make it through your hour."

Eloise smiled as she zipped her formfitting jacket.

"I forget sometimes everyone was not a ballet student used to hours of holding form and position."

"Well, it was awesome. I may not be able to walk up the flight of stairs to my bedroom tonight, but I'll remind myself how much better my jeans will fit, and a night or two on the couch won't be too bad."

"Oh, Tessa, you always were a funny one." She giggled. "I'm so glad we've been able to reconnect through class." Sliding her rolled mat under her arm, she tilted her head. "Are you busy? Would you like to have a coffee and maybe a treat at *Only the Basics*? I'd love to hear more about your life since you left Gibson's Run. It must be so exciting to be a writer. Living in such a wild city."

"I don't think I really experienced the wild side of New Orleans, but it's a beautiful place to live. Always a character around the corner with a story to tell."

"Oh! So exciting. I'd love to hear more. Can I treat you to a cup of coffee?"

Tessa wanted to do anything except talk about her life, but her only other option for the day was wallowing alone in front of the television with a friendly pint of rocky road for companionship. "Sounds great."

Twenty minutes later Tessa and Eloise stood in a four person deep line waiting to place an order for coffee at Maggie's little café. Throughout the chilly walk from the community center to the shop, Eloise peppered Tessa with questions. *Is living in New Orleans like the movies? Did you have loads of glamorous friends? Did you write Noel Trainer's biography? Do you still sing? How do you like teaching?*

The walk took less than five minutes, and Eloise discovered more about the last eight years of Tessa's life than her father, Lily Mae, and Ella combined. Through the questions Tessa realized how much she missed New Orleans. How easy it would be to turn and run back to the life she knew before she fell in love.

Edging a step closer, Eloise chattered about the launch of her new ballet classes at the center.

Tessa nodded at what she felt were well-timed intervals, but without the distraction of answering the endless string of questions her mind started to float to Ryland and Emma. Yesterday she'd planned to spend this afternoon with Emma working through ideas for another Guard-Ann Angel story. She thought they could spend an hour ideating, and then while the sweet little girl napped Tessa would have the opportunity to spend some quality time with Ryland. How did one's life become so empty in less than a day?

"...and I thought I could offer classes for the mothers, too. Ballet is an outstanding workout, you know."

Tessa nodded, although she'd only taken one ballet class. After the recital her mother thought she might be better suited for art lessons.

"What can I get for you lovely ladies?" Jenna Arnold, a kindergarten teacher who worked for Maggie nights and weekends, stretched a welcoming grin.

"I'd like a latte with three shots. Non-fat milk, please." Eloise tugged her credit card from her jacket pocket.

"Just a coffee." Tessa said.

"I just brewed a new Columbian roast." Jenna slid a white to-go cup to Tessa. "It's in the far right carafe. You'll have to tell me what you think. Maggie's testing a new distributor."

"This is my treat." Eloise said, patting Tessa's hand. "Why don't you find a table while I wait for my drink?"

"Will do."

The shiny carafes drew Tessa. Standing in a double wide row along a table near the west side of the café, she filled her cup to the brim. Blowing against the rising heat from the steaming coffee, she pivoted and smacked full force into the unmistakable chest of Ryland Jessup.

"I'm so sorry!" Grabbing a wad of napkins from the table, she began patting his chest dry. "I'm such a klutz."

"Tessa, it's fine." His voice was low and melted over her like butter.

"Did I burn you?" She searched his eyes for a flicker—a tiny ray of hope last night was a fluke. An imagined nightmare she could write about in her journal or give to Lily Mae to fuel her next Young Adult novel. But his eyes were blank. Devoid of emotion. No laughter. No sorrow. Nothing.

"No." His sigh floated over her messy bun.

"Miss Tessa!" Emma's shout cancelled the murmured pocket conversations in the café.

Tessa spun from Ryland, kneeling to welcome the outstretched embrace of the one Jessup who loved her unconditionally. "Hey, Miss Emma. Are you getting a special treat?"

"Yep. Daddy cames home and said I deserves a Saturday special."

"What's a Saturday special?"

"Miss Maggie's chocolate chip cookie with a glass of chocolate milks."

"Oh, that is special." She stretched to her full height, keeping her focus on Emma and not allowing the tug of her heart to control her vision.

"You gots to sit with us. We's gonna talks to Miss Maggie abouts making my birthday cake. You'll come, won't you? You and Pastor Tom hafta come to my party."

"Emma," Ryland's correctional tone sent swift hammers to her heart. "Miss Tessa can't sit with us today."

"But whys?"

"Because she's here with someone else." He glanced over his shoulder, toward the counter with a growing line—Maggie, Jenna, and two assistants wove around each other like a choreographed dance. "And it looks like Miss Maggie is too busy to talk to us about your cake today. We'll catch her on Monday."

"But you promised."

"Sometimes we can't keep promises." His gaze darted to Tessa. "Let's get your cookie and get back home. I have tape to watch."

"But I wanted my Saturday special with Miss Tessa."

"Sorry, E. You'll have to be disappointed. Learning to live with disappointment is a good life lesson. Good bye, Tessa." His voice held the soft burn of bitterness.

A final good bye. The end.

No!

"Wait. Ryland, can I talk to you for a minute." She waved to Eloise who watched the scene unfold from a near distance. "Emma can go wait in line for her cookie with Miss Eloise."

"Miss Emma," Eloise said, stretching her long,

lean fingers to the stubby four year-old fist. "I think I saw Miss Maggie put fresh Better-Than-Your-Momma's cookies in the case. Do you want to see if they're as tasty fresh from the oven as they are the rest of the time?"

Emma looked from her father to Tessa, her oversized gray eyes tilting in concern. Nodding to Eloise she laid her hand in the waiting palm. They shuffled through the crowded café and went to the broad bakery case to select their delicacies.

Lacing his arms over his chest, Ryland stared down at her. "Talk."

Scanning the space for an open, private table, she caught four sets of patrons gawking at their unfolding drama and one set of eyes belonging to Sissy Jenkins, senior member of her dad's advisory board and unofficial town tattler. Trying to do something private in Gibson's Run was impossible. God and Sissy would know. And throughout most of her childhood, Tessa was convinced Sissy knew first.

"Not here," she whispered, tugging his forearm to follow her. "Hi, Mrs. Jenkins." Tessa waved, but did not break her stride until she was standing across the street by the dilapidated fountain. Sucking in a breath she turned. "I don't know what to say."

"You're the one who wanted to talk." Ryland's legs were braced. Ready to take a hit.

"I know..." Chewing her bottom lip she tried to think of something to convince him she was not the nefarious character his mind convicted her of being.

"Tessa, I don't have time for this."

"Time for what, Ryland? Time to talk to a woman you claimed to have loved your whole life? Time to figure out how to heal the wound? Time to listen to a woman who discovered she can't live without you or your daughter? What don't you have time for, Ryland?"

Shoving his broad hand through his cropped hair, he turned from her, expelling air like a caged bull. "Do you know how hard this is for me? I've waited since I was six to have a chance with you and when I finally do I find out you've been using me for a story. A story." The last words spat from his lips.

"I'm not after a story. I would never do that to you or Emma. I love you too much."

"But you haven't always. You used to hate me. Admit it. You blamed me for your miserable childhood."

"I guess. But I never hated you. I wanted to hate you. The teasing. The endless hours of disappointed glances from my mother because I wasn't popular. I admit I irrationally blamed you for that experience. But I'd never allow that pain to justify causing you or anyone else a moment of anguish."

"I find that hard to believe since I've reporters calling me on every number I've had since high school."

"What? How? When?"

"That's what they're trying to figure out. Tanner's a big deal. His divorce is on the front page of every sleazy magazine in this country. Anyone associated with helping to fuel the divorce is front page news. Which means Macy. And by association, me and Emma." Resting his forearms against the iron fence, he cupped his head in his hands. "There were only six people who knew about Macy's involvement with Tanner. Where she was headed the night she died. Tanner, his wife, Macy, my mom, you, and me.

"Tanner wouldn't want any fuel for his divorce. His wife, Aubrey, promised me at Macy's funeral she'd protect our secret for Emma's sake. And since she hasn't said anything in all this time, why would she now?" Lifting his chin, his eyes threw daggers at her. "That leaves my mom and you, and I seriously don't suspect my mom. She'd never do anything to hurt me or Emma."

A lone tear zipped down her cheek. Swiping it away, she reached in her pocket for her vibrating phone.

"Hello?"

"Tessa?"

"Jim?" The voice of her former publisher burned through her.

"I'm so glad to catch you on a Saturday. Do you have a few minutes to chat?"

"Jim I think we talked everything through a few weeks ago. There isn't a place for me at E&E anymore."

"Things have changed, Tess. You're hot, hot, hot now. That picture in the *Times-Picayune* was gold."

Ryland shoved away from the fence and started to leave.

Tessa was as desperate for him to stay. "Hold on a second, Jim." Clenching her jaw she stepped closer, feeling the heat of his anger billow off of him. She covered her phone. "Ryland, I don't know how many different ways I can say I didn't do this. You'll have to trust me. Trust I'd never deliberately hurt you or Emma." Trying to avoid the tragedy of the prior evening, she stretched out her hand, willing him to engulf her tiny fingers in his beefy callused laden ones.

Seconds ticked by.

Neither moved.

Her breath held tight.

Ryland turned and crossed the street to the bakery.

Closing her fingers, her hand clasped only air. The heart she thought was already shattered, splintered into thousands of new fragments. Swallowing against the growing tightness in her throat, she slid the phone back to her ear. "Jim, what were you saying?"

38

Ryland ripped open the door, launching the welcome bell into a fit of jingles. He couldn't believe he'd fallen for her plea. The last several hours had been the hardest of his life. Harder than grappling with his career-ending injury. Harder than telling Emma Macy died. Closing the door on the one woman who fulfilled every dream he'd dreamed since kindergarten felt as if his beating heart was being torn with deliberate malice and torture from his chest. How had they landed here?

The reporter's call at the house had rattled him, but one look at Tessa and thoughts of Macy's infidelity and Everett Tanner's divorce floated out of his mind.

And then the reporter.

The picture.

The story.

And the realization Tessa wasn't many shades away from Macy's green ambition.

Every cell of his body was engaged in a bloody civil war. Half for his brain and the logical reason concluded Tessa's determination to return to her career trumped everything. The other half of his body raised arms for his heart, unwilling to accept their love could be anything less than epic.

But when she'd reached for his hand, Team Brain roared to a victory.

Macy's lies wove with the vision of Tessa melting down in Terrell's office over her career. And then the series of events leading to the showdown in the alley unfolded in his mind. The newspaper article in her adopted hometown paper. The book about Tanner being printed by her old publishers. The answers to questions only she knew.

Too many arrows pointed in Tessa's direction. He had no choice but to protect himself and his daughter. His heart screamed for him to take her outstretched hand, but the discipline he relied on to transform him from a gangly teenager into an elite professional athlete won. He couldn't risk his daughter or the pain of his own heart. Not again.

And yet, his heart yearned for her. Every non-Team Brain fiber of his body strained to be next to her. Without thinking, he was standing behind her resisting the urge to yank her into his arms. Crushing her to him; ignoring Team Brain until the end of time. Why didn't he just take her hand?

Macy.

The road of selfish ambition ruled his marriage, and he promised himself he would never allow another's desires to overshadow what was best for Emma. He'd never have thought Tessa would have any selfish interests. She seemed to really love his daughter. She listened to Emma. Made her a priority. Spent time with her when no one was around to watch. When no one was keeping score. The love he saw between his daughter and Tessa was real. But apparently it wasn't enough to choose Emma over an opportunity to get back in the game.

Emma waved to him from her window seat next to Eloise.

He kneaded the base of his neck. He needed caffeine.

His impromptu babysitter would need to wait a few more minutes.

Tugging his wallet from his wind pants, he ordered a large black coffee to go.

"Here you go, Coach." Tyson, a junior running back, handed Ryland a white paper cup with a smile.

He nodded and swiveled into Sissy Jenkins. At just five feet tall, the woman barely made his waist, but the fear she'd instilled in him since childhood shivered through his veins. "Mrs. Jenkins."

"Don't Mrs. Jenkins me, Ryland Jessup. I saw you with the Tarrington girl. You should be kinder to the woman you've been in love with since that awful gift in kindergarten."

The realization Sissy knew about his love life, including his awkward attempt at romance at six, churned the acid lining his stomach. "Mrs. Jenkins, I'd rather not talk about Tessa. I need to get my coffee and my daughter."

Waving off his protest, she tugged him to a corner table forcing him to sit with power that belied her petite frame. "Listen here. That poor girl has been through it. I may have had my questions about those books she was writing, but every one of them I read was beautifully shared and eloquently written. This nonsense about her trying to pit you and that imbecile Joey Taylor against each other is ridiculous. I told Bitsy Grey, just this morning after Jazzercise, she needed to take that Taylor boy in hand. She's been the closest thing to a mother that hooligan has had since his poor mother passed away. He's one mistake away from not being able to reform his life."

Sissy continued to berate Ryland, simultaneously sharing every bit of gossip drifting through town about

Joey, Tessa, and him. For good measure, she threw in some snippets about Sean and Maggie's wedding and the sad realization about Macy's death. She knew things about his life, he wasn't certain he knew. But if Sissy knew something, it was fact. Truth was relative. How had she known about Macy? Her Google alerts must have NSA rated security clearance. And if she knew, maybe someone outside his circle of trust was the source behind the dreaded book. Maybe...

"Listen here, Ryland Jessup. You were always a good boy. Not like those other mess-ups you called friends. *Pfft!*" She shook her head as she cupped his chin in her hand. "You have a soft heart. You try and keep it steeled away behind a gruff football exterior. But unlike those idiot friends, you fail.

"You've been in love with the Tarrington girl longer than most people in this town have a memory. I figure you have two options. One, you can believe her and the two of you can have that white picket fence dream you've harbored. Or two, you can keep on turning your back to her apologizing for something she didn't do. And she'll take a hint and stop offering."

~*~

Two hours later, Ryland cupped his sixth coffee as he glided on the back porch swing alone. With Mabel visiting a friend for a well-deserved night off, and Emma on a play date with the five-year-old who lived across the street, Ryland was left with no distractions from his thoughts.

Staring at new buds struggling to bloom, his mind swirled with the accusations Sissy had hurled at him. Six cups of coffee in, he could admit she was partially right.

But trusting Tessa—believing everything was coincidental—was more than his bruised and beaten spirit could muster.

The sun dipped low behind the twenty-year-old maple which stood guard to the west of his lawn. With its departure, the small burst of early spring warmth slipped from the Ohio afternoon. He zipped his fleece-lined GRHS track jacket, rested his head against the back of the swing, and prayed. "Lord, I need guidance from You. I believe You brought Tessa and I together, but have I misjudged her? Has her character changed from childhood? I want to believe she is the beautiful spirit I knew from afar. But the evidence points in one direction. How can I not be leery? Once bitten. Twice shy. I wanted to believe all of the awful things Emma and I endured over the past few years would fade like a sunset, but I don't think that's the road we are on. Lord, why can't I believe her? I want to. My heart wants to but my head just can't."

"Or just won't."

With a jolt, Ryland sat military straight. Coffee went flying. Again. Down his shirt. "Aww Mom. Did you have to sneak up on me?" He swiped at the liquid, beading against the fabric. At least he'd chosen water repellant instead of just water resistant like earlier.

She slid onto the swing beside him. "I'm sorry, but it sounded to me as if you needed a little startling."

With a sigh, he muttered, "Sissy."

"Yes. I know she can be a little too much in everyone's business, but this time her heart is squarely in the right place. You're being an idiot."

"Uh, thanks? Just what every only son wants to hear from his mother."

"Darling, I've only ever spoken truth to you and your sisters. I'm too old to start changing my ways."

"Still, idiot is kind of a strong label."

"When the label fits…"

"Thanks for the talk, Mom, but I need to go get Emma. I'm sure the Wilsons weren't planning on feeding her dinner." He moved to stand, but his mother's quick hand stopped his progress.

"Young man, you're not too old to turn over my knee."

He glanced at his bulky six-foot-six frame next to his mother's five-foot-four inches and stifled a belly laugh. At the ripe old age of eight he'd learned the lesson of laughing at one of his mother's outrageous statements. And although he outweighed her by well over one hundred pounds, he figured she would find a way to stretch him across her lap and break a paddle just to prove a point. "Ryland, I don't know the details of what happened between you and Tessa."

"Sissy didn't provide a detailed punch list?"

"Snarky is not an attractive quality, son."

"Sorry."

"As I said, I don't know what happened between you two. But I do know I've never seen two young people better suited for each other. If you allow her to slip out of your life, you'll be missing an opportunity at bliss."

"Mom, she knows about Macy."

"Good. She should know."

"And now there's a tell-all book detailing Macy's relationship with Tanner."

"What's that to do with Tessa?"

"She's a ghost writer. Of memoirs and tell-all type books."

"I'm not seeing the link. Correlation does not equal causation."

"Yes. I took statistics as well, but there are too many other things."

"Such as?"

He told her about the article and the reporter. The questions and the picture. He tried to glaze over the car and the park, but his mother was a woman of details.

"And based on all of those highly circumstantial pieces of 'evidence'—and I use the word loosely—you've convicted her?"

"Who else could have dredged up the past?"

"What about Tanner's wife? I imagine something scandalous such as his affair with Macy would be quite a boon to her divorce settlement."

Ryland shook his head. "After the funeral, Aubrey promised she'd keep the secret. She has kids, too. She wouldn't want to hurt Emma or her own children."

"But you think Tessa, the woman who spends three days a week with Emma, would want to blatantly hurt both her and you?"

"No...I don't know."

"Baby boy, that woman messed you up."

Even after all the time since her death, his mother still struggled with Macy's Name.

"In the head and the heart," she continued. "She messed you up more than I ever knew. I want to hate her, but I can't. She gave you a beautiful, smart, wonderful daughter whom I'm busting-at-the-seams proud to call granddaughter. So no, I can't hate her. But I can hate every action she did to cause the wounds in you. The deep ones. Below the surface of the scars that flash healing, but whisper the devastation your soul has endured.

"You are a good man, Ryland. Your daddy would be proud of the father, coach, and man of faith you've become. Don't allow one person's self-hate and selfish ambition rob you of the happiness you deserve. Tessa is part of your happiness. She and Emma. They're your gift. And they'll help you heal the deep wounds if you trust them and yourself enough to try."

The sting of unshed tears burned the corners of his eyes.

Cupping her hand over his, she squeezed. "Call Tanner's wife. Start with the logical. Not the farfetched. Logic. Reasonability is what makes good fiction. And trust me, I know good fiction. I'd have to believe the same holds true for real-life."

39

Ryland brushed Emma's hair—a final bedtime ritual before prayers, story, and lights out. Resting her head against his thigh, he brushed while she played with the ribbons trimming her heart pajamas.

"Daddy?"

"Emma?"

"Do you love Miss Tessa?"

His hand stopped mid-brush. Her innocent question splashed unseen ice water in his face. Did he love Tessa? Yes. Easy answer. Did he trust Tessa? Not the easiest answer. "Why are you asking?" *Delay. Delay. Delay.*

Emma shrugged and wriggled to make eye contact. "I love Miss Tessa and I thought if you loves her too, she could come lives here with you and me and Mabel."

"It's not quite that simple, E."

"Why not? G-ma says if people loves each other theys family."

"I am certain your grandmother did not say 'theys'."

Her little brow pinched across the bridge of her nose. "Daddy…"

"Sorry. You were saying…"

"I love Miss Tessa, and I know she loves me 'cause she showed me. And I thinks you loves her, too."

"Why do you think I love her?"

"'cause you are always worried about her."

"Worried about her?"

She sat straight, nodding and sending the brushed hair flying in static directions. "You always make sure she has what she needs. Likes when you went to find her in New O'leans. She neededs you and you went. You don't wants her to get hurts. I think you loves her a whole bunches." She laid her cheek back to his thigh and drew tiny circles with her chubby finger.

His mother was right.

When wasn't she?

Tessa was a part of his happiness. And he was blaming her for wounds she didn't inflict. Projecting Macy's hurt onto Tessa. Allowing the negatives of one to cloud the positives of another.

His mother was also right about not being able to hate Macy. For all her faults Macy gave him a beautiful daughter and a couple good years of memories. Just because she'd allowed her wants to override everything and everyone else, shouldn't diminish the good she'd helped create. And her selfishness shouldn't cloud the good in Tessa. He wouldn't allow Macy's malice to control him a minute longer. The letting go would be an everyday process. Until it wasn't. But he wouldn't fully be able to let go of the pain of the past without stepping into his future. With Tessa. She was his future. His and Emma's. He'd allowed his insecurities, doubts and pain enough footholds.

No more. No more drudging up what had been. He was determined to start fresh. To choose love. To choose Tessa. He needed to see her. In person. To tell her he loved her. To beg for her forgiveness. Hope she would accept it.

With Mabel gone for the night, he'd have to wait until the sun came up before he could go to Tessa's, but he could wait.

Emma tugged him from his revelation with her sweet voice. "And I think Miss Tessa loves you too." He could only hope the wisdom of a four year old was as true as the Gospel.

~*~

With an hour and a half workout, breakfast, shower, and dressing a half-sleep toddler checked off his morning list, Ryland whipped his SUV into one of the last remaining parking spots at church. He unlatched Emma from her booster seat and she slipped her hand in his as they walked the few steps to the clapboard white structure older than the town itself.

"Daddy, y'think I can run ahead?"

"No, darlin'. But I do think you might want to go to Kids Church today."

"Really? Why you think that?"

Oh, so many things wrong with the grammar. "I believe it would be nice to worship with kids your own age. You're almost five. Ready for kindergarten. You're ready to graduate to worship with the big kids."

"But I like listening to Pastor Tom. His voice is reals deep and when he's tryin' to make a point it gets reals loud. But not scary. Just loud. Makes me giggle."

"I'm certain Pastor Tom would love to have you laugh at his serious moments, but I think you should try Kids Church today. OK?"

With a sigh she nodded and tugged Ryland toward the side entrance splattered with confetti paint and an arched sign screaming, 'Kids this way.'

The drop-off took a few extra minutes and he slid in the back row while the announcements were being read. Scanning the congregation he couldn't see Tessa, but she had to be there. Her father was back to preaching full time. He couldn't imagine 'skipping' was allowed even when the PK was an adult PK.

Straining for a glimpse of Tessa, he missed the additional latecomers piled into his pew. He was shocked to see Jane Barrett and her husband, Lindy, as well as Sean and Maggie, who tended to split their time between the hometown church and a mega-church near Columbus.

Jane gave him a broad smile. "Whew!" she whispered. "I was worried we'd be walking in during the prayer." She kissed his cheek in greeting. "I always forget how long the drive is from downtown."

"Why are you sliding in the back row like a bunch of sinners?"

"Because we are?" His former babysitter gave him a wink. "Daddy's talking today. Giving his testimony. Bitsy insisted we all attend. I'm sure Molly and Jake are somewhere near the front. They never disappoint Bits. Me, on the other hand…" She shrugged.

He hadn't been aware they were beginning testimonies again, but with Tom back in his pulpit the change to worship made sense. The pastor loved to have examples of God's hand displayed for his congregation. And the loving father, farmer, and friend, Henry Grey, was a prime example of the love God had for everyone.

Settling into his seat, he bowed his head to pray and hoped wherever Tessa was in the church her heart was still open to him. To them.

As the offering plates began to pass down the pews, a high school student sang a reverent solo, plucking at his heart strings.

Jane nudged the plate against his shoulder. He dropped his envelope in the offering before refocusing his attention on the music.

Jane leaned over to him. "Where's Tessa? I hear things hit a rough patch between you two. Did you make up?"

"What did you hear?"

"Just the typical. You two were in a fight. Blah, blah, blah. You're an idiot. Blah, blah, blah."

"Jane," her husband covered her hands with his. "We should probably listen to the music. Not focus on Ryland's love life. I think the Lord deserves one hour of undivided attention."

Giving him an I'm-sorry shrug, she shifted in her seat and focused on the soloist. She leaned into her husband's side as he stretched an arm around her shoulders. Like a choreographed play, Sean mimicked Lindy's move, kissing the curly head of his future wife, who snuggled against his him.

Suddenly, the hallowed place of worship hollowed Ryland. With the outward expression of love and contentment, he felt lost. Searching the congregation, his heart ached to see the face of the one he loved. Once he saw her, once he sought and graciously received her forgiveness, his world would be righted. He'd be at peace; just like his dream. Glancing at his watch, he only had forty more minutes until he could freely search.

At the end of worship, Ryland gave Jane a quick hug good-bye agreeing to another group dinner in an effort to extricate himself from the barrage of questions. Slipping past several friends and acquaintances, he caught his mother's eye as she was deep in conversation with Sissy Jenkins.

Debating the obligatory hug his mother required from each of her children and another confrontation with Sissy he slowed his steps. But six feet six inches did not ever get paired with a short stride and he couldn't avoid hearing Sissy's whispers to his mother.

"He said she left this morning. Some publishing deal out of the blue. It's a real shame your boy couldn't lock her down." The words ripped at his heart. He was too late. How could he be too late? It had only been forty-eight hours since he'd slipped her the note about dinner. He'd thought he had the rest of his life. Apparently the rest of his life ended at noon on Sunday.

"Ryland, I didn't see you." His mother stepped into his embrace and whispered. "We don't know anything for sure. Don't jump to conclusions. OK?"

He nodded and stepped away from his mother.

"Wish you hadn't made her mad," Sissy said. "Having her in town certainly made for a happier pastor. I heard Jamison offered her a fulltime position. The kids seem to love her. But she called yesterday and turned him down." She narrowed her gaze on Ryland. "You certainly messed up things for everyone. I'll see you at Jazzercise, Nancy." And off she went to spread more Sissy Jenkins cheer.

"Ryland, don't listen to her. You know she judges every situation as if she is running a TV courtroom. Maybe Tessa has another reason for not being here."

"Sure, Mom." But he was sure of only one thing.

Tessa Tarrington had left Gibson's Run without saying good-bye.

40

The *swoosh* of the street-sweeper cleaning in front of her apartment pushed Tessa from her reoccurring dream. More of a memory than a dream. Swaying in Ryland's arms.

Twisting to her side, she dragged her feather pillow to her chest and squeezed. Glancing at the bedside calendar, she noted the marked star heralding the street sweepers. Three weeks since Ryland had walked away from her. Three weeks after she'd left Gibson's Run for good.

Three weeks since Jim Evanston called her with an offer. An offer she told him to stick. He and his ugly-hearted wife wanted her to write the untold story of her "tragic" romance with Joey and her torrid "affair" with Ryland. They hinted at the book they were fast-tracking about Everett Tanner and his many women—including Macy. But they wanted a bookend deal. Both sides of the spousal betrayal story. Macy's and Ryland's.

The vileness of suggesting anyone—including her—would write such trash made her see the truth in Ryland's accusations. She rapidly shut the door on a possible story and threatened legal action if any book about her, Ryland, Joey or anyone in her circle was floated by E&E. She'd worked for the Evanston's long enough to know what made them quake. Cash flow moving in any direction but into their pockets was unthinkable.

At the end of the call she wished she'd been on a house phone and could have slammed the receiver into the cradle with a crack. Hitting the off button didn't have the same soap opera effect.

Before she could lift her gaze across the street to see if she could catch Ryland, Terrell called. As surreal as an offer to write her own life story was, Terrell's call could have been filmed for a science fiction movie. He'd casually pitched the Guard-Ann series to a few of his publisher friends.

"Nothing formal, mind you. Just wanted to see if it would hold water."

Within days he was fielding offers from three of the biggest children's imprints in the country. She had her pick of who to sign with, but he recommended the one with a four book deal including an option of a cartoon based on the story. Clearly the biggest pay-out for him, but the potential of writing under her own name was mind-blowing.

Shocked, she'd slid to a bench and asked Terrell to set up meetings for the following week. After hanging up the phone with him, she'd called Lily and asked if Beau's daddy would loan the plane to her for another round-trip to Columbus.

Even after her father had scolded her for running away again, and she denied it, she knew the truth. She'd run. Again. But without Ryland's willingness to trust her, to believe in her, their relationship couldn't move forward. And facing a life in Gibson's Run without Ryland or Emma —knowing the outcome— she just couldn't muster the energy.

Her new phone—new number; new life—buzzed on her bedside table and she answered it with a swipe.

"Yes, Lily."

"Open your door right now."

Before she could toss back her covers, the pounding started.

Slipping on a robe, she knotted the belt as she slammed open the door.

"Good morning to you, too."

"No time for small talk." She thrust a coffee in her hand. "Drink. We have much to discuss and I need to have you fully awake and alert."

She followed a frenzied Lily to her couch and sipped the rich chicory coffee steeped with creamy milk. Medicine for her weary soul.

"I know how she did it." Lily said, slamming her coffee on the ottoman.

"Careful with the furniture. Didn't do anything to you." Tessa sipped from the to-go cup. "How who did what? I'm barely coherent Lil. Let the coffee find my blood stream."

"Bobbi Ann."

Coffee burned through her nostrils and over her lips. "Warn a girl before you use a name like hers. Nearly tore the inside of my mouth out."

Pushing off the couch Tessa padded to the kitchen and snagged a glass of water to cool the scalding. "Now what did the nefarious nitwit do this time."

"She's the source. The leak. The thief."

Lowering to the couch, Tessa drew her legs to sit cross-legged facing Lily. "She's my burglar? You've got to be kidding me. How? Why?"

"The why's pretty easy. She hates you and thinks you have everything her blessed little heart deserves. Writing career. Double digit manuscripts. Cozy relationships with dozens of stars. Trust of everyone in the industry. Two star athletes fighting over you. And there's always the Billy situation. You know how she hates that he liked you before he ever made a play for her."

"So not true. We were in class together. Friends. He needed help. That's all."

"*Hmphf.* Doubt the feeling was mutual from Billy's side, but you made your position pretty clear and direct. So he moved on to more welcoming pastures."

"Regardless. She and Billy are married now. She can't seriously still be jealous over college."

"She can, and she is. She's made it her life mission to ruin everything you have."

"Well, that's a dumb mission."

"Bobbi Ann."

Tessa nodded. Enough said.

Lily went to the print of New Orleans she'd given to Tessa as a house warming present. It was the lone hanging piece she had. Brick walls were no joke.

She tilted the painting and revealed a tiny hole in the mortar. Tessa moved to stand beside Lily and slid her finger inside the hole. It was empty. "Why are we poking our fingers in old building holes?"

"This isn't an old building hole. This is an expertly drilled *new* old building hole."

"And this is important why?"

"Because of this." Lily reached in her pocket and pulled out a tiny black cylinder—barely bigger than her fingertip.

"And this is?"

"A recorder. She's been spying on you. On all of us. Probably since her daddy so generously gave us that big discount."

"What?"

"When I was packing up my apartment, I noticed a few perfect holes in the walls—behind pictures—I was certain weren't there when I moved in. I contacted Mr. Risdy because I was concerned about my security deposit, and he said not to worry. Real quick. Had my security deposit back in my account before I was officially moved out of the apartment.

"And then last week, I stopped at Ella's to pick up her mail. Water the dozens of plants. Etcetera while she's working on her new contract, and I noticed one of her paintings was askew."

"You just happened to notice?"

"Hey, I'm super observant. Why do you think my young adult novels are so intense?"

"Because you have the maturity level of your readership?"

"Mean." But her twinkling smile recanted the admonishment. "Regardless, I straightened the painting and noticed the hole. Only this little guy was stuck inside. Ella added extra security after your burglary. Triple deadbolts, so on. I think the incident freaked her out more than she was willing to say. Anyway, breaking in—even if you were the owner of the building with a master set of keys—would be impossible now. "

"And because of holes in our three apartments you concluded that Bobbi Ann—I don't sweat for anything but shopping—Risdy became a mastermind criminal whose been tracking our every move and listening in on our conversations? Destroying my life bit by bit?"

"Well, yes."

"Lily, this is a harebrained idea even for you. What evidence do you have—besides the holes which could have been there when we moved in and didn't notice, and a recorder that could have been put there by anyone? People are generally innocent until proven guilty in this country."

"I researched the serial number on the recorder. With a little finagling of my father-in-law and Beau, I was able to use some of their contacts in the police department to confirm the purchase. Made by one Ellen Risdy. Bobbi Ann's mother. Who—God bless her soul—is in a hospital in Northern Louisiana for the mentally ill. Bobbi Ann is using her sick momma to wheedle her way into our private lives."

The tiny hairs on the back of Tessa's neck stood at attention.

"But why? I can almost get the 'she hates me' reasoning, but this seems like an awful lot of hoops to jump through just to hear a few conversations with clients. Even if she did steal my notes, what did she get out of it?"

"Other than ruining your life?"

"Other than that."

"She secured a contract with F&F. Days after your life was in shambles because of your break-in." Lily began to count out on her fingers. "Your career ruined. Sent you packing to Ohio. Decimated your love life."

"Fair enough. Let's just suppose for a minute she is the culprit behind *the terrible, awful day*."

"She totally is."

"Easy, Detective Lily Mae of the made-up-law-enforcement-agency, guilty until proven innocent."

"Guilty," Lily muttered.

Tessa shook her head. "Listen. I know you are all hyped up on a mystery solving high, but let's just be logical and reasonable. No conclusion jumping."

Lily sighed. "Agreed."

"Let's start at the very beginning."

The two friends began to walk through the last several months.

Tessa debunking. Lily prosecuting.

The scale tipping to Lily.

"She wanted you humiliated. I'm sure of it. I think she's been listening to you for well over a year. Think about some of those leaks. Your senatorial candidate client a year ago. How could anyone know about his daughter's problems with depression and near suicide? Or the teeny bopper rocker's eating disorder? You didn't write about any of it. But somehow the tabloids found out? You didn't even tell me until it was out in the papers."

"Gossip is a hard beast to keep wrangled." Tessa said. "They all have assistants. Anyone could have leaked those stories. And just look at how rabid the idea of making Bobbi Ann into a villain has made you. Besides, even if she was spying on me, why would she spy on you and Ella?"

"It makes sense. We're your best friends. If you were venting or sharing anything with anyone it would be us. Simple logic. It's totally Bobbi Ann. And I have more proof." She sucked in a deep breath, pressing the air back through her lips in a whistle. "Yesterday, I cornered Ronny Rapaport down at the *Picayune* and after a little arm twisting, he confirmed Bobbi Ann was the source behind the article on Joey. They corroborated her story with the driver, but when it all synced up, they ran with it." Lily's voice lowered. "She followed you to the hospital and took the picture of the two of you out front."

"I just can't believe it." The room swam before Tessa's eyes. The pieces of the mystery began to click in place. The leaks on books she was writing based on interviews she'd conducted in her apartment. The flood of additional untold information on her clients after the burglary of her apartment. The conversations about Macy and Joey she had with Ryland in her apartment. Her apartment. She was sitting in the epicenter of her own demise.

"Wait a minute." She snapped to standing. "The day after Joey's accident. The day of the photo."

"Yes, *cher*, we've already covered the lowdown, dirty shenanigans that led to the photo."

"That's not it. Ryland came to my apartment before he went to the hospital. He didn't know I was at church."

"Please. How could he not know *you* were at church? You were practically born in one."

"OK, Drama. Listen. Ryland came to the apartment, but Bobbi Ann told him I was at church."

"Again. Not a shocker. You. Preacher's Kid. Church. Sunday morning. Not a big leap, *cher*."

"But he saw her here. Coming out of my apartment building."

Lily shot up. "What? And we are just now getting to this vital detail? *Cher*, we really need to work on your detecting skills. You are entirely too trusting. And you really don't pay attention to the little details. This is why you'll need me to plan your wedding from the shower to the bower."

"Lily, stop berating me for a second. I think this is like a real clue."

"And what would you call all of my detective work?"

"You're right." She gave her a two armed bear hug. "Thank you. Even when I wanted to crawl into bed and hide under the covers for a month, you believed in me. You kept poking and looking. Digging and searching. How can I ever thank you?"

"Delta Alpha Psi until we die."

41

Twenty minutes later, a torn vinyl seat cover scratched Tessa's left leg as her right pumped on the second floor of the 2nd Police District.

"Will you settle down? We didn't do anything wrong," Lily said with a snap of her compact.

Tessa tucked her skirt around her thighs and focused on the stacks of paper and jumbled array of photos attached to Lily's detective friend's desk. With the force of hurricane winds, Lily pressed him to take their case against Bobbi Ann to his sergeant in under two minutes. The detective and sergeant were now locked behind frosted glass walls.

"We shouldn't have come here, Lil."

"Yes, we should. This is your life. You have to stand for yourself. No one else will."

"Except you."

"Well, that's a given. I love you more than moon pies and a cold Coke on the Fourth of July."

She squeezed Lily's manicured fingers.

The door scraped open and Detective Marcel Dupris ambled across the police station.

"Well, ladies," he said, lowering onto his chair with a creak. "Seems the sergeant was already looking into Mrs. Risdy-Jones."

"What?" Lily and Tessa asked in unison.

"Some weeks ago, the sergeant's chief friend— from Ohio—asked him to look into her in connection to his brother."

"Sean? Chief Taylor, I mean?" Tessa asked.

"Seems he's a friend of yours, too."

"What does Bobbi Ann have to do with Sean and Joey Taylor?"

Detective Dupris shrugged. "Can't say for sure, but the lady's name keeps swirling around trouble. When your friend called Sergeant Nguyen to look into the accident around his brother, Mrs. Risdy-Jones had already put a request in for the report. When Nguyen went to meet Chief Taylor before he left N'awlins, he witnessed Mrs. Risdy-Jones skulking around asking nurses and orderlies for information."

"And based on those two facts he started looking into her?" Lily asked.

"Seriously, Lil? You were ready to hang her on flimsier research."

"Yes, but I've nearly a decade of her deceitful and duplicitous actions as background."

"Well," Detective Dupris interrupted, "he's the head of our unit for a reason."

"Sorry, detective, you were saying. Your sergeant's been investigating Bobbi Ann, err Mrs. Risdy-Jones?"

Lifting the folder of notes and details from Lily, he nodded. "He did a little off the record digging, as a courtesy to Chief Taylor, and when Nguyen caught her digging for information she shouldn't need, he poked around a little more. Your research on the history of the recorder, coupled with what the sergeant uncovered, makes it seem that Mrs. Risdy-Jones is the most likely culprit."

"What do we do? Can we ride in the squad car when you go arrest her? Will there be sirens and a perp walk?" Lily's voice trilled.

"Unfortunately, there's little we can do. Every piece of information we have is circumstantial."

"No perp walk?" Lily asked.

"No. But the sergeant's work does support an injunction against the book Mrs. Risdy-Jones was in contract to write."

"What book?" Tessa asked.

"Not sure entirely, but Evanston and Evanston had a contract voided with Mrs. Risdy-Jones earlier this week. I can't tell you what the book was about because the court records were sealed, but the injunction was amended last Friday to include Mrs. Risdy-Jones in the suit."

"Are you sure you can't take a lil' peek and see who filed the injunction?" Lily's southern belle oozed through her sorority smile.

Detective Dupris was ill-equipped to defend against it. Turning to his computer he punched through a series of screens and windows. "Obviously, I can't tell you the details of an ongoing investigation, but the court docket is public record. Mrs. Risdy-Jones is scheduled to appear in fifteen minutes.

42

Tessa shoved the door to her apartment to the right with a clink. Following Lily, she kicked off her sandals with a sigh.

"I can't believe we missed it." Lily flopped onto the couch.

"The proceedings were closed. We don't know what we missed."

"We missed seeing Bobbi Ann grovel. Oh, I'd have paid all the money in my trust fund to see her eat the crow being served to her today."

"Lil, I know you want justice…"

"Vengeance. I want vengeance."

"That's reserved for The Lord. But it sounds as if justice was served. Bobbi Ann's contract is toast with E&E. Jim and Cheryl confirmed as much as they were leaving the courthouse."

After a break neck car ride from the 2nd District to the courthouse, Lily flipped on her hazards and raced through the front door, nearly plowing into the Evanstons. For the first time in the four years Tessa had known the couple, they looked contrite. Husband and wife apologized to her for any hardship in which they'd been complicit. "You know we always thought of you like the daughter we never had." Cheryl said with a weak armed hug.

Tessa barely stepped back from her before Jim jumped in with an offer for a new contract. "Bobbi Ann is not the writer you are. You have compassion and empathy for your clients. We need you."

"Thank you, but you're not who I need. I thought my career defined me, but over the last few months I realized only The Lord can define me. And I can't allow what I do to reflect poorly on Him. I'm afraid working for you would."

Cheryl broke away with a huff and followed Jim around the corner. Out of her life forever.

"I can't believe you didn't get more scoop from the E's," Lily said, drawing her back to the present. "Don't you want to know who finally sued them? Do you think it was Joey? Don't you want to know what'll happen with Bobbi Ann?"

Handing Lily a bottle of water, Tessa slid onto the couch beside her. "Bobbi Ann will bounce back. She always does. But how much richer are our lives?"

"But I just want to see her squirm."

"Lily Mae."

The buzz of the street speaker drew their attention.

She pushed the front door release and returned to her seat.

"Did you really just buzz someone into the building without asking who they were?"

Tessa shrugged. "The buzzer's been broken since I moved in. Generally it's Remy from upstairs when his hands are too full. If I didn't buzz him the first time, he'd keep buzzing until he succeeded."

"I still say you could have let a serial killer into your apartment building. Talk about the therapy sessions after that decision."

Bang! Bang! Bang!

"Told you," Lily said. "Sounds like a killer knock."

Tessa yanked open the sliding door.

Leaning against a cherrywood cane stood Joe Taylor. Hair trimmed, and with a slight pallor, but the twinkle in his eyes was all Joey.

"Hey T.T. long time."

"Not a serial killer, Lil. Serial charmer," Tessa said over her shoulder. She stepped into his open arms. "How're you? How's the hospital? How're you even here today?"

"Do you mind if I come in and take a load off? Leg's not what it used to be."

She ushered him to the couch. Straight into the unfortunate interrogation of Detective Lily Mae.

Within two minutes, Lily had Joey's brow sprinkled with beads of sweat as he loosened his buttoned collar, and filled in the blanks from the night of his accident to his arrival at the apartment.

"I'm just here to be supportive. My lawyer thought it would help the case if I showed up. That Bobbi Ann is one determined...person. If she wasn't being sued for libel already, I'd seriously consider it."

"You didn't seek the injunction?" Tessa asked.

"If I sought an injunction with every story pitched about me and my umm...choices. I'd never be out of court."

"Then who?" Tessa asked.

"Aubrey Tanner."

"Who?"

"Everett Tanner's wife," Lily said.

"How do you know who she is?" Tessa asked.

"As I said, I've been doing some research. Bobbi Ann joined a few new philanthropic organizations over the past year. Two are headed by Aubrey Tanner. I thought it was weird. Bobbi Ann never liked to give to anyone but the charity of Bobbi Ann, but now it makes sense."

Joey nodded in unison with Lily.

"What makes sense? Why should Bobbi Ann's choice of charities make a difference?"

"Catch up, T. She joined them, and then magically there's a scandal about Tanner's extracurricular activities? His divorce proceedings become front page for every newspaper, magazine and gossip website across the country. E&E is in contract on a book detailing his affairs. You don't see the connection?"

A wave of nausea crashed through Tessa. How could anyone be so cruel and solely ambitious? At the rehearsal dinner Bobbi Ann had slipped about knowing Tanner's wife. All of the little things added together to complete the puzzle. Tessa's life hadn't fallen into a toilet. Bobbi Ann had ripped it apart and dropped it bit by bit creating a splash. And she'd tried to do the same thing to others—families she didn't know. All for what? A book deal? Ghostwritten. A book no one would ever know she wrote.

"I just don't see how anyone, even Bobbi Ann, could be this cruel."

"Ambition is a drug," Joe said.

"But how did you get pulled into the situation? If she's not writing a book about you?"

"Pattern of behavior. The lawyers used her slander around the accident and the surrounding story. You, me, and Rys. As an example for how her behavior escalates." Joey laid his hand over hers. "The book proposal was about Tanner and all of his extras. Including Macy. I owe Jessup my life—twenty times over—I had to try to save Emma from having the whole world know about her mother's poor decision."

"Ryland?"

He nodded.

Lily slipped from the room.

"Tessa, Rys has been trying to get in touch with you for weeks. He knows he messed up. He told me he doesn't deserve you."

Tears pooled in Tessa's vision.

"He's right. He doesn't deserve you." Joey cupped her chin. "But he needs you. Emma needs you. And you need them. Forgiveness is impossible to earn. It has to be given freely. A pretty lady told me that once."

She swiped at her eyes. "I just don't know. I can't live tiptoeing on eggshells always wondering if this one choice will make him believe I'm a monster. I can't keep trying to prove myself every day, questioning if today is the day it all falls apart."

"He won't ask you to."

She spun in her seat at the sound of Ryland's deep voice. A flood of tears swamped her cheeks, blurring the sight of him.

Feet braced apart, he stood just inside her apartment.

"That's my cue." Joe struggled to stand and hugged Tessa. "Just listen. Don't judge first." He smacked a kiss on her cheek, clapped Ryland on the shoulder, and closed the door behind him.

Silence draped the room.

Tessa turned to the windows staring toward the Mississippi. She wished she could float away on the slow, muddy current, preferring the certainty of the Gulf to the uncertainty of the next few minutes. *Help me, Lord. Help me.*

"Please listen." Ryland's voice was barely a whisper above her head. "Listen to what I have to say. If you want to close the door, I promise I'll stay on the other side."

She looked into his stormy eyes. Every cell in her body screamed to reach out, wrap her arms around him and never let go. But her mind fought her, replaying the images of Ryland's rejections. Both of them. Hugging her arms across her middle, she leaned against the bank of windows and lifted a single eyebrow.

"I'm sorry isn't enough." He released a slow sigh and began to pace the small space in front of her. "I've thought of dozens, hundreds, of apologies, but none came close to expressing how truly sorry I am for not believing you. For not believing in us. You're the best person I know. You help people share their stories. To heal by sharing their truths. You helped a little girl deal with her sadness by giving her support. You gave up your whole life to take care of your dad. You forgave me all of the childhood torture. You care in ways I don't understand, but want to."

He stopped pacing, closing the few steps between them. "I love you, Tessa Tarrington." Resting his hands on her shoulders, he forced her gaze to meet his. "Yes, I've loved the idea of you since I was six, but in the last few months I have fallen deeply and irrevocably in love with you. And you love me, too. I know you do.

"Please don't let my blind stupidity rob us of the future God has planned. For us. For Emma. I know I have more work to do on myself than the average guy, but you didn't fall in love with him. You fell in love with me. Please forgive me. Forgive me and help me to learn to forgive Macy."

Tessa's chin dropped to her chest. A single tear splattered on the floor next to her foot. She loved him. The aching deep down in your bones forever kind of love. The kind of love that transformed tart, bitter lemons into sweet, fragrant lemonade and rescued lives from the toilet.

She reached her arms to wrap around Ryland's waist, resting her cheek on his heart. "I love you. And love means I'll always forgive you."

A shudder rippled through him. And slowly her feet left the floor as he lifted her to eye level. "I'll never let you go again."

"Promise?"

His lips brushed against hers. Gentle yearning flowing through her body. She clung to him, deepening the kiss which overflowed with the promise of endless tomorrows.

Epilogue

Tessa and Ryland strolled along Main Street, hands interlocked, leaving the back yard rehearsal dinner before more toasts to Sean and Maggie could be raised. Half the town was at the celebration in Sean's cramped backyard leaving Gibson's Run peaceful and still for a Friday.

The weeks since they'd reunited in New Orleans had been filled with a multitude of changes.

Tessa agreed to finish out the semester for Mrs. Monahan, but remained firm on her decision not to assume a fulltime position.

Jamison was crushed. Convinced Ryland was minutes from accepting an offer from a local university or high school in Columbus, he floated him a five year contract with the district as the Athletic Director and Head Football coach.

As far as Tessa knew, Ryland hadn't yet signed the contract, but he wouldn't tell her why. She hated any secrets between them, but he was adamant he needed to be certain before he committed to the school.

The artist tapped to complete the Guard-Ann illustrations had finalized her pieces two weeks ago and after meeting Emma, the character of Shelby bore a striking resemblance to the little girl. The book was set to release just before Thanksgiving—ready for the perfect holiday treat under the tree.

A few rounds of interviews, book signings, and

potential talk shows were in Tessa's future, and she couldn't wait. She was so excited to have her work—Emma's and her work—in print she wanted to shout with joy from every rooftop.

The news around Bobbi Ann's duplicity topped the headlines for a few weeks, with both Everett Tanner and Joey releasing statements seeking privacy for themselves and respect for Bobbi Ann. Greater generosity than she had shown either of them, but as Joey said, "She's a child of God, too. None of us are perfect and everyone deserves a second chance."

Tessa wasn't convinced, but her heart warmed at the spirit beginning to bloom in Joey and the renewed communication the scandal created between Tanner and his wife, Audrey. They put their divorce hearing on hold to try and work on their family.

Ryland slowed their pace, stopping in front of the town fountain. He lowered to the wrought iron bench on the sidewalk and tugged Tessa's arm to sit beside him.

"I don't want to stop. Mabel made those shortbread cookies with the toffee bits and dropped some at my dad's house. I was hoping to snag a couple before he got home."

"Sit with me." His voice low.

She cuddled into his side.

"Tessa, I've loved you since the first day I saw you on the playground in kindergarten. I was so in love with you I agonized for weeks over what gift to give you. Consulted my friends, and my sisters over what to buy."

The memory of those "Days of the Week" underpants and her subsequent response rolled through her mind. But no longer was the memory spiked with fear and anger. Now an involuntary smile tugged at her lips. "I remember them well."

"Out of that day you received a nickname I wish a million times over I could take back, but I can't. What I can do is offer you a new nickname."

He rolled, kneeling just in front of her. In his wide palms he held a small black leather box tied with a bow.

Tears sprang to Tessa's eyes. "Ryland?"

"Open the box, T.T.," he whispered.

Lifting the box, weighted with meaning, she tugged on the ribbon. A latch cracked open, revealing a single band of diamonds, no more than an eighth of an inch wide. She pinched the ring from its nest and raised it to the street light to watch the sparkle. And on the inner edge she saw a slight mark. Pulling it closer she read the inscription.

T ~for every day of the week, for the rest of our lives. My love, R

Tears blurred her vision as she launched herself into Ryland's arms.

"I love you," his voice was a choked whisper. "Sunday to Saturday and all the days we have to together. You, me, and Emma. Please marry me."

She nodded, unable to speak through the blooming of her heart.

Cupping her cheeks, nearly engulfing her face with his hands, he lowered his lips to hers. With a brush of a kiss he sealed their lives.

"I love you," she whispered.

"I love you, too." He slid the ring on her finger and a grin stretched across his face, lighting his eyes. "And I'll love using your new nickname."

Admiring her ring, she glanced up at him with a

single lift of her eyebrow.

"Wife."

And this time, Ryland Jessup got the perfect nickname right.

Thank you

We appreciate you reading this White Rose Publishing title. For other inspirational stories, please visit our on-line bookstore at www.pelicanbookgroup.com.

For questions or more information, contact us at customer@pelicanbookgroup.com.

White Rose Publishing
Where Faith is the Cornerstone of Love™
an imprint of Pelican Book Group
www.PelicanBookGroup.com

Connect with Us
www.facebook.com/Pelicanbookgroup
www.twitter.com/pelicanbookgrp

To receive news and specials, subscribe to our bulletin
http://pelink.us/bulletin

May God's glory shine through
this inspirational work of fiction.

AMDG

You Can Help!

At Pelican Book Group it is our mission to entertain readers with fiction that uplifts the Gospel. It is our privilege to spend time with you awhile as you read our stories.

We believe you can help us to bring Christ into the lives of people across the globe. And you don't have to open your wallet or even leave your house!

Here are 3 simple things you can do to help us bring illuminating fiction™ to people everywhere.

1) If you enjoyed this book, write a positive review. Post it at online retailers and websites where readers gather. And share your review with us at reviews@pelicanbookgroup.com (this does give us permission to reprint your review in whole or in part.)

2) If you enjoyed this book, recommend it to a friend in person, at a book club or on social media.

3) If you have suggestions on how we can improve or expand our selection, let us know. We value your opinion. Use the contact form on our web site or e-mail us at customer@pelicanbookgroup.com

God Can Help!

Are you in need? The Almighty can do great things for you. Holy is His Name! He has mercy in every generation. He can lift up the lowly and accomplish all things. Reach out today.

Do not fear: I am with you; do not be anxious: I am your God. I will strengthen you, I will help you, I will uphold you with my victorious right hand.

~Isaiah 41:10 (NAB)

We pray daily, and we especially pray for everyone connected to Pelican Book Group—that includes you! If you have a specific need, we welcome the opportunity to pray for you. Share your needs or praise reports at http://pelink.us/pray4us

Free Book Offer

We're looking for booklovers like you to partner with us! Join our team of influencers today and periodically receive free eBooks and exclusive offers.

For more information
Visit http://pelicanbookgroup.com/booklovers